WOLF BANE

HUNTERS OF THE FOREST, BOOK ONE

M.P. STARKWEATHER

PHOENIX ECLIPSE PUBLISHING

I want to dedicate this book to my two biggest fans, my husband Josh and my son Thom, who will probably never read any of my books. Thanks for pushing me to chase my dream. I love you both to the moon and back.

CONTENTS

BLOOD WOLF

A Vampires at Midnight and Hunters of the Forest Crossover Novella

ONE – GETTING READY

GARNET

How did I let Kayden talk me into training with him when we should have been getting ready for Delilah's birthday party? Instead of standing in a long, hot shower, I was crawling through the mud while being chased by his stupid wolf ass. "Kayden! At this point, we're going to be late!"

The sable brown wolf shook its head at me and ran off. I knew that he wanted me to chase him, but I wasn't about to follow him into the woods again and get tossed around in the mud even more. I turned and headed back to the cabin, where a hot shower and a dress I didn't want to wear awaited me.

I picked up my phone, tempted to text Delilah and tell her we'd be late. But I knew how much this night meant to her. That was why I was actually considering wearing that damned dress. It wasn't that the dress was ugly, I just didn't like dresses. I'd never really had any reason to wear one until now. The teal silk was my favorite color and I wanted nothing more than to force myself to put it on. But that would have to wait until I got this mud off.

I wasn't a prissy girl; mud didn't bother me. Disappointing people who were important to me was my issue. I really liked Delilah, and didn't want to be the one to ruin this birthday for her. I felt bad for her run of bad luck. For the past three years, since she became mated to Kayden, something horrible had happened on her birthday. I blamed him. He had the bad juju from rejecting his claim as head alpha of his pack and turning his back on the wolf clans. When they mated, he passed it to her.

I didn't believe all the superstitions that Grammy shoved at me either, but I'd seen this one at work. So, I knew it was his fault. "Red? Is that you?" My sweet grandmother insisted on calling me that, even though she knew I hated it.

"Yes, Grammy. I have to shower and get ready for Delilah's party. Are you going?" I called through the house, wondering where she was and how she'd known I came inside. She seemed to have heightened senses, even for a wolf.

I didn't get any of that. I couldn't even shift. So, I fought harder and longer than anyone else. Our wolf tribe was made up of four different packs that were local to the area. They'd decided centuries ago to work together to survive instead of competing against each other. Because of that, there was a competition every twenty or thirty years to decide who the tribe's head alpha would be. Right now, that was my father, Gunnar. I tried to think of him as Dad, really, but it was hard. He was more of a drill sergeant than a dad.

"Oh, child. I'll be along a bit later. I have some things to do first." Her response sounded further away. The cabin was only so big. Where was Grammy hiding? I shook the thought away, along with the regret that my dad wasn't a better one. I locked my bedroom door and took a shower in my en suite.

The hot water felt like a gift from the goddess after traipsing around in the mud all morning. I understood why Kayden pushed me, but I knew it didn't matter. If I couldn't find a way to break my curse, I'd never truly fit in. I let myself get lost in the heat and scents of the shower, trying not to think about how much I'd let everyone down.

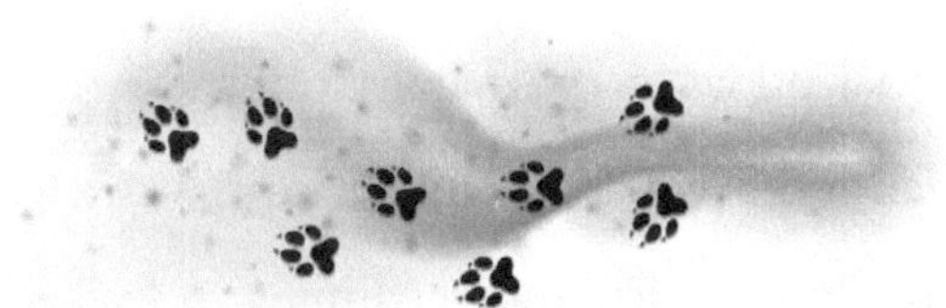

DELILAH

I smoothed my hands down my form-fitting red dress and winked at myself in the mirror. If this didn't get me all the attention at karaoke tonight, nothing would. My guys had been distracted for a while, and I was starting to get upset about it.

I knew there was some unrest in the city the past couple of weeks. How would there not be when the humans were finding out about us? Every day, more and more of them realized that the supernatural was real. This could be a huge problem for us. Because of it, the Council had been calling meetings and begging Kayden to join them.

Of course, he refused. Who could blame him? He'd been controlled by them for years without knowing it. They'd started reaching out to me as a way to get to him. I enjoyed telling them to fuck off way more than I should have. Then Vik called them back and decided to join. That threw us all off. I shook off the bad mood that was settling, and walked out of the bedroom to find Anna. She was dealing with the menu and staff for our event tonight. And all of my guys were due home later. We would finally all be under the same roof at the same time.

Karaoke was becoming a big deal at Midnight again. I smiled to myself as I strolled through the suite I shared with my men. It was strange that none of them were home right now. Eli was in Tokyo for business, Vik was with the Council, Dec was at his office across town, and Kayden had been called back to the forest village he grew up in. They hated leaving me alone, but Steph and Scott had my security covered. Besides, I was a bad ass hybrid. If I couldn't tear someone apart as a vampire, I'd shift into my wolf and do it that way.

"Anna? Where are you?" I called as I stepped into the living room and looked around for her. *Weird, I wonder where she's gone off to.* I let the thought trail off as I walked into the kitchen to grab a blood bag before looking for her. Maybe she went downstairs to talk to Scott or Steph about something. They'd all become close recently. I suspected that Steph and Scott were together, but couldn't prove it yet. He looked at her like a man in love, but she kept her feelings hidden and maintained as much distance as she could in public. I'd walked in on a few stolen moments, though, and pretended not to notice. At some point I would ask her about it and see if she would tell me the truth.

I drank my dinner leisurely, grabbed my phone, then strolled to the elevator that would take me down to the bar. Fear pricked along my spine, and I had to hold myself back from shifting. I refused to shred this gorgeous dress. I knew that Kayden had at least one extra hidden somewhere, because he knew how much I loved it. And although I'd been getting better at controlling my shifts, I couldn't stop it completely if there was danger.

On the elevator, I let myself marvel in the craziness that was my life. I'd gone from broke working for my uncle at his dive bar to being shot and turned into a vamp, then fought against my brother who wanted to take over the world, and ended up becoming a hybrid. I only knew of a couple of others like me who were vamp and wolf shifter. I'd been visiting Grammy regularly for the past few months, trying to get a handle on my new abilities.

The doors opened and pulled me away from my thoughts. I'd finished the blood bag and dropped it into the trash outside the elevator. The bar was dark, which was unusual. Even in the daytime, there were neon lights that lit Midnight up. It was always warm and inviting. But today, it was cold and dark, reminding me of the day I'd met Vik.

Had something happened to Anna? I would feel awful if my one human friend got mixed up in our problems. There was a faction of humans who had learned of our existence and wanted to rid the world of "the abominations" as they called us. Lucky for me, they had no idea how right they were about me. I was the worst of them all.

I stopped for a moment to push down my urge to shift. My mind swam with thoughts of Anna being harmed simply because she was friends with me. I couldn't allow that to happen. I would protect her with everything I had, including my wolf side, if it came to that.

"Anna? Are you down here?" I called softly, slipping my heels off to walk silently through the bar in search of my friend. I would never forgive myself if anything happened to her. I'd lost sight of her safety once, and refused to let it happen again. I heard a muffled noise coming from the stock room. I dropped my heels next to the bar and went to check it out.

I padded silently to the stock room door and paused with my hand on it. I needed a breath to calm myself before my wolf completely took over. I could feel the pull of the shift trying to take over. With a slow shove, the door opened and I gasped.

In front of me was Anna, being devoured by a man I didn't recognize. And by devoured, I mean he had her sprawled across some crates and his face was between her legs. I covered my eyes with my hand while leaving enough room to see what was going on. The moment she saw me, she squealed and pulled the man up to cover herself with him.

"I'm sorry to interrupt. I just wanted to make sure you were okay. It scared me when you disappeared while I was getting dressed. I'll leave you to it." I turned and raced from the room, not stopping until I was sitting at a table next to the front door. While I was glad she was okay, I was annoyed that she was hooking up with someone in secret. Why hadn't she told me?

I glanced at my phone and saw that I had messages from Vik and Kayden. Vik's meeting was going to run over, and Red didn't like the dress I'd sent her. Of course, she didn't. Because I hadn't sent it. That golden monstrosity was all Vik. My guys insisted that she have something glam to wear to the bar and refused to listen to me when I told them that it wasn't her style. I would have put her in something like I had on, but in a deep teal color. But Kayden had insisted that she would wear it if he told her that it was from me.

Before I could respond, Anna was standing in front of me with the guy she'd been about to fuck in the stock room. "I'm so sorry D, I didn't want you to find out like this."

"To find out what exactly? That you've been hiding things from me? I'll admit, it was a shock. But you're an adult and can do what you please with whoever you want. Just not in my bar, okay?"

"I wasn't trying to hide it," she sighed. "Rowan has been busy, and you've been training. Besides, it's not like he's a stranger. You know him." She gestured to the man as if he and I were friends. And now that I was looking at his face instead of the back of his head, she was right. I did recognize him. Rowan was part of Kayden's pack. He'd been involved in my training with Grammy.

"I'm sorry, I didn't recognize you," I said to him before turning to her. "You could have told me."

Anna pulled me into her arms and hugged me tightly. "I know. I'm the worst. Will you forgive me?" Before I could answer, the front door opened and Kayden strolled in with Garnet Trion on his heels.

He pulled me from Anna's arms into his and pressed his lips to mine. I wrapped my arms around his neck and momentarily forgot that Anna and Rowan were there. I poured my emotions into the kiss, letting Kayden feel how much I'd missed him through our psychic bond. He backed me up and pressed me against the wall, letting me feel exactly what I did to him. He was hard and ready. Unfortunately, we were downstairs in the bar instead of upstairs in our home. And we had an audience.

Down boy. We can't exactly fuck right here in front of company. The moment he heard the thought in his head, he tensed and froze.

Are you sure? The response made me laugh, then I pushed him back so I could get some space. There was no way I would be able to resist him if he tried to carry me upstairs. I'd missed all of my men so much the past few weeks. I was looking forward to having some time together to relax and enjoy each other.

"I'm sure. Besides, you didn't tell me you'd be coming with Garnet. I thought you had business to attend to," I accused.

"I already handled it. Now I'm here. Am I first?" He looked around as if searching for the others. Then Kayden looked at me hopefully.

"Yes, you're the first. But to be fair, Dec is the only one who could have beat you. Vik is at a Council meeting and Eli is on a plane," I explained. Then I watched as he pulled out his phone and sent a text. A moment later my phone pinged, letting me know that he'd sent the message in our group chat.

I win, fuckers. Pay up.

Not a chance, asshole. I'm on a plane. There was no way I could win this one.

Shit, I lost track of time. On my way.

I'd expected a response from Vik, but it was obvious he'd turned off his phone for the meeting. I understood why he did it. But part of me loved knowing that he was at my beck and call all the time. Moments like this made me miss him even more.

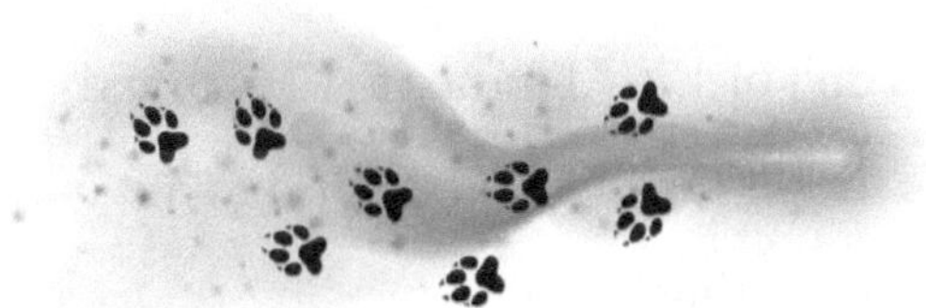

GARNET

Watching Kayden greet Delilah stirred something inside of me. I'd always wanted to find my mate, but my father insisted that I needed to learn to hunt the monsters instead of chasing love. I'd grown up as one of the boys, even though I let my flame-colored curls grow nearly to my waist. It was the only feminine thing about me, besides my figure. The dress Delilah picked for me was beautiful, but it wasn't me. So instead, I wore a pair of black pants and a teal silk button up shirt. The shirt was nearly the same color as the dress, so maybe that would make her happy enough to not get hateful about the stupid thing.

After she finally fought him off, D turned to me. "I see you decided against the dress." She looked over her shoulder at Kayden. "I told you. Pay up."

"You didn't pick it?" I turned to Kayden and growled. "Kayden, you dick. I can't believe you lied to me about that. I felt bad for not wearing it."

D laughed and pulled me into a hug. "Don't worry, I'll punish him later." Her whisper in my ear caused me to erupt in laughter. She joined in until he growled. "Super hearing. I forgot." D looked at him sheepishly, but I knew they were mostly playing around. He wasn't angry with her at all. If anything, he was feeling territorial because I had my arms around his mate. Which I knew wasn't okay, but also I liked D, so I didn't fight her on hugs anymore.

"So, when does this party start? I could use some refreshments and relaxation after that training session," I announced.

"As soon as the rest of my guys get here. I'm sure they've invited half the city too," D answered. She looked beautiful in her red silk dress. To be fair, she looked beautiful no matter what she was wearing. Those were the perks of being a vampire. Because being a wolf shifter who couldn't shift didn't come with those benefits. I looked homeless most of the time because I worried more about training than fashion.

My entire life had been about training. My father insisted that I train with the boys, and Grammy agreed. "There's something different about her," she would say. That would piss my dad off and they'd argue. I didn't understand the language they used. I knew it was the old tongue that had been passed down through wolf packs for generations, but my dad didn't want us to learn it. They fought about that too. It seemed like he and Grammy fought about everything. I hated being unable to shift like the others in my pack. There was something different about me, but Grammy nor Dad would tell me what it was.

I wasn't going to focus on fighting. Tonight, was about celebrating Delilah.

TWO – INTRUDERS

DELILAH

I knew something was off a moment later, when the door swung open and Declan sauntered inside without even a word. His eyes were glazed over and he stared at me hungrily, but not in a sexual way. "Dec? Are you okay?" I glanced at Kayden, hoping he would realize there was a problem.

He stepped between us and Dec swung at him. "Ah, shit, not this mind control stuff again." That would explain the look on Dec's face. He clearly wasn't happy to see me.

"Get out of my way. I have to take her back to them," Dec growled in Kayden's face. They struggled, and for a moment, I thought Dec was going to break free. Then Garnet stepped in and smashed a crystal vase over his head, knocking him out. Dec slumped over in Kayden's arms.

"Upstairs—the restraints," I shouted at him, not thinking that everyone here would be learning something about our sex life. I shook the thought away and followed my wolf mate to the elevator. I was surprised when Garnet entered right behind us.

"You'll need me if he starts to wake up again," she said with a shrug. I nodded and we hit the elevator button to take us to the penthouse. As soon as the doors opened, Garnet grabbed

Dec's feet and Kayden held under his arms. They followed me to the bedroom and placed him on the bed while I got the straps ready. Once Dec was tied down with the vampire-proof leather, I breathed a sigh of relief.

"I'm not even gonna ask," Garnet smirked. I knew she'd tease me about this forever, but at this point she had no idea if I was the one who liked to get tied down or not. And I wasn't about to tell her.

"So, what do we know?" I began, then realized that Anna and Rowan had followed us up here. Great, now everyone will have theories about my sex life.

"We know he wasn't alone," Rowan said, not even glancing at where we had Dec tied up. "As soon as you headed up here with him, a van tore down the street. I followed them for a minute, but didn't want to leave Anna unprotected." He pulled her into his arms and held her close. I might have to approve of this relationship after all. At least he wanted to protect her.

"Any idea who it was?" Kayden asked, staring at Dec as if willing him to wake up. Rowan shook his head. "Damn."

The elevator doors opened again, and we all braced for whatever was coming at us. The bedroom door swung open and Vik strolled in. "Just what the fuck are all of these people doing in our bedroom? And why is Declan tied up? Tonight isn't his turn."

My cheeks turned as red as Garnet's hair, and I shook my head at him. "He attacked me, or tried to. Something or someone was controlling him. She knocked him out and we tied him up."

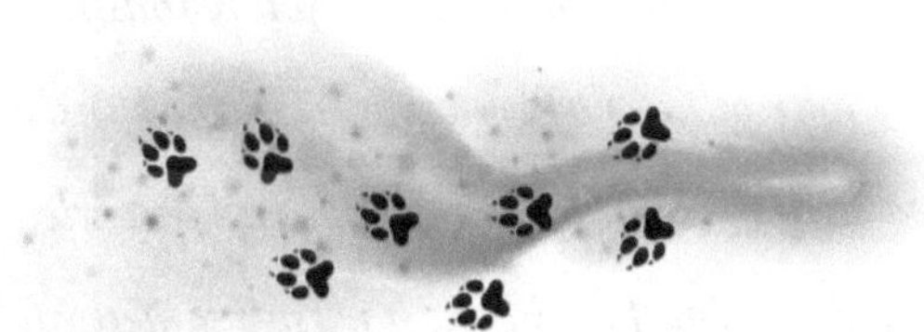

VIK

Walking into our bedroom and finding extra people there was strange. Realizing that someone had managed to mind-control Declan was worse. At least Kayden had been here and had some help to subdue him. Upon seeing Garnet was one of the guests in our room, my mind flashed back to the meeting I'd just left.

"I cannot agree to that. I've told you, I will be a part of your Council, but I am not giving up my family or my life outside of this," I insisted again. Since the incident with Delilah's brother, the Council had been completely revamped. It now included vampires, witches, wolf shifters, and humans. Declan's brother, James, was seated beside me.

"We can't deal with this threat if you're constantly leaving to go back to your other blood-suckers," Gunnar insisted. I wasn't impressed with the Shadowtail alpha, and intended to stand my ground against him. I could tell it wasn't something he was used to.

"Mr. Trion, I was invited here just the same as you were. We are to be colleagues on this Council. That does not give you the right to order me around," I spat. Gunnar Trion growled, his wolf dangerously near the surface. He needed to learn control, or he would be of no use to us here.

"Gentlemen, please. Let's not fight. Vik has a point, Gunnar. You are not in charge here. Stop trying to take over. This isn't your pack," a witch named Amber stated, not the least concerned that she'd called him out in front of everyone.

"Then let's get this meeting started. I have places to be very soon," I agreed. I walked over to the large oval conference table and took my seat. I was perfectly happy to let Amber lead the *meeting. She had already proven herself to be a powerful witch who could easily keep everyone in line. It helped that her values aligned with mine.*

I didn't think much of her father, and that was no secret. The man was cruel and desperately in need of an attitude adjustment as Eli called it. "Eli isn't back yet?"

Delilah shook her head. The tears in her eyes hurt me, but I knew that they were for whatever imagined pain Declan was in. I'd never been under someone else's control, so I had no idea if it hurt or not. "Well, there's not much we can do until Eli gets back. None of us know anything about mind control or the tech that would be needed to find the source. So, let's make sure Midnight is secure while we wait."

I hadn't meant it to come out as an order, but Kayden's face told me that was how it sounded. He had been helping me work on that for a while. There were times, though, when I couldn't help it. *I know you're worried, but you have to tone it down with the orders. You're not in charge here.*

I closed my eyes and took a breath. He was right. I wasn't the one in charge here. We had unanimously decided to let Delilah run Midnight with our assistance, not that she needed much. This would be her call. "I'm sorry, Myshka, I'm not trying to step on toes. What would you like for us to do?"

Much better, Fangs. I didn't mind Kayden's voice in my head, but sometimes he was a dick. A handsome one, but still. I ignored the comment and the nickname. I was aware that he meant it affectionately, but it still annoyed me sometimes. I grabbed her hand and pulled her into my arms. She leaned her head back to kiss me. I took full advantage of the offer and kissed her like my life depended on it. I wanted to kick everyone out and have my way with her while forcing Dec to watch. That would be his punishment for getting himself taken over. *Fangs, I know what you're thinking, but you have to let her tell us what she needs. You can't just kick everyone out.* Why did he know exactly what I was thinking? Eli's damned implant. Fuck.

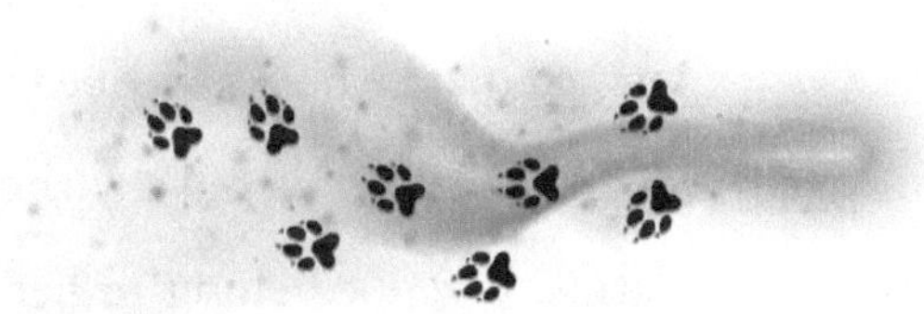

GARNET

Viktor Maxwell was a force to be reckoned with. I knew that my father butted heads with him constantly at council meetings. That made me like him even more. I didn't care that he was brash and cold. He obviously loved Delilah and would kill to protect her. I could only hope that the moon goddess blessed me with such an amazing mate. If I were being honest, I might have developed a slight crush on him. But I would never act on it. I respected Delilah too much. That didn't stop me from watching him kiss her and wishing it was me.

But no, that would never happen. Besides, no daughter of Gunnar Trion would ever stoop so low as to have a relationship with a fanger or a human. My father was the most racist man I'd ever known. Not that I'd had much chance to know people, since I'd been stuck in our compound for my entire life. At least until Kayden insisted that he needed my help.

A knock at the door pulled me from my thoughts and Delilah from Vik's arms. I stepped closer to her as Kayden walked over and answered the door. My first instinct was always to protect Delilah. It didn't matter to me that she was probably stronger than I was. I'd trained for this my entire life. She was still learning to control her shift.

My heart actually skipped a beat when the door opened. The man on the other side had to be related to Dec; they looked so similar. I glanced from him to where Declan was tied up, then back. The man's eyes widened but he didn't speak. Kayden ushered him inside.

"He's fine, James. Well, mostly. There was an issue, so we had to knock him out and tie him up. He was trying to hurt Delilah," Kayden explained.

The man raced past me and knelt beside the bed. Everyone relaxed as soon as they realized who was at the door. I should have taken that as a good sign, but it made me nervous. Who was this guy?

I didn't realize I'd stepped toward him when he walked over to Dec. I thought of these people as family, and couldn't resist the urge to protect. Delilah put her hand on my arm to stop me. I looked over my shoulder at her and she smiled. "James is Declan's brother. Yes, he's human, but he's family." I took a breath and let my body relax. No one here would be in danger from this sexy man. My eyes locked with his for a moment and I felt a zing of electricity run through my body.

Wait, why was I checking out Dec's brother? He was another one who was on Gunnar's "do not approach" list. I didn't care. He was hot.

James checked his brother, and I wondered what he did for a living. He seemed to know what he was doing. Could he be a doctor? Fuck, I needed to get laid. I was standing here picturing Declan's brother in scrubs, and he was even sexier than in his jeans. I met Delilah's gaze and knew I'd been busted in my little daydream.

"Why don't we go into the other room while James checks Dec out? He's an EMT, so he can make sure there's nothing else wrong with him. Then when Eli gets here, he can figure out what caused the mind control," she offered. I nodded, blushing. I heard her talking to Vik when I walked out.

"You and Rowan should check the perimeter. Kayden can help James. Anna, come with us. We'll have some girl time. I'll let you know as soon as I hear from Eli." I glanced back and saw her kiss him again. For some reason, this time, I wasn't jealous at all. Strange how five minutes could change everything.

I waited for Delilah in the living room. Anna walked out before she did, but Delilah was right behind her. "So, James, huh?" Anna turned to me as she spoke, and I felt my cheeks turn even more red.

"I don't know what you're talking about," I deflected. I knew that there was no denying that I found him attractive, but I wasn't about to tell Anna and Delilah that. What if they told Gunnar? That was the last thing I needed.

"Don't tease her too much, Anna. You remember Gunnar? That's her dad," Delilah offered. Anna grimaced.

"I'm so sorry. I was just teasing. James is hot. It's impossible not to notice. I won't say anything else," she promised. Apparently, my father had a reputation. I wasn't sure if that was good or not.

"I appreciate that, but there's nothing to say. I mean, yeah, he's attractive. But he's human, and my family would not be okay with that. I mean no offense—I don't hold the same ideals as my father in those regards, but for me to go against the head alpha would be suicide," I explained. Anna nodded as if she understood.

"Garnet, it's okay. Don't worry about your dad. You have to give yourself a chance to find love. And if that's with James, your father will have to get over it. The heart decides who we love, not the brain," Delilah insisted. I knew that she was right. But that didn't mean I was ready to face my father and object to his opinions.

"Can we just focus on what's going on here, and leave my non-existent love life alone?" I didn't want to be rude, but I wasn't going to have this conversation with them. I had felt something strange when I looked into James' eyes, and I wasn't ready to talk about it yet.

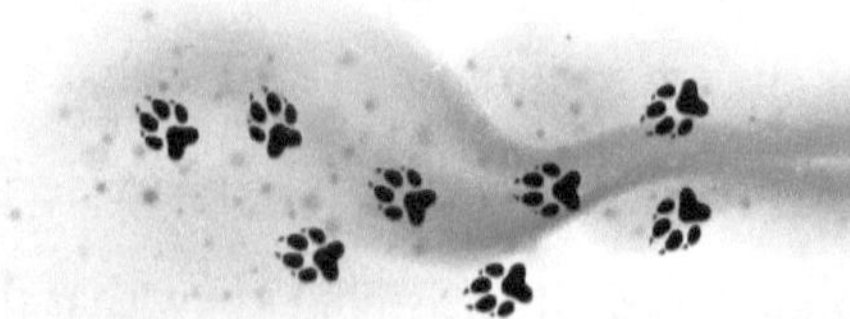

DELILAH

"We can do that. Let's see if we can figure out what happened tonight. I'll tell you what I know and maybe you can fill in the blanks?" I would do my best to stay calm, even though I was worried about Dec and what would happen if Eli couldn't figure out how he was being controlled.

I explained to Garnet and Anna that Declan had a meeting earlier with a top-secret client. I had no idea who it was or what it was about. The only thing he would say was that it was a commission for a new furniture piece. There had been no indication that he was in any type of danger. And his studio was only a few blocks away. He walked to work and back every day.

While I was telling them what I knew, the power started to flicker. That was odd. Midnight, and our apartment above it, had its own transformer. Then there were the backup generators. The only way the power could go out is if someone took the generators out first, the cut the power. "What the fuck was that?" Garnet asked as the power went out again.

Anna squealed and I darted across the room to her, only to find that Rowan had her in his arms. He must have rushed up here when the power went out. It was dark, but with my enhanced senses, I could still see enough to catch movement. "Garnet? Was that you?" I turned toward the movement and heard a grunt before someone hit the floor. I rushed toward the noise and found Garnet knocked out.

"Shit, Rowan? Get Anna out of here; keep her safe and don't come back until Eli tells you it's safe." I could hear her crying and knew that she was freaking out about the situation. She hated the dark. It was a tragic story from her childhood that she probably hadn't shared with him.

"I can't leave you alone, Delilah. It's not safe. We don't even know who broke in," he argued. Typical man, expecting a woman to need his help.

"Rowan, listen to me. I'm a hybrid and I can shift if I need to. Please, just take Anna home and stay with her. Besides, Vik and Kayden are probably headed this way since the lights went out. I'll take Garnet in the bedroom with Dec and James. We'll lock the door. It'll be fine." I hated arguing with him, but I couldn't focus on protecting myself if Anna was here.

"Fine, but if Vik comes after me for this," he started.

"He won't. You have my word," I cut him off. I wouldn't let Vik go after him for listening to what I wanted. Rowan sighed, then scooped Anna up and raced off. Once that was taken care of, I picked Garnet up and moved into the bedroom.

"James? Are you okay in here?" I called quietly. I had no idea where the intruders were or what they wanted.

"Ugh, my head," he answered. "I think they took Dec. I tried to fight them off, but it was so dark and I have no idea how many there were. I'm sorry, Delilah." His apology touched me, even though he hadn't done anything wrong.

I dropped Garnet on the bed as gently as I could, then walked over to my dresser. I knew there was a flashlight in the top drawer. "I need you to check Garnet and make sure she's okay. I have no idea how hard she got hit. We'll find Dec, don't worry."

I turned the flashlight on as soon as I grabbed it. Turning back, I saw James on the floor at the foot of the bed. He must have decided it was safer to stay there than to try and move in the dark. I remembered how hard it was to see in the dark when I was human, so I didn't blame him. "Here, this should help." I handed him the light and stepped back as he stood up and walked over to Garnet.

"Looks superficial; she should come to in a few minutes. And she'll probably have a worse headache than I do. What the hell is my brother mixed up in?" he asked candidly.

"I wish I knew," I admitted. This whole situation was strange, and reminded me too much of what happened when my brother was after me. I knew that wasn't possible anymore, but the idea still terrified me.

Before he could ask me any more questions, Garnet started to groan and covered her eyes with her arm. "So bright," she muttered. James was staring at her as if he'd lost himself, the light still pointed at her face.

"James, the light," I urged. He turned to me with a strange expression, then seemed to realize and pull himself from his thoughts.

"Oh, right. Sorry," he said as he turned the flashlight away from her face and pointed it at the wall. "Are you okay? Don't move too fast."

THREE – DAMN YOU, VINCENT GARNET

Once the light was no longer blinding me, I took a good look at the man leaning over me. James was so close I could have leaned up and kissed him. What was I thinking? I threw my arm over my face as fast as I could so he wouldn't see the blush creeping over my cheeks. After he turned the light away, I saw that Delilah was standing behind him.

"What happened?" I asked, focusing on her instead of the insanely hot man who was still too close to my face.

"Someone took Dec," she answered before walking toward the door. I could tell she was looking for some sort of clue, and I desperately wanted to help her. I just wasn't sure how. What good was a wolf who couldn't shift?

I tried to sit up, but James put a hand on my shoulder. "Not so fast. You probably have a slight concussion and the lights are still out. Just lie back and rest." I could have shoved him away and gotten up, but since my head was swimming a little, I decided to take his advice.

"Where's Kayden? What happened to Anna?" I still had a ton of questions, and it didn't seem like I would be getting answers any time soon. Although, the view from here was nothing to complain about. I put my hand on James' and explained, "I need to sit up. I'm not taking off, I promise."

He helped me sit up against the headboard, and I felt weird being in Delilah's bed. I knew that she was probably the one who'd put me here, but still. "Kayden is with Vik—I'm guessing that they're still checking the perimeter. I sent Rowan to take Anna home. She wasn't safe here, and I needed to focus on getting you taken care of."

Delilah's words stung. If I'd been more focused, I would have been able to fight off my attacker. Instead, I'd let myself get knocked out. Of course, she's going to feel like she needs to protect me. Damn, I could not catch a break. Until tonight, I was convinced that Delilah saw me as an equal. But now, that was ruined. One stupid mistake, and my delusions were shattered. I would have to fight twice as hard to regain that respect.

But that was a later problem. James was right, I had a concussion. The room was spinning and my head was throbbing. "Can't you do that freaky mate thing where you talk to Kayden in his head? Tell him that someone took Declan and then he'll come back up here faster."

"I tried that. He and Vik are convinced that they can find whoever did it if they keep searching. And he insisted that they can get the lights back on. They want us to stay here," she responded. Delilah sounded annoyed at being dismissed that way. I didn't blame her; a mate was supposed to put you before anything else, and that didn't seem to be what Kayden was doing. Maybe my father was right, perhaps Kayden had strayed too far from the old ways.

I didn't get to dwell on that for very long, because he and Vik showed up. "We need to call Gunnar. The wolves are our best chance here. They can track better than we can, and can get by undetected."

Vik didn't like that idea, and countered with one of his own. "I think we should involve the council. This is clearly a matter for them. They are trying to fix past wrongs, after all. What better way than to help track down a missing vampire?"

For a moment, I thought there was going to be a fight. Kayden and Vik stood chest to chest glaring at each other. Delilah stepped between them. "Stop. We're not fighting about which group can do a better job at finding Declan. Kiss and make up, then call both." I jumped at her words, thinking she was teasing them, but Vik reached out and grabbed Kayden by the neck before pulling him close over Delilah's shoulder. When their lips met, I realized I was staring, and quickly turned my attention back to James, who looked nearly as uncomfortable as I did.

Don't get me wrong, I have no problem with a little guy on guy action, I just wasn't expecting the uber growly alpha male to let a vamp manhandle him that way. If I were being honest, it was pretty hot. I didn't want to gawk, so I kept my attention focused on James. His blue-gray eyes locked with mine, and I wanted nothing more than to lose myself in them. A wave of dizziness came over me again, and he stepped forward to catch me.

My lips were mere inches from his, and I had to fight the urge to close the distance. I let my eyes flutter closed and waited for him to kiss me. Instead, he pulled me close and laid my head on his shoulder. "I've got you, Red. You're okay." Shit. I hated that nickname, and now the hot new guy picked up on it. Well, I had two choices here, call him out on it and admit that I'm okay—which would be admitting I thought he was going to kiss me, or play like I didn't hear him and let him hold me for a moment longer.

Of course, I opted to keep his strong arms wrapped around me. His scent reminded me of the woods right after it rained. Before I could stop myself, I buried my face in his neck and breathed deeply. At that moment, I didn't care what my father would say. I felt a strange zing of electricity when James touched me, and I wanted to keep feeling it.

"Is she okay?" Delilah's words preceded her brushing my hair off my face. Damn, I couldn't even get five minutes alone with James.

"I think she just got a little dizzy. She should be okay in a minute," he answered, obviously not ready to let go of me either. Hmm, that was an interesting thought.

"Well, if you've got her, I'll go referee Kayden and Vik. Otherwise, they'll be fighting again. Scott is supposed to get the lights back on. Hopefully that doesn't take too long. You two are safer in here than anywhere else. I'll be back in a few minutes," she said, and I peeked through my lashes to watch her leave. I was finally alone with James, and terrified of what could happen. Or what could not happen, depending on how I looked at it.

I waited a minute after she left to lift my head. "I'm okay, really." James leaned forward and pressed his lips to mine. My breath caught and I froze for a second before giving myself over to the sensation. I wanted to lose myself in him. I parted my lips and let him deepen the kiss. My heart was racing at the forbidden sensation. I knew it could get us both in trouble if we were caught.

Emptiness washed over me when he pulled away. "I'm sorry, that was completely inappropriate. I shouldn't have kissed you without permission." James ducked his head and looked at me through his full lashes. That scamp! He wasn't really sorry but neither was I. I'd wanted to kiss him and was relieved that he felt the same.

"No need to apologize. I enjoyed it. I can't let that happen again, though."

"Oh, you have a boyfriend?" I was glad he wasn't giving up so easily. It did make rejecting him harder though. I wanted to rip his clothes off and fuck him on Delilah's bed, but that wouldn't be a good idea.

I shook my head. "No, no boyfriend. An overprotective father who doesn't approve of humans in general, much less dating his only daughter." He nodded.

"I've met your dad. He's definitely something. I didn't realize he was that prejudiced, though. I mean, since he's on the council with me and all." James smirked at me.

"You're on the council? Then why didn't you go with Vik to talk to the others?" I hadn't expected James to be on the council. Even with our secrets getting out to the public, I would have thought the council would recruit an older human to fill that spot.

"You needed me more than he did. Besides, they won't make a decision without me. Vik will let me know when they're ready for me. I wasn't about to leave you until I knew you were okay," he admitted. It was sweet, even if he was being completely stupid. "So, you're really not going to let me kiss you again?"

I leaned toward him as he spoke, my lips seeming to have a mind of their own. I stopped myself just before we touched. "I can't."

"Don't you want to?" He was killing me with his teasing, and I didn't even think he was doing it on purpose.

"I do, but I can't. We can't. My father," I began, but he cut me off by pressing his lips to mine. I put my hands on his chest to push him away, and ended up sliding them up to wrap around his neck and pull him closer. He deepened the kiss, and I let myself drown in the sensations for a moment. Electricity zinged through me and I wanted to hold onto that feeling.

"Don't let him decide if you'll give me a chance or not. Please," he whispered against my lips when he pulled away.

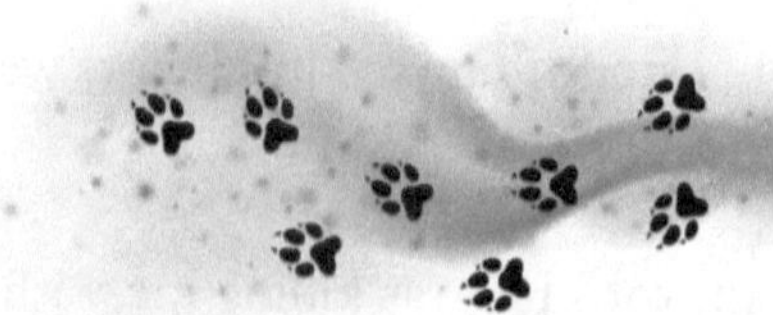

KAYDEN

I hated fighting with Vik. That wasn't true; I loved fighting with Vik. It was always heated and ended up with Delilah pulling us apart just before we started duking it out. I pretended to be upset when she started the 'kiss and make up' thing, but I didn't mind exploring my feelings for Vik. The five of us were a family, and there was no reason we couldn't all enjoy each other, as long as Delilah approved. And she definitely did.

She encouraged us to explore whatever we were comfortable with. So, when she'd insisted that Vik and I stop fighting, I let him lead. My heart skipped a little faster when he grabbed the back of my neck and pulled me in for a kiss.

I wondered what Garnet thought about it, then decided that I didn't care. I let myself relax into the kiss, with Delilah pressed between us, feeling what we did to each other. I wasn't ashamed that I enjoyed kissing him. The feeling of his lips on mine and his tongue stroking mine was enough to make my dick stand at attention. Unfortunately, we had other things to attend to before we could explore those sensations further.

Delilah had convinced us to call the wolves and the council. I knew Gunnar wouldn't be happy, because he would have to represent both sides. Luckily, I got to call him first. I knew from what Vik had told us about the council meetings that Gunnar wasn't fond of vampires, and didn't bother to hide his disdain for humans, either. Of course, that just meant that he hadn't changed from when I was a kid.

Gunnar Trion was the most grumpy alpha I had ever met. He hated the fact that I was stronger than him, and that my family had more of a claim on The Whispering Thicket than his did. The moment I turned down becoming the head alpha for the combined packs was the happiest in his life. It left him without a true challenger. Sure, other alphas had tried, but I was the only one who was strong enough to beat him. I didn't want it, though. I didn't know why at the time, but it was because the moon goddess intended me for Delilah.

Everything good in my life revolved around that woman. Well, I guess hybrid was a more appropriate term. Because of me, she was no longer just the vampire that Declan had turned her into in order to save her life. My bite had transformed her. I thought it would kill her, but she was stronger than that. Grammy had helped her through the transformation, and she was adjusting well to the changes. I was impressed that she'd held off her wolf with all this stress.

I held the phone to my ear and waited for Gunnar to answer. "What the fuck do you want, boy?" Ah, Gunnar. Always the charmer.

"Well, old man, I wanted to let you know that your daughter is fine. And we need the wolves. Dec was taken. We don't know who did it. We're coming to you; be ready." I didn't wait for his response, but could still hear him cursing as I disconnected the call.

I turned to Delilah, who was sitting on the couch between where I was pacing and where Vik was pacing. "He'll be there. And the packs will be gathered."

"You didn't give him much choice, did you?" she asked with a chuckle.

"That's how it's done, babe," I assured her. I didn't worry much that Delilah didn't get the inner workings of a wolf pack. The stronger wolf always gave orders and the weaker wolves always did what they were told. It's just the way things had always been done. I also failed to mention that I'd pissed Gunnar off by talking to him that way. It didn't matter. I needed the wolves, so they would be there.

A moment later, Vik hung up the phone. "The council will meet us at Whispering Thicket. I assume that's where you arranged for the wolves to be?" His expression told me that he knew I hadn't. But two could play at this game.

"Of course. They'll be there when we get there. We need to take Red with us," I said confidently. I knew that Gunnar would never let me live it down if anything happened to his daughter. I started to walk toward the bedroom where James was making sure she was okay from the concussion, but Delilah raced past me and stood in front of the door.

"I'll get them. You stay out here with Vik. Figure out what you're going to say to the council and the wolf packs. Then call Eli and make sure he knows what's going on," she insisted.

That seemed strange, but I let it go. Everyone was so stressed today, and people were acting odd.

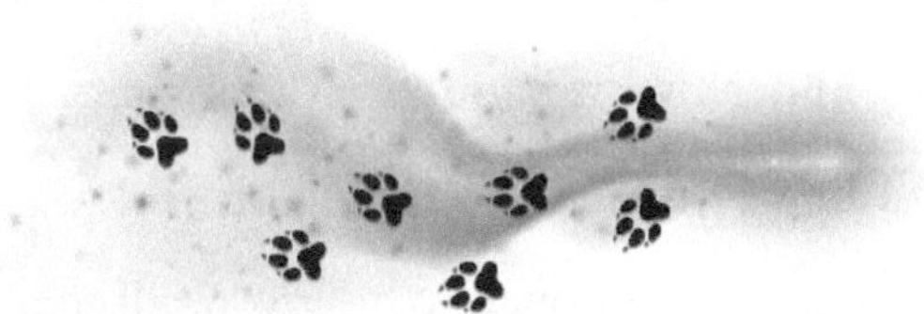

DELILAH

I barely stopped Kayden from barging in on Garnet and James. If he'd seen what I suspected was happening, he would feel obligated to tell Gunnar. And I wasn't about to let that happen. I could tell that James and Garnet were attracted to each other. I, for one, would fully support them getting together, even though James was human, and technically Garnet was not. The fact that she didn't have the ability to shift made her nearly human, and they seemed like a good fit. I'd gotten to know them both since we started rebuilding the council.

I tapped on the door and waited a second. I didn't think they'd be having sex, but I wasn't taking any chances. "Garnet, James, we're getting ready to leave. I'm coming in." I pushed the door open and found them in each other's arms. She jumped and pushed him away, but he held on, obviously still concerned at her almost fainting spell earlier.

"Don't be weird. I'm not spying on you for your father. Nobody is going to know anything you tell me, and no one is telling Gunnar anything." I had to reassure her so that she wouldn't be freaked out by the whole situation. "We do need to load up and head out. Unless Garnet can't travel?"

James shook his head. "She'll be fine. I'm coming with you, though." He held up a hand to Garnet to stop her protest. "Two reasons—number one, your safety; number two, I'm on the council, so I'll have to be there for talks."

"I figured you'd both ride with us. We should go. Hopefully Eli will be able to meet us there," I added. I hated his overseas flights, but understood that the business didn't run itself. We walked back into the living room to find Kayden and Vik gathering supplies. "What are you two doing?" It looked as if they had dragged half of Eli's office into the middle of the floor and they were sorting through it.

"Eli gave us a list of what he needs. We're trying to figure out what some of it was," Kayden answered. Vik growled.

"None of this stuff fits the description he gave us," he muttered. Although he was cute when he was frustrated, I wanted to get this over with, so I leaned over and looked at the list. I'd actually been working with Eli on some of this tech, and might know what they were hunting for.

"What's next on the list?" I barely got the words out as Kayden started rattling things off. I sifted through the pile and picked out a few things. Then I motioned for him to continue while I placed the items in a box next to me. Once we had everything Eli had requested, I handed the box to Vik and gestured to the door. I felt like everything was taking way too long, and Declan was in danger.

We raced to the clearing in Whispering Thicket, where the wolves were waiting for us. As we climbed out of the SUV, I scanned the crowd for Eli. He was standing next to Gunnar and having a heated conversation. I hated fighting with the old wolf, but he was so set in his ways.

"Eli!" I squealed and ran for him. He grabbed me and spun me around as he pressed his lips to mine. "You were gone too long this time."

"I know, love. But I'm here now, and we're going to get Dec back," he promised.

"Yes, my son Vincent will help you find your mate," Gunnar announced as the others joined us.

FOUR – REJECTION AND OBJECTION
GARNET

"What do you mean, Vincent will help them?" I asked, suddenly furious. These were my friends, and I would be the one to help them. Not my idiot brother. That asshole was incompetence personified. Amusingly enough, he had the same reaction.

"What?" Vincent asked, turning to look from me to our father and back. "Why do I have to help?" Leave it to my brother to sound completely self-centered and lazy in front of company.

"Because I'm your alpha, and I said you would. Do not disrespect me, boy," Gunnar threatened. I shuddered, but wasn't giving up so easily.

"Sir, why can't I help?" I stepped toward him as I spoke, putting myself between him and James. I didn't need him to focus on the fact that I'd gotten out of the car with a human.

"Because I offered your brother. He's stronger and can track better than you. I'm getting tired of this disrespect," he growled. Kayden stepped forward and held up a hand.

"Gunnar, you know I mean you no disrespect. Garnet will be helping us find our mate. She's been training for this type of thing for months now. And I want her help, not Vincent's."

Kayden dipped his head in a mock bow, that was supposed to be a show of respect. My father may have taken it that way, but I knew better. Kayden was preparing to challenge him.

"Boy, you don't get to make those decisions. This is my pack. You abandoned us years ago and forfeited the rights of head alpha." Gunnar's tone had turned even colder than usual, and I knew they were about to fight. Instinctively, I took a step back and pushed James behind me.

I turned to Delilah and whispered, "They're going to fight it out. I suggest we get out of the way." I motioned with my head to where Grammy was standing at the cabin door. Slowly, Delilah, Vik, James, and I moved toward the cabin. I didn't want to catch my father's attention.

As soon as we were close enough to the cabin, Grammy stepped out and held the door open for us to go inside. "You all just come on inside here. Those two are itching to fight, and now they have a reason. I'm sure it'll all be sorted in a minute."

I stepped forward and hugged my grandmother tightly. I'd missed her, even though I'd seen her two days ago. She disappeared into the woods sometimes without explanation. "I wasn't sure if you'd be back or not."

"Well, here I am. Now let's get some tea so we can watch the show," she said as she walked to the kitchen and grabbed the steaming tea pot. Grammy made quick work of sorting out tea for all of us and passing cups around. Before she was done, Luca walked in without knocking. That was his usual with Grammy. He and I had grown up together, and nine times out of ten, where one of us was, the other wasn't far behind.

Luca grabbed a cup and helped himself to some tea, then joined us by the window. He slid between James and me, wrapping an arm possessively around my shoulders. "Hey, James." Weird, I didn't realize they knew each other. We watched as Gunnar and Kayden circled each other, having a heated conversation. I waited for my father to throw the first punch, since he was the one who started this whole thing. Sure enough, he swung at Kayden and missed. I wondered how long it would be before they shifted.

"Are you okay?" Luca asked in my ear, touching his nose to the knot on the side of my head. I winced and he pulled me closer to press his lips to it gently. That seemed a little odd, but I didn't question it. We'd been best friends since we were young.

"I'm good. James said it's just a concussion." I didn't turn to see his expression, but it seemed like that upset him for some reason. That would be a mystery to solve another day. I needed to focus on what was happening outside. Sure enough, both men shifted into their wolf forms, and were trying to rip each other's throats out. "Should we do something?"

"They have to solve it themselves, Red, you know that," Grammy insisted. There was that damned nickname again. I shrugged it off and watched my father fight against my friend. It was hard to tell who was winning. A few minutes later, they both shifted back and shook hands. Grammy walked out and handed them each a pair of sweats to put on since their clothes were shredded. It wasn't an odd sight out here for men or women to walk around naked, so I knew she only did it because we had company.

Kayden walked in the cabin first, with my father behind him. "Gunnar has agreed to let you help us," he began, pausing to look over his shoulder. "But Vincent is coming too."

"What? No. Come on, that's ridiculous!" I objected, then realized that I was out of line and could get punished for it.

"Sir, may I help with the search as well?" Luca stepped toward Gunnar and bowed slightly. The two of them exchanged glances with Kayden, who smirked. My father nodded at him and Luca stood tall once more.

"Keep Red out of trouble. And get this done so you're all back here where you belong," he grumbled.

"I will, sir. You have nothing to worry about." Luca's promise was nothing out of the ordinary, either. He'd been 'protecting' me for years, ever since my father decided that I wasn't capable enough to do anything.

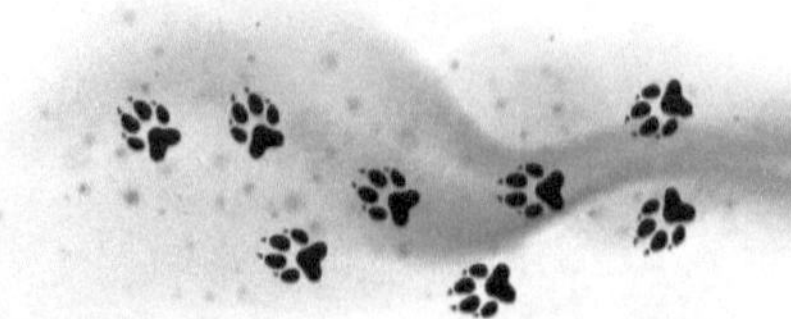

LUCA

I hated kissing Gunnar's ass to get my way. It helped that Red had already managed to get herself entwined in the search. Honestly, she was the only reason I wanted to help. It had looked like James was getting cozy with her, and I needed to find out what was happening there. If she was interested in him, that would explain why she'd basically brushed off all of my advances. Also, Gunnar would have a fit if his only daughter was dating a human. So, if she was, I would have to help her hide it.

James was a good guy. Kayden introduced me a couple of years ago, and we hung out regularly—at Midnight. He'd never come to our camp before. But if his brother was missing, I could understand why Gunnar would allow it. Moments after I got permission to keep Red company, a van pulled up and more people got out. They must be the council Vik and Delilah were talking about before Gunnar and Kayden came back inside.

I didn't pay much attention when Gunnar talked about the things he did within our community or outside of it. I knew that he hated his trips into the city and preferred running us through training after training while screaming that we would never amount to anything. I felt bad for Red, since he was harder on her than anyone else. The only thing that made her different was that she couldn't shift. She had the same abilities as the rest of us, except that one.

I left my arm around Red when she turned back toward the window to watch as Vik walked out with her dad to greet the newcomers. I wasn't really thrilled that they were all meeting here. I felt like it would be an excuse for Gunnar to put us through the ringer later over something. It didn't matter. He would do what he wanted, and if we objected, we'd pay. All I could do was try to stay between him and Red so she didn't bear the brunt of his wrath. I wondered if she realized why I did it. Someday soon, I would have to make a move that she couldn't ignore.

"Should we follow the others?" she asked, pulling me from my thoughts. Everyone else, including James, had gone outside to the picnic tables in the circle. I'd let myself get distracted, again.

"If you want. I was just thinking about what we could be missing with Dec's abduction," I lied. I wasn't about to tell her that I'd been daydreaming about kissing her. That would not go over well. I'd been flirting with her subtly for years. I couldn't just come right out and tell her that.

"Did you come up with anything useful?" I had her full attention now. No doubt she wanted to figure this out so she could impress her father.

"Not really. But I think we should pay attention to every detail. What if it was an inside job?" I didn't think Delilah had anything to do with her mate trying to kidnap her, but couldn't get past the idea that someone within the council could be responsible.

"Like Delilah, or another of her guys? Why would they do that? It doesn't make sense." Red was suddenly pissed. I'd definitely stepped in it with my piss poor explanation.

"That wasn't what I meant," I tried to backpedal and explain, but she slugged me and walked off. I was left to chase after her and try to get her to stop. She kept walking until she reached the tables where everyone else was, so I stopped trying to talk. Instead, I took a seat near her and listened to what the others were discussing.

"Who would want to kidnap Delilah?" one of the council members asked. I didn't know who any of them were, but this one smelled like a witch. She wasn't a shifter, and didn't have the same scent as the vamps.

"The only person we ever had a problem with is dead. So, I have no idea," Delilah insisted. Vik and Kayden agreed with her. When the witch started to talk again, another vehicle pulled up. Everyone turned to see who had arrived.

Eli stepped out of the car and strolled over to Delilah. I felt like a perv watching them make out, but at the same time, it took Red's attention away from how angry she was at me. And it proved a point. There was no way Delilah or any of her guys could have been in on this. And if Red would just hear me out, I could explain exactly what I'd meant. Although the more I thought about it, the less sure I was that someone here could be behind it.

"Where are we with the search?" Eli asked as he sat down and pulled Delilah into his lap. She settled in while Vik and Kayden explained what they knew. Honestly, I'd expected them to know more than they did. No one had any clue why someone would want to brainwash Dec to kidnap Delilah.

Once he was filled in, he took charge. I respected a man who could come into the middle of a situation and take over. "We need to go back to Midnight and regroup. My lab is there, and it's possible they'll return or send Dec back. We have to be there if that happens." Apparently, I wasn't the only one who respected his take charge attitude. Everyone loaded up and followed him back to Midnight.

Upon our arrival, Eli split everyone into pairs and had us checking the perimeter inside and out. I was lucky enough to get paired with Red. She didn't seem thrilled, but I could tell she wasn't as angry with me as she had been. We walked the alley behind Midnight, looking for any sign of who had broken in. We collected some strange fibers and I decided to try my apology again.

"Look, I'm sorry about earlier. I didn't mean that the way it came out. Of course, I don't think Delilah or any of her guys are responsible. But can we really trust this council?"

"I don't know," she responded, as she slipped her hand into mine, just like she always did. We walked together and chatted about her training with Kayden and how her dad had been volatile when she stopped training with him. "I know that I should be worried about him, but I'm not. I don't want him making my decisions for me anymore. I want to be my own woman."

I understood her feelings and agreed. She was old enough to make her own decisions. Perhaps this was the moment I was waiting for. I turned to her, planning to pull Red into my arms and kiss her, but the back door opened and her brother stormed out. "There you are! I should have known."

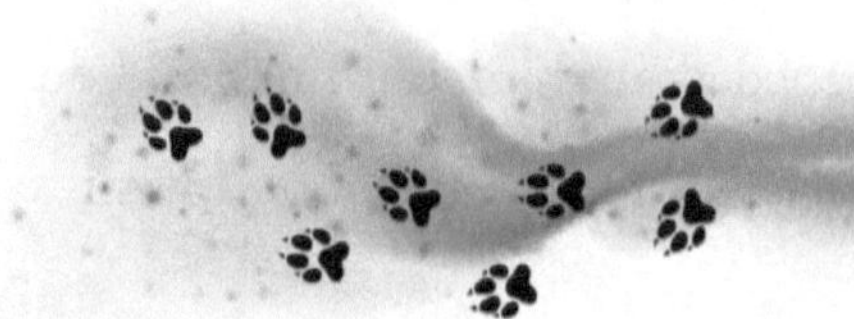

DECLAN

"What do you want with me?" I asked again. I couldn't see the people who had taken me from my home, but I knew they were nearby. When I woke up in our bed, tied up, I wondered what had happened. Before I could ask, the lights went out and I was knocked out again. I woke up here in this chair, tied up and alone.

I didn't remember anything after Scott left me at my studio. Wait, that wasn't right. I remembered texting the group chat that I was on my way. What the fuck had happened between that text and me waking up?

It didn't matter, because now I was in a tough spot and had no idea how to get out of it. I was tied to a chair in the middle of a room with no windows. Although there was something familiar about this room, I had no idea where I was or who had taken me. Delilah must be frantic. I tried to reach her through the telepathic link Eli had installed for us, but something was jamming it. All I got was static.

There had to be a way to get a message to them. Or somehow get them a clue about where I was. I had no idea how, though. I was starting to feel less groggy. Whatever they had used to knock me out was almost completely worn off now. My stomach grumbled. Shit, when was the last time I had a blood bag?

I tugged and pulled at the ropes until I could feel them burning against my wrists. The coppery scent of my blood hung in the air as the ropes dug into my flesh. Great, my abductors knew enough about vamps to use the ropes I couldn't break. This was getting worse by the minute.

"I know you're there. I can smell you. Unless you want a feral vamp on your hands, you need to let me go. Or bring me a blood bag," I growled. I'd only gone feral once, and that was right after I was turned. Kayden had been the one to track me down and bring me back. He and Grammy had tied me up and kept feeding me blood until I was me again.

I swore then that would be the only time I let that happen. I didn't have much say in things right now, but maybe I could convince my captors to at least feed me. Was that shadow moving? Did I hear footsteps? I wasn't lying when I said I could smell them, but I couldn't tell where they were. This room was too big to just be a room. I had to be in a basement or warehouse or something. But where? And how was I going to get out of this?

Wait—that was definitely footsteps. It sounded like they were getting closer. I tried to turn my head to see who it was, but I was met with a bag of blood and a straw. As nervous as I was that I would be drugged again, I was too hungry to stop myself. I sucked down the contents of the bag and waited to see if I would remain conscious. When I didn't get groggy or pass out again, I decided that perhaps asking nicely had worked.

"Please, just tell me what you want," I insisted.

The voice that responded was distorted making it impossible to tell if they were male or female. "We need something, and you're going to help us get it." This was getting ridiculous. I had to find a way out of here.

"Tell me what it is and why you need it. Maybe we can compromise. You don't have to keep me tied up." I hoped that I could convince them to let me go with the idea that I'd help them. I wasn't holding my breath though.

"You'd never willingly give us what we need," the voice said. That was creepy. I had no idea what they were after, though, and no way to contact my family. No doubt, they were searching for me. It was only a matter of time before Vik, Eli, or Kayden stormed this place to rescue me. I was certain they would keep Delilah away for her safety.

"Why not just tell me what it is and let me decide?" I pushed, silently praying that they didn't decide to put a bag over my head or a gag in my mouth. I needed to keep them talking. Maybe they would give something away about their plan or where I was being held. Of course, without a way to get that info to the others, it wouldn't help me much.

"And why would we tell you anything? We can't let you stop us. Especially when we can make you help us." It seemed like they were really enjoying keeping their purpose from me.

"How will you make me help you?" It seemed like I was missing something here, but I had no idea how they would force me to help them.

"We already have." Laughter filled the room and I wondered if this had anything to do with the time I was missing from earlier. What had happened? "We can control you, and there's nothing you can do to stop us."

Wait, what? They'd been controlling me? How was that possible? I had so many more questions now, and knew that I wouldn't get answers. I kept trying to reach out over the implant Eli had created, but there was no response. All I got was static. That had to be a clue about where I was. I just couldn't connect the dots.

"What are you talking about? How can you control me?"

FIVE – NOW WHAT?
GARNET

Luca pulled me close and leaned down as if he were going to kiss me. Was this finally the moment when he would admit that he felt the same for me that I did for him? Or was I reading too much into the situation? He dragged me closer and closed his eyes. I tilted my head back and closed my eyes, silently urging him not to stop until he'd claimed me. I knew that I shouldn't want him the way I did, but I couldn't help it.

Before our lips could meet, the back door of Midnight slammed open and a voice ripped me from the bliss I was imagining. "No wonder you didn't find anything. You've just been out here making out with your boyfriend. I told Dad to make you stay home. Too bad he had to listen to Kayden and bring you."

Luca and I jumped apart as if we'd been caught doing something wrong. "Vincent. Did you find something?" Luca stepped in front of me. I glanced around him and glared at my brother.

"What's this? First you can't shift, now you can't talk for yourself? You really are a worthless bitch," Vincent snarled. I shrank back from his words as if I'd been slapped. I watched as Luca raced toward him.

Without warning, Luca's fist connected with Vincent's jaw, snapping his head back and making a vicious cracking noise. "Watch yourself. No one, and I mean no one, talks to Red that way." In the next moment, Luca and Vincent were rolling around in the alley, fists flying. They moved so fast that I had trouble figuring out which one was which.

I stepped forward, planning to get between them, when the door swung open again and Delilah walked out. She growled low, and they both froze. It was strange to see two alphas submit to a female, but I supposed it had more to do with her being a hybrid. Delilah could easily rip both of them in half without breaking a sweat, and they knew it. It didn't hurt that she had my father behind her.

His angry disapproval was apparent the moment our eyes met. He'd already decided that this was my fault, and I would be the one to pay. Generally, when this happened, I would have to do extra training sessions until he was satisfied that I would behave. The vicious growl emanating from him froze me in place. I started to shake, and before I realized what was happening, my father had the three of us against the wall screaming at us. We'd shamed him and the pack with our behavior. It was ridiculous of course, but there was no way to argue with him.

"Perhaps we should focus on finding Declan without the wolves' help. If you can't stop them from fighting amongst themselves, Gunnar, they're of no use to me." Delilah's words were cold and dismissive.

"If that's what you want, I'm happy to oblige," he snarled. Kayden stepped forward and my father backed down. There would be no additional power struggles here. I wanted to apologize to her for making things harder than they needed to be, but Delilah wasn't interested in speaking to any of us. She turned and went back inside Midnight without another word. My father and brother walked around the front of the building and got into the pack SUV. Kayden gave me an apologetic look before motioning that we needed to go. Luca followed me, climbing into my father's vehicle next to me. At least I wasn't alone. The ride back home was miserable. Vincent had given Father his account of what had happened, and of course, it was all my fault. It didn't matter that he'd disrespected me and Luca was defending my honor. I was used to it, and had to squeeze Luca's arm to keep him from smarting off.

"Get back to training, Red," Father growled when he parked next to the cabin. Vincent barked a laugh and I glared at him.

"But it's dark out and we don't have lights," I protested. I knew better than to say anything, and barely flinched when his hand connected with my cheek. Luca's low growl didn't go unnoticed by me or my father.

"You can join her. The two of you need to learn how to obey your alpha. Three hours should do it." He walked away muttering about these damned kids as Vincent chased after him. I hated how I got punished for my brother's behavior, but it had been the way of things ever since we found out that I can't shift.

"Are you sure he's really your father?" Luca asked quietly as we headed to the obstacle course. I snorted a laugh. "He doesn't act much like one."

"I'm as sure as I can be. I barely knew my mother. Who else but my father would have bothered to raise me, especially after learning that I'm defective," I said, trying to keep the irritation and sadness out of my voice.

"You're not defective. Just because you can't shift, that doesn't mean there's anything wrong with you. What if you're not his kid? What if you're not a wolf at all?"

"Luca, what does that even mean? If I'm not a wolf, what am I?" As much as I wanted his words to be true; as deeply as I wanted to be something else, someone else, I knew that I wasn't. Even if by some miracle, Gunnar Trion wasn't my father, he was still my alpha and I had to do what he said.

I let my mind wander as Luca and I worked our way through the obstacle course that taught wolves how to use all of their senses and figure out their strengths. I wondered if he might be right about Gunnar not being my father. What would that mean for me if he wasn't? Could it even be possible? I knew that I was more than human, but if I wasn't a wolf, what was I? Distracted, I tripped and face planted in the mud.

I lay there, debating giving up, until Luca raced up to me in his wolf form. I winced as he licked my face. It shouldn't bother me, as he'd done that exact thing since we were little. But for some reason, it was different now. I felt like it meant something else. He ran behind a tree and shifted back, slipping on a pair of shorts before coming back to help me up. Part of me hated that he started doing that, but another part of me understood. Since I couldn't shift, everyone was awkward about being naked around me.

I'd never been comfortable with pack nudity, and once he became head alpha, Father had insisted that everyone remain dressed when I was around. Everyone blamed me for the new rule, and I got hazed for it. A lot.

Luca strolled back over to me slowly, as if he knew I was checking him out. "Let's get you cleaned up," he said with a smirk. He scooped me up and headed for the waterfall. I couldn't explain why or how I knew, but somehow, I did. Luca was going to drop me in it.

The night was warm enough, the cool water wouldn't bother me too much. I was more worried about what I would do if Luca jumped in with me. Would I be brave enough to finally tell him how I felt? I already knew the answer to that. Every time I tried to tell him that I was in love with him, something stopped me. I spent the afternoon berating myself for letting James kiss me, and for wanting more. Polyamory was common among wolves, so that wasn't an issue. I could have feelings for both men, and neither should care. But James was human, and that would be a big problem. Gunnar Trion was a traditionalist, and refused to think that species should mate with other species. Simply put, wolves stay with wolves. I hated his outlook on things, and wanted to make changes when I took over after him. If I got to take over after him.

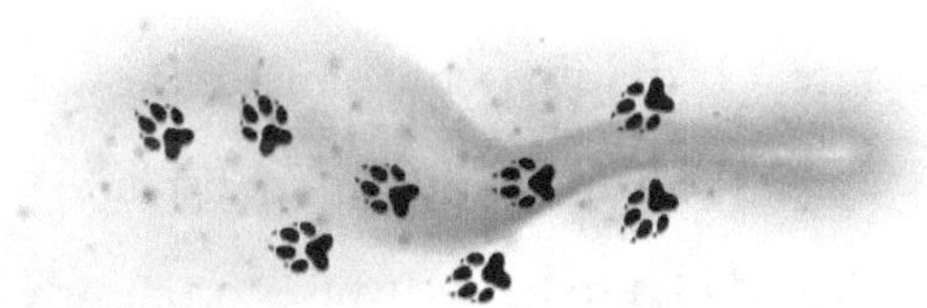

KAYDEN

"Look, I know how bad that was, but we can't just leave them out of it. Red can help us. Gunnar is just being an ass," I insisted. I needed Delilah to listen to reason. She'd been pissed that Luca and Vincent had started fighting. After they left, she refused to listen to any explanation I tried to give. It didn't matter to her that Vincent was a slimeball, she didn't want to deal with the conflict while looking for Declan. Nothing I said to her was helping.

Vik turned around and stared at me. "Do you really think you can keep them from fighting long enough to focus on finding Dec?" Delilah glared at him, as if she'd already realized I could sway him into agreeing with me.

"I think they can help. Maybe not Vincent, but Red and Luca for sure." It didn't seem to matter how many times I repeated myself. Delilah didn't want to listen.

"It's not a bad idea to let the wolves help, Love. I'm having no luck tracking him by his implant. Maybe they can do it by scent alone. I say we let them help us." Eli finally chose a side. He'd been considering all the information while trying to track Dec's telepathy implant for nearly an hour.

"Fine, but they're your responsibility. And if they can't stop fighting long enough to find him before..." Delilah let the statement drop. We all knew what she was thinking. If they couldn't stop fighting long enough to find Dec before something happened to him, Delilah would kill them all. I had no doubt my mate would do it. She could be vicious, especially where one of us was concerned.

I nodded and pulled her off the couch and into my arms. "I'll take care of it. We'll find him." I kissed her quickly before passing her to Eli. I had to call Gunnar and arrange things. It would probably involve kissing some ass, and I hated that idea, but I needed the wolves to help find Declan. I agreed with Delilah, we didn't have time to waste.

I took the elevator down to the nightclub before pulling my phone out to call. Since Dec's kidnapping, we decided to close the place for the night. It was the easiest way to get Delilah to agree to go upstairs with us. She wanted to tear through the city and find him. I didn't blame her; I felt the same way. But I didn't have an unpredictable vampire side to deal with, and I had full control over my wolf.

Gunnar answered before the third ring. "What do you want?"

"Pleasure to speak with you as well, Gunnar. I need the wolves to help me find Declan." I waited, not giving him any more information than that.

"Your woman sent us away. Why should I let them come back? What's in it for me?" His voice was gravely and his tone serious.

"Well, I would owe you a favor, for starters. If that's not enough, I'm sure we could settle on an hourly rate for us to pay them for helping." I wondered if that would get his attention.

"You can pay me an hourly rate for each of them to make up for the scene your woman made tonight. Then I'll consider letting Vincent and one of the others help you."

"Gunnar, you know her name is Delilah. I'll pay your rate, but only if Red and Luca are among the wolves you send. If you agree, send them over in the morning. If not, I guess we're done here." I disconnected the phone without waiting for his answer. He'd send them. Gunnar Trion was an asshole, but I knew that the easiest way to get his cooperation was to pay the outrageous fee and move on. Goddess knew we had the money, so that wouldn't be a problem.

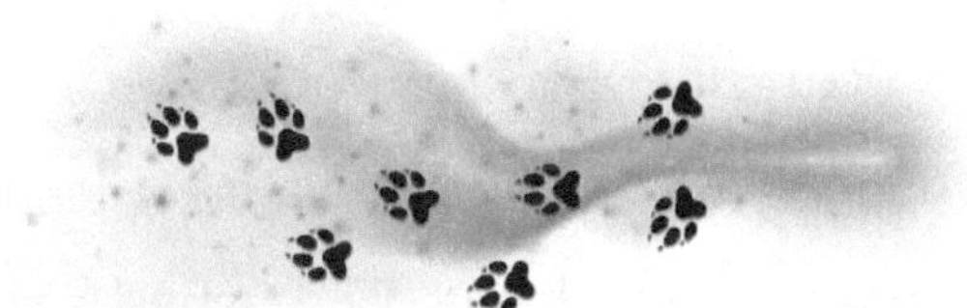

LUCA

I carried Red to the waterfall with her body pressed against mine. I'd dreamed of this moment for as long as I could remember. Being in love with the head alpha's daughter was complicated. I had to stay on his good side, but that put me on her shit list a lot. All I ever wanted was to take care of her. I wondered if that would ever happen.

Could she feel my heart pounding against her? Did she understand what it meant? I had no way to know other than to ask her, and I couldn't bring myself to do that right now. I hated how Vincent had interrupted us earlier. I was finally going to kiss her. That would have told me everything I needed to know about her feelings.

At the top of the waterfall, I stepped to the edge. "Luca, you wouldn't." Red gasped, glancing over the edge. The moon was barely a sliver, shining its pale light on the water. I knew that there were no big rocks below us. We'd jumped from this spot a few hundred times over the years. The water was deep enough without being too deep, and it would be cold. I wondered if she'd be mad at me for tossing her over the edge a moment before I did it.

I watched her drop, waiting until she was almost at the bottom before I jumped. There was no way I was letting her go that easily. I wanted to proclaim my love for her. My wolf wanted more than that. My animal side had already decided that Red was ours. I had no say in it, and wouldn't have objected anyway.

I fell into the cold, dark water, landing near Red but not on top of her. She was scrubbing the mud off when I swam over to her. "I can't believe you dropped me off the waterfall at night!"

"It's not like we haven't done that before," I insisted. I thought back on all the times we'd snuck away just like we had tonight. Her father could be a lot to deal with, and sometimes Red needed a break. If I couldn't be her boyfriend, at least I could be her best friend and take care of her by tending to her needs.

"Usually, we had towels when we came here, though," she shot back. I hadn't considered anything after getting the mud off her. Damn.

"I'm sorry, Red. I wasn't thinking. I can go get you a towel. My cabin is right over there." I gestured in the direction of my home, even though she knew where it was. I seemed to always say the dumbest things around her.

"It's warm enough out here. We'll be fine. If my father doesn't catch us slacking," she laughed. As if her words had summoned him, I heard Gunnar's voice calling us.

"Fuck," I muttered.

Red whipped her head around, obviously not hearing what I did. I'd begun to suspect that she wasn't a wolf after all. She didn't have our senses, and couldn't shift. Grammy talked of curses and such, but I wasn't sure I believed in all of that.

"What is it?" I wanted to pull her into my arms and kiss the fear from her voice. This wasn't the time for grand gestures, though.

"Gunnar is calling," I replied, making a sour face. She groaned and scrambled to the bank of the pool. We raced back toward his cabin, carefully running through the muddy obstacle course. He would know we hadn't been training because we were soaking wet, but maybe, just maybe, I'd be able to distract him from that.

"Where have you two been?" Gunnar growled. "Nevermind, it doesn't matter. You're going back to Midnight tomorrow morning to help look for the missing vamp. And Vincent is going with you. There will be no fighting. Do you understand?" He looked from Red to me and back again. It figured he'd take Vincent's side and blame us for the fight earlier. I would bet he didn't even know what his son had said to his daughter to start it all.

"Understood, sir," Red and I replied together. I wondered what had changed his mind. Then of course, he explained it as if he wanted us to know we were being used.

"They'll be paying me for your services. I expect you to find that guy and show them what a wolf pack is worth. Do what Vincent tells you and there shouldn't be any trouble." I stifled a laugh. He wanted us to let Vincent be in charge. The thought of that was hilarious.

I was shocked that Red didn't even offer to argue. She was twice the tracker her brother was, even without wolf senses or the ability to shift. And of course, Kayden would offer him money to get us back on the team. He understood what motivated Gunnar better than any of us.

"Now run the course again, then get to bed. He wants you there early." Without another word, our head alpha turned and stormed back toward his cabin. Red and I exchanged a glance, then slowly walked back to the start of the course. No doubt, Vincent would be hiding somewhere and report back to his father if we didn't actually run the course, especially since we hadn't been doing it when he came out.

"Red, I'm sorry about earlier. I shouldn't let Vincent bait me like that."

"Are you really apologizing for standing up for me? Because that's ridiculous, Luca. Besides, it's all working out, right? Kayden smoothed it over and we get to go back." Her optimism seemed almost forced. Was she hiding something?

"It was my fault we got in trouble. If I had waited to fight him," I started. But she cut me off.

"No. Just no. Vincent is a slimeball who deserves every single punch he gets. You didn't do anything wrong. I'm just thinking about Dec. Why would someone kidnap him? What could they want with him?"

SIX – FINDING CLUES
GARNET

Luca and I spent an hour going through the obstacle course as slowly as possible and discussing all the reasons why someone would have wanted to kidnap Declan. The only thing that made any sense was that they were using him to get to Delilah. "It's the only thing that makes sense. Declan came after her, but didn't actually hurt her. So, it stands to reason that he was going to take her somewhere."

"But where? And why?" We'd been debating those questions the entire time we climbed ropes and walked across beams. Now that we were at the end of the course, I felt like things should have been falling into place. For some reason, we had more questions than answers.

I shook my head at him. "I don't know. There has to be some clue that will lead us to those answers. I just need Vincent to stay away from us long enough to find it."

"We should get some sleep. I'm sure Gunnar will want us to start early so we can get back. And we'll probably have extra chores, too, since we're helping someone who isn't part of the pack." Luca sounded annoyed at that prospect. For me, it was just part of my every day life.

He was right, though. Vincent beat on my door before sunrise, announcing that it was time to go. "Get up! We're leaving in ten minutes, with or without you." Somehow, I doubted that. As angry as my father was last night, I was certain that Kayden had told him that I had to be there. I threw on a pair of leggings and an oversized sweatshirt, then pulled my hair into a knot on top of my head. Vincent was still pounding on my door when I slipped into my boots and jerked the door open.

"Stop beating on my door, dumbass. I'm ready to go as soon as I use the bathroom," I growled, shoving him to the side and heading to the bathroom. When I was finished, I walked outside to find my brother already in Luca's Jeep with him. That meant I was riding in the back, but I didn't care. At least Vincent wasn't driving. On the way into the city, I stared out the window, trying to figure out who could have taken Declan. Those thoughts melted into memories of James kissing me, and Luca holding me close in the alley, when I thought he was about to kiss me. *Fuck, Garnet, this isn't the time to fantasize.* I chided myself, then realized that Luca had just parked at Midnight.

Kayden was waiting for us behind the building. "No fighting today. Vincent, I need you to stick with me. We're going to comb the inside for clues while Red and Luca look out here."

He gave me a knowing look before he turned and walked back into the building.

"Let's start away from the building and work our way back. You take that side of the alley; I'll take this one. We'll show each other anything strange, okay?" Luca nodded at my suggestion. I wanted nothing more than to stay by his side, but there was no way we'd get anything done if I let my hormones run the show.

I watched him for a minute, while he was distracted. Was he thinking about me the way I was constantly thinking about him? I had no way to tell, except that he glanced over his shoulder at me and chuckled when I quickly looked away. My cheeks were pink, and my heart raced. *Focus, Garnet. There will be time for all of this later.* I hated that I had to remind myself of that so much. I'd let myself get distracted and nearly missed a clue.

Next to the building, there was a muddy footprint. That by itself wasn't very helpful, as we'd all been through the alley several times since Dec was taken. What caught my attention was the moss in the tread of the print. That particular moss only grew deep in the Whispering Thicket, out by Levi's cabin. No one went that far into the forest anymore—not since Levi chased us all off during our plant lesson with Grammy. Levi didn't even come to pack meetings or gatherings. He was still pissed that my father defeated him and took the head alpha position away from him. But he couldn't be behind this, could he?

"Luca, come look at this," I called as I squatted to get a better look at the moss. It had been years since I'd seen it, but I was certain this was the same moss that grew near Levi's cabin. I would have bet my reputation on it. I felt, rather than saw, Luca squat next to me. I used a stick to scoop a piece of the moss up and show him. "Does this look familiar?"

"That only grows out by Levi's cabin. How did it get here?" he wondered aloud. It was a good sign that Luca had the same thought I did about the moss.

"We need to show Kayden and the others. It looks like Levi is involved in Dec's abduction. I'm not sure exactly how or why, though." Luca offered me a hand and pulled me to my feet with him. We took the sample of moss and headed inside. Kayden and Vincent were crawling around on the floor of the nightclub, obviously chasing scents. "We found something," I announced, getting their attention.

Kayden muttered something, and a moment later, Delilah, Vik, and Eli stepped out of the elevator. He must have been calling them. Luca and I walked further into the nightclub and followed Kayden into a room behind the bar. Once everyone was inside, I presented the moss. "This particular moss only grows in one place." I handed the stick to Kayden.

"It looks familiar, but I don't know where it's from," he replied. It didn't surprise me, since he'd lived in the city for so long.

"Levi's cabin," Luca said flatly. Kayden's eyes went wide, and Vincent coughed.

"Are you saying that Levi took the vampire?" My brother truly was a moron. Who else would insult the people who were paying us to help them? No one paid any attention to him, and he shrunk back against the wall.

"We'll have to go out there and talk to him," Kayden said. Then he explained to his family exactly who Levi was and why this was a strange thing to find here.

"Then let's go," Delilah ordered, heading toward the door. Eli grabbed her arm, stopping her.

"We need a plan first. We can't just rush in and accuse the man of taking someone captive. What if it wasn't him? What if this is a set up to make us think it was him?" Eli's theory made sense, but I had a nagging feeling that Levi was involved somehow.

"We can't go out to Levi's without Dad's permission. We should go talk to him first, then check out Levi's place. I know Dad will say it's okay, since it was my idea," Vincent insisted. I wished that our father had let Luca and me do this without dragging him along.

Kayden and Luca exchanged a glance, then turned to me. "We'll go with your plan, but I think all of us going to talk to Gunnar is a bad idea. We don't want to make him think we're going to Levi's without his approval. So, I'll take you to talk to him," Vik interjected. He'd been mostly silent this morning, so it was strange that he'd offered to take Vincent to talk to our father.

Vik ushered my brother out the door, turning back and nodding at Kayden as he left. "What was that all about? Are we really going to wait here while my brother asks Daddy-dearest for permission?" Sarcasm dripped off the words as I said them.

"Hell, no. I just needed to get him out of here, and Vik volunteered to babysit for a while. The rest of us are going out there and searching around Levi's cabin. I'll deal with Gunnar if I have to after the fact. So, let's load up." He led the way out the back door, since Vik and Vincent left through the front. Within a few minutes, we were headed out to the forest.

It felt strange doing this behind my father's back, but at the same time, so freeing. I felt as if a weight had been lifted from my shoulders. I knew that we would find something to lead us to Dec out here. I had no idea why, but I knew it.

A tingle shot up my spine, and I itched to jump out of the SUV and run inside the cabin. I knew it was dangerous, but I wasn't scared. Not like I should have been.

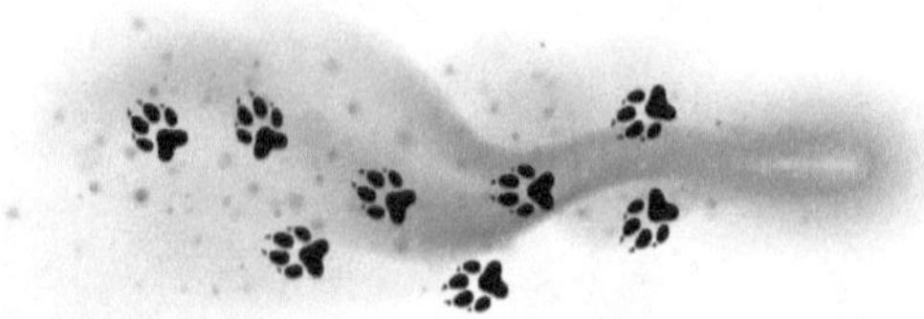

DELILAH

I was feeling annoyed that my guys had decided we needed the wolves to help after I'd sent them away. I didn't see any reason for them to get involved again. I spent the morning keeping Vik and Eli busy with my pouting, until Kayden called for us to see what Garnet had found. I really needed to remind Kayden that she hated being called Red. The discovery of that weird moss filled me with hope, which was promptly dashed when Vincent said they had to ask Gunnar for permission to talk to the previous head alpha.

I didn't want to ask Gunnar for anything, especially not permission to have a conversation with some random old man wolf who didn't want anything to do with his pack anymore. Relief washed over me when Kayden asked Vik to distract Vincent by taking him to his father. I knew that meant we were going rogue and would find the answers ourselves.

Kayden took us out into the forest, driving like a maniac down some dirt road that seemed like it belonged in a horror movie. I sat in the front with him, ignoring Garnet's attempts to talk to me. I wasn't in the mood for apologies or excuses. I just wanted Dec back and to know why these people, whoever they were, had taken him.

When he stopped the SUV, I didn't move. I'd thought the road was menacing, but it was nothing compared to the dilapidated cabin that stood before us. I'd never been a fan of slasher films, but this looked exactly like what you'd expect from one. If a man with a chainsaw had met us out front, I would not have been shocked at all. A shiver ran down my spine as Kayden opened the door for me.

"Are you sure this is the place?" I asked, making a disgusted face. It gave me the creeps, and I couldn't shake the feeling that someone was watching us.

He nodded, but Garnet answered me. "This is Levi's cabin. Don't be surprised if he comes out with a shotgun. Or shoots first and asks questions after. He's been on the outs with my family since my father took him down in a one-on-one battle and refused to kill him."

I knew that wolves battled for power, but didn't realize that they went so far with it. "He's mad because Gunnar didn't kill him?" I wondered aloud. It was ridiculous.

"Crazy, I know, but that's wolf culture. The winner is supposed to kill the loser and take his place. It's actually considered disrespectful if the winner doesn't," Luca explained, stepping forward to stand beside Garnet. He seemed to be trying to stay between her and the cabin. That led me to believe that her warning may not have been exaggerated. A loud crack sounded just before a large branch fell from a rotted tree, barely missing our car.

"Fuck!" Eli swore as we ducked away. After the dust settled, we stayed where we'd crouched on the ground. Waiting to see if a crazed old man would come out and shoot at us was not my idea of fun.

When no one greeted us, and there were no gunshots, we cautiously stood up. "Do you think maybe he's not here?" I wondered aloud.

"It's possible, but he doesn't usually leave his cabin. Gunnar has wolves that deliver food and run errands for Levi," Luca replied quietly.

Kayden led the way to the cabin, motioning for us to follow him. I tucked myself behind him, worried that the gunshots could still come.

When we got to the door, Luca eased it open, and Garnet strolled inside, clearly not concerned about Levi or his temper. "Wait here," she ordered.

"Levi? We need to talk to you. Are you here?" she called as she walked through the small cabin. There was no response, and just when I started to worry that she'd been captured, Garnet shouted. "Delilah, Kayden, come quick! Back bedroom. The place is empty."

I raced toward her voice, terrified of what I might find. My heart stopped as I entered the room. There, in the middle of the room, tied to a wooden chair, was my last love. Declan's head drooped. Was he knocked out or worse? I couldn't force myself to ask the question, instead rushed to wrap my arms around him and kiss his head.

"Is he...?" Kayden couldn't say it either. Garnet shook her head.

"He's unconscious. He still has reflexes, so I know he's somewhat okay," she answered. I breathed a sigh of relief as tears streamed down my cheeks. I wanted to take him home, but wasn't sure if that was the best idea.

"What can we do for him?" I begged. I wouldn't survive if anything happened to him. My heart ached at his absence and pain stabbed through me as I took in his injuries. He'd obviously been tortured before whoever had taken him had abandoned him here. But why? What did they want with him?

"We need to take him to Grammy. She'll know what to do," Garnet insisted.

I shook my head. I didn't want to chance leaving him in this forest, even if Grammy was the only one who could heal him. "She can come to us." It was my turn to insist.

Kayden glanced from Garnet to me, then nodded. "We'll take him home, and Grammy will come with us. Garnet, you and Luca can go get her. We'll get Declan loaded up and clear the cabin. Ten minutes."

I watched as Eli carefully cut the ropes that held Declan in place before helping Kayden pick him up and carry him to the SUV. "I've got a scanner in the back that will tell me if they gave him something to prevent healing. He probably just needs a blood bag," Eli said, gesturing to the hatch. I opened it and stepped out of the way so they could lay Dec down.

"He can't drink it; he's out cold," I reminded them. Eli nodded and took supplies out of a kit that I hadn't seen before. He inserted and IV and hooked Dec up to a blood bag while he scanned him with a handheld medical device. The sight of the needle made me a little nauseous, so I stepped away while Kayden helped Eli. I stumbled away from the SUV, lightheaded. I didn't understand why the needle bothered me this time. I'd never had that reaction before. I couldn't fight the feeling I was going to be sick as I backed away, trying not to trip.

The woozy feeling didn't go away as I moved away from the SUV and closer to the woods behind us. Maybe if I sat down for a minute, it would go away. The hair on the back of my neck stood up and I turned my head to look around. Something was wrong here.

A hand covered my mouth as two strong arms wrapped around me. I felt something slice into my arm as I struggled. I tried to reach out to Kayden through our mate bond, but only got static in return. Eli's implant tech had the same result. I jerked and twisted, but the arms holding me were like steel. I couldn't move. Was this person holding me until I bled to death? It seemed unlikely that I would die from a cut, since I was a vampire, but I was also a wolf shifter, so I wasn't sure. Then, without warning, everything went black and I felt myself falling. I thought I heard Garnet yelling as I fell, but couldn't be sure. Then there was nothing but darkness.

SEVEN – THE MYSTERY REMAINS
GARNET

"What do you mean, you found him? You were supposed to follow my plan and wait for permission. Why can't you ever do anything right?" Vincent laid into me the moment we arrived at the cabin.

"We're not talking to you, Vincent. We need Grammy to come with us. So shut up and get out of my way," I ordered, shoving him back. I knew it was a mistake, but I didn't care. I'd had it with his bullying, and had decided to finally stand up for myself. I'd take my punishment and move on. He gripped my arm hard, and Luca stepped forward to stop him.

"Vincent! Leave your sister alone. You know you're not supposed to lay your hands on a woman. Don't make me get the wooden spoon," Grammy warned him as she walked outside. "What's this I hear about you finding the missing vamp at Levi's?"

"I know we weren't supposed to go there without permission, and I'm sorry. We couldn't wait. He wouldn't have made it. Honestly, he still might not. They want you to come with us to Midnight and take care of him there. Please, Grammy, we need to go," I begged. Vincent had stormed off, no doubt to go tell our father how Grammy and I had spoken to him. I didn't care. He was being a dick, and Grammy had called him out on it.

"Okay, child. I'll go with you. I'm sure we'll figure out what's wrong with the poor boy." Grammy walked back into the cabin to grab her healer's bag. The moment she walked back out the door, panic hit me.

Something was wrong. That tingling feeling was back, and I couldn't explain why, but I knew Delilah was in danger.

"We have to go, now." I turned and started to run, not waiting to see if they were following. Of course, I knew they were, because I heard Luca ask for Grammy's bag, then could hear their footfalls behind me. Would we get there on time? I raced back to Levi's cabin with Luca and Grammy following me. "Delilah!" I shouted as I ran.

"Red, slow down. Her men are with her. They'll protect her from anything out in the forest." Grammy's words pushed me faster. It didn't matter that her men were with her; she was in trouble. Something was wrong.

I broke into the clearing where Kayden had parked and watched in what seemed like slow motion as Delilah fell to the ground. I barely saw the three figures in black that had been holding her up when they melted back into the trees. Crimson stained her arm and the ground where she landed. How had Kayden and Eli not realized that she'd been grabbed?

I slowed to a jog and kept moving until I was at her side. "Delilah, please wake up." I was terrified that she'd been drained of her blood. The cut on her arm was healing so slowly. She moaned, but didn't open her eyes. Her fangs clicked into place and I knew that she could smell me. I put my wrist in her mouth and forced it against her fangs until the skin broke and my blood spilled onto her tongue. A moment later, Eli was by my side.

"What the fuck happened? Kayden and I were checking Dec's injuries out and it was like time froze. Is she okay?" He was scared and confused. I wished I had a better answer for him.

"I don't know. She's barely swallowing my blood, but her cut is healing faster. Wait, I think she's starting to come back," I managed to say before Delilah grabbed my arm and started to drink with more force. A moment later, Kayden replaced my arm with his, and Delilah opened her eyes.

"I'm okay now," she muttered, pushing Kayden's arm away. She looked down at her blood-soaked arm and shuddered. "Did you catch them?"

"Who?" Eli asked, nudging me aside to help Delilah to her feet.

"The people who attacked me. I'm not sure how many there were. One held me, another covered my mouth, and another sliced my arm open. I have no idea what they were doing," she admitted.

I looked around, not seeing anyone in the forest nearby. "Whoever it was, they're long gone by now."

Kayden cursed under his breath. "And we've obliterated any possible evidence." He gestured to the dirt at his feet, where the three of us had effectively messed up any footprints that had been there.

"Shit, I didn't realize that someone had attacked her. I just saw her down and was trying to help," I groaned. I felt horrible that someone had ambushed Delilah while I'd gone to get Grammy.

"It's not your fault, please don't beat yourself up about it. Kayden and Eli were less than ten feet away, and had no idea what was going on either." She turned to them and continued, "That doesn't mean that either of you should feel bad about it. Something blocked me from reaching out along the bond or the implant. Eli, will you check mine and Dec's to make sure they're still functional?"

"Absolutely. Let's get back home first. Everyone load up. We can come back later and search the place better if needed." Eli carried Delilah to the SUV as he spoke. None of us wasted any time getting in and heading back to Midnight. The thought that someone had tried to kill Delilah was terrifying, even for me, and I'd grown up wandering those woods alone at night.

The ride back to the city took less time than I'd expected. Once we were all upstairs and settled in, Grammy checked Delilah and Declan out. After her assessment, Eli took his scanner and checked the implants to make sure they were in working order.

"I'd feel better about it if the three of you stayed here tonight," Delilah said. I was shocked. She'd wanted us to let her find Dec by herself, and now she was asking us to stay. I wondered if that was because of Grammy, or if there was something else on her mind.

"We'll stay, then, if it'll ease your mind," Grammy responded. She grabbed her bag and walked down the hall to Kayden's room, claiming it for herself.

"Where do you want us to go?" Luca asked, gesturing between the two of us. My cheeks flushed and I wondered how Delilah would take his question.

"Well, there are four other bedrooms besides this one, so you can stay together or separate. It's up to you. No one here will judge you either way. The five of us will be sticking together, though," she replied, glancing over her shoulder at Declan where he lay sleeping.

"I'm glad he's going to be okay. I'm sorry that this happened. We'll figure out who's responsible, I promise." My words would do little to ease her fears, but they were all I had to offer. I would make it my mission to find the people who had taken Declan and who had attacked Delilah. Then I would make them pay. Because they didn't deserve any of this. They were a good family that gave back to the community and had created support programs for wolves and vamps alike.

Luca and I walked out of the room, and Delilah shut the door behind us. "So..." I turned to him and he grinned.

"Which room do you want?" he asked with a sheepish grin.

"I don't care. I think Grammy took Kayden's, so anywhere we go, you'll be wolf-scenting the place up." I hadn't realized that I'd implied we were sleeping together until I watched the shock spread over his face.

"Okay, how about this one?" He opened the door across from Delilah's room and I looked inside. From the posh décor and shelves of books, I was certain this was Vik's room.

"Too fancy. I'd be afraid of messing up his stuff and pissing him off." I turned and opened the next door down. This room was more casual, with drawing supplies on an adjustable desk and rolled up papers leaning against the wall. Definitely Declan's room, and my choice for now. "This one. Dec won't care if we're in here."

Again, I'd implied that Luca would stay with me. I glanced at him when I realized, but he didn't look embarrassed or shocked anymore. I realized that I didn't want to be alone tonight. I knew that nothing would happen between us. Luca was my best friend, and I didn't think he even felt that way about me. So, it wouldn't hurt anything for us to share a room. We'd done it as kids, so it shouldn't be a big deal, right?

"Sounds good. We should get some sleep. Tomorrow is gonna be rough. I'm not sure how we're gonna keep the promise you made, but we'll figure it out." I hadn't realized that he was listening when I'd promised Delilah to find the people responsible. That had been my promise, and now Luca was making it his as well. I wasn't sure how I felt about that, but it was nice to know I wasn't going to be working alone.

Exhausted, I dropped onto the bed. I was bone-tired, and expected to fall asleep quickly. At least until Luca flopped down next to me. "Don't worry, your virtue will remain intact.

I figured neither of us wanted to be alone tonight. Can I just hold you?" His words were sweet, and his tone was different than usual. He wasn't teasing or joking around.

I scooted over and rested my head on his shoulder with his arms wrapped around me. It felt like home. I'd wanted this for as long as I could remember, but I'd always thought I was too broken for him to feel the same. Now I wasn't sure if I'd been right. "Luca?" I asked, sleep making it difficult to speak.

"It's okay, Red. Just sleep." There was so much I wanted to say to him, but I couldn't stay awake long enough to get the words out. I fell asleep with Luca's arms around me. I hadn't expected the dreams to come again.

I was no longer in the bed with Luca. Instead, I was standing in the forest, in a clearing deeper in than where Levi's cabin was. I had never been this deep in the Whispering Thicket, but I was certain I knew the exact spot in which I stood.

Hooded figures circled a fire, and were chanting softly. I couldn't make out the words, but I felt drawn to them. Somehow, as is the way of dreams, I knew that I was watching the Silverbark Coven perform a ritual. Moments later, three of the hooded figures transformed into wolves, still covered by the cloaks that hid who they were from me.

If they sensed my presence, none of them made a move to stop me when I inched closer to get a better look at the fire and what they were doing. This dream was strange. I could feel the heat from the fire as I approached, but still couldn't make out what the figures were saying. They had to be witches, with wolf shifters—but how? Most shifters stayed away from witches because we were taught to fear them.

I knew there was a witch on the council, but hadn't ever interacted with her. I wasn't even sure if I would recognize her if I saw her again. She could have been one of the people around the fire, even. But I didn't feel like she was. That was impossible to explain. It was as if I sensed these people and could rule out their identities. No, that's crazy. I didn't even have the wolf senses I was supposed to, much less something more advanced.

At first, this dream was just like the others. I watched the witches chant while the wolves seemed to sway along with it. The wolves were always there, just like the witches. It was the same six people every time. What did it mean? I'd tried for years to figure out the significance of the dream, with no success. Something about it made me shy away from telling anyone. I didn't want them to think I was crazy. After all, who dreams about witches and wolf shifters doing some strange ritual around the fire at the full moon?

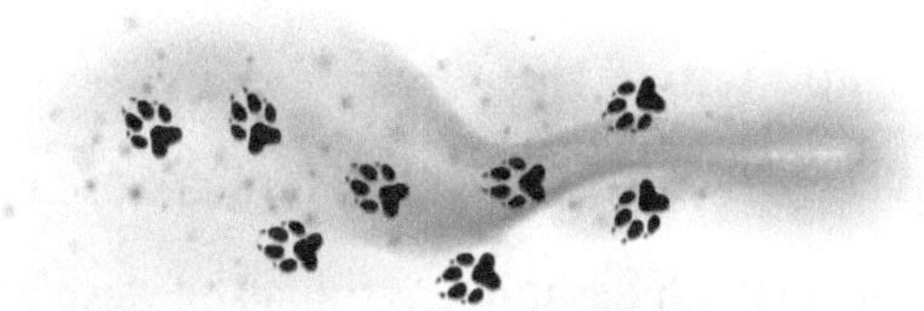

LUCA

Red jerked and whimpered in her sleep, obviously having a nightmare. I shook her gently, trying to wake her up. She groaned, but didn't open her eyes. Shifting her into my arms more, I sat up and tried to rouse her again. "Red, wake up. Please." What would I do if I couldn't pull her out of the dream? Shit. I needed Grammy, but wasn't sure what time it

was. I knew better than to wake her if this wasn't an emer-
gency.

I leaned down and gently pressed my lips to hers. Electricity
shot through me, and my wolf growled. Something about that
seemed to work. I straightened up just as her eyes fluttered
open. "What happened? Why am I in your lap?"

"You were having a nightmare. I couldn't get you to wake
up, so I held you until it was over." I didn't see how the small
lie would hurt anyone. I wasn't sure how she felt about me, and
didn't want to push her into anything she wasn't ready for.

"It was the strangest dream. I don't even know if it was a
nightmare, but I'm exhausted now," she breathed.

"Do you need me to get Grammy?" I asked, terrified that
something was wrong with her. She shook her head and snug-
gled closer on my lap. I had to fight hard to keep my cock from
reacting to how close she was. I failed miserably, but she didn't
say anything about it, so I pretended it hadn't happened.

"I just need to sleep a little longer," she murmured as she
dozed off again in my arms. Panic washed over me. She was
too pale. I gently laid her on the pillow and tucked the blanket
around her. At this point, Grammy could rake me over the
coals, I just needed her to figure out what was wrong with
Red. I raced down the hall and knocked on the door, trying to

be quiet enough that the vampires and Kayden wouldn't hear what was going on. I didn't need them doubting our ability to help again because of this.

Grammy opened the door and glared at me. "What is it, boy?" The question hung between us for a minute while I tried to catch my breath.

"Red. Please, she's not waking up. Well, she did wake up for a second, then she passed out again. And she was having a nightmare just before I managed to wake her." The words spewed from me, all running together as if it was a race to get out.

"Let's go take a look," the old woman said simply, then started down the hall. "Which room is she in?" She didn't mention the fact that Red and I had obviously shared a room last night, since I knew she was having a nightmare and had tried to wake her. I wondered when the questions would come.

I led the way back to Dec's room where we'd spent the night. When I opened the door, Grammy rushed inside. Red was standing at Declan's mirror writing something on it with a marker. I didn't understand what the symbols were, or how she could be in a trance like that. "Don't touch her, boy. We have to wait and see what she writes. It could be a vision, or something more sinister." I took a step back at Grammy's warning and waited. Red was frantically scribbling the symbols across the large mirror above the dresser. I wondered if I should get someone else to help, but wasn't sure what they'd be able to do.

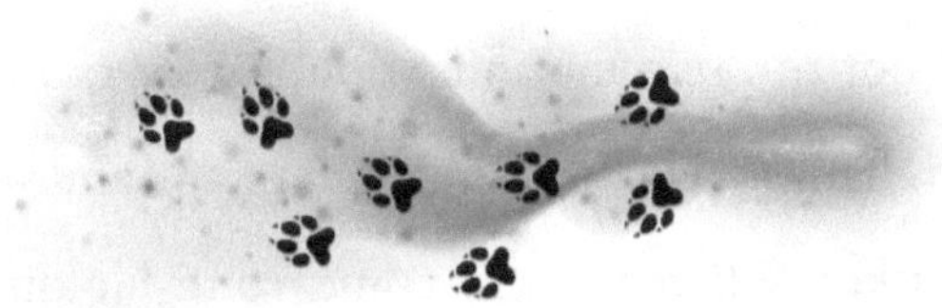

GARNET

I briefly remembered talking to Luca before I slipped back into the dream. When I got back to the circle, it had changed. The six figures were still there, but one of them had begun to write strange symbols in the dirt. I moved closer to see what they were. The symbols looked familiar, but I had no idea what they were or why I recognized them.

I stared at the symbols, tracing them in the air with my finger. Bright light surrounded me, swirling and dancing in the darkness. The longer I traced, the more the light moved. What was happening? This didn't make sense. It was almost like magic, but I didn't have powers. I was a wolf shifter who was cursed to not be able to shift. There was no magic in that. I'd been skipped over by the goddess on that one.

Pain shot through me and I doubled over. Somehow, my location changed. I looked down at my hand and was holding a black marker. Where had that come from? Holding my stomach, I glanced around the room. In front of me, on Declan's mirror, was a copy of the symbols the witch had been writing. Along with that, I could see in the reflection that Grammy and Luca were staring at me.

"What happened?" I asked, turning to face them. I could tell from their faces that they had watched me make the marks on the mirror.

"You were sleepwalking again, dearie," Grammy said simply. This was way more than that. There was no way I was just sleepwalking. I'd been in the forest, witnessing that ritual. I'd seen the witch write the runes that I'd copied onto Declan's mirror. Wait—runes! Those strange symbols were runes. At least that would help me figure out how to translate them.

"I don't think so, Grammy. I saw things, in the forest. It felt like I was really there. How is that possible?" I needed to explain everything, but couldn't find the words to use.

"Don't fret over that right now. We'll figure out exactly what happened. Why don't you go take a shower to calm your nerves?" Grammy's suggestion seemed odd to me, but I didn't argue. Perhaps a shower would help. I knew that Delilah and her men wouldn't mind. They'd welcomed us into their home and asked us to spend the night.

"Okay, you're probably right."

I paused just inside the bathroom door and listened as Grammy spoke to Luca. "Take pictures of this. Make sure you get every symbol and the order they're in. This is a message; we just have to decode it. Once you have the pictures, clean it all up. I'll discuss it with our hosts over breakfast. We need to keep Red's mind off it, though." Why would Grammy insist that I not think about the symbols, the runes, that I'd scribbled across Declan's mirror?

ONE
DISAPPEARING WOLVES

GARNET

I GLANCE AROUND THE clearing, the moonlight allowing me to see the smallest details. Six figures dressed in dark robes circle a fire, chanting. They don't see me. I know they will soon, but not yet. I've been here several times, and it's always the same. They chant, then draw the symbols in the dirt. Magic swirls around them. I have no idea who they are or what they're doing out here. I'm not even certain where here is. Exactly like last time, I watch from the shadows.

I'm not close enough to see the symbols, but I know them by heart. This dream comes to me so often now that I wonder if it's a repressed memory. None of it makes sense, but magic is a strange thing. And it could be the key to unlocking my shift. Everything fades to black and gray and I sit up, cursing. Fuck. I was so close this time.

I wake in my bed, with no new writing on my wall. It doesn't matter. If I had written the symbols again, Grammy would have destroyed the evidence again and convinced me that I had dreamed the whole thing. I can't figure out what she's hiding. But I don't have time to ponder that; I have chores.

Since I disobeyed my father, I have to take care of everything that the young wolves were responsible for until now. Which means I'm watering plants, harvesting herbs, cleaning up the training grounds, and maintaining weapons that I'm no longer allowed to use.

I argued against the punishment at first, but all that did was piss him off. And Gunner Trion is not the man you want to be pissed at you. I suppose he's handsome enough, with his salt and pepper hair and full beard. He stays in shape by pushing the wolves as hard as he can in their training. I used to be one of them.

Not that I've ever been able to shift. Grammy swears there's no curse, but what other reason can there be? I'm a wolf shifter who can't shift. That screams curse to me.

Anyway, I argued with Gunnar (my father) and pissed him off worse, so now I'm not even allowed to talk to Luca. He's my best friend, and honestly, I've been in love with him for as long as I can remember. It's hard to confess those feelings, though, when you're not allowed to be in the same location. Besides, I'm pretty sure that Luca doesn't feel the same way about me. There was the one time we almost kissed, but my idiot brother ruined that for me.

Vincent is good at ruining things for me. Growing up, he always told me that I'm adopted. He almost had me convinced for a long time. It would explain why I look completely differ-ent from the rest of my family, and why I can't shift.

None of that matters right now, though, because I overslept this morning. I throw on clothes and race from the cabin to get my chores done. I can't be on the course when the wolves arrive, or my punishment will be worse.

As I race around the camp, I hear people talking about wolves going missing. That sounds a lot like the situation that got me in trouble. Maybe I can sneak my phone later and call Kayden. He might know what's going on. Kayden should have been the alpha over all the packs, but he didn't want it. Instead, he found his fated mate and abandoned the packs. That allows my father to be in charge.

Not long ago, one of Kayden's brother mates went missing. He hates it when I call them that, so I make sure to do it as often as possible. His mate, Delilah, insisted that I help find Dec. Kayden went up against my father to make it happen. The whole thing was a huge mess. And because I'm not good at following orders, I'm being punished.

I don't fight it now, instead, I enjoy the solitude of the work. Once the plants are watered, I start gathering the list of herbs Grammy gave me last night. It'll take me hours to get them all, but I don't mind. That gives me time to think about this missing wolf situation. Who would want to take them? Where could they be? And why would someone take wolves?

Those are the questions I'm trying to answer. After an hour, I still have no theories. I need to talk to Luca and maybe Kayden. But I know that my father won't allow it. Everyone in the pack has been told that I am to be ignored. They're treating me as if I don't exist; it's like I'm not even one of them anymore.

I don't feel like I belong here. I never have, except for when I was with Luca. Great, now I'm thinking about him again. Luca Walsh is a delicious specimen of a man. And I've been around him since before the awkward teenage years. His chestnut brown hair falls below his ears, much to my father's chagrin. His golden-brown eyes are warm and inviting, and he almost always wears a smile. Being kept away from him is the worst punishment of all.

Until this, I spent at least a part of every day with him. We trained together, talked about everything, and just enjoyed each other's company. For the past week, I have not talked to him. I've only seen him in passing, but with my father's watchful eye on me, it wasn't safe to even say hello. I'm lost in my thoughts and barely register the footsteps creeping up behind me.

A hand clamps down on my shoulder and I squeal in surprise. Another hand covers my mouth and I struggle against the strong arms holding me still. "It's okay, Red. It's just me. Shh, you have to be quiet or he'll catch me."

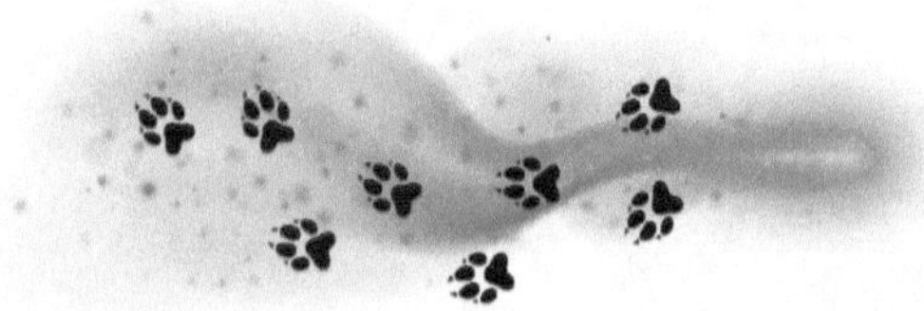

LUCA

I can't resist sneaking up on Red as she collects her list of herbs.

It's been a week since I've been close enough to touch her, and

I can't take it anymore. I'm dying to tell her that I'm in love

with her, but I can't seem to get the words out. So, I sneak up on her and grab her, pressing her body against my chest as I encourage her to keep quiet.

When I turn her to face me, her eyes light up even though they're filled with tears. "Luca, I've missed you!" she whispers as she throws her arms around me and hugs tightly. Moments like this make me think she feels the same way I do. I press my forehead to hers and look at her for a long minute. I'm close enough that I could press my lips to hers. Before I realize what I'm doing, I catch myself leaning closer. I turn my face away and hug her again, pressing a kiss to her cheek.

I can't make myself tell her how much this punishment is hurting me. I can tell from her reaction to me that she feels the same way. "I missed you, too." I can, however, admit that I missed her.

"You're going to get in trouble. You have to get out of here," she insists, pushing me away before grabbing my arm and pulling me back to settle again with my arms around her.

I shake my head. "Gunnar and Vincent went into the city. Everyone else is training. We don't have long, but I had to see you."

She relaxes a little. "What do you know about the missing wolves?"

Of course, she's heard about that. "I know that it sounds a lot like when Dec was taken. Other than that, I'm not in the inner circle, so I don't know anything."

"Fuck, I was hoping you'd have some answers." That's my girl, ever searching for answers. I mean, she's not my girl, but I want her to be. Damn, I need to let this go.

"I'll see what I can find out, and I'll meet you again tomorrow afternoon at the falls." If we work it right, we can get into one of the caves without anyone seeing us. Then we can spend more time together without Gunnar knowing.

"That's so dangerous. I'm surprised you're offering to do it," she laughs. Am I usually more cautious? Yes. Do I care right now? No. I'm desperate to spend more time with her. I've been craving her scent for a week now. I thought I was going to die without her. If I didn't know better, I would swear she's my fated mate. But if she was, then she would be feeling the same way. Clearly, she's not, or she would have been suffering as much as I was. Right?

I hug her again, then run off, hurrying to shift and get to the training course before anyone realizes I was gone.

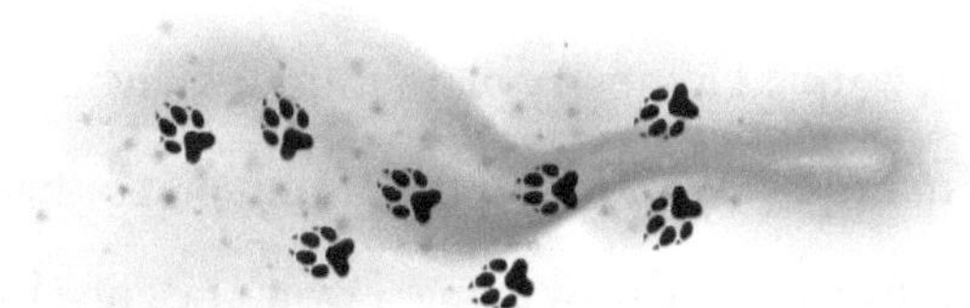

GARNET

I'm relieved when Luca runs off. I don't want him to get in trouble for me. My chest aches as he leaves. I press my hand to it and rub. That's an odd feeling. It physically hurts me to be away from him. I wish I could tell him how I feel. But I can't. He obviously doesn't feel the same. Does he?

I feel like I'm spiraling. I can't process anything right now. I grab the basket of herbs and head back to the cabin. With my morning chores done, I'll have some free time to work out on my own, since I'm not allowed to use the training course anymore. I'm sure Grammy will let me go a little deeper into the woods to run and climb trees.

After all, what good was all this training my father insisted on as I grew up if I lost every bit of muscle I have because of this punishment? I carefully plan my argument so that I'm ready for anything she can throw at me. I won't be gone long, I know I have evening chores, and I won't go near the other wolves. That should be enough to get her to agree.

She'll never say it, but I know she's as annoyed with my father as I am. She hates that he's punishing me for doing what Vincent couldn't. I know it's more of a respect issue than me actually doing anything wrong. I embarrassed my big brother and by proxy, my father. I should feel bad, but I don't. Thus, the punishment.

I race to the cabin, careful not to lose any of the herbs. The camp is mostly vacant right now, since everyone is training and my father is away. I find Grammy in the kitchen. "I have your herbs," I say, depositing the basket on the table. "What are you doing?"

She stands at the stove, stirring a pot. "I'm restocking the medicines. It'll take me a full day to get everything brewed and steeped. Did you get everything I asked for?"

"Yes, ma'am. It's all there. Where's Father?" I suddenly remember that I can't know he's gone without giving away my little visit with Luca.

"He's in the city, talking to Kayden. I have a feeling you already knew that, though." My eyes go wide and I stare at her. How could she know? "The boy smells of sandalwood, dear. It's not hard to pick up on if you're paying attention."

"You won't tell on me, will you?" I want to beg her. I probably will if she doesn't agree to keep this between us.

"I understand your father's need to discipline you, but I disagree with his methods. Keeping you away from your friend is cruel. I won't say anything. But be careful. You know how angry he'll be if he finds out." I take her warning to heart. I don't want Luca to get punished for talking to me.

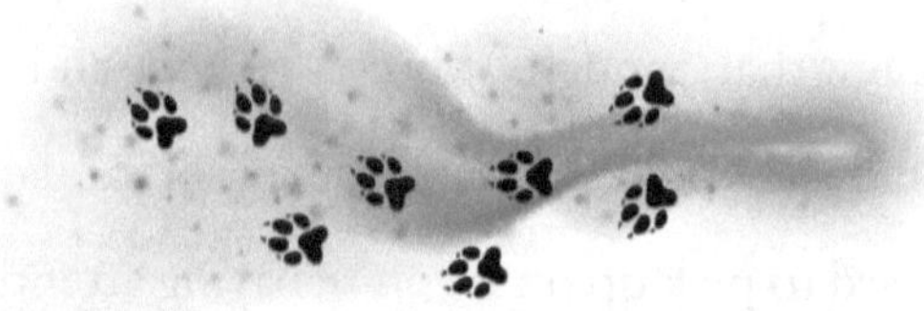

JAMES

I duck into my brother's room when the wolves arrive. First, I don't like Gunnar. He's a dick and I don't want to deal with him. Second, I want to hear what's being said. After Dec's kidnapping, I spent a little time with Gunnar's daughter, Garnet, and I'm kind of smitten. She's gorgeous with all those dark auburn waves, those green eyes, and that attitude. But more than that, when I kissed her, I felt something I've never felt before.

I can't get her out of my head, so I don't even try. I actually came to visit today to see if Kayden could get me a date with her. I hold no misconceptions about her father and his hatred of humans, though. So here I am, standing just inside the door to my brother's room, eavesdropping.

Wouldn't Mom be proud? I almost laugh at the thought, then stop myself. Pay attention, James. I know that Dec has steered them into the living room where he can help me hear it all, and I love my big brother for it.

"Wolves are missing. I'm going to send Vincent to find them, since he did so well with finding you," Gunnar says to Dec. I have to stifle another laugh. Vincent did nothing but attack Garnet, physically and mentally, while she and Luca searched for my brother. Why couldn't Gunnar see that his son was a waste of space? He'd find the wolves faster if he let Garnet and Luca look.

"What exactly do you want from us, then?" Kayden growls the words, and I can hear his feelings for this man. Loathing is too light of a word to describe it.

"I want you to provide vampire assistance, of course. When Vincent finds the responsible party, he'll need backup to retrieve the missing wolves. I'd like that to be your people." I can tell from the way he says it that he's carefully considered his words. I wonder if his facial expression gives away his true meaning.

"You mean, my people are expendable and yours aren't," Viktor snarls. I'm glad I'm not the only one who sees it that way.

"It is much easier to replenish the vampire population than the wolves." The flippant way he talks of lives pisses me off. I want to rush out of the room and beat the hell out of him. But I don't have to.

Delilah clears her throat. "Gunnar, I suggest you tread carefully here. You wouldn't want to lose your seat on the council for bigotry and prejudice, would you?" I'm immensely proud of my sister-in-law for how much she's grown into her power since she became the only known hybrid. *We* know there are others, but it's not common knowledge among the vampire or wolf shifter communities.

"I am simply a man asking for help. How does that make me a bigot?" He's baiting her, and I hear her low growl. If she shifts and attacks him, it'll be her who pays.

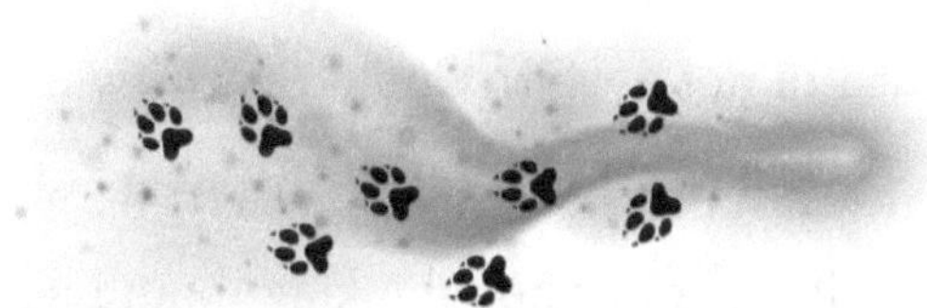

GARNET

I can't believe I talked Grammy into letting me train. I can't use the course that the wolves do, because I've been grounded from it. I swear, Father treats me like a child. I can't stand it, or him. As I practice my fighting stances, my mind drifts back to a conversation with Luca.

"You're not defective. Just because you can't shift, that doesn't mean there's anything wrong with you. What if you're not his kid? What if you're not a wolf at all?" He said those words to me as we worked through our punishment, three hours of running the course in the dark, because we'd disobeyed my father. When really, the issue has always been that Vincent is an asshole and we take the blame.

What if I'm not a wolf? Could that be what the dreams are trying to tell me? I don't have anyone to ask about it, so I should let it go. I can't stop thinking about Luca's question. What would it mean for me if I wasn't Gunnar Trion's daughter? Who would I be?

I ponder those questions as I work through as much of my training as I can on my own. The words play through my head as I run through the forest, keeping to the trails that I know will be deserted. That pushes me further away from the camp and safety. I'm not thinking about that, or about how vulnerable I am since I can't shift. I'm thinking about what I could be if I'm not who and what I've always thought.

I remember my dream. It keeps repeating, only changing slightly. I see the same things every night. Those symbols that I can't quite decipher. They're familiar, but I know I've never studied them. What if I'm a witch? I could talk to Amber about it. She's on the council and would probably be able to help me. But that would lead to Gunnar finding out. I can't do that.

I shake my head, chasing the thoughts away. Thinking about Luca's ominous question leads me to think about other things that happened while we were searching for Dec. His brother, James, kissed me. And I liked it. I told him that nothing could come of it. Once again, Gunnar stands in my way. This time it's his hatred of humans that will keep me from my happiness.

It's not uncommon for women, human, vampire, or wolf, to take more than one mate. I lose myself for a moment in the thought of Luca and James, together, with me. Now that is a sandwich I'd like to make. I wonder if either of them would be into the other. I'll save that one for when I'm safely locked in my room and can explore it more.

For now, I need to pay attention to where I am. I can no longer hear the falls, and I'm not sure how long I've been running. It's as if I've been in a trance, running toward something without realizing what I was doing. Now that I've stopped, fear creeps in. I'm used to the sounds of the forest. I grew up here. I've never been scared of the noises it makes or the animals that live here. But the silence that surrounds me now has my heart racing.

My body is damp with perspiration, so I'm not sure if my hands are clammy because of that, or the fear that's digging its icy fingers into my heart. I turn in a circle, trying to find the reason for the silence. I don't see anything. I can't sense anything. It's further proof that Luca may be right about me not being a wolf. Unless my curse cuts me off from my wolf senses.

I don't care how many times Grammy tells me I'm not cursed; I still believe I am. And with that belief comes doubt. I doubt my abilities and my worthiness. If only the Goddess would give me some kind of sign that I'm doing the right thing, or that I'm where I'm meant to be.

I pull myself from those thoughts as the silence bears down on me. A twig snaps to my left, and I race off to my right to escape whatever danger is hunting me. Because that's what this feels like, being hunted. I just wish I knew what it was so I could figure out how to fight or evade it.

I dash down the path, hoping that I'm headed back to the camp. I glance over my shoulder and don't see anything. I slam into something large and hard. Fuck.

Two strong arms wrap around me, keeping me on my feet. "Red? Are you okay?" I know that voice. My breath is coming in ragged bursts. I can't form words. I look up and lock my eyes to the man who holds me to him. Ryland Turner.

Fuck, why did it have to be Ryland? My lungs burn as I try to regulate my breathing. I need to pull myself together so I can get out of his embrace. Ryland is tall and lean, all muscle and sex appeal. His dark curls and beard beg me to run my fingers through them. I'm certain he'd let me, as he's made it clear that he's interested.

His large hands rub my back, encouraging me to calm down. "Deep breaths, Red. I've got you. You're safe now." It's as if he knows what I was running from, and he's decided to play my knight in shining armor.

I don't want to be attracted to him; he's too much like Gunnar. Add to that the fact that he knows how handsome he is, and it's a lethal combination. His arrogance is the one thing that turns me off. That's not entirely true, but it is what I tell myself. In reality, his growly alpha persona has me wondering what submitting to him would feel like.

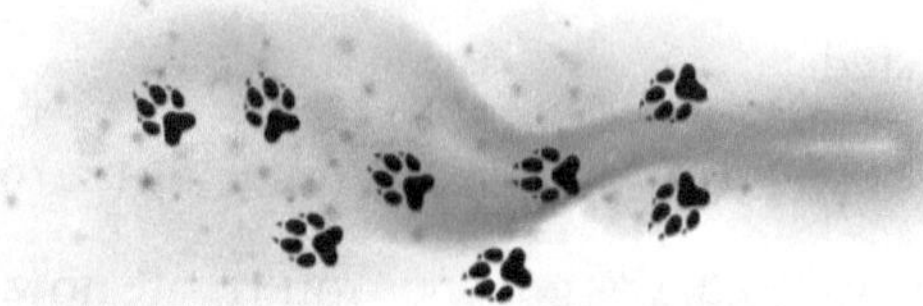

RYLAND

As I head back to my cabin from training, I scent something on the wind. It's Red, and she's scared. I would know her scent anywhere. She doesn't know it yet, but she's mine. And not just because she's beautiful and I want her. She's my mate. I felt the pull on my eighteenth birthday and have kept those feelings to myself ever since. I'm not sure why she hasn't realized it yet, but I'm patient.

I shift and race through the forest, following her scent. If she's in danger, I will be the one to protect her. I can't stand that she spends her time with Luca. I don't have a problem with him, I'm just more than a little jealous of their easy affection.

I stop in the middle of a path and shift back just as Red slams into my chest. I wrap my arms around her to keep her from falling back.

"Red? Are you okay?" My eyes search her face, or what little of it I can see. She's burying it in my chest. Her breaths are too ragged, and I know she can't speak. I need to calm her down before she pushes herself to unconsciousness.

I start to rub her back, encouraging her to breathe. When her eyes meet mine, I feel the mate pull again and barely stop myself from claiming her lips. I've made my interest in her no secret. She knows that I want her. The only thing she doesn't seem to know is that we're destined to be together. That's why I can be patient. I'll let her come to that conclusion on her own.

"Deep breaths, Red. I've got you. You're safe now." I hold her tightly without hurting her. I refuse to let go, even when she pushes against my chest. She's still not steady on her feet.

I know that I'm looking at her like I want to eat her up, because I do. I want to drop to my knees in front of her and worship her with my tongue. I can't tell her that, though, because this is not the time. She's terrified and needs me to protect her. After all, a wolf who can't shift doesn't have as many defenses as the rest of us.

She breathes my name, "Ryland," and my control wavers. I tighten my grip on her and drop my face to hers. Our foreheads touch and I search her eyes.

"Red," I growl, unable to keep the raw need out of my voice. I may not be able to tell her that we're mates, but I can let her know that I still want her. She shivers against me, and I realize that she's cold. No doubt, she's going into shock as well. I need to get her out of here, somewhere safe, where I can find out what happened. Something scared her, and I intend to find out what it was so I can take care of it.

TWO
QUESTIONABLE DECISIONS

GARNET

R YLAND WASTES NO TIME scooping me up and carrying me away from the perceived danger. If he senses it too, that means it's real, right? If he had looked at me that way for one more second, I would have kissed him. I want to, even now. I don't understand the aching pull I have toward him. Part of me wants to just give in, but the practical part of me pushes that away.

I can tell the moment we get far enough from whatever was chasing me. My chest relaxes and my breathing comes easier. "Where are you taking me, Ry?" I ask, my mouth close to his ear with the way he carries me. I see the goosebumps pepper his skin and relish the thought that I have that effect on him.

"My place. It's the closest, and I know it'll be safe. Then we can talk about what spooked you," he answers without turning to look at me. He's singularly focused on getting me to safety, and I appreciate that. Even if he's not always the kindest man, he's never been cruel to me.

I know that he isn't Luca's biggest fan, and he can't stand Orym, either. That's probably because Orym has expressed interest in me as well. These alphas are pretty territorial, even if they don't have a reason to be. I'm my own person, and no one owns me. I'll talk to whoever I want, and flirt if I feel like it.

I don't argue about going to his cabin, though I should. I should not want to be alone with this big, bad wolf. I have no idea how my father would feel about it, but I get the impression that he thinks I'm either too good for any of the wolves in our extended pack, or not good enough. I can never tell which it is. I push that thought away before annoyance can set in.

Ryland crosses the threshold of his cabin, closing and locking the door behind us without putting me down. He carries me to his couch and gently drops me onto it. He doesn't speak, disappearing into the kitchen. When he comes back, he has a bowl of ice cream and a glass of water. "Water to hydrate, ice cream for your nerves. Then you can tell me what you remember."

He sits in silence, just out of reach, until I drink some of the water and start to eat the ice cream. It's strawberry, which is my favorite. The smell of the ice cream is in direct contrast with his scent. Ryland smells of sage and makes my mouth water. I can't focus on that, or I'll realize that we're alone in his cabin, locked away from the rest of the world.

When I finish the ice cream, he moves closer, turning my face to look at him. The way he's looking at me nearly makes me combust with desire. I can picture him on top of me, giving me what I want and need. I'm certain my cheeks turn pink as his pupils go wide.

"Red," he starts, swallowing hard. "I need you to tell me what happened. I have to know why you were so scared." I don't reply immediately, and he leans closer, grabbing my chin. "If you don't start talking, I may not be able to control myself."

It sounds like a threat, but in the best way. He wants me; that's no secret. The secret is that I want him too, just as badly. If I were anyone else, I would have given in to those desires by now. But I'm broken. I don't deserve him, or Orym, or even Luca. I don't think that James would mind my inability to shift, but he's so far out of reach that I can never have him. Gunnar would not let that happen.

I take a ragged breath, then tell him about training and running. I leave out my dreams and what I was thinking about as I ran. He doesn't need to know my fantasies or nightmares right now. When I finish, he pulls me into his arms and holds me close. I try to pull away from him, but he slides me onto his lap with ease, turning me to face him. I'm straddling Ryland Turner and can feel his hard length pressing against my already soaked pussy through my jogging shorts. It's almost too much to take.

"Do you trust me?" he asks, running his hands from my shoulders to the center of my back, down and up again.

I can't speak, so I nod instead. He pulls me down, capturing my lips with his for a searing kiss. I feel a stab in my heart, but it's not painful. It's as if something clicks into place. I let down my guard and melt into the kiss. I relax and let Ryland guide me through this exploration, sliding my hands into his hair.

"Fuck, Red. I could kiss you forever," he groans against my mouth. He presses his forehead to mine and stares into my eyes. "Please let me taste you. I feel like I'll die if you don't."

I know I shouldn't, but that jab in my heart pushes me to nod. "Yes." I want this as badly as he does. And why shouldn't we? There are no laws in the packs against sex before mating. I might as well let Ry do as he pleases, even if I regret the decision later.

He gently pushes me back against the couch cushions, dropping to his knees in front of me. He slowly drags my shorts and panties off, then stares at me. "So beautiful," he mutters, making me blush again. His hands trail up my thighs and pull them further apart. Then, without preamble, he buries his face in my pussy. I swear I hear him say something that sounds like, "mine," but I can't focus to say for sure.

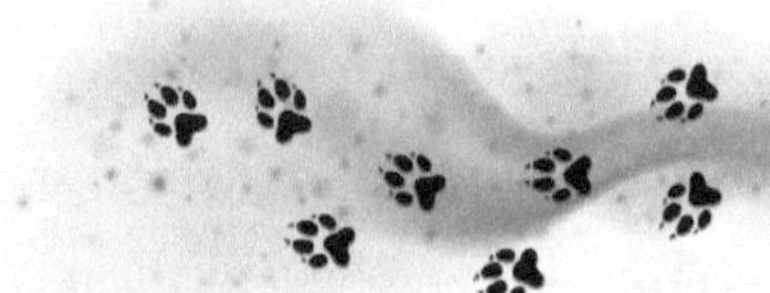

RYLAND

I'm being pulled to Garnet. It's been a constant since I realized we're fated mates. I can't resist asking her for a taste. I expect her to say no, but she agrees. Perhaps she wants me as badly as I want her. I know that a taste won't be enough. Nothing will ever be enough when it comes to her. I want to be gentle and tender with her, but I can't control myself. Hopefully there will be time for tender later. Right now, I need my mouth on her. I stop for just a moment to appreciate how beautiful her body is. "So beautiful."

I trail my tongue along her slit and growl possessively. I can't stop the word that comes out next. "Mine." Fuck, I hope she was too distracted to hear that. Otherwise, I'll have some explaining to do.

Her pussy tastes as good as her mouth. I wasn't joking when I told her I could kiss her forever. I'd love to have the opportunity. I'm sure that she has more than one mate, but no one else has said anything. I can't think about that right now.

Instead, I focus on pleasuring her with my tongue. I lick in slow strokes, alternating pressure to see how she reacts. I want her to know exactly what she does to me. I want to worship her like the queen she is. I don't care if she can shift or not, Red is all I want.

I wish that she felt the call the way I do, but I can't force the issue. Maybe I can seduce her until she realizes what's between us. I flick her clit with my tongue, drawing slow circles on it until she cries out. I'm dying to have her hands on me. I want her to touch me, to fist her hands in my hair again, anything.

I don't have to wait long until she starts stroking her fingers along my shoulders and upper back. She trails them along my arms, up to where my hands hold her hips still. If I wasn't holding her, I'm certain she'd be bucking against me. I shiver at the contact, wanting more.

I'm always going to want more from her. But I'll take what she gives me and pray it's enough. The Goddess chose her for me, and I will not turn away from that. I continue to worship her, as if I'm starving and her pussy is the only food I'll ever need. At this moment, I feel like that analogy is true.

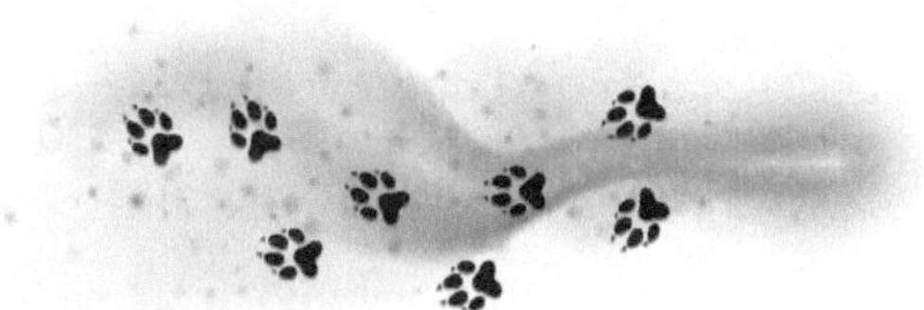

GARNET

I know that doing anything with Ryland is a bad idea. But it's hard to think with his face buried between my legs. His tongue slides along me in slow, possessive strokes. I can't stop my hands from slipping into his curls and guiding him to the exact spot I want him. He groans as I tug on his hair, his breath warm on me. Ry builds me up until I'm sure I can't take anymore. I cry out, but he doesn't stop. Instead, he slides two fingers inside me as he continues to lick and suck my pussy.

My next orgasm tears through me. How is he so good at this? I'm panting and gripping his hair so hard I worry I'll rip it out. He doesn't seem to notice. He's a man on a mission, and that mission is my pleasure. I feel like I'm falling apart. Everything is too much. "Ry, please." I don't want to beg, but I'm almost at a point where I think it's the only way he'll stop.

His hands grip my hips and he looks up at me. Oh, fuck. His dark brown eyes are so intense. "Please what? You have to use your words, Red. Tell me exactly what you want from me." It's like he's pushing me toward something, but I have no idea what it is. My body feels like it's going to combust if he stops touching me. Yet I want more. I want him.

Where did this sudden desperation come from? It doesn't matter. I'll figure it all out later. Right now, I'm lost in those chocolate eyes staring at me as if I'm the center of the universe. "I want you, Ry. Please."

He shakes his head. "Not good enough. More words. You want me to what?" He's baiting me to see if I'll tell him exactly what I'm thinking. Part of me wants to shrink away from him. Instead, I hold my gaze to his and strip my tank top and sports bra off. He licks his lips as he watches me. I'm naked, lying on his couch, with him between my legs.

"I want you to fuck me, Ryland." My voice is breathy and filled with need. He growls, then pounces on me, his kiss as desperate as I feel. That reassures me. At least I'm not the only one feeling this way. He breaks the kiss long enough to unfasten his jeans while I pull his shirt over his head. I watch when he stands up, sliding the jeans and his boxers down his legs slowly. He's watching me watch him. I can tell it excites him.

I take him in as he stands naked in front of me. His tan skin is darker than mine. My eyes take in his chest and arms, following his abs down to his cock. Fuck, he's bigger than I thought. This is going to hurt, in the best way. I reach for him and he comes to me without hesitation. I wrap my fingers around his dick and stroke him before guiding him to my entrance.

"Red, look at me." He waits for me to meet his gaze. "Are you sure this is what you want? We can't take this back." It seems like a strange thing to say, but he's right. We can't take this back. There will be no going back to the way things were before.

"I'm sure, Ry. I want this. I want you. I don't understand it, but I'm drawn to you." He smiles and kisses me again, teasing me with his tongue. I guess he likes my answer, because he lets me guide him to where I crave.

As soon as we're lined up, he thrusts into me, sheathing himself in one move. As wet as I am, I was not ready for that. I cry out in a mix of pleasure and pain. His kiss swallows the noise, and he starts moving his hips. Fuck, this feels amazing.

Ryland pumps his hips, thrusting into me faster and harder. I throw my head back as I come, and he trails kisses and nips down my neck. I'm getting close to another orgasm, and I can tell this one is going to be bigger than the last. I dig my fingers into his back, urging him to get closer. He drops his head and starts to suck on my neck. It feels so good that I tangle my fingers in his hair again, holding him there.

I know if he leaves a mark, I'll have some explaining to do, but right now, I don't care. I just want him to keep doing what he's doing. It feels amazing, and I never want him to stop. I could stay here forever. I feel him tense, and know that he's close to coming. He slows down for a moment, then slams into me, hard and fast until we come together. "Ryland!" I scream and he bites down on my neck where it meets my shoulder. Fuck. Did he just mate mark me? Oh, shit.

My eyes go wide as he pulls away from me. "What the fuck did you just do?" I know that I'm as much to blame as he is, but I can't help being upset. I wasn't ready for this.

"Red, please. Let me explain. I'm sorry. I know it's too soon, but we're fated mates." I look at him in shock. Fated mates? What the fuck?

"Ry, what makes you think we're fated?" I ask cautiously. I know he wouldn't have marked me just because. He's difficult, but he's not the type of guy to force a girl into a mate bond.

"My chest hurts when we're away from each other. I sensed you were in danger earlier. It was a desperate need to find you and make sure you were okay. I should have told you on my birthday, but I didn't want to make you feel like you don't have a choice. You don't have to mark me. I'm so sorry. Please just say you'll forgive me." The pain in his voice makes my heart ache.

I hold up a hand to get him to stop. I grab his hand and pull him down to lie on top of me. "Just give me a minute," I say as I brush my hand through his hair.

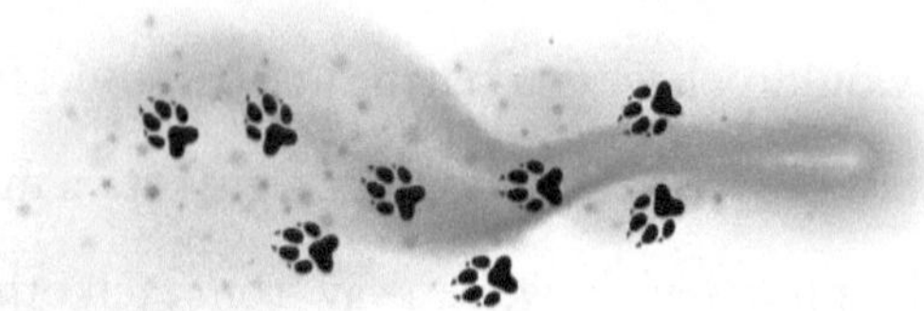

RYLAND

I should not have bitten her. What the fuck is wrong with me? If she doesn't bite me back, the bond will be incomplete. I know that I'll slowly go crazy, and I deserve it. She's always going to wonder if I did this on purpose, when it was an impulsive move. I didn't plan it out. Panic grips me as she blows up at me. I deserve her anger.

Then I watch as her expression changes. She's more shocked than angry. I think I still have a small chance when she asks me why I think we're fated. After I explain, she pulls me to her and holds me, stroking my hair as she thinks. But what the fuck is she thinking about?

Just when I think I'm going to go crazy from the silence stretching between us, she speaks. "Do you think a person can have more than one fated mate?"

I try to move to look up at her, but she holds me still. I can hear the tears in her voice. "I do. I've seen several who share mates. Your vampire friends, for example." I don't personally know them, but I've heard and seen enough to know that Kayden's fated mate is the vampire hybrid, and she has three other mates as well.

"Would you be upset if you had to share me?" Excitement tears through my heart at her words. Does this mean she's decided to accept the bond? I can't be sure until she says the words and marks me herself.

"I don't like to share." I pause, certain that my admission has made her cry. "But for you, I would learn how to. I promise you, Red. I will do whatever you need me to. I will be the best mate ever." I know that no matter what I say, she has to make this decision herself.

"Why didn't you just tell me?"

I sigh against her breast. "I was scared you'd reject me." The truth spills from my lips and it costs me. Pain shoots through my heart at the thought that this amazing woman won't want me to be hers and won't want to be mine.

"Oh, Ry," she says, and I can hear her tears. I try to lift my head again, and this time she relaxes her hold on my hair so I can. I slide up her body and press my lips to hers. This kiss isn't about desire or desperation. This one is about love. I need her to feel what's in my heart.

I kiss her tenderly, our tongues dancing as she opens her mouth to give me access. I don't want to stop kissing her. I pour my heart and soul into the kiss. When I pull back, I wipe the tears from her eyes with my thumbs. "Please don't cry. I don't ever want to make you sad. I'm sorry. For all of this. I should have just taken you home."

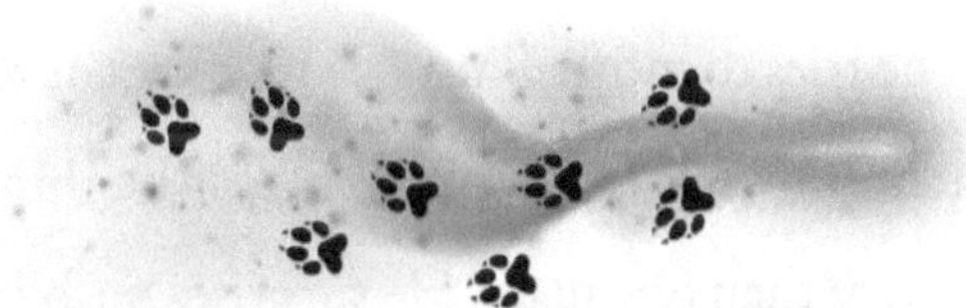

GARNET

While I stroke Ry's hair, I think about things. If he's right, the mate pull is why I've been feeling so off lately. I suspect that he is, because the pain in my chest gets better when he's around. But not just when he's around. I've had the same feeling around Luca and Orym, too. And I get that feeling when I think about James. So, how do I know what it means?

I close my eyes as I stroke his hair. *Goddess, grant me the strength to make the right choice here.* Am I crazy for considering marking him? Am I even more crazy for wanting to make sure I don't have to give up the other men I'm attracted to? Fuck, this is hard. Tears stream down my cheeks, and I hold him to me when he tries to move. I just need a moment to think.

I can't stop myself from asking him if he thinks a person can have more than one mate. He surprises me by mentioning Delilah and her men. They do seem to be fated. Then he indulges me when I ask how he would handle sharing. I've known Ry as long as I've known Luca and know him nearly as well. He doesn't like to share and isn't afraid to fight for what he's decided is his.

But I won't have that if the others turn out to be my fated mates as well. Would the Goddess give me four mates when I can't even shift? Would that be a reward for everything I've gone through?

When Ry admits that he was scared of rejection, I lose it. Tears fall faster, and he does the only thing he can to stop them. He kisses me. I feel every emotion that he pours into it. And I realize that he's right. This feeling isn't something I can push away or ignore. He is one of my fated mates. I have no idea what is going to happen, but the bond is already halfway done. If I don't claim him, he'll slowly start to go crazy.

He startles me by breaking the kiss and telling me that all of this was a mistake. No. I won't let him think that for a moment longer. I push him hard, rolling us onto the floor. "Ow. You could have just asked me to get up."

I straddle him, laying my body on top of his until we're touching nearly everywhere. "I will not tolerate that kind of behavior. Do you understand? No mate of mine will ever be allowed to talk down about himself like that." I don't give him a chance to respond, capturing his lips with mine briefly before I lick down his neck and bite him in the same spot he marked me.

I feel the magic of the bond snap into place. It's strange, but warm. I can feel him inside my head. *Ry? Can you hear me?* I can't resist testing to see if our bond is similar to Kayden and Delilah's.

Fuck, Red. Did you just claim me? I'll take that as a yes. I sit back and grin at him.

"I did. Is that a problem?" I ask, feeling a little bratty.

"No. I just thought—" I cut him off with a look.

"Well, stop that. The thinking. You're doing it all wrong." I pause and grab his hands, pressing them to my breasts. "But the touching is good. Keep doing that, okay?"

He laughs, still unsure of himself, but not willing to stop touching me yet. And if I'm being honest, I'm not ready to stop touching him either. I pause for a moment, considering how this will affect everything. My father will be pissed. The moment Gunnar comes into my mind, any lingering sexual desire fades away.

I forget that Ry can sense my emotions now. His hands fall from my breasts, and he sits up, dragging me into his arms. "It's okay, Red. I'll take care of you. Even Gunnar can't fight against fated mates." His attempt at comfort helps a little, but there's no way I won't be punished for this.

"It won't matter. You were told to shun me, and I was told to stay away from everyone. He won't care that I was scared or in danger. He'll care that we disobeyed him."

Ry presses a kiss to my forehead and holds me a little tighter. "Then we'll leave. We're both adults, and can leave the packs the same as Kayden did. We can move into the city and make a life there." His willingness to give up everything for me was more than I could handle. Tears started to fall again. Ry obviously wasn't good with tears, so he kissed me again, tenderly and leisurely this time.

Once the waterworks stopped, he eased me back. "I know you don't want to leave. But are you really going to let Gunnar control your life forever?"

"What choice do I really have? He's the leader of all the packs in the Whispering Thicket. I can't leave. I can't even shift. What good would I be to anyone?"

Anger sparks in Ry's eyes. "If I'm not allowed to be down on myself, you have to stop that. You are not less just because you can't shift." He pauses as if he's just considered something. "Luca may be right. What if you're not a wolf at all?" Fuck, now he's using the bond against me. I have to learn how to stop him from reading my thoughts.

"That was a personal conversation, Ry. Please don't go poking around in my head without permission. I promise I won't do it to you, either." I try desperately not to think about Luka, Orym, or James. I know that I've failed when Ry glares at me.

"Seriously? Those two? And who's the other guy?"

"Ry, we are not having this conversation right now."

THREE
AFTERMATH

LUCA

I'm just finishing up training when Gunnar and Vincent
come back. I can tell that he didn't get the answer he wanted

from Kayden by the way Gunnar screams at Vincent and sends him off to the training course. Fuck, I hope Red doesn't get in his way. She's suffered enough recently.

Just the thought of her has me rubbing my chest, over my heart. I'm starting to suspect that this feeling is more than simple desire. It's not like we've been told what the mate bond feels like. So I have no way to confirm that's what this is. Unless I talk to Grammy. Which I can't do, since the person I'd be asking about is her granddaughter. Talk about awkward.

I watch from the shadows as Gunnar storms into the cabin, then see Red on the other side of the clearing. She obviously saw her father and is hiding. Who is that with her? I can't see clearly, but whoever he is, his shadow is familiar. I dash through the trees and come up behind them.

"I can't do it, Ry. He won't understand. I won't let you get punished for me," Garnet says, wrapping her arms around him. Fucking Ryland Turner. What happened here? I'm frozen in place, staring at them as my heart cracks in half.

"Red, love, please. Just let me talk to him. You and I both know that you can't fight the mate call. He'll understand that. It'll be okay, I promise," Ryland reassures her, pressing a kiss to her forehead before gently brushing her arms off and walking toward the cabin.

She stands there, reaching for him but not moving. As soon as he's out of earshot, I step forward, snapping a twig under my boots. I stop, standing perfectly still, as if that will hide me.

Red's head whips around and our eyes meet. I know she can see the pain in my eyes. "Luca," she says my name and my chest constricts. I can't respond. She knows that I've seen her with him, and that I'm destroyed. Before she can take a step toward me, I shift and race through the forest.

I can't handle her pity, or her excuses. I could smell him on her. I know they've been intimate. I have no one to blame but myself. I love her more than I can stand, but I was too scared to tell her. Now it's too late. Because who can possibly have more than one fated mate? I mean, sure people have more than one mate, but not the other half of their soul.

I run until I can't run anymore. I have to go somewhere that she can't find me. I know that if I don't, she'll figure out a way to come to me and explain. I can't handle that right now. I won't be able to look at her the same. She belongs to him now, and I'm relegated to the friend zone. Fuck my life.

I stop near the waterfall to catch my breath. I know that the adult thing to do is turn around and have this conversation with her. But I can't. My heart feels as if it's being torn out of my chest. The further I run, the more it hurts. I won't be able to stay away from her for long, but I need some time. I shift back and climb a tree, settling down in the center for the night. I'll talk to her in a few days. Until then, I'm perfectly happy staying right here.

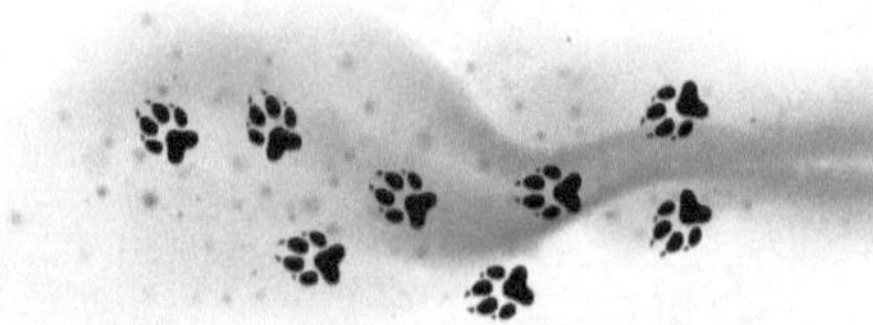

GARNET

Fuck. I shouldn't have let Ry walk me home. But he wouldn't let me out of his sight until we were behind the cabin. I should have found Luca and explained everything. The pain I saw on his face eats at me. I know Ry can feel it through the bond, but I don't know how to block it yet.

I stand there, defeated, and wait for Ry to finish talking to my father. I know this is going to end badly, but there is nothing I can do to stop it. I'll be punished, and Ry probably will too. It's not fair. If the Goddess sees fit to put us together, no one should stand in the way of that. I should have gone with him so I could at least hear what they're saying.

Ry? Are you okay? I ask through the bond. He doesn't answer, but I can feel his irritation. Things are not going well with my father. Should I go in there? I can't force my feet to move.

A moment later, Grammy comes out the back door and heads straight for me. It doesn't matter that I'm hidden in the tree line, she knows exactly where I am. She stops directly in front of me and pulls me into her arms. "Oh, child. I wish I had known this was going to happen. I would have stopped you from going to train. Your father is pissed, but what's done is done. He can't keep you from your mate. Since you've sealed the bond, you'll be going with Ryland."

My face lights up for a split second. "There's more to it than that. What's wrong?"

"Your father wants to exile you. I'm fighting him, and I won't hesitate to fight dirty. Don't worry, child. Grammy's got you." There's something in her voice.

"What aren't you telling me?" I know there's more to this that she's not saying. I have to pull it out of her.

"I don't think he's your only mate. All I can tell you is that there will be more." She hugs me tightly.

"How do you know?" I push away from her, wanting answers more than comfort.

"I can't tell you that, child. Just know that there are more mates for you to find. Don't give up on another because you've found one. You'll need them all before the end." What the fuck does that mean?

"Before the end of what, Grammy? I don't understand what's going on here." At this point, I'm so confused and torn about everything.

"You'll understand when the time is right. I have to go now. Your father will want to talk to you, then you'll have to gather your things." She turns and walks back to the cabin. I have no choice but to follow her. If what she says is true, then my father will be looking for me soon anyway. There's no point in hiding.

I walk in the door, and he glares at me. Ryland is standing in front of him, and it looks like he's been punched in the face. *Ry? Are you okay?* He gives me a slight nod, then turns his attention back to my father. What the actual fuck is going on here.

"I'll have a word with my daughter now. You may wait for her outside." My father dismisses Ry, and he walks past me without even looking at me. I'm terrified of what's about to happen, but I can't regret finding my mate. I won't let him guilt me about this.

"Father," I say, standing tall as he faces me.

"You dirty whore," he starts, and his words are like a slap in the face. "How dare you claim a mate without permission! I should have you exiled for this. You show nothing but contempt for me, after everything I've done for you."

I can't take another moment of this. I feel as if I'm about to explode. "And just what have you done for me, Father? Treated me as less than everyone else because I can't shift? Allowed Vincent to treat me like shit and punish me for it? Please, tell me exactly what I should be thanking you for." I know that I'll pay for the words, but I'm leaving this house tonight and I will never return. Even if Ry decides that he doesn't want me anymore, I'll find somewhere to go.

I'm pretty sure Delilah would take me in if I needed it.

I'm not prepared for the hand that connects with my cheek. Fuck, that hurt. I won't give him the satisfaction of my tears, though. "You ungrateful bitch. I took care of you after your mother left. You need to show some respect," he growls, extremely close to shifting inside.

"I'm beginning to understand why she left. I'll never understand why she left me with you, though," I snarl back at him. I turn to walk away, and I'm jerked back by the hand that's fisted in my hair.

"You don't get to walk away from me until I say." I can see that his restraint is barely holding on. I shouldn't push him, but I can't help myself.

"I know pack law. You can't keep me from my mate, and you can't deny an already completed bond. You want me to show you respect? Then earn it." I jerk my hair out of his hand and stomp back to my room.

I slam the door and fall back against it. I can't believe I finally stood up to him like that. Fuck, that was scary. I hear a tap on the window and rush to see if it's Luca. I try to hide my disappointment when I see that it's Ryland. I push the window open and stare at him.

"You were so cold. And you blocked me. Or ignored me. Why?" I can't stop myself from asking. I need reassurance from him, and I hate myself for it.

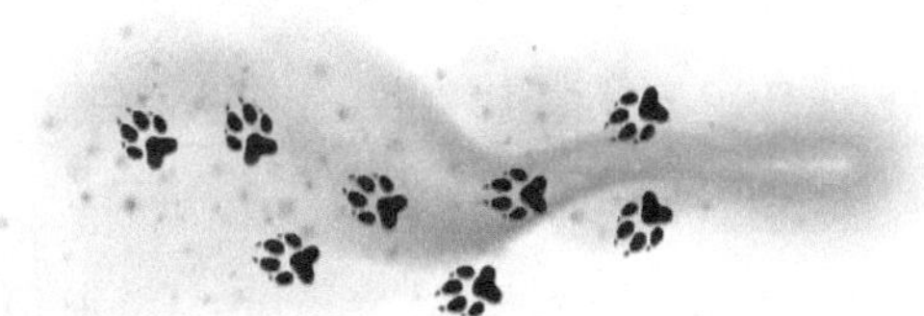

RYLAND

I know she's pissed. I don't blame her, but I had to block her out so I could deal with her father. I did everything I could to be respectful until he called her a whore. Then I swung on him. Unfortunately, he's older and a little faster than I am. He clocked me in the eye before my fist could connect. And she walked in before we could finish our discussion.

"Are you okay?" I ask, seeing the red handprint on her face. "I'll kill him."

She laughs. "You weren't too concerned when I was trying to check on you." Tears fill her eyes, and my heart aches.

"I was trying to protect you, love. Please. Come home with me. He can't stop you," I beg her, almost going down on my knees.

"Well, I can't stay here," she breathes. I sigh in relief. For a moment, I thought she was going to. I watch as she fills a bag with her clothes, zips it and tosses it out the window at me. I catch it, carefully place it on the ground and wait for her to give me something else. Two more duffels follow, then she starts to climb out the window herself.

"What the fuck are you doing?" I can't stop the question, but instantly regret it.

"I'm not facing him again tonight. You can either catch me, or get out of the way," she says as she launches herself from the window. Of course, I scramble to catch her. Once she's in my arms, I press my lips to hers for a quick kiss. I won't let her go again.

I set her down gently and pick up her bags. "Come on. I'll make you dinner." Her eyes go wide, and I can hear her stomach grumble. I didn't think she'd eaten enough today, even with the ice cream after her training. I know she's still pissed, but I can't tell if it's directed toward me or her father.

I don't try the mate bond, because as she pointed out, I blocked her earlier. It wasn't fair of me, but I didn't want her to see my reaction to her father. I wanted to kill him. Part of me still does. But I'm mate bonded to his daughter, so that makes us family.

We walk back to my cabin in somewhat comfortable silence.

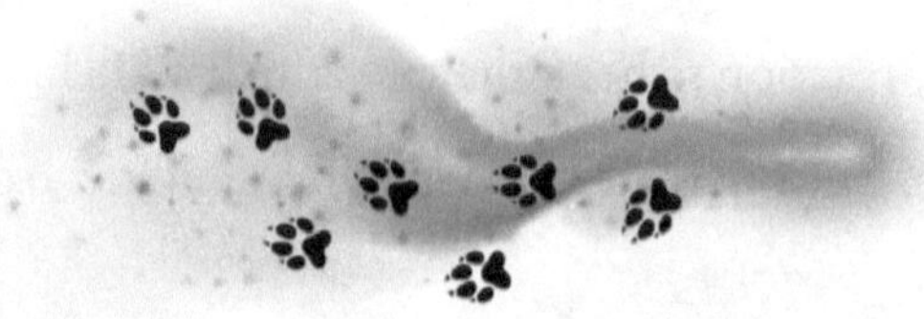

GARNET

I know it's ridiculous to be angry with Ry for trying to protect me, but I can't help it. He ignored me when I was worried about him. That isn't going to work for me. But I understand why he did it, so I'll forgive him. I also need to tell him about Luca. I have to go find him and explain.

Fuck, why does finding my fated mate seem to be screwing my life up? I will not regret this. I refuse to. The Goddess has a plan, and we are all part of it. So these guys need to straighten up and focus on what we need to do.

"Are you going to tell me what you talked about?" I ask when we get to Ry's cabin. He sets my bags in his bedroom and returns to the living room where I'm lounging on the couch. I might as well make myself at home.

"He's sending Vincent out in search of the missing wolves tomorrow. Before I told him about us, he was going to send me. After, well, his fist had something to say to my face. I hate to admit it, but you were right. I should not have told him. But I couldn't just leave you there with him. We belong together. You're mine." He looks at me and winks. "And I'm yours."

It's a good thing he finished that thought. I would have blacked his other eye. I do not belong to anyone like that. I am not property. But if it's mutual, I'll accept it. I love that he already knows me well enough to know how I feel about that. It shows that he's been paying attention all these years.

While we know each other pretty well, we don't know everything. I let him take my hand as I sigh. This conversation isn't going to be easy. But it's necessary. "Luca knows about us. He saw us before you went inside at Gunnar's. He ran off before I could explain."

"Why does it matter that Luca ran off?" It takes him a second, but Ry finally realizes what my problem is. "Oh. I see. Do you think that he's one of your other mates? If you even have more."

"Grammy says I do but won't tell me how many. She said that everything will work out the way the Goddess wants. I can't leave Luca like that. He needs to know that I think he's one of my mates." I don't want to admit that I hope he is, then I remember that Ry can hear my thoughts.

I'm sorry. It doesn't make what we have mean less. But I love him. I have for as long as I can remember. I hope he understands. This situation is all kinds of fucked up. I can't imagine how he's feeling right now.

I know. I didn't need the mate bond to know that you're in love with Luca. It's obvious to everyone but him. I don't mind sharing your heart, as long as you have room for me too. His sweet thoughts make me smile. I tug on his hand and pull him over to me for a sweet, lingering kiss.

Always. He smiles against my mouth before breaking the kiss. I pout at him, but he kisses my forehead and stands up.

"I promised you food. You haven't eaten enough today. Anything special you want to eat?" Oh, yeah, he's gonna cook for me. I had no idea Ry could cook.

"What are my options?" I stand up and follow him to the kitchen.

"I can make you a salad, which I don't recommend. I also have steaks that would come with baked potatoes. Or frozen pizza. That's all the dinner stuff I have until supplies get here tomorrow." As much as I want to make him cook for me, I decide on the pizza. He's right, I didn't eat enough today. I don't want to wait for steak tonight.

"Can we do the pizza?" At his nod, I ask what I've been dying to. "Then can we go look for Luca?" Ry tenses for a second, then relaxes.

"Of course, love. Whatever you need. We'll eat, then track him down and drag him back here so you can talk some sense into him." I can tell he wants to ask me something else, but he's hiding it from me.

"What?" I put my hands on my hips and stare at him, waiting.

"What if he doesn't want to be found? Or doesn't want to be your mate? Then what?" He has enough sense to look embarrassed at his questions. "I'm not saying any of that's true, just playing devil's advocate. What if? You know?"

"I understand. I've been asking myself those questions since he ran off. I can't give up on him. We're connected. And if that feeling I've been having related to you was the mate call, then I've had it for longer with Luca. You men and keeping secrets. I should beat you both." I make the empty threat and laugh as Ry thrusts his ass toward me in invitation.

I swat it playfully, then go back into the living room and fall back on the couch. I wonder how long it will be before I figure out how many mates I have. Then I have to figure out how to make things work with more than one man. I may have to call Delilah and ask for advice.

Ry puts the pizza in the oven and joins me. He grabs the remote and turns on the TV. "Wait, how does your TV work out here?" Gunnar told us that satellites couldn't reach us out here. That fucker.

"I have a signal booster. I got it from Eli when we went to the city the last time Gunnar took me with him to meet with Kayden. He felt sorry for me not having any way to wind down at night."

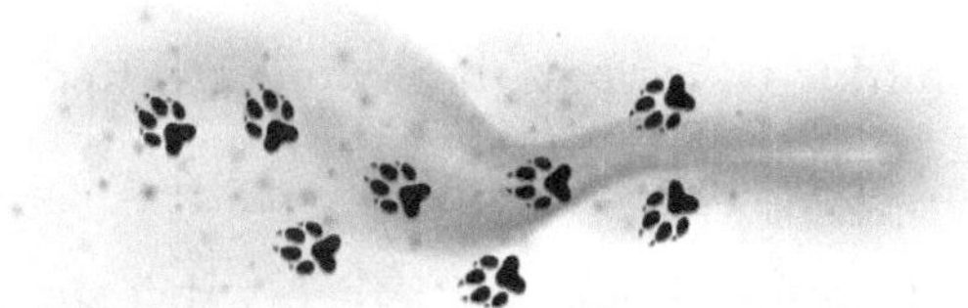

RYLAND

I don't want to go searching for Luca in the dark, but I will not refuse a request from my mate. What Red wants, Red will get. I'll do everything in my power to make her happy, even if that means chasing down men who could be her other mates. And it could be worse. She could have her sights set on that dick, Orym, instead of Luca. At least Luca was a decent guy.

I watch as she devours half the pizza. I knew she was hungry, but damn that girl can eat. I'm impressed. Most women don't want you to know how much they can put away. That's my girl. Luckily, I have snacks stocked for when she gets hungry again later. Wolves have to consume a lot because of how much energy shifting takes out of us. I wonder if Red eats as much as the rest of us, since she can't shift.

I start to think about Luca's theory that she's not even a wolf. I wonder what she could be. It's obvious that she's more than just human. Not that I have a problem with humans, I just know she's not one. There's something supernatural about her, which is probably why she's been able to hide here her entire life. I wonder if that's why Gunnar treats her different from the rest of us.

What if she's not even his? I shake the thought away as she starts to stare at me. I can't hide my thoughts from her again, so I let my guard down and change my line of thinking. I start to consider where Luca could be. I'm sure he won't be at his cabin, although we'll check there first.

"The falls. That's the most likely place. Probably in a tree. He'll want to make it harder on me to find him." She seems to know him so well. Why hasn't he made a move on her? I don't understand how he could think she wasn't interested in him.

She finishes her pizza and stands up. "Are you good?" I nod, watching as she laces her boots and ties them. "Then let's go. I could be wrong, so we should check his cabin on the way to the falls." I agree with her. The best place to start is his home.

When we don't find him there, I follow Red to the falls. I'm paying close attention to everything around us. I can't afford to get caught off guard again. I have to protect her at all costs.

We walk a few yards past the falls and I scent Luca. My nose twitches and Red notices. "Where?" She doesn't ask me if I've found him, just where he is. I point at a tree a few more yards away. She dashes toward it, then turns back to me for confirmation. I nod and she starts to climb. Fuck, I wish she chased me down like that. Her determination is hot as hell.

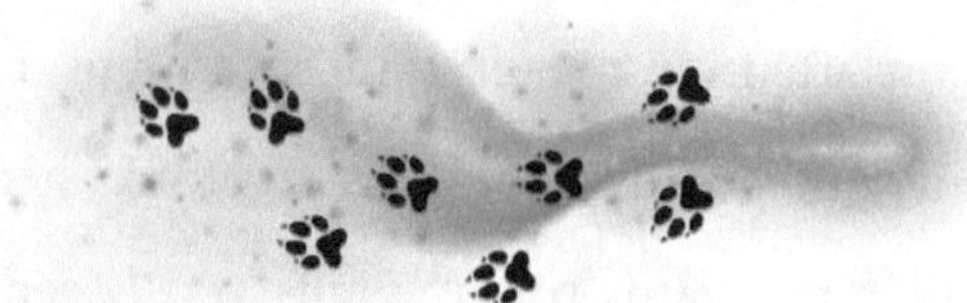

LUCA

I'm awakened by Red flopping on top of me in my hiding spot. "What the fuck?" How did she find me? I glance around and see Ryland at the base of the tree. Of course, she used her guard dog to hunt me down. "What do you want, Red?"

She stares at me for a long moment, then leans forward and presses her lips to mine. I gasp and she maneuvers her tongue into my mouth to stroke against mine. I shouldn't touch her; she belongs to someone else. But he's standing just below us, and is watching this without saying a word.

That's enough to make me relax into the kiss. I can feel my control start to snap as my cock hardens under her. Red moves her hips against me, grinding her hot pussy against my dick. Oh, fuck. I can't think straight. I want her more than I want to breathe. I push her away a little and groan. "What are you doing?"

She looks at me and laughs. Ryland calls up to us, "I told you he'd be shocked. Can you two come down now? I'm a little worried that you'll fall and I won't know who to catch." I know he's being sarcastic, because he'd catch her.

"Come on, Luca. Please. Come with us and let me explain. It's not exactly what you think," she begs. Why is she begging me when she's already mated? I don't understand. But going back to Ryland's with them would be better than sleeping in this tree all night.

"You don't think it's gonna be a bit awkward since you just kissed me?"

"Nope. Ry knows. Please let us explain so you will too." Her tone is calm and relaxed, even though I can hear her heart racing as much as mine is.

"Okay, I'll go with you. As long as he's not going to fight me." She laughs again. I follow her down from the tree. As soon as we're in the moonlight, I see the hand print on her face and his black eye. "What the fuck happened to you two?" I know the answer already and it makes my blood boil.

"Gunnar didn't exactly approve. But it's okay, pack law is on our side," Ryland explains. I nod, still confused about this situation. I have no choice but to follow them back to his cabin.

Once we're inside, he gestures to the couch. I sit on one end and Red sits down next to me. Ryland brings bottles of water and drops down next to Red. I'm expecting an ambush, so what comes next is a shock.

"I think we're fated mates," Red says.

"You and Ryland, I know," I say dryly. She shakes her head.

"You and me," she insists. "But also, Me and Ry. And there's another one or more out there too. I don't know how many. Grammy wasn't very specific."

"What? This is a lot to process, Red."

FOUR

ANOTHER MISSING WOLF

ORYM

THIS MEETING IS RIDICULOUS. Gunnar won't listen to reason, and I'm tired of his incessant whining about people being disrespectful. "Why did you call us here today, Alpha? What aren't you telling us?" I ask, forcing him to refocus on the issue at hand.

"Vincent was supposed to go looking for the missing wolves yesterday. He went to train last night, but never came home. I need a team to find him." Was that anger or pain in Gunnar's voice? I couldn't tell.

"I'll volunteer, Alpha, if I can select my own team," I offer with a kind smile. And I know exactly who I'll take. Besides easing this pain in my chest, I'll enjoy the search much more.

"Yes, fine, take whoever you like. Just find my son. He's my heir after all. I'm certain he's following a lead and just forgot to check in. Go as soon as possible."

I'm relieved that he doesn't ask who I'm taking. Now I just have to find them, because they should have been at this meeting. I wait until Gunnar walks away, then turn toward his cabin. Grammy is hanging clothes on the line when I get there. "Good morning, Grammy. Do you know where Red is today?"

"Good morning, sweet boy. She's with Ryland at his cabin. Perhaps not alone; I can't be sure. If you need her, you'll have to go there." She watches the face I make. "Don't worry, child, you'll get your chance."

I thank her and run off in the direction of Ryland's cabin. I can't stand that pompous asshole, and hate that Red is spending time with him. But if that's where Grammy says she is, then that's where I have to go.

I knock on the door and wait, annoyed that I'm going to have to be nice to Ryland. I'll do it if it means I get to spend time with Red, but I don't have to like it. What is she doing here anyway? And what did Grammy mean, maybe not alone? The whole thing seems strange, since Gunnar keeps her under lock and key. I knock a second time, and the door swings open.

"Luca? What are you doing here?" I'm not sure who I expected Grammy to be talking about, but I didn't consider Luca at all.

"It's complicated." He looks over his shoulder and motions for me to come inside. "Come on, I'm sure you're here for a reason. We can talk inside."

I step into the cabin, looking around for Red. I don't see her, but maybe she's in the bathroom. I can't shake this strange feeling that I'm missing something here. I know she's here, since the pain I've had in my chest all night finally eases. Mate calls are no joke. I just don't have the guts to tell her about it, since her father would kill me instead of letting me have her. That doesn't mean I have to like her being in another man's cabin, much less one I despise.

"Have a seat. Do you want me to get Ryland?" I didn't know they were friends, which is strange. I nod.

"Yeah, I guess so. Is Red here, too?" The puzzled look on my face must give me away.

Luca chuckles and walks toward the back of the house. I can hear a muffled conversation, but can't make out what's being said. A moment later, Ryland walks out in just a pair of sweat pants. Red follows after him, obviously wearing one of his t-shirts. There is no fucking way this asshole stole my mate. I'll kill him.

I'm on my feet and across the room with him shoved up against the counter. As I reach for a knife to deal with this mess, Red grabs one of my arms and Luca grabs the other. They drag me off Ryland and step in front of him.

"I told you we wouldn't have to wait long to find the other one," Luca teases. The other one what?

Red blushes and threads her fingers through mine. I'm suddenly relaxed and on edge at the same time. "We should talk," she says, dragging me to the couch. Once we're settled, she gives me a long look. Then turns to Luca. "I think you should tell him your part first. If things line up, we can tell him the rest."

I growl as Ryland settles next to her on the couch, sliding his arm around her protectively. Luca drops on the floor in front of us and smiles. "Pain in your chest when you're away from her? Annoyingly drawn to be as near her as possible as much as possible?"

I glare at Ryland and nod. "She's my mate. I'm sorry, Red. I should have told you. I didn't want to overwhelm you since I'm certain your father won't allow it."

"Except that he doesn't have a choice," Ryland says with a laugh. "And I don't have to like you to share if that's what she wants."

"What are you talking about?" I still have no idea what's going on here. Red untangles her fingers from mine and threads them again, as if testing something. There's a zing of static that jabs at me, but in a good way.

"I know it's a little different, especially since it's not generally easy to find your fated mate..." she pauses and locks eyes with me. "But I have more than one fated mate, and I believe you are meant to join us."

"I'm meant to join you. *Us.* Who is us? You and Ryland?"

"Don't forget me," Luca chimes in. "It's not as bad as it sounds, Orym. There are plenty of times when this has happened in the past. It just means that Red is special and needs us all."

"What happens if I don't agree? What happens if I do?" I'm spiraling, and need something to hold onto. I grip her hand harder.

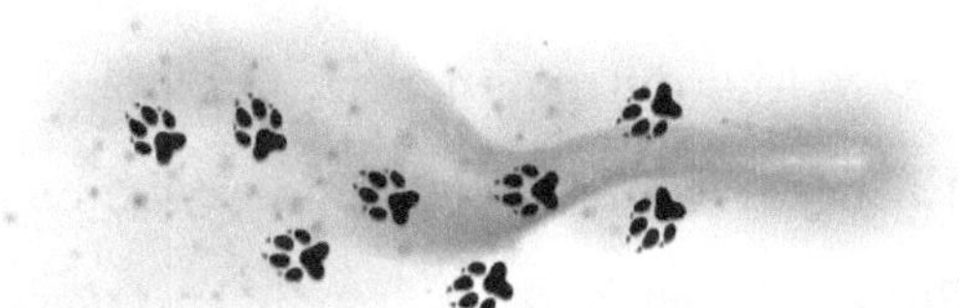

GARNET

Luca, Ryland, and I spent half the night talking about the possibility of other mates. Since I have no idea how many I'm looking for, I don't know what to expect. Luca swore that they would find me, and fast. He may be right.

"It's all overwhelming, I know. If you don't want to share, or if you don't want me, I'll deal with it. If you do, then you and Ryland will have to stop fighting." I stare at his lips as I speak, my cheeks turning pink as he catches me.

"You said you're not sure how many mates you have. Do you feel the pull?" he asks, watching me watch him.

"Honestly, I didn't know what that feeling was. I've felt it connected to four different people, and thought I was going nuts." I glance at Ry and Luca. "I'm sorry I didn't tell you last night. But after some thinking about it, I may know how many and who." I turn back to Orym. "There's only one real way to know, though."

I lick my lips, watching him. If I had known all I had to do to realize the pull in me was the mate call was to kiss them, I would have done it ages ago. I lean closer to him and breathe in his fresh cedar scent. He's holding onto my hand as if it's the only thing keeping him here. His tousled sandy brown hair begs for my fingers to be in it. I stare at his green eyes, waiting to see if he understands my meaning.

When he doesn't move, I glance at Luca and Ryland. I know they won't go far, but I need a little privacy here. *Please, Ry, give us a minute?*

Anything for you, love. I'll take Luca with me. Let us know when it's safe to come back. He stands up, presses a kiss to my temple and nudges Luca on the arm. They leave without a word. Of course, Ry will explain to Luca that I asked for a minute. But the fact that no one argued, and that Ry didn't even try to fight back when Orym attacked him is a huge step.

"Okay. What's the one way? And where did they go?" he asks. I can tell he's confused and I completely understand. I carefully unthread our fingers and flip my leg across his lap. Once I'm straddling him, he takes in a sharp breath.

"I can show you, if you want. And they had something to do," I whisper, leaning closer to him. His hands automatically grip my hips and I can't tell if he's holding me on his cock, or keeping me still. His breath is coming faster, just like mine. I rest my hands on his shoulders for a second, then can't resist running them through his hair.

He groans, and I twine my fingers together behind his head. Then I lean forward and press my lips to his. A shock of electricity passes between us. I gasp and that's all the encouragement he needs to start exploring my mouth with his tongue. As I suspected, Orym is another of my mates.

I've kissed boys before, but never had this sensation with any of them. Only with the four men I've kissed most recently. And

I know what that means, even if I'm not ready to think about it yet. Gunnar might just kill me for it. As long as I stay in the forest, it shouldn't be an issue.

Orym grinds me against him and I can feel his hard length press against me. Oh, Goddess, I want this man. But I'm not ready for three people in my head at once, so I have to hold back. Luca understood, so I hope Orym will too.

When I finally break the kiss, we're winded but sated. "Red, I've never felt like that before." I smile at him.

"That's how I know. If this isn't what you want, or if it's too much, we can break the connection. Please understand, though. That's not what I want, but it has to be what you want too."

Orym looks at me for a long moment. "I don't know, Red. I want to, but I don't know about him."

"You don't have to decide right now. The pull is uncomfortable, but manageable. Especially if we're spending time together."

"Who is the fourth?" I'm not prepared for the question and don't know how to answer it. I don't think he will flip out to learn that my fourth mate is a human, but there's no way to know for sure.

"I'll let you know when I have that completely figured out," I evade the question. "Now, I'm sure you didn't come here today because of the mate bond, right?" When he nods, I call out to Ry with my mind.

You two can come back now. Thank you. I slide off Orym's lap but don't move away from him. If he wants space to figure things out, I'll give it, but he's going to have to use his words. Otherwise, I'll keep touching him.

Ry and Luca come back inside, taking the places they vacated before. Orym threads his fingers with mine and it seems as if he's trying to bait Ry into a disagreement. Or maybe he's testing the waters. I can't be sure yet.

I look at Ry over my shoulder, and he's smiling at me. *I'm being good, love. Besides, I'm the only one you've completed the bond with.* I guess that would give him a sense of satisfaction, no matter who I hold hands with or kiss.

"Orym was just about to tell us why he came this morning," I announce. Our attention shifts to him, and he looks uncomfortable.

"Vincent is missing. I've been tasked to form a team and find him. Honestly, I volunteered to form a team, as long as I could select whoever I wanted."

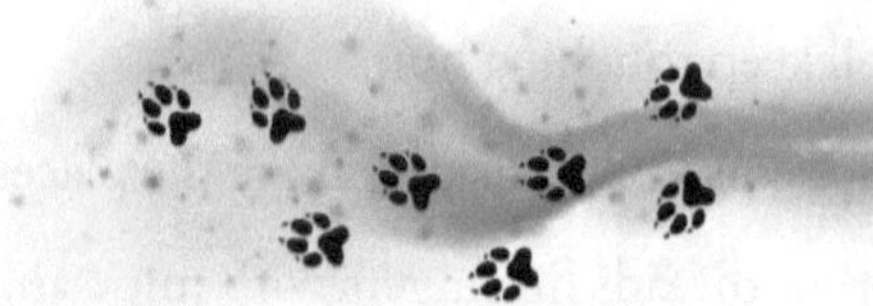

LUCA

"Does he know that you selected Red for your team? Because I'm sure you didn't come here for us," I say, gesturing to Ryland and myself.

"He said whoever I wanted. There were no restrictions. I just have to find Vincent. And I plan to do that—as long as you three help me," he responds. Orym sounds determined, and I have no doubt that he can find Vincent and bring him back. I also know that Gunnar will have a complete and total meltdown about it.

"Then we're gonna need backup. Let me go talk to Kayden and see what he can do to help. I know that will piss Gunnar off even more, since Kayden refused to help him. But they like us, and I think I can get us at least a little more help. If that's okay with you, Orym." I make the offer, knowing that Kayden isn't going to allow any of the vamps to help us. It's a long shot, but Red isn't the only one who has an idea of who her other mate could be. I think I can get him to come back with me, and I can test my theory.

"More help would be good, if you think Kayden will do it," he responds.

"Okay, I'll head that way as soon as Gunnar is busy. I don't need him coming at me over an unplanned trip to the city." Really, I don't want to have to explain why I missed the meeting and this morning's training. But after staying up half the night with Ryland and Garnet, I was too tired to manage that this morning.

I thought it would be awkward sleeping in Ryland's bed with them, but they both insisted. Since I'm her mate too, there was no way I could say no. I would prefer to have our mate bond completed, but I understand why Red isn't ready yet. I'm sure having extra voices in your head is a lot to manage, especially when you aren't ready to share everything yet.

I wonder if Ryland has figured out who she thinks the fourth mate is. I'm actually shocked that he accepted Orym so easily. They've always fought and competed over everything. And that's probably why the Goddess gave them both to Red. She will have them straightened out in no time.

I won't let either of them push her around. And I'll encourage her to embrace the last mate as much as she needs. I'll stand between her and her father if I have to. I know from our conversation last night that he isn't happy that Ryland claimed her without permission. I wonder how he'll react when he finds out about her other three mates. Because I won't be the one to tell him. Let him find out on his own.

We talk strategy for a while longer, then I get ready to leave. I have to go to my house before heading into the city.

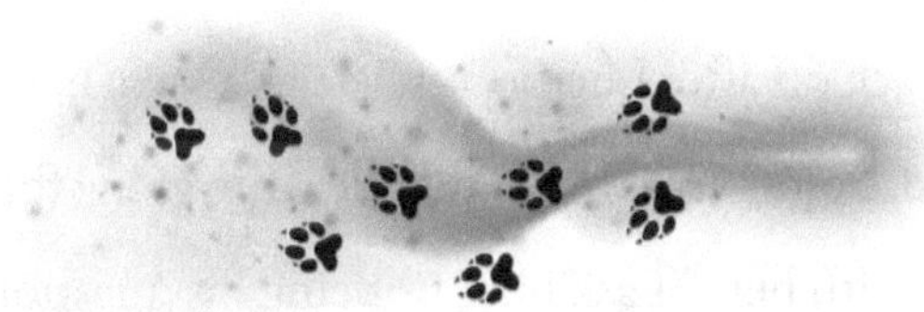

RYLAND

I don't want Luca to leave, because then I'll have to deal with Orym by myself, or leave him alone with Red. I'm pushing my desire to punch him down and playing nice because it's what Red needs. And I will take care of her, no matter how badly it pains me. I'm not even sure what it is about him that pisses me off. We've just always butted heads.

I know that I shouldn't be jealous, but part of me is. I don't want to share her, but I understand that if she has four fated mates, it's what the Goddess wants. There is always a purpose. We have to be willing to do what the Goddess desires. Even if we don't understand the why of it.

So, I back off after Luca leaves, letting Orym have some time with Red. I press a kiss to her temple. "I'm going for a run. Will you stay with her?" I ask him, noticing his questioning glance at the politeness in my tone. *I don't want to leave you alone after what happened in the forest yesterday.* I tell her.

"If you want, I'll hang out for a while," he says to her, not answering me directly.

Thank you. I would prefer not to be alone, either. Enjoy your run. I hope that she doesn't decide to complete the mate bond with him in my cabin, but I trust her judgement. She told Luca that she wasn't ready to have so many voices in her head, and he understood. I can't help feeling that if she's not ready for him, she won't be ready for anyone else.

I try not to be offended that Orym ignores me. I guess that's better than trying to fight me all the time. There has to be a way past our issues, but I don't know what it is.

Leaving them alone, I shift as soon as I'm outside. I race toward the spot in the forest where I found Red yesterday. I want to look around in the daylight and see if I can figure out what spooked her. When we talked about it after completing our bond, she said that she was drawn to that area. She had no idea where she was heading and didn't realize anything was wrong until silence fell. Then she felt as if she were being chased. I want to find what was chasing her.

I run until I reach the exact spot where she plowed into me. I can still smell hints of her fear lingering here. I slow my pace and sniff around, searching for something, anything, that will allow me to protect her better. I wonder if she'll tell Orym about what happened, or if she'll keep it between us. She didn't want to tell Luca yet, so it feels like something just for us.

If I need their help, I'll have to tell them, even if she's not ready. I hope it doesn't come to that.

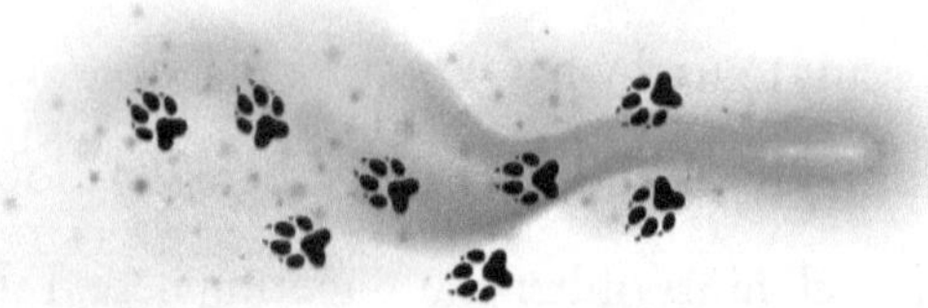

GARNET

As soon as Luca leaves, Ry decides he has to go too. It's not obvious at all that they think Orym needs some alone time to adjust to everything. I'm glad Ry asked him to stay with me, though. Being chased through the woods yesterday was not a feeling I want to repeat.

And if something is after me, it'll come for me when I'm alone. I wouldn't put it past Ry to make sure that I'm not alone at all until we figure all of this out. I don't really want to tell Luca or Orym about that yet. I don't even want to think about it.

"So, tell me more about this multiple mate bond thing," Orym interrupts my thoughts.

"What do you want to know?" I barely have more information than he does, but I don't say that. All I can do is try to be as honest about it as possible.

"How are you planning to make it work? If there are four of us, and one of you, that seems a little unbalanced, doesn't it?"

I stare at him, unsure how to answer his question.

"I'm sorry, I wasn't trying to make you uncomfortable. I just don't really understand it all, you know? Like, I'm dying to bond with you, but there are three other guys to consider. And I get the impression that even though you've bonded with Ryland, you're not ready for the rest of us." How did he know we'd bonded?

My expression must give away my thoughts because he takes my hand gently. "I'm not sure how I knew, but there's something between the two of you. It's almost like you're communicating without speaking."

"Oh, that. Yeah. That's actually why I'm not ready to bond with everyone yet. I didn't realize that the reading each other's thoughts thing that Delilah and Kayden can do is actually a thing. I want to bond with all of you, but I'm still learning how to block my thoughts and keep Ry's out of my head."

His eyes go wide. "Oh, wow. That would be a lot to deal with. I'm sorry I brought it up. I'm not trying to pressure you into anything. I just want to understand before I decide what I want to do." He pauses and stares into my eyes for a beat. "That's not true. I'm sorry, Red. I have to be honest here. I want you, no matter what. If you're not ready to bond, that's fine. I'll wait. And I'll figure out how to deal with Ryland, too."

"Really?" I was beginning to think he would turn away from us since the one person he can't stand is one of my mates.

"Really. I can't promise that we won't fight. We've been doing that since we were kids, so that will take some time to smooth out. But I promise I'll try."

I grab his shirt and pull him toward me, crashing our lips together in a desperate kiss. I know that I can't let things progress much further without risking him losing control and accidentally claiming me like Ry did. But I can allow myself to enjoy his mouth against mine.

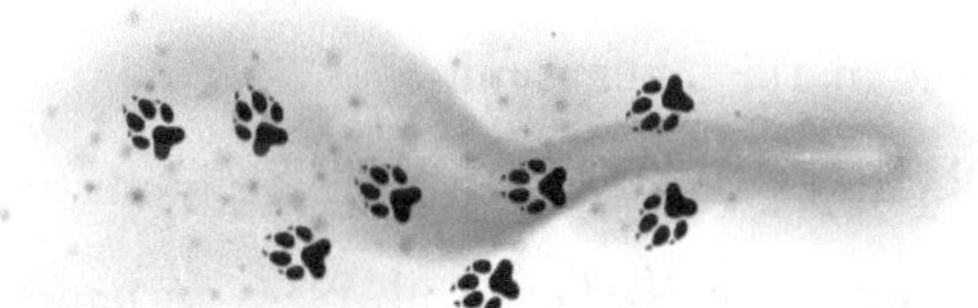

ORYM

Kissing Red is as natural as breathing. She tastes like what I would imagine sunshine tastes like, if it had a flavor. That is the single stupidest thought I've ever had, but it makes sense to me somehow.

I meant it when I told her I won't pressure her into anything, but I won't stop her from taking what she needs. Right now, that means kissing her and letting her touch me in any way she wants. I groan against her lips as her hands fist in my hair. I love the feeling of her against me, and I desperately want to get her out of Ryland's t-shirt. Which is exactly why I won't. I refuse to lose control. If I do, I'll end up taking her in another man's house, and marking her as mine.

I let Ryland's sage scent, that fills his home, deter me from acting on my impulses. I carefully place my hands on her hips, gently holding her in place when she tries to climb into my lap again. I don't know that I can hold out if I let her straddle me.

When she finally pulls her lips from mine, she trails kisses and bites down my jaw and neck. I barely stifle a moan at how good it feels. I can't let myself do the same to her, because I know that I won't be able to stop myself from biting her and making her mine.

She starts to unbutton my shirt and I grab her hands. "What are you doing?" The question comes out harsher than I intend and she flinches.

"I just wanted to touch you. I'm sorry," she whispers, pulling away. Fuck. I can't deny her, even if it's a risk. I slowly unbutton my shirt and open it for her.

"I'm fighting the urge to rip your clothes off and make you mine," I warn her. The expression on her face tells me that she already knew that, and has been enjoying my suffering. "I won't do it, though. You have my word. No matter what you do to me today, I will not fuck you, and I will not claim you. Not today." Our eyes meet. "Tomorrow may be a different story, though."

With my warning in place, she spreads a hand over my chest, pushing my shirt off my shoulder until I peel it off. Now that she has access to my chest and stomach, she pulls back and stares for a moment. Her appreciative hum is all I need to keep me still for her. Every cell in my body wants to drag her to me and impale her with my painfully hard cock. But I gave my word, and I refuse to lie to her.

FIVE
SEARCHING

JAMES

When Dec calls and asks me to do him a favor, I agree. When I get to his place and find out exactly what he wants me to do, I understand that he's the one doing me a favor. I shake hands with Luca and listen as he explains the situation.

"Wait, you think Garnet and I are fated mates? Isn't that a supernatural thing?" I stop him to ask.

"Usually, yes, but she has three others, so I'm thinking the Goddess has made an exception for her." I nod absentmindedly at his explanation. I wish my brother hadn't taken off the second I got here. I could use some advice.

"Three other mates? So, she's got her own little harem, just like Delilah." I laugh at the thought. Could I really be fated to be hers? I don't really believe in all that stuff. But if there's a chance that Garnet is interested in me, I'm all in.

"It looks that way. She hasn't told us that she suspects you are the fourth. But I know her better than she knows herself, and I'm sure of it. Will you help us find her brother?"

I can't say no to a chance of spending more time with her. She's all I've thought about since we were searching for my own brother. "I'll do it."

Luca drags me to him and hugs me. It should be awkward, but it's not. He follows me back to my place to grab supplies, then I ride to the wolf camp with him. "Is Gunnar okay with me being part of this? He doesn't seem to like humans much."

I can't stand the pompous alpha, and hope that I don't have to interact with him at all. But I won't let him stop me from seeing Garnet.

"We're going to avoid him, but he told Orym to assemble his own team. So, if he gets mad, it's his own fault for not expecting us to reach out. I'm sure he'll be pissed when he realizes that Red is going too." Luca laughs.

"You know she hates being called that, right?" I shouldn't interfere, but I've seen how she cringes at the nickname. It's the reason why Delilah and I call her Garnet.

"Does she? I've called her that for as long as I've known her." He shrugs. From his facial expression, he knows that she hates it, and he likes to annoy her with it. Great.

We pull up to a cabin, and I grab my bag when I step out. "Follow me. We're going to Ryland's. That's where Red is." Luca leads the way down a path.

"Who is Ryland again? And Orym?" I know he's mentioned both, but I'm sure we haven't met.

"They're Red's other mates. Don't worry, you'll love them. Maybe." He stops suddenly. "But they kind of hate each other, so watch out for that."

Awesome. I'm going to meet two guys who hate each other and are both Garnet's mates.

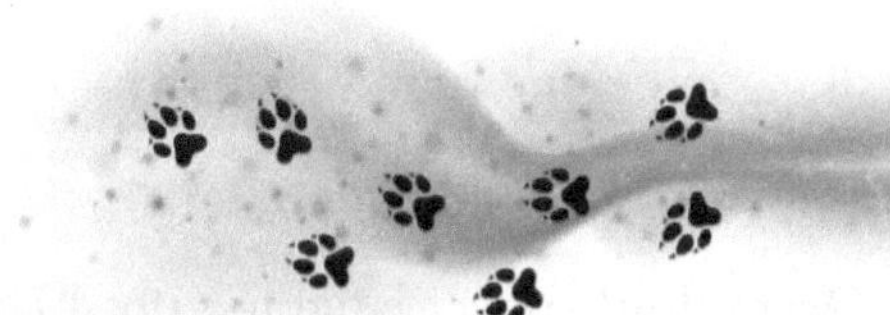

GARNET

Ry, you can't avoid coming home just because Orym is here. I'm trying to reason with my somewhat annoyed mate. He's been gone for hours. I'm starting to worry, because he's barely responding to me.

"Still not talking to you?" Orym asks.

I shake my head. "I know he's okay, but it's annoying. First he runs off like a child, now he's ignoring me like one too." I know that I shouldn't say anything bad about one mate to another, but I'm so frustrated that I could scream.

The door opens and I pounce, planning to yell at Ry for being a jerk. "Oh, I'm sorry," I say when I realize that I've just spider monkey jumped on James Roarke. Fuck my life. Then I see Luca walking in behind him. I glare at him as I untangle myself from a very embarrassed James.

Luca and Orym double over laughing until I give them a dirty look. I know they won't push me to bond, but I can scare them into being nice by making them think I'm never going to do it.

"James, please come in. I'm sorry. I thought you were Ry. He's been gone too long and I'm starting to worry." The flimsy excuse is met with an understanding nod.

"It's fine, Garnet. Luca brought me to help find your brother."

I see Luca and Orym exchange a glance, and realize that I've been figured out. I can't have one fucking secret, can I? "Thank you, Luca." I can't stop the hint of sarcasm in my voice, but judging from James' look, he knows why he's really here.

"I guess he told you then?" James nods, his cheeks turning pink. "Great. Well, let's get introductions out of the way then, shall we?"

I turn to Luca and wait. He catches on to what I want from him. "James Roarke, this is Orym Key. Orym, this is James. Perhaps I should go find Ryland and we can talk about finding Vincent." And just like that, the weasel runs away, leaving me to deal with this awkward situation.

Orym and James exchange pleasantries. "I'm happy to help in any way I can. My brother was taken a while ago, and it could be the same people. Garnet helped us find him, so I'll do whatever I can." Why does James have to be so damned sexy?

As he talks with Orym, I find myself staring at the two men, comparing them. James is blond with blue eyes, his hair cut short. Orym's hair is a bit longer, but not as long as Luca's. What the hell will I do with four men? Goddess help me, I want to find out.

We sit back on the couch, Orym on one side of me and James on the other. I don't know what to do with my hands, so I twist and untwist my fingers until Orym peels them apart and works his fingers through mine.

I give him a small smile, relieved to have something to do with my hands that isn't awkward. "I'm sorry. This is just a lot for me. I'm sure it's just as bad for you guys. I can't imagine how you feel about it all."

Orym looks from me to James. "You could just do the test and know for sure. I can go find Luca and help him look for Ryland. Then you'll have some privacy." He kisses my cheek and walks out the door. Fuck. James and I are alone now, sitting close on the couch, barely touching.

"What test?" he asks. "Like to see if we're mates? How do you even test for something like that?" His genuine curiosity makes my heart race.

"Well, since you're human, I'm not sure if it will work. But I knew with Luca and Orym from kissing them. It was like a mild connection that felt a bit like static between us." I pause and watch his face.

"Like with our first kiss?" Fuck, that's exactly what I was thinking of. It's almost like he can already read my mind. I'm in trouble here.

"Yes, exactly like that. That's why I'm pretty sure about this." There's nothing more to say. Now he knows that I didn't tell any of my other mates that I've already kissed him. I think that will be the end of that conversation, but James gently grabs my chin and tilts my head toward him.

His lips meet mine and I can feel the static racing through my body. He makes a noise, and I'm sure he feels it too. I run my hands over the back of his neck, and he fists his hands in my hair, pulling me onto his lap. I straddle him easily, not bothering to fight the draw between us.

I'm not as worried about James claiming me as the wolves. I'm not even sure he'll be able to unless one of them explains it to him. So, making out with him right now is pretty low stakes. His tongue tangles with mine and I sigh against him.

I know that I should pull away, but I don't want to. I want to strip him down and fuck him hard. Logically, I know that I shouldn't do that. Not here, and not right now. This is Ryland's home, and I have to respect that. Someone should tell my traitorous pussy that, because she's way too excited at James' hands roaming my body while his mouth tastes mine.

Just as I have the thought, he eases me away from him. "I know this isn't the time or place, but I want you, Garnet."

The way he says my name, all growly with need, shoots straight to my clit. I know my panties are soaked, and he knows it too. I haven't exactly gotten dressed today, so I've been hanging out in Ry's t-shirt and my panties. That does nothing to help my restraint.

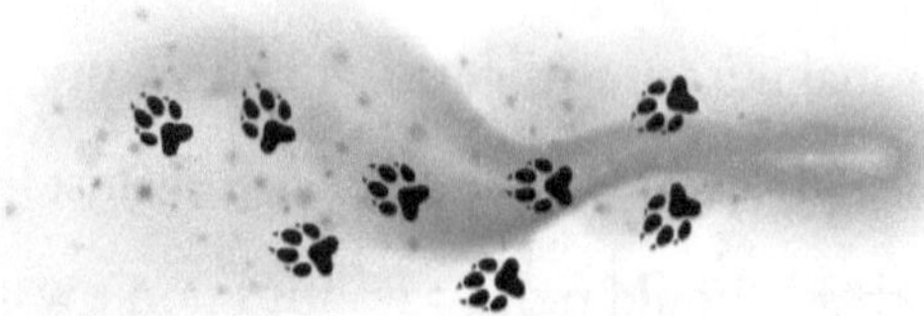

ORYM

I can tell there's some awkwardness between James and Red, and I don't think it's because he's human. It's probably better if I give them some time to talk without me in their way. After I excuse myself, I search for Luca's scent and chase him down.

"Any sight of Ryland?" I ask.

"Not yet. I can smell him though. I think he went deeper into the forest. I don't understand why, though."

"They're hiding something. There was a lot of internal conversation while you were gone. They used the mate bond to talk about something they didn't want to share with me." I shrug. "I'm not mad about it. I don't like him either. But it means I don't know where he went."

"You and Red didn't. Never mind, it's not my business." Luca turns away from me. I know what he's asking, and I understand his need to ask. She didn't want to mate bond with him yet either.

"We didn't. We did kiss for a bit. And we talked. Nothing more. She isn't ready to have all of us in her head yet. I understand that, and why you needed to know." I'm not ashamed to talk to him about this. I wouldn't tell Ryland anything, but that's just because he pisses me off.

"Thanks, man. When you find out that the girl you've been in love with your entire life is your fated mate, but has three other mates, it's not easy to deal with. Especially when she bonds with one and decides not to bond with you."

"Agreed. It doesn't help that Ryland was the first, either. That's enough to make anyone question her sanity. There has to be more to why she chose him first. I know we can't ask, but maybe after we're bonded with her, we'll find out." I know that the offer isn't ideal, but it's all I've got.

He nods. "Do you smell that?" We've been walking the entire time we talked, and I pick up the scent he's talking about.

"I do. He's up ahead." We shift and race down the path, finding Ryland sitting in the middle of the path, staring into space. "What the fuck?"

"Ryland? Are you okay? Hey, man. Red is getting worried," Luca tries to get his attention. Nothing seems to be working. He looks like he's in a trance.

"This is not ideal, and I know I'll pay for it later, but I have an idea." I draw my fist back and slam it into Ryland's face before Luca can stop me. Ryland's head jerks backward and he cries out from the pain of it.

"What the fuck was that for?" He glares at me. "Since when do you sneak up on a man and sucker punch him?"

"When it's the only way to get him out of whatever kind of trance he's in, I think it's acceptable," Luca offers. We each hold a hand out to help him to his feet. He accepts Luca's, swatting mine away.

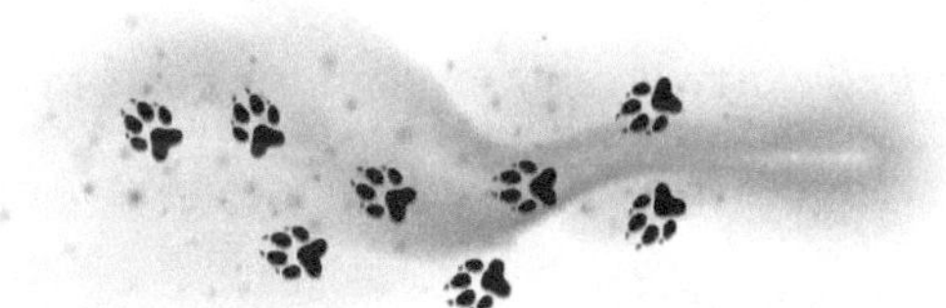

RYLAND

Damn, my face hurts. What the fuck happened? I was chasing that scent from the other day, looking for whatever had scared Red so badly. The next thing I know, there's a fist in my face.

"Where's Red?" I start to panic. I can't believe they would leave her alone. It's not safe. Of course, they don't know that because we didn't tell them the whole story of how we realized that we're fated mates. Fuck. Now I have no choice.

"Relax. She's fine. James is with her. He's the fourth mate," Luca says easily, and Orym nods.

"What? How did he find her so fast? And who the fuck is James?" I feel like I've missed something important.

"He's Declan Roarke's brother, and he's human. So, you don't have to worry about him claiming her. I'm pretty sure he doesn't even understand what it all means yet." Why is Orym trying to reassure me?

"This is too weird for me. James, a human, is her fourth mate. Fuck, this is complicated. Okay, we need to get back to the cabin. Something weird is going on here, and I'd rather let Red explain it all." I refuse to tell them anything else, turning and heading back home. With any luck, my girl won't be fucking another man when I get there.

"Ryland, we need to clear the air. If we're both Red's mates, we should at least try to get along," Orym insists. I want to punch him so bad, and I don't even know why. I agree with him.

"You're right, we should try. I don't know what else you want from me, though. You attacked me in my own house today, and I didn't even try to fight back. If that's not trying to get along, I don't know what is." I know I've made my point when he shrugs and backs off.

"Tell us what's going on then, Ryland," Luca orders. I shake my head.

"Red will have to explain. All I can tell you is that I knew we were fated before she did. I felt her fear and panic, and tracked her to that exact spot I was just in. Something was chasing her through the woods. I didn't see anything, but all the signs were there. Including her panic. There was no noise, not even her footsteps on the path. She was running, panting, crying, and nothing made noise until she ran into me." I shiver as I realize that's exactly what happened today when I went to check that spot out.

"Why didn't you tell me that last night? Or us this morning? One of us could have gone with you to check this out." Luca scolds me like I'm a disobedient child. I laugh at him.

"I wasn't about to leave her alone, no matter how safe I think she is at my cabin. Whatever is after her could just as easily get her there as out here."

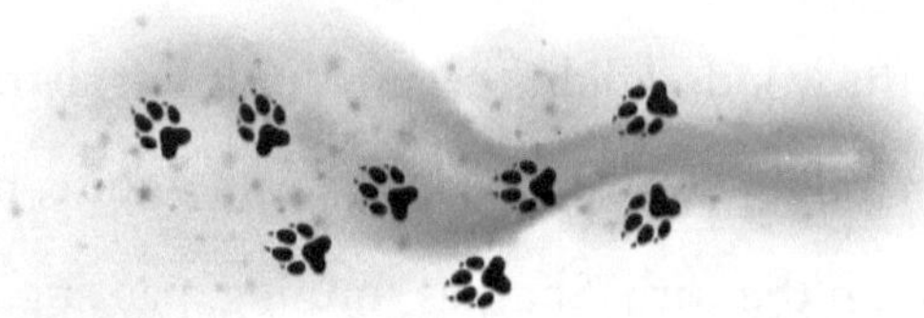

LUCA

I want to punch Ryland for keeping this from us. If I had suspected that Red was in danger, I would have called Dec and asked him to send James to us instead of driving all the way out there. I'm pissed. "If you had told me, I could have gone with you."

"But you had to go get mate number four. How did you figure that out anyway? I have access to her head and couldn't get to it." He sounds annoyed that I know her better than he does. I smirk.

"I know her. And I could feel the tension between them when I helped look for his brother. It was a safe bet that he was number four. Or one, depending on if she kissed him then." I can't help teasing Ryland, especially since he makes a face. I'm still annoyed at him for being the first to bond with her.

I had hoped that it would be me. But I couldn't make myself tell her how I felt. So, I have no one to blame but myself. "Wait, is that how you ended up bonding? Because you sensed her fear and saved her from whatever it was?" Orym's eyes are wide when he asks the questions.

Ryland nods reluctantly. "I didn't save her to force the issue. It just kind of happened. And I claimed her before I realized what I was doing. I had to convince her that we were fated. After she thought about it, and realized that we'd been feeling the same thing, she claimed me. Then she realized that she was having those feelings for you morons too."

Of course, he has to insult us while admitting that he fucked up. The only reason he completed the bond with Red was that he did it before she knew to expect it. If she'd been expecting it, she would have chosen me first. I know her, so I'm certain of it.

With that little secret packed away, we continue back to Ryland's cabin. "Should we knock?" I ask as we climb the few steps to the front door.

"It's my house. I'm not knocking on my own door," he growls, throwing the door open and storming inside.

"Ry! Where have you been?" Red jumps up and launches herself at him. To his credit, he catches her and presses a kiss to her lips without missing a beat.

"I'm sorry, love. I went to check the area where I found you yesterday, and something weird happened. I need you to tell the guys about it, so I can tell you what happened to me." He looks at her as if he's completely broken her trust and can't stand letting her down. Wow, I guess he does care for her.

She swats his shoulder and he sets her down. She drops back onto the couch, threading her fingers with James' before she turns to us. "Get comfortable. I'll tell you and then Ry can fill me in."

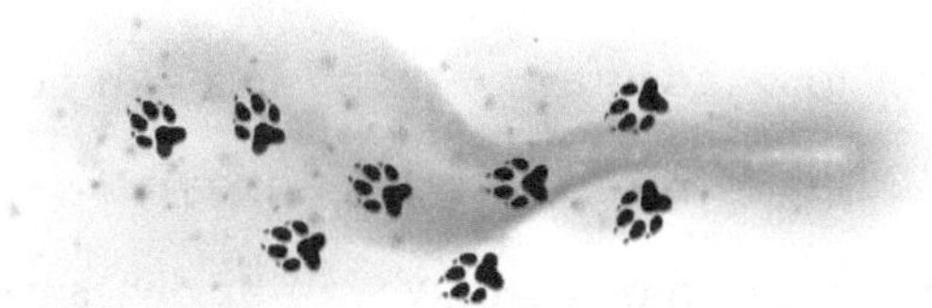

GARNET

I don't want to talk about what happened yesterday. I don't want to relive that feeling of losing control. But I don't have a choice since Ry told Luca and Orym. It's not fair to James to keep it from him. Ry sits on the couch next to me, then pulls me into his lap and scoots closer to James so I don't have to break contact. Luca sits on the floor at my feet, allowing Orym the spot next to me on the couch.

Before I can start my story, Ry introduces himself to James. "Sorry, love. Your story," he tells me, wrapping his arms around me. Luca rubs my calves, and Orym tentatively reaches for my other hand. I link our fingers as I start to tell them what happened.

"I went into the forest to train, since I'm not allowed to use the course anymore. After my workout, I went for a run. I completely zoned out, and when I finally came out of it, I had no idea where I was. It was too quiet, though. That was the strangest part. I didn't know which direction was home." I pause and lay my head on Ry's chest.

"Something was chasing me. It would have caught me, too, if Ry hadn't showed up when he did. I don't know what it was, but I could feel it reaching for me. It had to be some sort of magic, but I have no idea where it was coming from. By the time Ry found me, I was in a full panic. I couldn't talk, could barely breathe. He scooped me up and brought me back here. Then he took care of me until I was able to think straight again."

I leave out the part that Ry distracted me from my panic by fucking me with his tongue, and the details of him claiming me without permission. I wasn't really mad at him about that anyway. It was more frustrating to learn that my mates knew that we were fated, but I didn't. Since I'd gotten a similar story from Luca and Orym, I felt like the Goddess was fucking with me a little. Even James seemed to know.

It doesn't matter now. We need to focus on finding my brother. There's no way to know if the two things are related or not. "Now that everyone knows what happened, Ry, please tell me what happened to you when you went out there."

He starts to explain running toward the area, still able to connect with me. A pang of guilt rushes through me, even though I didn't do anything wrong. I had to kiss Orym to know if he was one of my mates. Did I have to make out with him too? Probably not, but that was fun.

Ry continues his story. "I got to the spot where I found you, and something happened. It was like I was there, but I wasn't. Something was trying to control me. I fought it off the best I could, but all I could do was sit down and force myself to stay there. I couldn't sense you anymore, and I was scared for a minute that something had happened to our bond, or you."

I press a kiss to his cheek. "Then these two found me and Orym punched me."

"What?" I look at Orym in shock.

Luca jumps to his defense. "He was just trying to get Ryland's attention. I had already yelled at him and gotten in his face. It was like he couldn't see us at all."

"I did what I had to in order to break whatever spell it was. And I would do it again, for any of you." Orym tries to make it sound like he didn't actually enjoy punching Ry, but I know better. They've always been rivals, and fighting is second nature to them. I hate it, but we'll work through it later. For now, we have to make sure none of us goes to that spot in the forest again. At least not until we have something to fight against that magic with.

"I understand that this is an issue, but shouldn't we be focusing on finding your brother?" James asks, pointing out that Vincent's disappearance should be higher on my priority list. "As long as we avoid that area, we should be good, right?"

I nod. "I agree. We should revisit this after we've found Vincent. With any luck, finding him will lead us to the people who took Dec, and we'll get justice for both of them."

"And find the other missing wolves. Hopefully everyone will be safe," Orym adds.

We shift gears and start to plan how to best search for my idiot brother and the other missing wolves. Apparently, Dec told James that there are some missing vampires too. So, we'll mount a search and rescue mission for all of them.

After a while, Ry slides me off his lap and into Orym's. "I'll get dinner going. You can move this to the kitchen table if you want. Then I'll still hear what you're saying."

James and Luca stand up and head into the kitchen with Ry. Orym wraps his arms around me and holds me for a minute. "I'm wearing him down," he whispers in my ear. I can't help but laugh.

"You two have to learn to get along," I insist. He presses a kiss to my cheek.

"We're working on it, Red. I promise."

"I'll hold you to that." I start to stand up, but he scoops me into his arms as he stands up. Then he kisses me hard and deep before walking into the kitchen and dropping me onto Luca's lap. I'm not sure how I feel about being passed around like this, but I could get used to the attention.

How am I already so attached to these men? It's crazy, but I am.

SIX

JUGGLING

RYLAND

I KNOW WE HAVE to focus on finding Vincent and the other missing wolves. And I guess vampires now too. But I really just want to spend some time enjoying my mate. I'm even warming up to the idea of sharing. I make dinner for everyone, realizing that Red probably didn't eat all day because of the excitement. I have to do a better job taking care of her.

We continue planning our search, deciding that the five of us staying together is the best option. I don't have to love the idea, but I do have to keep Red safe and happy. Keeping her happy involves taking care of these assholes, so that's what I'll do. The intensity of our emotional connection is almost too much at times.

I can feel her desire for the others, and for me. I wonder if that connection will be more or less overwhelming when she finally claims the others. Only time will tell. With everything planned and dinner eaten, we have to deal with where everyone will be sleeping tonight. Of course, Orym and James offer to sleep in the living room, but Red gives me a look, and I can't let that happen.

"Luca, what if you and Orym go get your bed, and we connect it to mine? That would make it big enough for all of us, wouldn't it?" I can't believe I'm finding a way to let more men in my bed with my mate. The smile on Red's face is worth it, though. Anything to make her happy. That is a very dangerous slope to be on.

"Yeah, that would double the size of it." He turns to Orym. "You wanna help me get it?" And back to me. "Can I borrow your truck?"

I nod and toss him the keys. I have to get used to sharing, might as well include my truck in it. None of it matters. As soon as Red claims them all, we'll be a pack, a family. I remind myself of this a few times, when I realize that James didn't pack any clothes. Mine will be big on him, but I'll still make the offer.

"I can find you something to wear if you want."

James smiles at me and shakes his head. "Not needed. Luca and I are close enough to the same size. He's already offered. But thanks, man."

Good. That's one less thing I have to deal with. Red hasn't even started to unpack her stuff yet, and I'm already moving three more people into my small cabin. Ridiculous but worth it.

Thank you, Ry. I really appreciate how cooperative you're being. Red speaks the words in my head.

Does that mean I get a reward? I know that nothing is going to happen with the other three here, unless I want to risk one of them claiming her too. I just can't resist flirting with her. I drag her out of her seat and press my lips to hers.

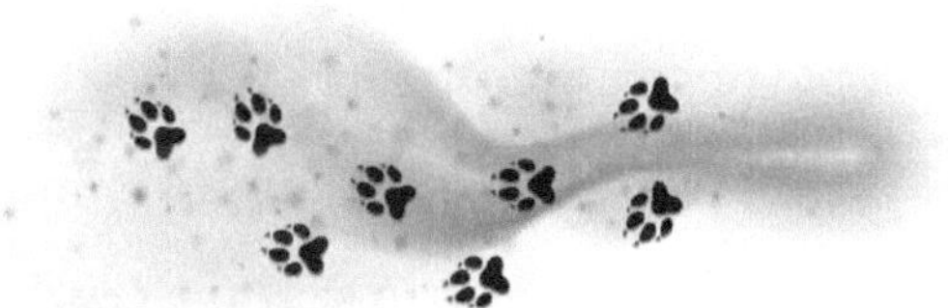

JAMES

I can't help feeling like a third wheel after Luca and Orym leave. I should have offered to go with them. When Ryland kisses Garnet, I step outside. I don't want to be a creep and stare at them, and I'm not sure what the protocol is for this. I've never been involved in this type of relationship. Will she expect all of us to be involved with each other? That is an interesting thought. I'm not opposed to it, but I can't say I'm excited about it either.

Even with the awkwardness, this feels like home. I don't know why, other than Garnet. Maybe there is something to this fated mates business after all. I mean, I didn't believe in vampires until my big brother became one. Speaking of Dec, I should call and update him on this.

"James? Is everything okay?" he answers immediately.

"Yeah, bro. We're prepping to start the search. There have been some developments, though, and I wanted to get your input," I start. How am I going to explain this?

"What's up? Do you need more backup?" Of course, my brother would think I was calling for more help.

"Nah, I think we've got that part covered. This is personal. Do you have a minute to talk?"

"Oh, okay. Give me a sec," he says, then I hear murmured conversation and a door click shut. "Garnet giving you trouble, little bro?"

I've missed him teasing me. Since I joined the council, I haven't had much time for anything. "Not really. But it is about her. How do you manage to share Delilah? Apparently,

I'm one of Garnet's four fated mates, and I'm struggling a little." There, I admitted it.

"That's easy. You take it one day at a time. But first, you should ask yourself if she's worth it. When the answer to that is yes, the rest falls into place. I can't tell you what to do, but I can tell you about my experience." I realize that this is exactly why I called him.

"Please," I ask, and he continues.

"When I met Delilah, she almost died. She didn't have her memories, and I'm the one who turned her to save her. Then Vik and Eli found us. It wasn't pretty. But she insisted that she loves us all the same. There was no way I could back down from that. I would have fought them for her—not to take her away from them, but to allow me time with her too. You have to be willing to do that. And to give her time with the others when you can tell that's what she needs."

"It's not all going to be that easy, though, is it?"

"Not even a little bit, bro. They'll probably test you. I'm guessing that the other three are wolves?"

"Yeah."

"Don't submit. Stand up for yourself, but don't let it come to a fight. You're good, but not that good."

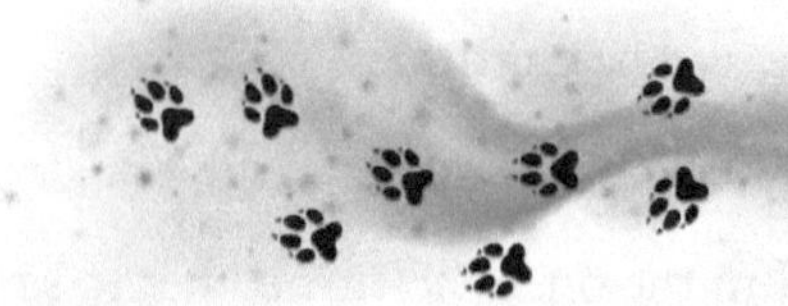

GARNET

I get lost in kissing Ry and don't realize that James is gone for a minute. "Where did he go?" I ask, pushing Ry away.

"I don't know, love, I was kissing you. I'm sure he's outside. He wouldn't go far." I appreciate that Ry has so much confidence in James, but if my father finds out he's here without permission, things may get ugly.

"I'll clean up after I get him back inside. We don't need Gunnar figuring out what Orym did. We have to stay under his radar until after we find Vincent," I insist heading for the door. As soon as I open it, I realize that James didn't go far. He's on the phone, which could be the reason he left. That would be better than him being uncomfortable with me showing someone else affection.

I pause for a minute, then decide that I'm my own woman, and I'll do what I want. I quietly walk over and wrap my arms around him from behind, laying my head on his shoulder. He tenses for a second, then relaxes against me.

"I get that, Dec. And yeah, she's definitely worth it. Speaking of, she just found me. I'll talk to you later." He listens for a minute. "Absolutely. Love you, too, big bro." When he hangs up the phone, he turns in my arms and holds me.

"You disappeared," I say quietly.

"Just needed to check in with Dec," he replies. I know it's not the whole truth, but I let it go. Or I nearly do.

"It's not an easy situation," I admit.

"True, but can you name one thing worth having that is?" I press a kiss to his lips. The more time I spend around all of them, the further I fall.

"How is Dec doing? I haven't really talked to any of them since we got him back. My father isn't exactly their biggest fan, you know."

"He's recovering. It's more the mental effects than physical. Those were fixed with a couple of bags of blood. But he's still hesitant to trust. Which is what surprised me about him helping Luca get me here. He made it sound like they needed me to help with the search. I took that to mean my brother wanted answers and didn't trust anyone else to get them. Turns out that was not the case."

"Oh, are you disappointed about that?" I can't help asking, and hoping that isn't true.

"Not even a little," he says as he brushes his lips against mine. Good. That's a relief. I hate thinking that any of them don't want to be here. "I'm looking forward to getting to know you better before you decide to mark me as yours."

"What?" My eyes go wide. How does he know about that?

"You know that I actually know Kayden, right? And that we talk? We've discussed fated mates and how that works before.

I can't imagine wanting to bite you like that, though, so you're safe. For now anyway."

I know my face is completely red, probably more than my hair. I assumed that since James is human, he wouldn't know anything about fated mates or claiming. It's a little disconcerting to find out that I was wrong.

"I'm sorry. I shouldn't have assumed." I'm tripping all over this apology.

James smiles at me. "It's fine. If our roles were reversed, I'd probably do the same. I know more than most humans, but I don't know everything. I'm happy to learn whatever I need to, though. Especially if it means more time with you."

Why are these men so sweet? I'm going to get cavities from all of this before it's over. Every time one of them says something like this, I want to claim them and put my mark on them. Maybe I should just stop resisting that urge.

No, Garnet, stick to the plan. Find Vincent, then claim the rest of your mates. I have to remind myself that there are bigger issues going on right now.

Love, you're projecting. Not that I mind, but I'd rather not have your desire for other men getting me all hot and bothered. Fuck, I have to learn how to shut this off.

Sorry, I'm working on it. I lay my head on James' chest and sigh.

"You guys were doing that telepathy thing again, weren't you?"

I nod. "I'm sorry. I keep screwing everything up today. I can't keep my emotions from attacking Ry, and I'm making everything awkward for you. I'm sure Orym and Luca feel the same way."

I drop my arms and turn away from him. I need some space from everyone for a moment. It's all just too much. I walk around the side of the cabin, then hear footsteps. Without looking, I know that James is following me. I glance over my shoulder at him.

"Not trying to stalk you, just not willing to let you out of my sight. I'll give you some space, but I need to see you. It's not safe out here alone, remember?" I nod at his insistence. I understand why none of them want me to be alone, it just makes processing my emotions harder.

I agree that it's not safe, though. That's why I came outside to find James in the first place. "Thank you." I sit on the ground and stare up at the moon. Praying may not help, but it can't hurt.

I settle in and talk to her. *Goddess help me. I don't know what I'm supposed to do here. I have to find Vincent, and I have to figure out why you've given me four mates. I feel like we have a bigger purpose, but I have no idea what that is.* I don't expect her to answer, but putting my thoughts out there helps me to process.

I know that James is watching me, and that doesn't bother me in the least.

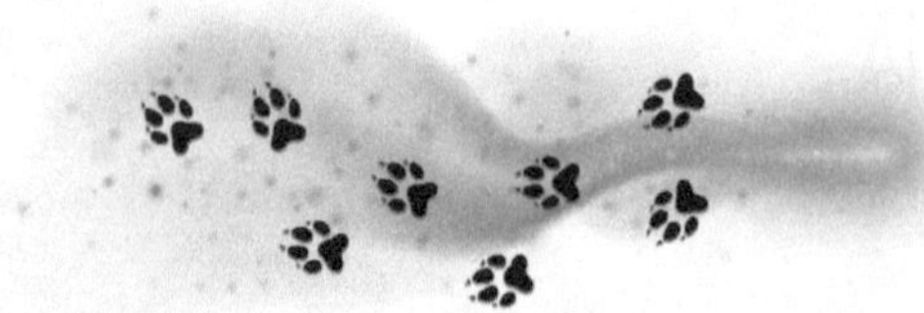

ORYM

Luca and I load up his mattress and bedframe, then drag it over to Ryland's house. With James and Ryland helping, it doesn't take long at all. I'm not sure how I feel about sharing a bed with my least favorite person, but the idea seems to make Red happy, so I'll suck it up and do what I have to.

"We'll head out first thing in the morning. I think it's smart to avoid the area where we found Ryland today, since it had a similar effect on Red when she was there. If we search everywhere else and come up empty handed, we'll figure out a way to search that area last.

I may still be a little hesitant about this situation, but I can't argue the connection we each have with Red. I really should try to call her Garnet. She beams at James when he says her name. That tells me that maybe she's not as fond of her nickname as I originally thought.

We have to get up early, but none of us is ready to sleep. Ryland puts on a movie and we settle on the couch with our girl. Luca sits on the floor in front of Garnet, while James and I sit on either side. As expected, Ryland gets upset that we've all settled in without leaving him a spot. He is such a baby. I start to offer my seat, but Garnet shakes her head. "You can't always sit next to me. You have to share."

I smirk at her response, and his reaction. He flops onto the floor next to Luca, determined to be close to her anyway. With the movie going, everyone starts to relax a little. We know what we have to do in the morning, and we're all prepared to do it.

As much as I want to whisk Garnet away and claim her as mine, I know that this time together is what she needs right now. I can push my desires away as long as she gets what she needs. There will be plenty of time for us to cement our bond once we find Vincent and figure out what's happening to the wolves.

When I start to doze off, I notice that Garnet's head is on James' shoulder. She's struggling to sleep as well. His eyes meet mine and I nod. Then I nudge Luca with my foot and gesture. He taps Ryland and within a moment, we've scooped her up and everyone is in the big bed. I don't expect sleep to take me, so I face the door with everyone in front of me, letting James and Ryland sleep next to Garnet.

I get the impression that Luca doesn't mind sharing because he knows where he stands with her. Ryland is a lot more possessive, and James seems to be just trying to figure us all out. I'll make sure I get my time with her when this is all over.

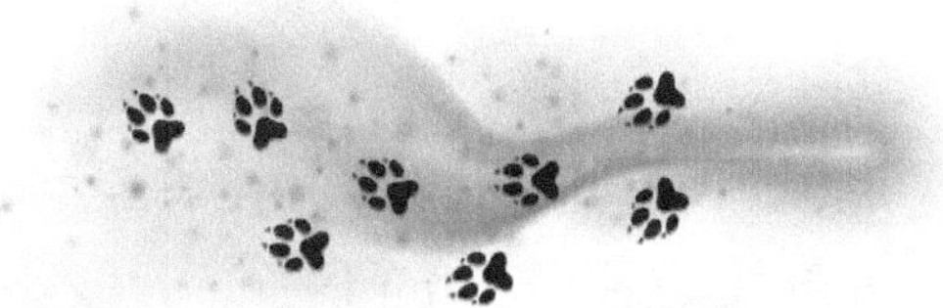

LUCA

Red sleeps through being carried to bed, and the chaos that ensues in deciding who will sleep next to her. Orym and I back off, letting James have one side and Ryland the other. It annoys me that Ryland thinks he has more right to be near her because he's already bonded with her, but I won't fight him on it. Red deserves better.

Now that I'm a hundred percent certain she's mine, I can wait. I hate it, because Ryland seems to be holding it over our heads that he was first. I watch her sleep, noticing that it takes Orym a while to settle in and rest. The difference is that while he's worried about outside threats, I'm worried about something else.

I know Red is still having nightmares. Grammy has had me come to the house and paint her room six times since we found Dec. Each time, we carefully document the symbols she's drawn, then I cover them up. At first, Red would ask about it later. I hate lying to her, but Grammy insists it's for her own good.

So, instead of talking to her about what she remembers, I have to lie and tell her that she must have dreamed it. I have copies of all the pictures. Grammy doesn't know, because I have them hidden and only pull them out when I know I'm alone. I've been trying to decipher what they mean, but I'm not getting anywhere with it.

I pretend to sleep until Orym's breathing starts to slow. It was easier to keep an eye out for the nightmares last night when it was just Ryland and me. Maybe I'm overthinking it. She didn't have one last night, but for some reason, I feel like she will tonight. Overstimulation, maybe? Finding out that you have four fated mates and trying to juggle their attention can be a lot.

I keep an eye on her, noticing the second the nightmare starts. I wonder if Ryland can sense it with his connection to her. He's sleeping like the dead, though, so I'm guessing not. She shifts in her sleep, a small cry letting me know that I'm right. If she draws on Ryland's walls, I'm not going to be able to cover it up. Then she'll know what I've been hiding from her.

Will it ruin everything? I don't know. I hope not, but there's no guarantee. I guess that will all depend on what she does next. The moment she climbs out of bed, Orym stirs. I shake my head at him, encouraging him to let her be. He looks at me, puzzled. When she doesn't move for the door, he relaxes a little. We lay there, watching her as she searches for a marker. I'm sure she has one in one of her bags that she didn't unpack today.

"Is she okay?" he whispers at me.

"It's like sleepwalking. I don't do anything to wake her, because I don't know what it will do."

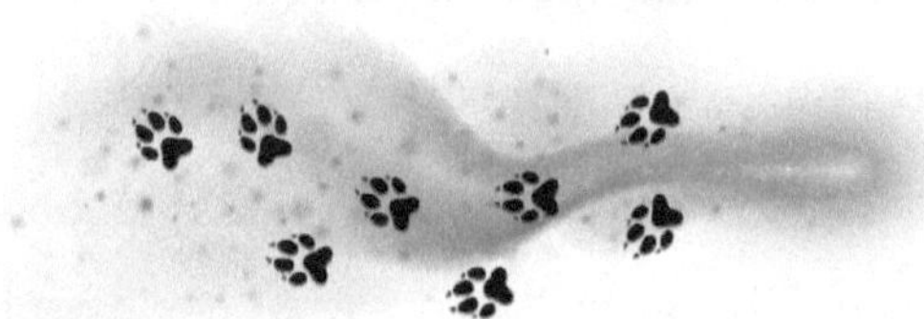

GARNET

I'm in the clearing again, watching the circle of six. They chant and dance around the circle, just like always. I know the words and find myself muttering them as I look for something. What am I looking for? I guess I'll know it when I find it.

The moment the six hooded figures in the circle start to make the symbols, my hand lifts on its own and copies them. I know that I've done this before. I should realize what's happening, but I don't. I should know this is a dream, but part of me believes it's really happening.

I draw the final symbol, and six pair of eyes turn in my direction. Each set is a different color. Red, Orange, Yellow, Green, Blue, and Purple. What does it mean? I know the colors have significant meaning, as do the symbols I've been drawing. But I can't connect the dots.

Their eyes bore into my soul and I scream at the pain it causes. When my eyes finally open, I'm standing in Ryland's bedroom with a permanent marker in my hand. Luca is wrapped around me, smoothing his hand down my back. "It's okay, Red. It's just a dream. You're safe. I've got you."

I drop the marker and kiss him fiercely. I feel as if Luca is the only thing grounding me to this moment in time. I hold onto him as tightly as I can. I jump when a second set of arms winds around me.

Orym coaxes me into his arms and kisses me gently. It's as if they know I was somewhere else and they want to pull me back to them. When he's done, I look at the bed, where James and Ryland are staring at us.

"I'm sorry," I say, knowing it's a lame apology. I turn back to the symbols I've drawn all over Ryland's wall. I expect him to get angry, but he looks more concerned.

"Are you okay?" he asks. "What did you write on the wall?"

"I don't know," I admit. "It's this recurring dream I have. I see a circle of six hooded figures in a clearing. They chant something, then draw these images. Every time I wake up, I've drawn them too. This time I didn't wake up until the symbols were all finished. The six of them stared at me, through me, and it hurt."

I shudder and Luca pulls me back into his arms. I can't admit that I know he's been covering up the symbols, because I know Grammy is the one who made him do it. But I can tell from his face that he's figured out that I know.

"When did this start?" James leans forward.

"The night we found Dec," I admit, holding onto Luca to steady myself. Orym presses up against my back and I'm thankful for the added support. I don't feel like my legs will hold out much longer.

"Can you describe the location?" James pushes for more information. This is probably a good thing. I finally have the chance to talk it out, and it's with my mates.

I give them as much detail as I can, telling them where the clearing is in the forest. I explain where every tree is, where the fire is located, and where each of the six figures stand, explaining about their eyes turning rainbow colors.

"I know that each part of the dream means something. And it's happened enough that I know it's a dream while I'm in it. I just can't alter anything that happens. This was the first time their eyes changed color. I don't understand the significance of the rainbow. It's a little hard to figure out the symbols, too, when they disappear every time I draw them."

Luca looks guilty and I'm certain the others know exactly why. I hold up a hand before they can say anything. "I know why it happened, and I'm not upset about it. I'm just explaining my point of view."

"I know. And I'm sorry. I have copies of all the pictures Grammy had me take before I covered the symbols up. I can get them for you in the morning if you want. I haven't had any luck deciphering them either," Luca admits.

"That would be great. We can take them with us and see what we can figure out when we camp at night. We have to keep to our plans. Finding Vincent has to be our priority. Once that's done, we can focus on whatever this is." I don't mean to sound as if I don't want their input, but I've already decided.

"What if it's all connected?" James stares at me. I don't know how to respond, so I shrug. Then he continues. "I'm just saying, what if the wolf disappearances, Dec's kidnapping, and your dreams—what if it's all connected? What if we have to figure out each part in order to get to the bottom of it?"

"That's not a bad theory," Orym says.

I notice that Ryland isn't saying anything now. Not since he asked me what I wrote on his wall. "Ry? Are you okay?" I take a careful step toward him and he flinches away from me slightly. I feel the sting of that movement like a slap in the face.

I pull my hand back as tears fill my eyes. Orym and Luca growl at Ry because they know he just hurt my feelings. "It's okay. I just defaced his wall. He doesn't have to talk to me if he doesn't want to."

James climbs out of the bed, scoops me up and carries me to the living room. I guess we're giving Luca and Orym a minute with Ryland. I can hear them yelling but can't make out what they're saying. It seems as though at least one of my mates is scared of me, though.

"Hey, Garnet," James turns me to look at him. "It's okay. We'll take care of you."

SEVEN
ALIENATION

RYLAND

AFTER BEING SCREAMED AT by Luca and Orym, I understand that my reaction upset Red. I'm not mad that she wrote

on the wall, I'm confused. I don't understand why she did it. And if this is something she knew could happen, why wouldn't she tell me about it?

"You should have told me this was an issue," I growl at Luca. He knew the whole time that she could do this, and didn't bother to warn me. I don't care about the wall, really. The fact that all of this was kept secret feels like a betrayal, and I don't like that.

"What exactly would you have done? Made sure there were no permanent markers or other writing utensils in the house?" His response pisses me off even more.

I can feel her fear and pain through the bond, and I know that I've fucked up. "Did you know about this too?" I turn on Orym, itching to punch him.

"No, I didn't. And Luca is right. It wasn't our business until Garnet decided to tell us about it. Now it is, because it happened right in front of us."

"So, what exactly do you want me to do about this?" I snarl. I know what I should do, but I'm not finished being angry yet.

"Apologize," Luca says.

"Make it up to her," Orym says at the same time.

I push my way out of the room and head out the front door. I'm not going to have them order me around in my own home.

I have to cool off before I can talk to her, otherwise, I'll just make this worse. I know that I shouldn't just leave, but I can't help myself. I want to scream at all of them for invading my space and making me share my mate.

And she is *my* mate. We've fully bonded. That should mean something. But it doesn't seem to. I'm trying to be understanding and supportive, but there is only so much a man can take. I shift into my wolf form and race away from my cabin. Maybe a swim at the falls will clear my head.

I can still feel her inside my head. I usually like the feeling, but right now, I need to be alone. I know that all of this is my fault. I was the one who pushed the bond on her. And now I'm the one who's suffering and being left without a choice.

It's ridiculous and I know I'm being immature, but I don't care right now. I can hear her calling out to me through the bond, and I ignore her. She's not happy about it, but I'm not happy that she's keeping secrets from me. Our bond is supposed to mean something, but it doesn't feel like she cares as much as I do. Since a bond is impossible to undo, I have to figure this out.

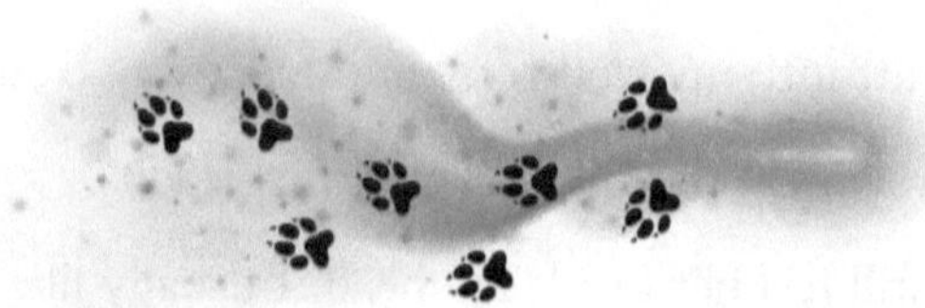

GARNET

I understand that Ry is upset, and that I should have told him about the dreams. But we've literally been bonded for a day. How can he be this pissed that I wrote on his wall? James tries to comfort me, and just when I'm starting to listen to him, Ry tears through the living room and runs out the door.

I try calling out to him over the bond, and I think he hears me, but he doesn't respond. I can feel his anger and irritation. *Ry, please come back. We should talk about this.* Nothing. *At least tell me where you're going.* No response.

"How can he ignore me like this?" I ask James, tears falling again. He pulls me into his arms, pressing a kiss to the top of my head.

"Garnet, I don't know. I can't pretend to understand the connection you have. And I'm sure it hurts that he's not talking to you right now. But maybe he needs a few minutes to calm down before he says something he'll regret." His argument is logical, and I hate it.

I know that he's probably right, but that doesn't make it hurt less right now. "James is right. You should try to get some more sleep. I'll go after him and make sure he's okay." Luca rubs a hand down my back and kisses my cheek.

Orym steps in front of him. "I'll go. You're the only one who really understands what's going on with Garnet right now. She'll probably sleep better knowing you're here. I can keep an eye on Ryland, and make sure he comes back in one piece."

His thoughtfulness touches me and I untangle myself from James to walk over to him. "You would do that for me?"

"If it helps you rest, absolutely, beautiful. I would do anything for you," he says. I wrap my arms around him and kiss him hard. He groans and relaxes against me. Then he realizes what he's doing and eases away from me. "I can't help if I don't go after him. We'll stay safe."

I watch at the door as he leaves, scenting the air to find Ry's trail and follow it. "I should be the one chasing him down. I should go after him and make him talk to me," I pout.

James pulls me back inside. "What good would that do?"

"It would teach him that he can't ignore me," I answer.

"No, it would annoy him and he'd blow up at you. The only thing that would accomplish is you getting your feelings hurt. None of us want that. Not even him. That's why he left. I'm sure he's going to cool off and come back. Then you can talk it out. Okay?" Luca's question sounds more like an order, so I glare at him. My gaze softens when he starts to laugh at me.

"Fine, I guess we should go back to bed, then."

I know I'm not going to be able to sleep knowing that Ry is out there, and now Orym too. Maybe I shouldn't be so scared to complete the bond with everyone, just so I can keep track of them. Then again, I see how well that's working with Ry. He has to get his jealousy under control or this will never work.

I have to make him understand that he doesn't own me just because we've completed the bond.

My body is dying to mate with each of them, but my brain is terrified. I can't take a chance that Luca or Orym will do what Ry did and bite me before I'm ready. It's why I've been resisting doing anything more than kissing any of them again since I found out I have four fated mates. Add to that Ry's possessive streak that wasn't an issue before, and I just can't do it yet.

Luca and James walk into the bedroom with me. Luca straightens the blankets and tucks me in like I'm a child. James snuggles in next to me. I wait for Luca to do the same, but he turns and looks at the wall again. "Something is different about this. I need to get the other pictures to compare." He turns to us. "Will you be okay to protect her while I run to my cabin? This is going to drive me crazy if I don't compare the pictures with these symbols."

"Yeah, man, whatever you need. Just be careful," James responds. I don't like the idea of Luca going out there alone, but I trust him to come straight back. And his cabin isn't that far away.

"Hurry back. I'll worry while you're gone," I tell him. He presses a kiss to my forehead, then takes off.

James looks at me for a minute. "Are you okay? Can I do anything to help you relax?" His offer is sweet and sincere, with no sexual inuendo. But damn do I wish there had been. He's definitely the safest bet, since I'm not sure how our bond will work. He's not a wolf, so he wouldn't bite me.

"I can think of something that might help," I tease, licking my lips. "If you meant it when you said anything."

Desire fills his eyes and I'm sure he's thinking exactly what I am. "I don't want to push you into anything or take advantage." This man. How is he so sweet?

I rub my hand up his chest, hooking it behind his neck. Then I pull him close for a teasing kiss. I can't figure out his slight cinnamon scent, but it's delicious, just like him. I trail kisses along his jawline and back to his mouth. I know that teasing him isn't fair, and it's just as torturous to me, but I can't resist.

"James?" I whisper his name, my voice all breathy with need.

"Yes?" The single word comes out strained. I think my teasing is working. I run my hand down his chest, stopping at the waistband of the sweats Luca gave him to sleep in. He draws in a ragged breath. "Garnet, we don't have to do this."

"What if I want to?" Apparently, that's all the encouragement he needs to flip me onto my back and kiss me. It's not a sweet kiss, it's one of possession, of claiming. I hum against his mouth, wanting more. I tease the waistband of his pants again, but he pulls away, grabbing my hands.

"Not yet. I want to taste you first." His voice is raspy with need, and I feel both powerful and desired. I can feel my pussy drip with his words. I want his mouth on me, and I don't want to wait any longer.

"Yes, please, James," I beg. I don't even care that I'm begging him. I need this. We need this. He pulls my panties off as I drag my shirt off. When I'm naked in front of him, he drinks me in with his eyes.

"You are perfection," he says, sliding his hands up my legs, stopping on my thighs. He stretches them apart, baring me open for him. He dips his head between my legs, his nose almost close enough to touch as he teases me with his breath. "You smell delicious."

I shiver at his words, and he runs the flat of his tongue along my slit. I was already soaked, and that just makes it worse. He hums as he tastes me, lapping at my entrance but not touching my clit. I dig my hands into his hair, trying to move him where I want. "James, please."

He chuckles against my pussy, refusing to go near my clit. What the fuck? "Not yet, beautiful." I growl at him, but instead of responding, he slides two fingers inside of me while his tongue makes lazy passes around my clit without touching it. He knows exactly what he's doing to me, and it's all intentional.

When I realize I can't move him or coax him where I want, I lay back and surrender to the sensations that he's causing. As soon as I stop trying, he latches onto my clit and sucks, making my back bow and come off the bed. He backs away, fingers still stroking in and out of me. James thrusts them inside of me again, then pulls them out and rubs them around my clit before sliding them back down and thrusting them inside of me again. It's enough to set me off, and I come hard.

"That's one," he says with a smirk. Is he planning to count orgasms? That's ridiculous, right? But the way he dives back into my pussy with his face tells me that's exactly what he's planning to do.

His amazing tongue joins the mix of what his fingers are doing, and it's almost too much for me. I cry out with another orgasm quickly. "Two," he mutters into my folds.

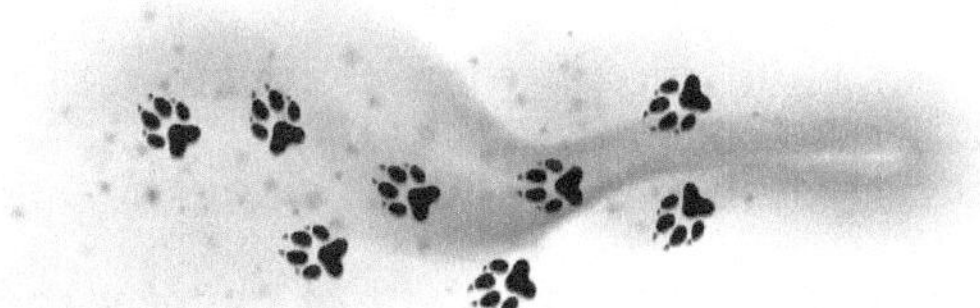

LUCA

I couldn't tell Red that I needed to talk to Grammy. I don't want to, but Red's description of this dream is worse than the last one. And without the memory potion, Red's not going to forget that dream. Grammy needs to know. I just hope Red will forgive me.

I walk up to the door and knock. If Gunnar answers, I'll have to make up an excuse for being here. Because I've been sworn to secrecy. No one else knew about this until tonight, when Red told her mates. Fuck, should I tell Grammy about that too?

The door creaks open and Grammy stands before me. "Can we talk?"

"Come in, child. Don't worry, Gunnar isn't here. He's out yelling at the younger wolves and making them do the chores he'd piled on Red." She steps out of the way and I enter the cabin.

She gestures for me to sit, so I do. When she drops into the chair next to mine, I take a deep breath. "It happened again, but this time, other people saw the symbols and she told them about everything. The dream has gotten more involved, and she's remembering it even after the tea. I got the impression that she's been playing along when we clean up and distract her."

"Well, that isn't good. But she is stubborn, and stronger than I anticipated. Well, if she's told her mates about it, there's nothing we can do now. As long as Gunnar doesn't find out, everything is manageable."

My jaw drops. "How did you know it was her mates? I didn't say who saw them."

"Who else would she trust enough to admit she'd been lying to you?" Yeah, I should have figured that she'd catch on to that.

"How did you know that Ryland wasn't her only mate?" I can't stop myself from asking.

"Each of us has abilities, child. Mine is to see the threads. They don't determine who we'll end up with, that's a matter of choice. But they do indicate where we'll be pulled. And she's been connected to you three since you were cubs. The human is a more recent development. Has she bonded with anyone else yet?"

"Not yet. We've agreed not to pressure her. So, when she decides that she's ready, we'll accept that. She's struggling with having Ryland in her head, and I'm afraid that four of us would overwhelm her."

"That's smart. I wonder if she realizes that her bond with the human will be different. I don't know how exactly, but it won't be a claiming bite that seals it."

Oh, shit. Maybe I shouldn't have left them alone together. I think Grammy recognizes the panic in my eyes. "Whatever happens will be what's meant to happen. You can't stop them. Even if it's unintentional."

"But she doesn't want to be bonded to anyone else right now. She'll be pissed if it happens accidentally. Especially if I know and don't stop it."

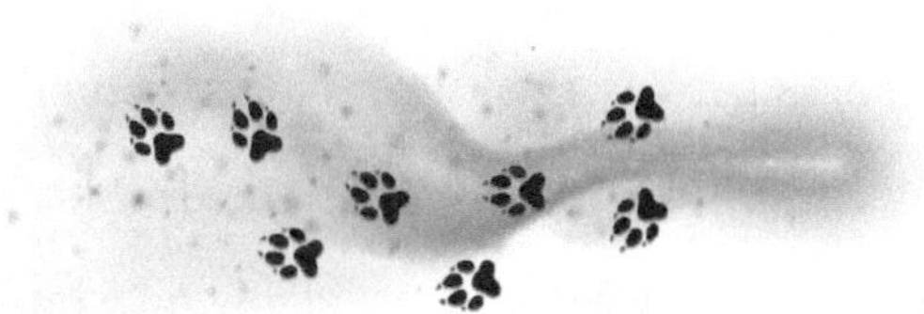

JAMES

After giving Garnet four intense orgasms, I wipe my face and kiss her deeply. I want to take things further, but I'm worried about pushing her too far. When I break the kiss, she reaches for my pants again. "Are you sure?" I ask, making her pause for a moment.

"I am. I want to be with you, James. This isn't something you're pushing me into."

If we're fated mates like she claims, I have to take her at her word. Even if I'm not sure I believe in fate. But I don't stop her when she grabs my pants again and tugs them down, freeing my cock. She hums her appreciation. I know I'm average at best, but it's nice to know she likes what she sees.

Garnet licks her lips, then shoves me back on the bed, stripping my pants off. Now that I'm as naked as she is, she climbs over me to settle between my legs. Her hand wraps around my dick and strokes it gently, as if she's memorizing every inch of it. I love watching her as she explores my body.

Without warning, she leans down and licks the underside of my cock, from base to tip. I pant at the contact. She sucks the tip into her mouth. "Oh, Garnet."

She starts to bob, taking me all the way into her throat, then backing off with a pop. "You like that?" She licks the tip again, then starts sucking me while rubbing her tongue along the underside of my dick.

I groan. If she keeps this up, I won't last. "That feels so good." I tense as I feel my orgasm coming on. Just before I get there, she stops. I have a moment of disappointment, then realize that she knew exactly what she was doing.

"I want you inside me when you come," she says breathily. Fuck, this woman makes me so hot. I reach for her, but she shoves me back on the bed and straddles me. She takes my hands in hers, placing one on her breast, and the other on her clit. Then she fists my cock and rubs it along her slit, coating it in her wetness.

"Fuck, Garnet, you're so wet," I breathe.

"Just for you, James," she replies, sliding me into her so slow that I think I'll die before she gets me fully sheathed. I let her control the pace, even if she wants to go torturously slow. But she surprises me a moment later by lifting her hips and dropping herself back on me. Garnet starts to move hard and fast, slamming her pussy onto my cock over and over until she notices that I'm not moving.

She gives me a look and stops moving. "Garnet, please."

"Please what? If you're not going to touch me, James, I'm not going to fuck you."

I pinch her nipple, and she rolls her hips. When I stroke her clit, she picks up her pace again.

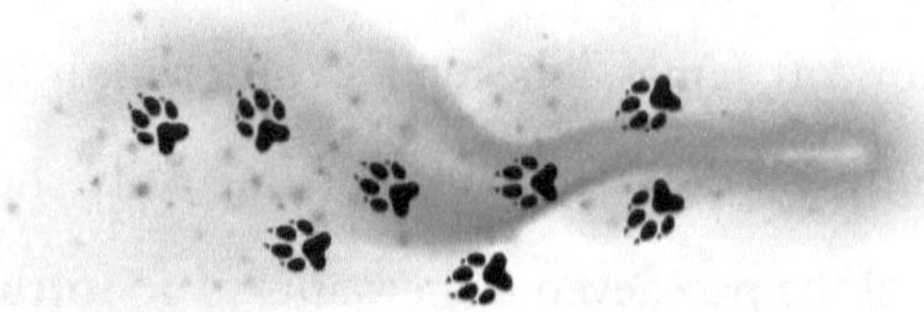

ORYM

I can't believe I offered to chase Ryland down and talk to him. What is this woman doing to me? Seeing her relief was worth it, though. As soon as I walk outside, I scent Ryland and follow the path he took. I can tell that he headed toward the falls. I feel like I'm invading his privacy, but Garnet is worried, so I'll do it.

By the time I catch up to him, he's diving into the river at the base of the falls. Should I jump in too, or wait for him? Probably better to wait. I drop to the ground and crisscross my legs under me. I watch as he swims a few laps. I don't know what his problem is, other than the fact that Garnet has four mates and he has to share.

The way he treated her is inexcusable, and I plan to tell him that. It doesn't matter if he likes me or not. It's not about me and him. It's about her. And she needs all of us. I wish I knew why, because the Goddess always has a reason. I think it has something to do with her dream. I've seen symbols like that before; I just can't remember where.

I get distracted by my thoughts and Ryland manages to catch me off guard. "I don't need a babysitter," he growls. I know he's close to shifting, and if he does that, he'll attack me. This was a bad idea. I should have let Luca come after him.

"I'm not here to babysit. I'm here to talk. You stormed off without talking to your mate, and she's upset. Rightly so. You keep blocking her from your thoughts but haven't bothered to show her how to block you. Then you get pissed when you glean something from her that you don't like." I know I sound like a dick, and I don't care.

"You wouldn't understand," he bites back.

"Then explain it so I can," I push. "How am I supposed to help our mate feel better if I can't convince you to talk to her? How am I supposed to make you feel better if you don't talk to me?"

Wait, do I want to make him feel better? That's weird. Why should I care if Ryland is upset? I realize that I do care more than I want to admit. It's as if this mate bond with Garnet has attached me to Ryland and the others as well. That's a strange feeling to get used to.

"Why would you care if I felt bad? You hate me." He tilts his head and stares at me, all animosity gone from his voice.

"Well, it's possible that I don't actually hate you. And that this mate sharing thing has some... interesting side effects. Like me caring that you're upset. And that she's upset. It makes me want to fix this. So, help me do that. Tell me what the problem is, and let's work toward a solution together."

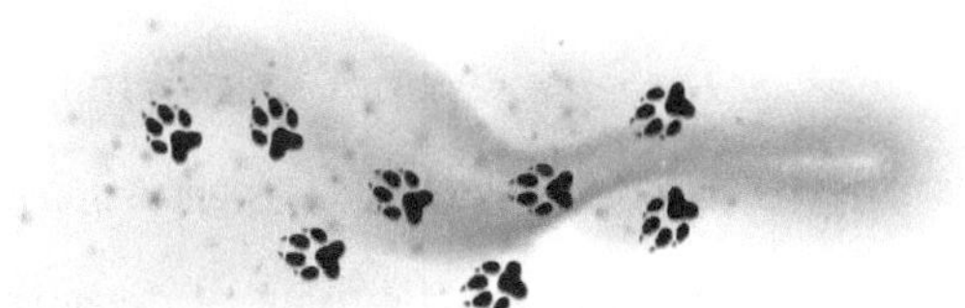

GARNET

James feels so good inside of me. I don't ever want to stop fucking him. He pinches my nipples as I ride him, and I can feel myself coasting closer to my release. He tenses, and I know that he's close too. I lean down and capture his lips in a kiss just as we both start to come undone.

The orgasm is so intense. For a minute I feel like something is wrong. My whole body feels like electricity is racing through me. I ride the wave of pleasure that borders pain, kissing James the whole time. When I finally ease myself away from him, I can see what looks like lightning wrap around my arm. It only lasts for a moment, then it's gone. *I had to have imagined that, right?*

I don't think so. I saw it too. James' voice is in my head.

Fuck. "What did you just say?" I ask, starting to panic. Please tell me I didn't just complete the mate bond with him too. I don't think I can handle more people reading my thoughts.

"I didn't say anything. But I can hear you in my head. How did you do that?" He seems as freaked out as I am right now. Good. At least I won't be alone in this.

"I don't understand it, but I think we just completed our bond." I should apologize, but it's not my fault. It's not his either, though.

"Oh. So, is this what it's like with Ryland?" he asks, then nods at the thought that goes through my head. "I get it. Having other people just know what you're thinking can be really frustrating. I'll do my best not to intrude on your personal thoughts."

I give him a pointed look. It should amuse me that he offers to not read my thoughts because he read my thoughts and knows that it annoys me when Ry does it. But right now, I'm too busy trying not to think about anything.

"I don't know how to turn it off. But I don't need everyone in my head all at once. That's why I wasn't going to bond with anyone else right now." I pause and see the pain in his eyes. "It's not that I don't want to be bonded to you, I really do. I just wanted to know how to have a little privacy too."

He nods as if he understands, then eases me off him. Without a word, he picks up his sweats and heads into the bathroom. I know I've upset him, but even he's doing a better job of blocking me out than I can do with either of them. Great. I've alienated two of my mates, and when the other two find out what just happened, they won't want to be around me either.

How am I supposed to find my brother if I can't even figure out my mates? I'm screwed.

EIGHT
REFOCUS

JAMES

I KNOW IT'S IMMATURE to run away, but Garnet hurt my feelings a little with her attitude about our accidental bonding. It's

not like I forced the issue. She came onto me. I was prepared to wait for as long as it took for her to be ready. And I've never had a fated mate before, so I have no idea how any of this works.

I storm off into the bathroom and turn the shower on. Hopefully she takes that as a message that I want to be alone. I can't talk to her right now. I need to refocus. This whole situation is too much, and now that I know how she feels about bonding with us, it's even more so.

I can't help feeling like Luca and Orym are the lucky ones. If her emotions have been this out of whack since Ryland claimed her, I completely understand why he's acting so annoyed. I didn't even believe in fated mates until now, and I'm annoyed.

I step into the shower and clean myself up. I wash my hair and body, then stand under the spray, just letting the hot water ease my tension. Even with my annoyance, I don't want to leave her unprotected for long. I'll just have to hang out in the living room until everyone else comes back. I have no idea if I can keep blocking her from reading my thoughts, or even if I should.

Garnet deserves to know how badly she hurt me, and how overwhelming this is for me too. She needs to know that she's not alone in this. Just because I'm upset, that doesn't mean I'm going anywhere. I turn the water off and grab a towel. As I dry myself and get dressed, I slowly lower the mental wall I've put in place.

I don't try to hide my annoyance or my hurt. I want her to feel both. But I also want her to know that I care about her. So, I stop holding back. I let her have access to all of my emotions and thoughts through the bond. If it's too much for her, she can tell me.

Maybe Ryland and I can work with her to block some of her feelings and thoughts from us, too. Of course, that may not be the best idea. I have a feeling that's why he left, though, because she can't shield herself and he heard something he didn't like.

If we're all going to be her mates, we have to find a way to co-exist and work together. I can't say that I'm thrilled about sharing the woman I'm falling for, but I also understand that not everything is black and white. We exist in shades of gray. I will do whatever I can to take care of Garnet and show her that she's valued.

But I refuse to let her act like I did anything wrong in this situation. I hope she's ready for this.

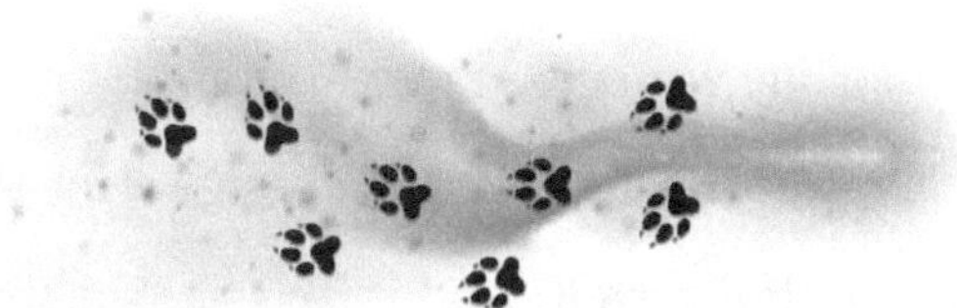

RYLAND

I know that I've been followed the moment I dive into the water. But if he doesn't want to say anything, I'll just enjoy my swim. When I climb out of the river and creep up on him, I realize that it isn't Luca. Orym. What the fuck would he be following me for?

After we argue, he floors me by saying that he doesn't actually hate me. Then he suggests that we work together to figure all of this out and fix things. What am I supposed to do with that? I've hated this guy since we were pups. It doesn't matter that I have no idea why I hate him; I just do. I'm allowed to feel how I feel without explaining myself to anyone. Even myself.

I can see that arguing against his logic is pointless. "Fine. I'm annoyed that she wants to ignore our bond. I'm dying to be close to her, but she acts like she doesn't want that. I don't know how to deal with it. And it feels like she's rejecting me for you guys."

"That's not it at all. She's really upset that you ran off. And that you're blocking her from your mind. I think she's just overwhelmed by the idea of all of us being inside her head. You have to talk to her. We can work this out. The rest of us will give you two some alone time, but you can't keep acting like you own her. You don't. She's her own person, and we're all connected to her." I hate that he's making sense. I want to be pissed and hate him, but he's right.

That's when I realize that I don't hate him anymore. I care if he's upset too, and I can tell that this situation is upsetting him. Am I about to start being nice to Orym? No, I won't go that far. I can't admit how I feel. Not now at least.

"Alright. I'll come back with you and talk to her. No promises, though. She may not want me around after we talk. You don't understand what it's like being bombarded by her random thoughts constantly. And then there's the dream. She tried to hide that from us. Luca did too, because he knew about it and didn't say anything. How can you just let that go?" I don't expect him to answer, but he does.

"Because I have faith in my mate and in the rest of you. If there's something that I need to know about, you'll tell me when it's important. If it's not relevant yet, why burden someone with it? I prefer to see them not telling us as that. It wasn't relevant until she had the dream and wrote those symbols on the wall. Now it is relevant, and they told us about it."

Damn this guy for making sense. I don't have to like it to agree with it. "Okay, let's head back, then."

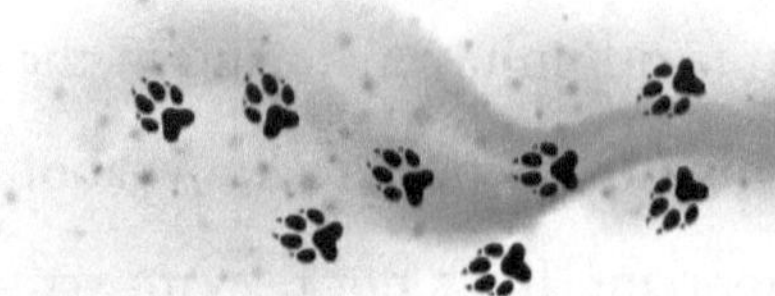

LUCA

Grammy looks at me and laughs. "You can't stop what the fates have in store for her." That sounds ominous. I don't understand how Grammy can be so flippant about Red's life.

"Maybe not, but I have to try," I say as I race out the door. At this point, I'm not sure if I'll make it in time to stop her from bonding with James. I don't know if she'll even want me to stop her. But I know that she was feeling overwhelmed by the bond with Ryland, so I have to try.

At this point, halfway back to Ryland's cabin, I realize that I didn't actually go to my cabin and get the photos that I'd used as an excuse to go see Grammy. Fuck. Well, it's too late now. I'll just have to come clean with her and hope she doesn't get too upset.

I rush back into Ryland's place and realize that something has to have happened. Red is sitting in the chair in the living room, and James is across the room on the couch. It's the most space I've seen between them since they met. Both of them look angry, but neither one is talking.

I can tell that they're upset with each other, and they keep glaring. Yeah, I'm too late to stop them from bonding. Now they're having an argument between themselves and I can't hear any of it. Great.

"Okay, I'm sorry I left the two of you alone. I get what's happening here, and it's going to be okay. But you're going to have to actually talk so I can help." I drop to the couch between them and look from one to the other. They continue to glare at each other as if taking last shots or something.

When no one speaks, I try again. "I understand that you're both upset about something. And I can tell that you've bonded. Please just talk to me, instead of screaming at each other inside your heads. Don't lock me out."

I hate resorting to guilt, but it works. James looks at me and gives me a guilty smile. "I'm sorry, Luca. Someone is upset that they've managed to accidentally bond with me after realizing how difficult this is with her first bond. And she's blaming me for not knowing how the bond would happen."

"That's exactly what I figured. So, let's talk about it. None of us knew how the bond would work with James, Red. You can't blame him for that. It's not exactly his fault that he's human, or that he's your fated mate." Reasonable isn't my strong suit, but I'm going to try to smooth things out here until Orym gets back.

"I'm not blaming him. I'm upset because I can't stop him from hearing all my thoughts. But somehow, he and Ry can both block me out. It's not fair. Why does he get privacy and I don't?" she pouts. This is starting to make more sense.

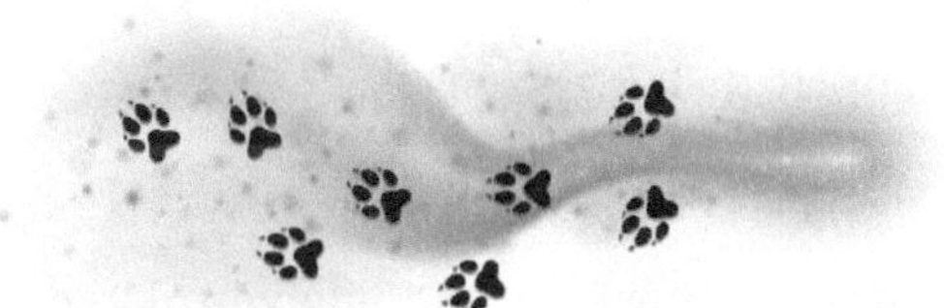

ORYM

Ryland and I walk back to his cabin. It's not a far walk when you head straight there. The only reason he was difficult to find was that he'd torn through the forest zig zagging around to throw Garnet off. It turns out he knew that she'd want to follow him.

I feel like we're making progress, though. He understands that he needs to talk to her. There has to be a way to help her shield her thoughts so that they're not being intrusive to him. And so that he's not getting things she doesn't want anyone else to hear.

When we walk into the cabin, I realize that something has happened. Everyone goes quiet when Ryland and I enter. "What happened? Is everyone okay?"

Luca shakes his head. "They bonded. It was an accident. None of us knew how her bonding with James would work. But they've been at each other since it happened. I just got them to start talking instead of glaring at each other and screaming in their heads."

"That is a new development," I respond. I walk over to the chair Garnet sits in, scoop her up and sit down with her on my lap. "I got Ryland to come back. Now we're all going to talk this through and get a little more sleep so we can go find your brother."

"Okay," she agrees quietly. I know that she's not happy about this, but we'll just have to make the best of it. And her reaction will definitely keep me from thinking about claiming her anytime soon. From Luca's face, he feels the same.

Knowing that everyone's problems center around this mate bond that we all share makes me a little sad. Bonding is supposed to be a joyous thing that happens to special people. I refuse to let my new family treat it any differently.

"Let's start with discussing the problem. Each of us has a reason to be upset, so we'll go around the room and discuss each person's problem." I look at each of the guys who are sitting on the couch beside me. "I'll start. I'm frustrated at how everyone is viewing this mate bond. I was taught that it's a gift, not a curse. But every one of you is treating it like it's an inconvenience. And I don't like that at all."

I see some guilty faces, but don't hesitate. "We have to work together. We have to be a family. We have to find Vincent and figure out who's taking wolves. So, let's stop acting like this is the end of the world and get ourselves focused on the goal here."

I don't expect anyone else to talk, but suddenly Garnet stands up and faces us all. "I'm upset that I didn't have a choice in any of this. I don't want everyone to have access to my personal thoughts and feelings without my permission."

And just like that, we have the root of the problem.

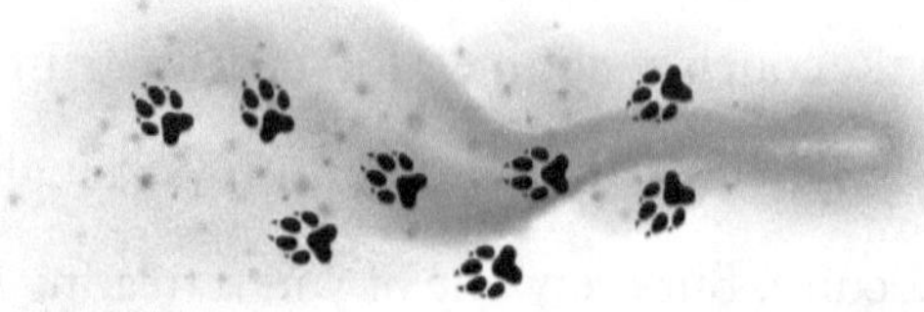

GARNET

I don't know why I shouted my feelings at everyone, other than the idea that I can't hide them from Ry or James now anyway. "I'm not blaming anyone for this. But I am allowed to have feelings and thoughts that I don't want to share. And instead of helping me figure out how to keep those things private, everyone took off. I'm not saying this is your fault. It's mine. I'm the one who decided I wanted James. He agreed to it. But it's *my* fault."

"You shouldn't have to deal with this alone. Maybe we can help," Orym offers. I wish there was something he could do, but I don't even know what sealed the bond with James.

"How?" I ask. I know I sound bitchy, but I'm just too frustrated to care. He stands up and walks the three steps to me, pulling me into his arms. He kisses me tenderly, with no indication that he wants anything from me besides to provide comfort. When he eases back, he gently cups my face.

"I don't know. But I would almost bet that you're not projecting your thoughts now." He turns to the other guys. "Is she?"

Ry and James both shake their heads. "I'm not getting anything from her right now, except a calm sensation," James offers.

"Same here," Ry agrees.

"There, it's settled. We just have to keep Garnet calm, and then she'll have control of what thoughts and emotions you two get from her," Luca says with a wicked grin. No doubt he's thinking of ways to keep me calm.

"It doesn't teach me how to block them out like they do me, though," I admit the bigger issue. "That's what I really want."

"Why do you want to block us out?" James asks. "Did we do something wrong?"

"No, I just feel so out of control right now. And it seemed like after I had that dream, Ry got more caught up in my thoughts and feelings while I was trying to process the whole thing. If he had just listened to what I was saying instead of focusing on my emotions and what was going on in my head, he might not have run away from me." Considering that he barely spoke to me after he came in, I don't know if he actually wants to be with me anymore.

"Garnet, you know that's not true," James responds, but his response isn't to my words, it's to my thoughts, to my worries.

"That's exactly what happened," Luca defends, as if James is arguing with me. I shake my head at Luca, and it only takes him a moment to understand.

I lock eyes with Ry, refusing to back down. If he's going to reject me, he'll have to do it to my face. *I understand that I'm being difficult, but you aren't telling me how you feel.* I push the thought at him as hard as I can, hoping to get through whatever block he's put up to keep me out.

I can't keep you out. I can only ignore you and clear my head so you don't know what I'm feeling. His response in my head is a relief. He hasn't completely closed himself off to me. But he admits that he's been ignoring me. That hurts, but we should be able to get past it.

"I get what's happening here, but it's not helpful to the rest of us if the three of you have a private conversation right now," Orym interrupts. I glance from Ry to James and realize that James has heard everything.

"You can hear Ry in your head too?" I can't help asking. James nods. "Wow, I hadn't expected that." I repeat what I said to Ry in my head, and he tells them his response.

"Did it work that way for you, too?" Orym asks James about blocking me out too.

"Kind of. I focused on shutting down my emotions and clearing my head by building a mental wall between us. Now that I've done it, I can let it down and put it back up if I need to." His explanation sounds so easy. I should be able to do that.

"Okay, so it sounds to me like that's what we need to help Garnet do. But that's going to involve the two of you sticking around and cooperating. Can you both do that?" It's pretty sexy how Orym completely takes control of the situation. Both James and Ry nod in agreement.

"Does anyone else have something they need to get off their chest? Now is the time." I shiver at his authoritative tone. I wonder if he'll be bossy in the bedroom. Ry groans and James turns red. Obviously, I need to work on that wall.

"I'm going to ignore whatever that was and move on. I need to tell you all that I've been working with Grammy to try and redirect Red from these dreams. I don't know exactly why, but I can tell you that Grammy isn't happy that Red told us about this one. The only thing she'll tell me is that we have to protect her. I can't get more out of her. And I lied about going to my place to get those pictures. I needed to talk to Grammy. That's where I went." Luca's admission is a punch in the gut, but I understand why he lied.

"Okay, I think we can work with that. If everyone is good here, we should get some sleep. We still have to find Vincent, and it'll be morning soon. There's no reason to let the trail go any colder." Orym kisses my cheek and heads toward the bedroom. Luca follows him, pausing to kiss my other cheek.

James and I exchange a glance before he goes with them. We can talk it out tomorrow while we're searching the forest for my idiot brother. Right now, I need to talk to Ry.

As soon as we're alone, I notice how uncomfortable he is. Good. I don't want this to be pleasant. For either of us. "We should talk," I start.

He nods. "I suppose so."

"I know that those dreams give me a lot to process. If you were in my head while I was trying to process, I understand why you took off."

He looks at me, tilting his head to the side. "I was pissed that you kept that from me. Then you tried to brush it all off because Luca knew about it. Just because he knows about it, that doesn't mean you don't need to tell the rest of us. We all care about you, Red. You belong to all of us, not just Luca."

"Woah, let's take a breath here. I do not *belong* to anyone. Yes, I am fated to the four of you. That does not make me your property. I'm sorry I didn't tell you. I wasn't exactly thinking about the dreams when we bonded. Until it happened, I wasn't thinking about it at all."

Ry stands up and walks over to me. He doesn't reach for me, though. I sense that this is him meeting me halfway. I'll have to close the distance if I want to touch or be touched. I only hesitate for a moment, then take the two steps that bring me close enough to press myself against him. I know that there will be a lot of compromise involved with having four mates. I'm not exactly looking forward to it.

"I'm sorry. I should have told you, but I didn't know how. It's a strange thing, having new people in your head. And those dreams don't help. I really thought you were mad that I'd written on your wall," I say softly.

He lifts my chin with a finger, forcing me to look at him. "I overreacted. And I'm sorry. I would love to promise that it'll never happen again, but I know better. There will be mis-communication in this relationship, and we're going to have to work on that. Please just know that I am trying." He leans down and gently touches his lips to mine. I'm not sure if it's the bond, or the passion he puts into the contact, but I can feel that he's sorry and that he wants to make it up to me.

I wrap my arms around his neck and let myself drown in his kiss. I don't care if I ever breathe again. I'll die happily if I can keep kissing Ry. He groans, obviously picking up on my emotions and desires. His arms wrap around me, pulling me closer to him and encouraging me to wind my legs around his torso. I let him pick me up, never breaking the kiss.

I know that we still have things to discuss and problems to work through, but I feel like we're on the way to mending our relationship. Ry eases his lips from mine and carries me to bed.

Orym and James are on one side of the bed, while Luca is on the other. They've left the middle for me. I wonder if they're going to fight over who sleeps where again. Ry sets me on the bed and I climb up between them. Each of them kisses me goodnight, then everyone settles in.

I'm a little surprised when Ry nudges Luca to sleep beside me, but it's a nice gesture. I fall asleep easily and wake fully rested. I don't want to get out of bed, but I know that we have to start looking for Vincent. It's hard to believe that he's only been missing for two days.

I stretch, then realize that I'm in bed alone. It's still warm, so my mates haven't been up long. I can hear murmured voices coming from the kitchen. I'm not feeling any distress from Ry or James, so I think they're just planning our search. Maybe I'll try this connection thing again.

Where did everyone go? It's so lonely in here. I giggle at the pouty voice I use in my head. I hear footsteps, but they stop just outside the door.

Are you okay, Garnet? I know you don't like communicating this way. My sweet James, always worried about me.

She's fine. Just seeing what she can get by with. Isn't that right, Red? Ouch, it looks like Ry has me figured out already. That stings a little. But since I was only teasing with them, I decide not to let that bother me.

I was teasing. But it is strange to wake up alone now. It's only been two days, and I already miss their body heat pressed against me while I sleep.

"Do you want coffee or not?" Luca yells. That gets me moving, because knowing him, if I don't come get it, he'll pour whatever is left out just to spite me. I jump out of the bed and dash to the kitchen, pushing James and Ry out of the way.

"If you even have to ask, then you don't know me as well as you think," I glare at Luca playfully and reach for his cup.

He shakes his head and holds the cup just out of reach. "Not my coffee. I'll get you a cup. Go find a spot. Orym is making breakfast." He swats my bottom as I scoot around him. I make it a point to give Orym a loud kiss as I pass him. I turn and stick my tongue out at Luca, then settle on the couch.

I'm a little surprised when he brings me a cup of coffee, made just the way I like it. I half expect him to deny me my morning drink of choice because I'm being a brat, but he doesn't. I kiss him as I take the cup from his hand. We all settle in and have breakfast together before checking supplies and heading out to start our search.

NINE
TRACKING VINCENT

ORYM

SINCE I'M THE FIRST one awake, I decide to make breakfast. With that taken care of, I continue to nudge everyone toward the door. I've checked and rechecked our packs. Knowing that we have everything we need, I'm anxious to get this over with. We need to find Vincent and figure out who took him, as well as the other wolves and the missing vamps. Once that's settled, we can figure out our relationship with Garnet, and each other.

Each of us carries a backpack loaded with food, water, and anything else we might need. I carry our tent, though I'm a little surprised that Ryland doesn't try to argue with me about it. He seems dead set on proving that he's the biggest, baddest wolf there ever was. I don't see this as a competition, so, I'm mostly ignoring him.

Garnet splits her time between the four of us, walking with each one for a bit before moving to the next. It gives us a little time to talk to her and each other. I mostly just listen to everything.

Tracking is my forte, and I'm completely focused on Vincent's trail. I lead the way, pretending not to notice that Garnet is by my side again. I want to spend time with her and get to know her better, but I have to find her brother first. I can't afford to get distracted. There are lives on the line here.

I'm sure that I offend her by not paying attention, but I can't worry about that right now. I have to follow Vincent's path through the forest and find out who took him. This is bigger than any of us now. When we stop for lunch, everyone is starting to get cranky. We've been walking for hours and don't seem to be any closer to finding any useful clues.

"Let's break for food now. We'll stop for an hour and rest, then get back at it," I instruct, easing my pack off my back and helping Garnet to remove hers as well.

"That's fine by me. I could use a rest," she says as she drops onto the ground next to her bag. A moment later, I hear her soft snores. She's exhausted and didn't say anything about it. I feel like an idiot for not noticing.

"We'll let her sleep for a bit, then we'll eat. If it takes more than an hour, it'll be okay." Luca's eyes meet mine and I nod at his suggestion. We should let her sleep for a bit. The past couple of days have been hard on her, and with her brother missing, she hasn't really had time to process.

James sits with her while Ryland, Luca, and I collect some wood for a fire and water to put it out when we're finished. We grew up in this forest, and we'll protect the woods as much as possible.

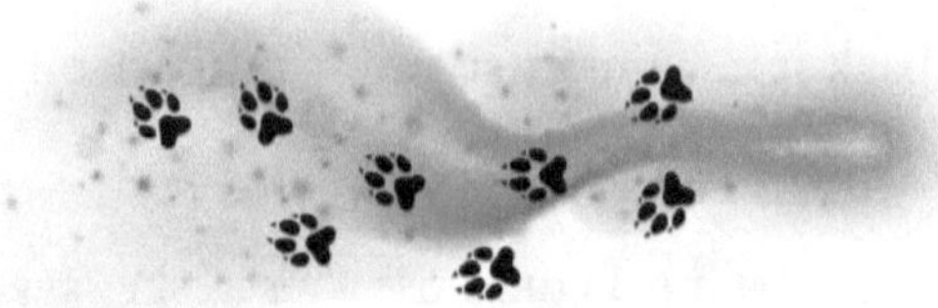

JAMES

I could offer to help gather wood or water, but I'd rather rest next to Garnet. She looks comfortable enough resting her head on her pack, so I leave her there. I'd rather have her in my arms, but if something happens, I won't be able to protect her that way. And protecting her is the most important thing right now.

I can't help thinking that her dreams have something to do with the missing wolves and vamps. What I can't figure out is why someone would take both. It doesn't make sense. Typically, wolves and vamps avoid each other, except for the council members. Other than Dec and Kayden, I don't think many wolves and vamps are friends. Since they were friends before Dec was turned, I'm pretty sure their relationship is not the norm.

From Garnet's description of her dreams, we're probably dealing with witches. I don't know much about them, other than what little Amber has mentioned during council meetings. I know that witches usually have elemental powers. That would account for the chanting around the circle. I need to make a list of questions to ask her about her dreams later. I should ask them when she's just had the dream, so we can get more information about what we're up against. I wonder if any of the others have made the connection, but I doubt it.

If Luca or Orym had, they would say something. Ryland is the one who's nearly impossible to figure out, even if he is in my head. I feel like if he knew anything, he'd try to hide it. I have nothing to support that idea, other than his attitude toward everything. It's like we're all inconveniencing him. And maybe we are. If not for us, he would have Garnet all to himself.

I can't say that I would mind having her to myself, but I understand that's not exactly what she wants. So, I'll cooperate and take what she's willing to give me. Hopefully she'll forgive me for our accidental bond, even though neither of us is to blame.

I watch over her as she sleeps, keeping an eye on our surroundings and making sure she's not having a nightmare. Her sleep seems restful and uninterrupted. When the other three come back, they build a fire nearby and start making lunch.

Within minutes, the fire roars to life and Luca has lunch prepared. Then Ryland and Orym make sure the fire is completely out. I can see how much they love this forest in the care they take with the fire.

Garnet starts to stir, and I place my hand on her shoulder. "Are you hungry?" I hold up a sandwich when her eyes meet mine. The melted cheese inside bread is simple, but delicious.

"Starved," she admits, taking the sandwich from me and scarfing it down. Once we've all eaten and had a few minutes to relax, Orym stands up.

"We should go. I feel like we're getting close to something."

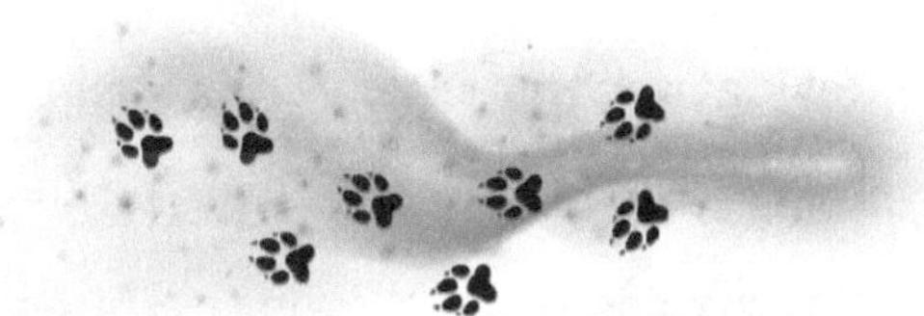

GARNET

I feel like we've been walking for days, though it's only been a few hours. When we stop for lunch, I fall asleep faster than I'd like to admit. I completely trust my guys to keep me safe, even though we're in the middle of the forest with no shelter. I know that they won't let anything happen to me. I wake to

James' hand on my shoulder and the offer of a grilled cheese sandwich.

Once we're moving again, I continue to split my time between the four of them. Orym doesn't say much, but I know he's doing most of the tracking. Ry and Luca are just as capable, but neither of them seems as invested as Orym is. So, we let Orym take the lead here.

"We're leaving pack land if we go any further into the forest," Orym says to us, holding up a hand for us to stop. "His scent goes this way, and we're following it. I just want everyone to know where we stand. If we run into the people who inhabit this land, they may not be friendly. We have to be prepared for that."

We take his warning seriously. Trespassing is not something our packs condone. But we have to find Vincent and the other missing wolves, not to mention the vampires. Everyone is counting on us to do this. It doesn't matter the danger; we have to continue.

It's dark here, the trees closer together than in our forest. The five of us stay close together, a ring of mates surrounding me and protecting me from the dangers we face. I would laugh, but this place feels different from home. More ominous somehow, but familiar. It's like I've been here before, but I can't remember it. The colors are more muted, as if something is subduing them.

"Is it just me, or does this place look completely different from where we were ten feet ago?" James asks. I nod, but have no explanation for it.

"It's the magic. This area is home to the witches, and you're seeing their power. The magic coats everything here. It looks and feels different than wolf territory, because it is. I have no doubt their leaders know that we're here. We still need to be quiet and stay out of sight." Luca's explanation sends goosebumps down my arms.

Even before he spoke, I knew that was what he would say. I can feel the magic in this area as it courses against my skin. It's a strange sensation, but it doesn't hurt. It feels as familiar as this area does. I have an odd feeling of being at home here. But that can't be. Wolves aren't usually welcomed into the witches' side of the forest. I've been working on blocking things from Ry and James, and take this opportunity to put those blocks in place. They don't need to be worried about my strange feelings.

"As long as we aren't doing anything wrong, they'll leave us alone, right?" I can't stop myself from asking.

"We hope so, but really have no way to know. If we're approached, please let Luca or myself do the talking." Orym's request doesn't seem unreasonable, but I can tell it pisses Ry off.

"It's okay, Ry. Let them take point on this. It doesn't mean you're any less of an alpha." He glares at me as if I've said something offensive. "I didn't read your mind. That thought is written all over your face." His glare eases a bit. But I know that I'm right about what he was thinking.

Ry has to be in control, and he doesn't like letting anyone else step up. It's part of why I'm hesitant to claim Luca and Orym right now. I don't want them fighting over control. Mostly I'm scared that the Goddess made a mistake giving them all to me, and I don't want them to be tied to me if they have a chance to be happy somewhere else.

I already feel bad about claiming James and Ry, even if they don't. I keep trying to figure out why I would have four mates. I mean, it's not uncommon. Delilah has four, but she's a hybrid, and three of her mates are vampires. It's hard to know if the Goddess of the moon decided to give her those mates, or if it just happened.

I shake that thought away. Orym is leading us further into the forest, still following Vincent's scent. We walk for a while longer, then he holds up a hand to stop us. "Look," he whispers. My eyes follow his hand. There's a cabin in a clearing in front of us. "His scent goes in that direction. I think we should camp here and watch the place for a while."

We all shrug off our packs and get started setting up camp. Orym and Ry put the tent up while James and Luca collect fire wood and water. I don't know how we'll have a fire if we're this close to that cabin. Surely, we'll get caught if we do. I have to trust that my men know what they're doing, though. I watch the cabin while they work. None of them wants me to help, so there's nothing else for me to do.

It looks to be abandoned, but there's no way to know for sure. I stare at it, wishing I could see inside. I must doze off while I'm watching it, because suddenly I have the sensation of being inside the cabin. I can see that it's empty, but there were wolves here. Someone was hiding them. There are chains on the walls that hold collars. I shudder at the image. I walk over to the kitchen and look around. It's weird, but I feel as if I'm actually inside the cabin. I open the fridge and see bags of blood and food. It's fully stocked.

Whoever took the wolves and vamps kept them here.

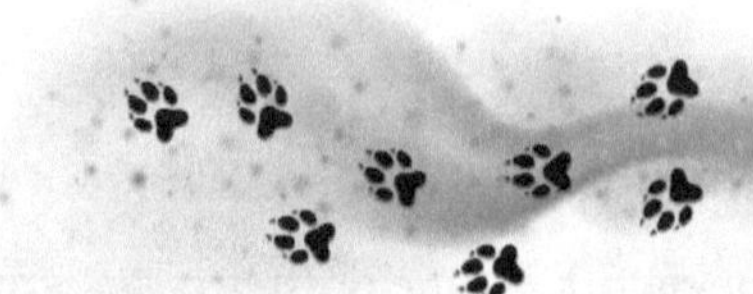

LUCA

James and I get as much fire wood as we can find, then fill our jug with water. I have no idea how Orym thinks we'll be able to have a fire without the occupants of the cabin seeing us. I don't argue, though. I want to stay as close to Red as possible.

There's something off about this part of the forest, and I don't like it.

When we get back, she's staring at the cabin, but it's like she's not even there. "Red? Are you okay?" She doesn't respond, and my heart starts to race. I grab her arm gently and give it a little shake. This reminds me too much of how we found Ryland the other day.

James waves his hand in front of her face, but she doesn't even seem to see him. "This isn't good, is it?" he asks. I shake my head.

"We have to get her to snap out of it."

Orym and Ryland notice that we're concerned and join us. "What's wrong with her?" Ryland asks, taking her hand.

"I'm not sure. It's like some sort of trance, but I don't understand it." Panic is gripping me hard now, so I pull her into my arms, turning her away from the cabin. "Red, please come back to me." I hug her tightly, not letting go until her arms wrap around me.

"What's going on?" she asks as she comes out of whatever had her frozen.

"You were just staring at the cabin, not moving. It was like how we found Ryland the other day. I'm glad you're okay now," I tell her, pressing a kiss to her temple.

"I don't know exactly what happened, but it was like I was inside the cabin. No one is here, but they were, and they will come back. It's empty now. We can go check it out if you want." Her words send a chill through me. She's so certain that what she saw was real. What if she's wrong?

I exchange a glance with Orym. "There's only one way to know for sure," he offers. "I can go with her and you guys can stay hidden in case we need you. Then she can call out to Ryland or James if we get in trouble."

"I'm going too, then," I insist. I won't let her go without me.

"Okay, we'll wait here," Ryland agrees. I don't have time to wonder what he's thinking, because Red is already heading toward the cabin with Orym following her. I have to run to catch up.

She opens the door without hesitation, and as predicted, it's empty. I can smell the wolves and vampires that were being held here, though. Vincent was definitely one of them. The chains on the walls make me shiver. I don't want to be one of the unfortunate ones who gets held here. We search the cabin thoroughly, but don't find anything or anyone.

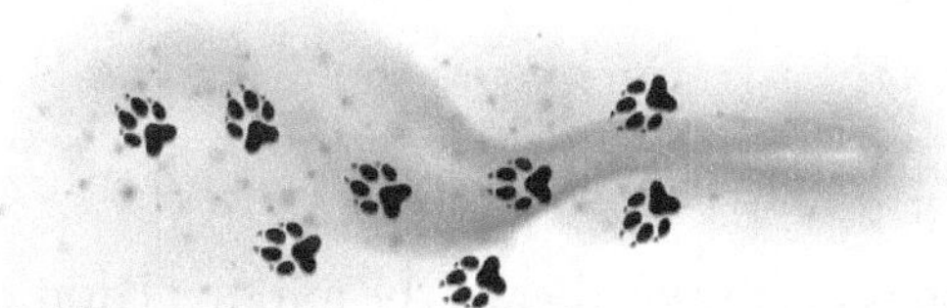

RYLAND

As much as I want to go with them, I agree to stay behind with James. Orym is right, it makes more sense for Red to go with the two who can't hear her in their heads. James and I won't even have to worry while they're gone, because we can talk to her the whole time.

We watch as they approach the cabin. *Are you okay?* James asks her.

I'm fine. The cabin is empty. You'll see. She has a strange calm thing going on right now, and it's freaking me out a little. James and I exchange a look, and I can tell that he's not sure about this either. Before we have a chance to think about what could be her problem, we see them heading back toward us.

Nothing? I ask, watching as she shakes her head. How can it be empty? How could she possibly know that it was? This situation is getting weirder by the minute. I don't push her for details, waiting until everyone is safe inside the tent.

"What did you find?" I ask when the tent is zipped closed.

"It was empty, just like she said," Luca offers. I can tell that he doesn't understand it any more than I do. Orym looks confused too. How did she know?

"There were chains to hold the wolves and vampires. And the fridge is filled with food, so they'll be coming back. Or bringing new prisoners. Either way, we have a little bit of time, since no one is here," Orym explains.

They give us a detailed description of every inch of the cabin. By the time they're done, we know every entrance, exit, and window. If the wolves and vamps are brought back here, we should be able to free them pretty easily. All we can do now is wait. It's starting to get dark, which is saying something since this part of the forest doesn't get much sunlight anyway.

When we're finished talking, we head out of the tent to light the fire and cook dinner. It's my turn, so I whip up a quick stew. Once it's finished, Luca and James put the fire out and we go back into the tent for the night. It's camouflaged, making it harder to see, especially in the dark. We're taking great pains to stay hidden here, even if the witches can sense that we've entered their territory.

It's not like we're here to attack them, so there isn't much they can do but ask us to leave. At least, I hope that's all they can do. Because otherwise, we're sitting ducks. I don't like that feeling at all. I have to be able to protect Red, and James, since he can't shift either. Sure, I have Orym and Luca to help me, but I'm the first one to bond with her. I take that responsibility very seriously, even if she doesn't. I will keep her safe, no matter what I have to do.

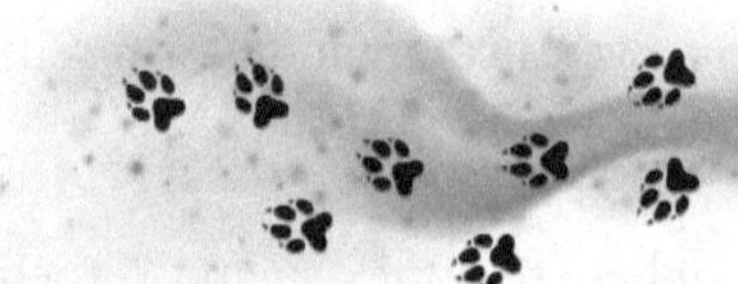

GARNET

I'm not sure how I feel about what we find in the cabin. Or more accurately, what we don't find. How is it possible to have a vision that clear about the inside of a building, then go inside and every detail be exactly the same? I feel like everything is connected.

I don't know why, but somehow, I know that my dreams have to do with these abductions, just like my inability to shift. But I don't understand how I know or what that connection could possibly be.

I have more questions than answers at this point. I know that Vincent was here. Orym scented him. But I don't think he was being held prisoner. Yes, there are chains on the wall that would be used to hold wolves and vamps. Vincent's scent was on every one of them. Why, if he was a prisoner, would he have touched them all? I suppose that his captors could have forced him to chain up other prisoners to keep their scent off things.

There's just something completely off about the whole thing. I know that I shouldn't obsess over those small details, but I can't help it. I probably shouldn't keep my thoughts to myself, but I don't know how to explain my certainty. So, I'll hide these thoughts and focus on the ones that I can share.

"Are you okay? You were convinced that the cabin was empty. But how did you know?" James scoots over next to me in the tent.

"I don't know. I had a vision, I guess. It's just strange how everything inside the cabin was exactly how I saw it. The whole thing is freaking me out. I can't think about it right now." I hope that he drops the conversation, because if not, I'll end up losing concentration and he'll know exactly what I'm thinking.

"Then let's focus on something else." He pulls out a map and spreads it out in front of us. "Orym thinks we should go this way in the morning if no one shows up at the cabin tonight." He points out a path that goes deeper into the forest. It's a solid idea.

"Should we go further into the witches' territory without permission? Does he really think that's the best idea?" I don't know why it scares me, but something about this plan feels wrong. Like we shouldn't be here at all. I can feel the forest warning me to get out. I desperately want to obey the warning and run. But I can't. I have to help find my brother.

James nods. "He, Luca, and Ryland are checking the area. He can explain it to you when he gets back if you want. But he's convinced that following the trail is the best way to find Vincent. Once we have him and the others, we can get back to your home."

"I understand that. I just don't know that going further into the forest is a good idea." I look at him pleadingly. I need him on my side here, but I can tell from his expression that he's not.

He gently lifts me onto his lap. "I'm not doing anything, I promise. I just want to hold you for a minute. This place gives me the creeps. I don't want to go further, but I understand why Orym thinks we should. And I'll follow you anywhere." I curl into him, turning to wrap my arms and legs around him.

I can feel his hard length pressing into my crotch through my jeans. And he said he wasn't doing anything. Maybe not intentionally, but he is definitely doing something. I press my lips to his cheek and hug him tightly. I can't wait until this is over and we can figure out this mate bond thing.

Please tell me you two aren't fucking. I laugh at Ry's voice in my head. He must have felt the wave of lust wash over me, or both of us. Sometimes I forget that they're connected now too.

James answers before I can. *No, we're not fucking. But you try spending any time near her and not getting a massive hard on. It's not possible.*

I laugh at both of them. My mates are definitely horny, almost all the time. If I'm not careful, I'll end up barefoot and pregnant before we get back home. Oh, shit. We haven't talked about any of this. Do they expect kids? Do I want kids? I don't know. Where will we live? I mean, sure, most of us are from the forest, but is James going to give up the city for this? Is it even fair for me to ask him to?

My heart starts racing and I feel like my lungs are closing up. Breathing is nearly impossible. James rubs his hand up and down my back. "It's okay, Garnet. Take a deep breath. That's a good girl. Now let it out. Good. Again. Keep going," he instructs. I do as he asks, noticing that the more I focus on his voice, the easier it is to breathe.

"Panic attacks are not unusual in times of stress. And I would say finding out you have four mates on top of your brother coming up missing, and who knows what else would qualify as stress. Just focus on breathing for now. You don't have to figure out the future just yet. We'll get there together."

How did he know what I was thinking? Oh, no. Did I drop my blocks? "James?" I start to ask, but he holds up a hand.

"It's written all over your face. I didn't hear your thoughts. Your reaction to my conversation with Ryland was enough to know that's where your mind went. Also, that's perfectly reasonable to wonder how things will work out. We can talk about it now if you want, or we can wait until we find your brother. Either way won't change my answer."

TEN
DEEP, DARK FOREST

LUCA

WE KEEP AN EYE on the cabin all night, taking turns staying awake. We don't want to be caught by surprise. There's no movement at all, and no one comes back to it. We wake early and Orym suggests that we break camp and keep looking. I agree with him, but I sense Red's hesitation. In the end, it's two votes against and three votes in favor of going further into the forest. James isn't excited about it either. Ryland is chomping at the bit to get into a fight with someone. I just want to find the missing wolves and vamps so we can go home.

Orym and Ryland take the tent down while the rest of us make breakfast. Once we're packed up and have eaten, we follow Vincent's trail further into the forest. The hike isn't easy. It's dark and there are exposed tree roots everywhere. I catch Red when she trips, keeping her from falling on her face.

Ryland growls at us because of the noise we made. He's being more of a dick than usual today, and I'm not a fan. "Don't worry about him. I have no idea what his problem is, but I'll take care of it," I whisper to Red as I set her gently on her feet.

"He's mad because we haven't found anything yet. I'm surprised that James is so patient with him. He's been bitching at us all day." Her explanation doesn't surprise me. I have a moment of jealousy over the bond that allows them to talk to each other in their heads. Then I remember why Red and I don't have that yet. It's just another reason to be irritated at Ryland.

I guarantee if she had bonded with me first, she would have been much more receptive to mating all of us instead of waiting. But I have to trust that the Goddess has a plan. I don't have to understand it or like it to cooperate. And let's face it, I would do anything for Red. So, waiting isn't that horrible. At least I know she's mine.

I'll make sure that our bond is worth the wait. That won't stop me from feeling jealous of Ryland and James. But it does help me to keep that in check. Red would be upset if she knew, and I won't be the one who does that to her. She's dealing with enough jealousy from Ryland anyway. It's obvious that he doesn't want to share her, even though we've all confirmed that we're her mates too.

I won't stoop to his level. I refuse to be that guy. I'll wait as long as it takes. I shake thoughts of jealousy and bonding away and refocus on helping to track Vincent. His scent is getting stronger, which should mean that we're getting closer to finding him. I hope it happens soon, so we can go home. I'm ready to be done with this camping trip.

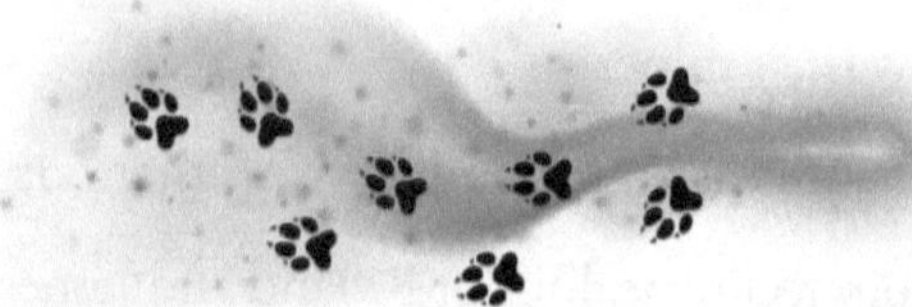

JAMES

Ryland's incessant bitching is driving me crazy. *We're not there until we find Vincent. Stop complaining about everything. It's ridiculous and a waste of time.* I finally snap at him, and he shuts up for a little while.

"I'm sorry," I whisper to Garnet. I know that she isn't fully adjusted to the bond yet, and that the voices in her head bother her sometimes. I'm not trying to do that, and I know I was harsh with Ryland.

She shakes her head with a grin. "He deserved that. And you're right, it is ridiculous and a waste of time. Maybe he'll settle down now."

We keep our voices low because Orym and Luca confirm my suspicions that we're getting closer to whoever has the wolves. I can feel the magic touch my skin, skating along, testing me. It's like the air can sense our intention. So far, we haven't had any problems, because our intentions aren't bad. I have no idea what will happen when we find the missing vamps and wolves. Everything may change.

Orym holds up a hand to stop us. We all freeze, except Ryland. He works his way around us to get in front with Orym. Of course, he has to see what's going on. I take a step backward, pulling Garnet with me. Luca stays behind us. Now that we're arranged pretty much in a straight line, it's easier to see why Orym stopped us.

There's a camp ahead. There are a few tents set up and there's a fire in the center. I can't tell how many tents or people there are, but I can see that the wolves are at attention now. I won't be surprised if the three of them shift so they are better able to protect us.

I can sense Garnet's hesitation at my thought. I don't block my emotions or thoughts from her anymore. If she can't keep me from hearing hers, then I won't keep her from hearing mine. *I don't want them to shift either, but it feels like they're going to.*

If they do, it'll be harder to talk our way out of this if we get caught. The witches will suspect us of hunting on their land. It won't end well.

I understand her hesitation, and while we're talking, I see Ryland's posture relax a little. He understands her concern, and even if he's not acknowledging it, he is letting her know that he'll control it. I can respect that. As soon as he starts to relax, Luca and Orym do too.

We all crouch down and watch the camp, trying to see if the missing wolves and vamps are being held here or not. I can't tell, but I'm not really sure what I'm looking for. I guess I'll learn soon enough, since I'm mated to one of the wolves. It doesn't matter to me that she can't shift, Garnet is still a wolf. I wish she saw it that way, though.

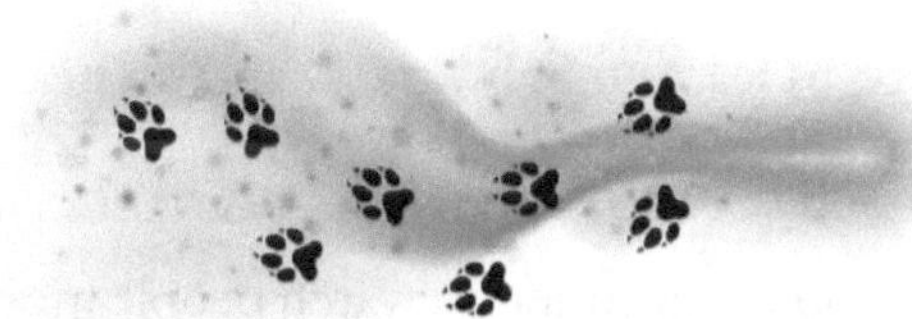

GARNET

Right now, I wish I was a better tracker. Orym, Luca, and Ry seem to think this is where Vincent is, but I can't smell him. It's just another wolf sense I got passed over by. James' thought that the three of them are going to shift scares me. I know they would do it to protect us, but I think it would draw more attention to us and make it harder to talk our way out of a fight.

I relax just a little when I see them stand down. There's activity going on in the camp, but from here, it's hard to tell if these are witches, wolves, or vamps. I'm sure my three wolf mates can tell, but I can't. It's hard not to feel a little jealous about their abilities, since I didn't get any of them. I've fought hard to learn to fight, track, and do nearly everything the wolves can do.

Kneeling on the ground, we watch people move around the camp. It looks like they're just setting up for the night. Everyone is preoccupied with their tasks, so they haven't noticed us yet. As I watch them, I see something disturbing. There are wolves protecting the camp. I recognize a few of them. "Isn't that Levi?" I ask, grabbing Luca's arm.

The elder wolf is one of my father's enemies, ever since Gunnar took over as head of the packs. He hates my family, but there he is, shaking hands with my brother. "Vincent!" I exclaim as quietly as I can. James covers my mouth with his hand and pulls me closer to the ground. I almost ruined our hiding spot. I have to control my outbursts better.

That is Levi, and he is with Vincent. They don't look like prisoners, though. We need to stay hidden and keep watching.

Ry's voice in my head instantly settles me down. He's right. I have to keep myself quiet and hidden so we can see what's going on. If my brother has joined these people, I'm not sure what we'll have to do to get him to come home.

We can't just leave them here. Some of those wolves are being held prisoner. We have to save them. And the vampires too. I'm insistent, but Ry shakes his head. Disappointment settles in, but I stay quiet. I don't want to be the reason anyone gets hurt. We don't know enough about where we are or what we're dealing with.

James keeps his arms wrapped around me, and I'm essentially sitting on his lap. He doesn't seem to mind, but I'm dying to move. I want to race over to my brother and ask him what the fuck he's doing here. None of this makes sense. I know that some of those people are wolves, and others are witches. I haven't seen anyone that looks like a vampire, though. They must be in the tents.

I wonder what these people are doing with them. Why kidnap wolves and vampires? Is it a plot to get rid of supernatural creatures? But how would that benefit the witches? They're supernatural too. None of this makes sense. I know that we can't just charge in there. So, I'll wait. At least I get to wait with one of my mates wrapped around me.

I don't know how long we sit there, watching the camp as the sun sets around us. It's not safe to stay here like this, but if we move, they could see us. "We're going to have to risk sleeping here. Two of us will stay awake at a time and keep watch. The other three will sleep. Ryland and I will take first watch," Orym tells us in a whisper.

I fall asleep easier than I expect to in James' arms, with Luca beside me. The three of us are backed up against a tree. Orym unrolls a blanket for us, and we snuggle close under it.

I'm not sure how the dream starts this time. I feel like I've stepped into the middle of it this time. I know this is some sort of ritual. Six hooded figures, each wearing a different colored robe, stand around a fire. I can hear the crackle of the wood as it burns. I feel the heat from the blaze. But this is just a dream, right? It's not real. It can't be. Yet, it feels a lot like that vision I had earlier.

I watch as they step closer to the flames and begin to chant. I can't understand what they're saying, but I know the words. How do I know the words when they're mumbling? None of this makes sense. I'm being pulled to step closer to the fire, but I force myself to stay put. I will not move.

I tense, fighting the urge to move. The chant gets louder, but I still can't make out what they're saying. It feels like they're calling to me. They want me to join them. To come back to them. Wait—to come back to them? I've never been with them. I'm so confused, but I feel the pull of their chant.

I know this is a dream, but it's the most real thing I've ever felt. I wish my mates were here. I need their strength to fight against this pull. Just when I think I can't hold out any longer, the chanting stops.

The hooded figures step back from the fire, and start to draw the symbols again. I know each one intricately, but I have no idea what they mean or why they're drawing them. Is this part of a spell? Could that be why I feel like they're calling me?

What could a coven of witches want with me anyway? I'm just a cursed wolf shifter who can't shift. I'm not anyone special. Other than having four mates, there is nothing overly interesting about me at all. I can't figure this out.

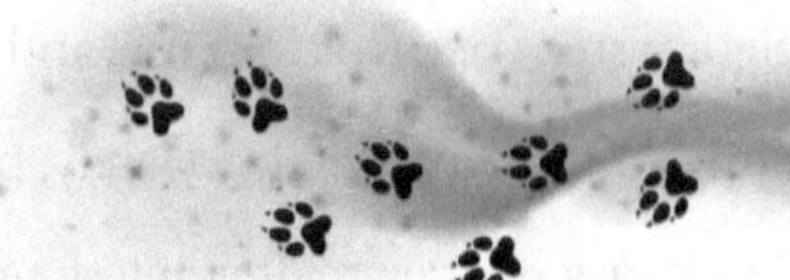

ORYM

I'm focused on the cabin when I hear a whimper. Garnet is obviously having another nightmare. Luca insisted that we shouldn't wake her when this happens, but I have to find a way to calm her down. If we're discovered because she's not being quiet, our mission will fail. When I get to her, she's kicked the blanket off and rolled away from James and Luca. I'm surprised that they're still sleeping, given the noises she's making.

I drop to the ground and pull her into my arms. I start rubbing small circles on her back to calm her. Just as she begins to relax, I hear a rustling noise behind us. Is that Ryland? He's wandered off by himself, and I suspect he's feeling jealous again. It serves him right for ignoring Garnet for most of the day yesterday.

"Come on, Ryland, that's not amusing," I mutter under my breath. A moment later, a wolf breaks through brush and growls at us. Garnet startles awake and backs herself closer to me to get away from her brother. I'm certain this wolf is Vincent, and she confirms it a moment later.

"Vincent? What's wrong? Let us help you," she whispers.

"I don't think he can hear us. He doesn't seem to be in control of himself," I say in her ear. She nods, careful not to break eye contact with the wolf that's staring her down. I can't believe how brave she is to face off with a full-grown wolf like this. Most people would hesitate, especially if they knew what a wolf like that is capable of.

James and Luca sit up, realizing that we're in danger. Luca shifts into his wolf form and steps in front of us to block

Vincent from his sister. There's nothing we can do right now without starting a fight. I can tell from Garnet's face that she doesn't want that.

Before I can figure out what we should do next, a blast of blue magic hits the ground in front of Luca. He jumps out of the way. There's no way we can defend against magic. None of us have powers. This won't be a fair fight.

Even as I have the thought, I sense a barrier of magic surround us. I can't tell if it's meant to protect or contain, and that makes me nervous. I don't like being trapped. But when the blue magic blasts again, it hits the shield, bouncing off. While it appears as if the barrier is for protection, there's no guarantee. I have no idea if it will shield against physical attacks too, or just magical ones.

I'm not sure that I want to find out. "We need to get out of here. Head back toward home. We'll regroup and come back with reinforcements." I hear myself shout the orders and scramble to help Garnet to her feet. As we retreat, Vincent lunges at us. Something tackles him, preventing him from grabbing Garnet.

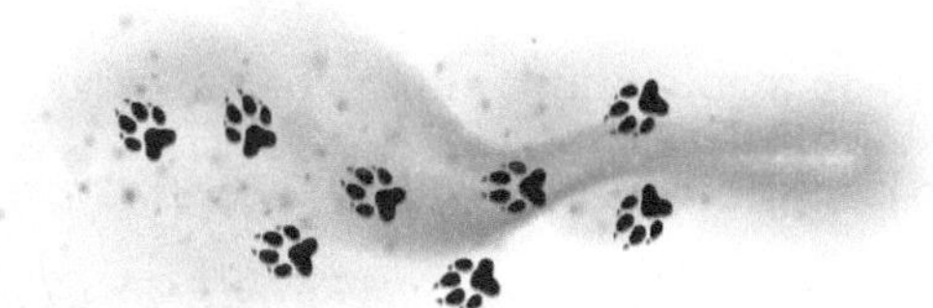

RYLAND

Everything happens so quickly. Orym will keep Red safe, but I have to stop Vincent. I see him lunge at my mate, and the world turns crimson. I dive at him, shifting in air. My body collides with his, rolling us both over a few times before we stop at the edge of the clearing.

My wolf instincts make me want to rip out his throat, but I know I can't do that. He's family now. I lay across him, flattening him to the ground with my weight, while I growl at him. He needs to understand that this behavior is not okay. He can't attack Red, even if he doesn't like her.

I think there's more to it than that, but I can't prove anything. I could shift and ask Orym for some rope to tie Vincent up, but that would allow him a chance to get away. And I refuse to do that. There has to be another way.

Red. Ask Orym if he has rope. We need to tie Vincent up to stop him from attacking. I need enough for a muzzle and to hog tie his legs. I throw the request along our bond, but silence greets me. I turn my head and look for her.

I see them retreating further into the forest. But why wouldn't she respond? It doesn't make sense. She's the one who got after me for ignoring her when she talks to me this way. I watch for another minute and realize that something is wrong here. It's too quiet. Just like the day I got sidetracked in the forest. And the day when Red was being chased by something.

Fuck, I'm in trouble here, and have no one to ask for help. Well, if I'm on my own, I have to fight whatever this is. First, I need to snap Vincent out of this trance he's in. I bite his leg hard, and he submits. I growl until he starts to shift back to his human form. "You fucking bit me, you asshole. I'll have you locked up for this, Ryland."

When I'm sure he's back to himself, I shift back as well. I don't let go of him, but my grip is looser than it was. "I had to snap you out of their control, you idiot. Did you willingly let them take over your mind?"

He looks at me blankly. "I don't know what you're talking about."

"Someone here was controlling you. They were making you attack us. You've been gone for a couple of days now, and your father is worried. He sent us to find you and bring you home." Even as I say the words, I know he's going to argue.

"My father sent you to find me? Really? Well, here I am. I guess we can go home now. Then you can explain to me how I got this far into the forest without knowing what was happening." Ever the dick, Vincent is only concerned with himself.

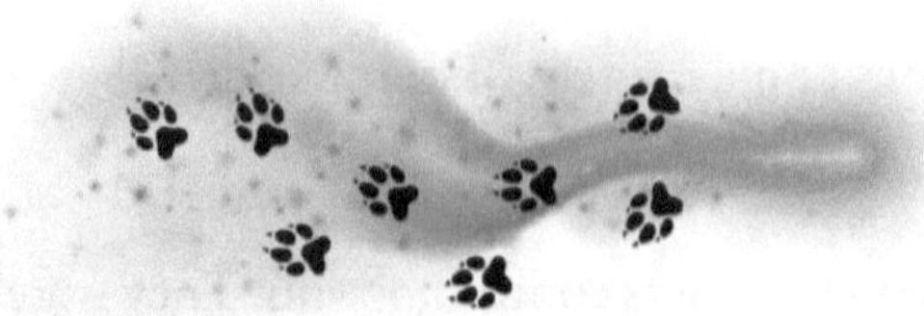

GARNET

I watch as magic bombs erupt around us. I have an over-whelming urge to protect my mates when I see a faint shimmer of magic encase us in a bubble. How did that happen? When a burst of blue magic bounces off the shield, I relax a little. At least we're safe here. But where is Ryland? And what happened to Vincent?

Orym asks us to head back home, and I don't hesitate. A noise gets my attention behind us as we turn to leave. I see Ryland tackle Vincent to keep him from biting onto my leg. "We have to go back for him," I insist as Orym drags me away from the fighting.

"We can't. He'll meet up with us when we get somewhere safe. I'll come back for him as soon as I can," he tells me.

Ryland! Please come with us. It's not safe out there. I scream the words in my head, but I can tell that he can't hear me. This is a huge mess. What if something happens to him? I would never forgive myself for leaving him behind.

As we dash through the woods, I keep an eye behind us for Ry. Instead of him, we run into someone else. The raven-haired woman who stands in front of us looks familiar, even though I'm sure I've never met her.

James steps forward and greets her. "Amber."

"James, it's nice to see you, though this situation is not ideal," she replies. I look from her to him and back again. Could this be an ex-girlfriend? I have to admit, I don't know as much about my mate as I'd like to.

"Amber, I'd like to introduce you to my mate, Garnet, and her other mates, Orym and Luca. Ryland is dealing with Vincent right now." James gestures to each of us as he makes introductions. Surprise crosses Amber's features before her expression goes neutral again. For a moment, I think she recognizes me. But how could she when I'm certain we've never met?

"It's lovely to meet you all. If you'll follow me, I'll take you somewhere safe."

I hesitate for a moment, then hear James' voice in my head. *It's okay, Garnet. She's on the council with me.* I relax a little, but keep my guard up as we follow her. I hope that Ryland finds us soon. I hate that we're leaving him behind.

Luca and Amber chat easily about our situation. He apparently feels comfortable telling her everything. I guess I shouldn't be upset about it, since James seems to trust her too. I find it hard to trust anyone right now.

"I understand that you weren't coming into our territory to start a war. I was not aware that there were more wolves and vampires missing than the ones we already knew about. And I had no idea that a coven in my territory was involved. I will definitely be investigating this." Her anger is palpable, and I hope that she means what she's saying.

But I don't know her, and I can't take her at face value. Not right now. But I can't afford not to follow her. She leads us to a cabin even further into her territory. "Please, come inside. This is my home, and you'll be safe here."

"What about Ry? I don't see him anywhere." I can feel my chest tighten as my heart starts to race.

Orym pulls me into his arms and holds me tightly. "It's okay. If he's not here in an hour, I'll go look for him. I promise this is going to be okay."

Amber leads us into the living room. "Please make yourselves at home. I'll get you all something to eat." She walks away, leaving us alone.

"I'm worried about this. Are you sure we can trust her?" I whisper to my mates.

"I don't think we have a choice," Luca answers.

"I've never had a problem with her on the council," James adds.

"I don't know. But we have to trust someone, or we'll be stuck here and captured like the others," Orym explains.

Well, at least it seems like they're not sure about her either. After she brings us food and shows us to a bedroom we can stay in, Orym decides to go looking for Ry.

"You should tell them about your nightmare while I'm gone." I look at him, confused. "I know you were having one just before Vincent showed up. Try to remember what happened in it and tell James and Luca about it."

"How did you know?" I ask.

He presses a kiss to my temple. "You were crying out in your sleep, and you distanced yourself from everyone. I'll be back as soon as I find him." I pull him down and kiss him.

After he leaves, Luca and James look at me expectantly. "What?" I ask, feeling self-conscious.

"Are you going to tell us about it?" Luca prods.

"Fine, but it was exactly the same as the last one." I think that will be enough, but he stares at me until I give him every detail of the dream, just like I did last time. Nothing is different. I explain it all again, though, just to keep him happy.

"Okay, well, at least it's not changing anymore. That's probably a good thing. We'll figure out what everything means. Let's focus on getting through this first." James takes my hand as he talks.

"I can agree with that. I don't want to think about those dreams anymore right now anyway. I wish they'd go away." I know that getting upset about it won't change anything. I take a deep breath and relax against the headboard while James and

Luca settle in on either side of me. "Is it bad that I don't want to sleep because I know the dream will come back?"

"We understand how you're feeling, even if we don't understand the dreams," James says.

ELEVEN

FINDING RYLAND

RYLAND

I WATCH AS THE others escape while I maintain my hold on Vincent. He doesn't struggle, which is good. "We need to follow them, but quietly." I hold his bicep as I practically drag him with me into the thick brush ahead.

Since he's no longer being controlled, he's actually more cooperative than usual. I'm not sure how I feel about it. If the witches are able to control wolves, how will we defend against that? I wait until the sounds of the forest are normal again to ask. "Can you tell me what happened to you?"

He looks at me as if I've grown a second head. "What are you talking about?" Well, this will be fun. I wonder if whatever control spell they used has a memory eraser portion to it.

"How did you get out here in the witches' territory? Gunnar said you were training but never came home. That was a few days ago," I explain.

Vincent still looks confused. "I was training. Then, I don't know, I remember waking up with you on top of me out here. That's it."

Fuck. This is bad. We need to catch up to the others before Vincent and I get captured. I reach out to Red again through the bond. *Red, love, can you hear me?* I don't expect a response, so we keep walking.

Her voice in my head catches me off guard. *Ry? Are you okay? Orym went to find you and bring you to us. Look for him.* I pull Vincent along with me and pick up my pace.

We're okay for now. I think we've gotten away from the fighting. Vincent doesn't remember anything. It's not safe for us out here. I can't track you guys for some reason. It had to be a magical barrier that went up around them and blocked us from talking. But how? The witches were attacking us, not protecting us.

Relief washes over me when Red starts to think about the path they took to the cabin they're in. I relax a little more when James' thoughts creep in as well. I never thought I'd miss sharing head space with him. "Come on, Vincent, this way," I order, still dragging him along.

A few yards ahead, I see Orym heading toward us. I duck behind a tree, worried that he's been compromised. It would be easier to tell if Red had just sealed the bond with him and Luca already. I'll have to talk to her about that later.

I peer around the tree we're hiding behind and I can tell that he's seen me too. I wait for him to catch up to us. "Ryland, are you okay?" My eyes rove over him, checking to see if there's any indication of witches controlling him.

"We're good. Were you followed?"

He shakes his head and looks at Vincent. "Is he okay?"

"He's not being controlled anymore, if that's what you're asking," I reply.

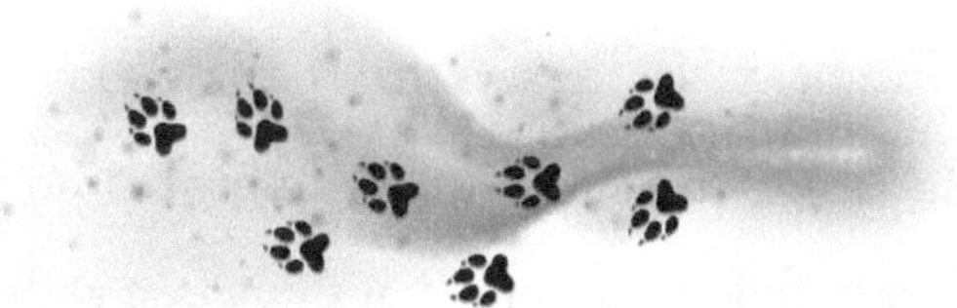

JAMES

The moment I'm able to connect with Ryland again, I sigh. He's annoying and frustrating, but he's ours. Hmm, I think I'll come back to that thought later. Best to focus on getting everyone back in the same location as quickly as possible.

I think about the path we took to get to Amber's cabin and send him the directions. Once I'm sure he's heading the right way, I explain to Luca that Garnet is talking to Ryland and that he's on his way with Vincent in tow.

That means that half of our mission is complete. He saved Garnet's brother. Now we just have to figure out how to save the rest of the wolves and the vampires who are being held here. I believe Amber when she says that she didn't know about this, but it makes me wonder about her ability to lead her people if they refuse to follow the rules that she, along with the council, laid out for them.

Being part of that council, though, means I have to show her respect. And I will. But I will also protect my mate from any of the witches here, including Amber. That is the one thing I will not compromise on. Garnet's safety is my number one priority.

I leave Luca to keep Garnet calm while she waits for Orym to get back with Ryland and Vincent. I should talk to Amber and find out exactly what's going on here. I don't know how we're getting out of this territory, or if there will be repercussions for us being here at all.

I find her in the library, a small room off the kitchen with bookshelves lining the walls. She's sitting on the floor with books spread out around her. There's a notebook in her lap and she appears to be taking notes from four different books at once. "Is this a bad time?" I ask, startling her.

"Oh, James. You scared me a bit. Of course, please, have a seat and we can chat." She gestures to a chair just inside the door. I step over her books and sit.

"What are you working on?" I glance over her and look at the books. Some of the pages are in English, but others are written in strange symbols that look a lot like what Garnet drew on Ryland's wall.

"Well, with what just happened, I figured I should consult my tomes and see if there's anything I can do to help. I meant it when I said that I didn't know what was going on. Witch law is very cut and dried about this. I will issue a statement, and they will be compelled to return the people that have been taken. If they don't comply, well, that's what I'm looking at now. I need to know my options." Her face looks pained, and I want to offer my help.

"Could this start a war?" I hate having that thought, but it's echoed on her face.

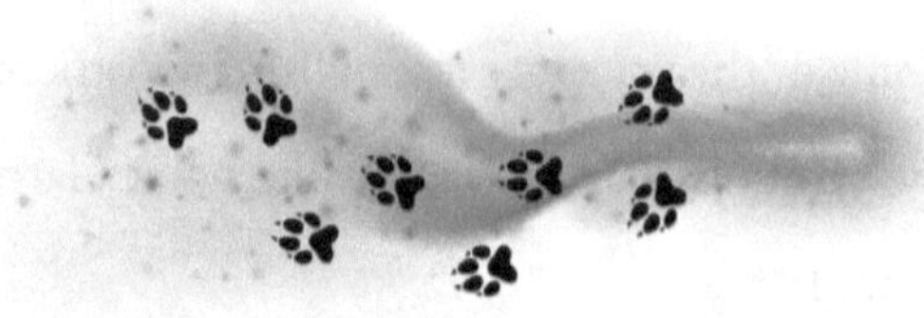

GARNET

I'm so relieved to hear Ry in my head that I start to cry. James has to take over giving him directions, and I sit back, listening to them while Luca holds me. Annoyance washes over me when James leaves the room to talk to Amber. Then I realize that I'm jealous. I don't want my mate talking to another female. It's ridiculous, especially since James isn't interested in her that way.

I snuggle closer to Luca. "I'm not good at this."

"At what?" he asks, rubbing my arm.

"At having mates. At being a wolf. Pretty much everything right now. This curse is vicious."

He presses a kiss to my temple. "Red, you are exactly who you're supposed to be. I told you before, I don't think you're a wolf at all. I don't think you're cursed. I just haven't figured out what you are yet."

I turn in his arms to look at him. I don't understand his insistence that I'm something other than a cursed wolf. "What makes you think I'm not a wolf who's cursed?"

"Don't take this the wrong way, but you don't exactly fit in with the rest of us," he says. While the words could hurt, I understand that they're true. I have never fit in with the wolves. I always thought it was because I was cursed.

I must make a face, because he holds up his hands in defense. "Red, I've loved you since we were kids. That was not meant to hurt you. Part of what drew me to you was that you're different. There's nothing wrong with that."

"So, you think I'm human like James?" It wouldn't be the worst thing if I was. I ponder the implications of that for a minute before Luca speaks again.

"I don't know. I think there's more to you than that. Nothing wrong with being human, either, I just don't think you are."

Before I can respond, James opens the door. "Amber needs to talk to you," he says. I can tell from his face that he knows what we've been talking about, and that he has an opinion that he's keeping to himself for now.

It should bother me, but it doesn't. He'll tell me when he's ready. Luca scoops me into his arms and carries me into the living room where Amber is waiting for us. My cheeks heat at her gaze. "Being taken care of by your mates is nothing to be embarrassed about." Her words make me even more self-conscious.

Luca sits on the couch with me on his lap. James sits next to us and takes my hand. "What's this all about?"

"I realized as I was doing some research that there are things you don't know, Garnet, and I would like to help you with that," Amber says.

"I'm not sure I follow." I can't express how confused I am by all of this. How could Amber have answers to questions I haven't asked?

"I understand your hesitation. Don't worry, I'm not offended. I really just want to help. Until I spoke with James on the matter, I thought you were aware. He's indicated that you don't know the things I thought you did. Let me start at the beginning," she pauses, takes a deep breath, then continues. "The witches of the Whispering Thicket have always kept ourselves separate from everyone else. Our territory is spelled so that only witches and their companions are able to enter."

"But we walked right in with no problems," I insist.

She nods at me. "I know. And since we know none of your mates are witches, what does that tell you?" Amber stares at me expectantly. I know what she wants me to say, but it can't be true. Can it?

"That's not possible. Besides, there are wolves and vamps in the woods here as well. How do you explain that?" I know that I'm being defensive, but I can't stop myself.

"Garnet, it's okay to be scared. This is a very new idea, and I sprang it on you with no warning. The wolves and vamps would have been brought in by witches. That's how they got through the defenses. But you five came on your own. There is no way any of you should have been able to get through the boundaries without a witch accompanying you."

My jaw drops in disbelief. "I'm not a witch. I'm a wolf. I just can't shift." I let the argument fade as I think about her words. Could she be telling the truth? How is this possible?

"I understand that you think that's true. I can assure you that it is not, though. I do sense a binding spell on your powers, but it's not strong enough. James told me about the shield you created in the forest before you got to me." She holds up a hand when I start to protest. "Yes, it was you. You protected your mates."

"But I don't understand. How can I be a witch? I grew up in wolf territory," I protest.

"I don't know the details, but I can tell you what I suspect, if you'd like," she offers. I nod, and she holds up a book. "This book holds the details of all the births and deaths of our coven over the past hundred years. In it, there is a listing for a baby girl born under the full moon. The details are incomplete for this listing, but the baby disappeared."

"Maybe you should ask the mother about her," I suggest.

"I would happily do that, but Ruby disappeared as well. I can't say if she's alive or not. All I know is that she is no longer in the forest."

"Wait, so, you're telling me that I'm the missing daughter of this missing witch? I don't understand what makes you think that." I know that she's right, even as I protest. I don't understand how I know, but I do.

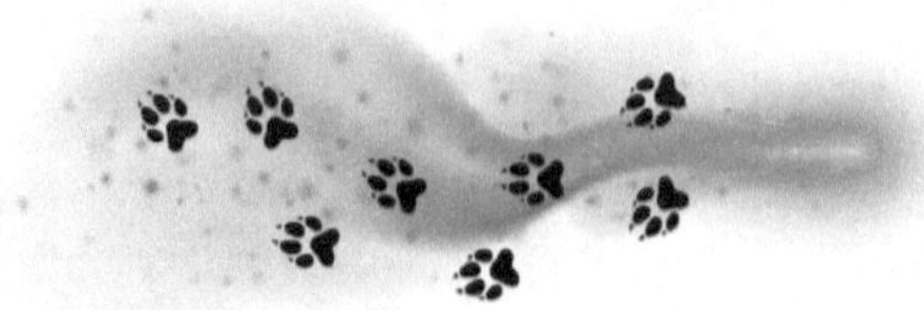

LUCA

Amber's revelation doesn't surprise me. I've suspected as much for a while now. I wasn't planning to spring the news on Red like this, but she needed to know. I'd been doing research for a while and had spoken with Eli about it. He has resources no one else had access to, and even he couldn't find proof.

"Yes, my dear, that's exactly what I'm saying. I knew Ruby, and you look a lot like her. I must admit, I didn't know that she had a baby. Of course, I was young then, and there are ways to hide such things." Amber's words are quiet but hold the weight of truth.

I hold up a hand. "I think we should talk this through as much as we can before Orym gets back with Ryland and Vincent." Red turns and gives me a puzzled look. "Yes, we need to tell them, but Vincent doesn't need to know. At least not yet."

"Oh. I hadn't thought of that," Red whispers. I ease her onto the couch between James and myself.

"How do you feel about this, Garnet?" James asks her, kissing the back of her hand for reassurance.

She doesn't speak for a long moment, and I'm afraid that she's talking to him in their heads again. It's another reason we should complete the bond as soon as possible. We would be able to have those private conversations easier.

"I don't know. I can't say she's wrong. There is something about this forest that feels like home. And I knew the minute we walked in that this place was different from the wolf territory. I just didn't understand what I was feeling. Did I really create that barrier? I don't understand how it happened," she says.

"In times of great stress or fear, a witch can do magic without thinking about it, or even without any training. I would like to teach you about your magic. That would involve removing the binding spell, and spending some time together. If you're not interested, I won't push the issue," Amber offers.

It's very nice of her, but I wonder what she has to gain from helping Red. It's obvious that my mate is confused about everything. Her allegiance is still with the wolves, though. I wonder how this news will change her relationship with Gunnar. So many things make much more sense now. He treated her differently because he knew she wasn't his. Grammy defended her because she'd been the one to bring her into our territory.

Amber offers more information, and Red asks a few questions. I ask Red to find out how close Ryland, Orym, and Vincent are, so we know when to cut off this conversation. Just before they arrive, Amber gives Red a book. It's a handwritten journal that had belonged to her mother, Ruby. Inside, there are a few pictures of Ruby and some spells, along with stories. It was clear that she meant the book for her child.

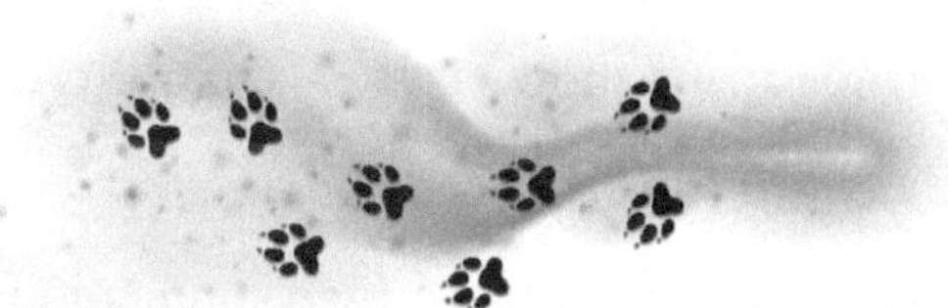

ORYM

Ryland starts acting strange as we get closer to the cabin. "Are you okay?" I ask. He tightens his grip on Vincent and nods.

"I'm just anxious to get back home. This forest gives me the creeps." I'm not sure I believe him, but I don't argue. The cabin is ten feet away and we close the distance quickly. When we enter, I can tell that they've been having a conversation that they don't want all of us to know about. Interesting. I'll have to get Garnet alone and find out what that's about. I wonder if Ryland knows already.

I won't push her to bond with me before she's ready, but that connection would definitely come in handy right now. "Why don't you get your mates settled in while I fix Vincent something to eat and show him to his room?" Amber offers. I expect Garnet to argue, but she nods.

Luca and James stay behind for a moment after she leads us into the bedroom that's been loaned to us. Garnet turns to us and pulls Ryland and me into her arms. It's only a little uncomfortable. I guess I'm warming up to him now.

"What's going on? I could tell that you all stopped talking when we came in," I say quietly.

"I'll explain in just a moment. Luca wanted to check on Vincent and James needed a moment with Amber. I won't lie—it's a lot to take in, and I don't know how either of you will feel about me when the story is told." Her ominous words scare me a little. What could she possibly say that would change how I feel about her?

Luca and James join us and close the door. "He has no idea how he got into the forest. I still don't want to discuss this in front of him," Luca explains.

Ryland looks as confused as I feel. "I could have told you that he has no idea what's going on. What is going on?"

Everyone turns to Garnet. "Let's all sit down and I'll explain." She waits for us to pile onto the bed. We sit in a circle, facing her. "Amber just informed us that—I didn't expect this to be so hard to say—I'm not a wolf shifter. I'm a witch who disappeared shortly after birth. My mother apparently disappeared around the same time. I have no idea who my father really is. But that shield earlier? That was me. I don't know how it happened and I have no idea why I believe her. I just know that Amber is telling the truth."

I look at Luca and James, then turn to Ryland. None of them look surprised by this revelation. How can Garnet be a witch? I guess it's not so farfetched, if you consider that she's never had the same abilities as the rest of us. And she's clearly not human. But what does this mean for us?

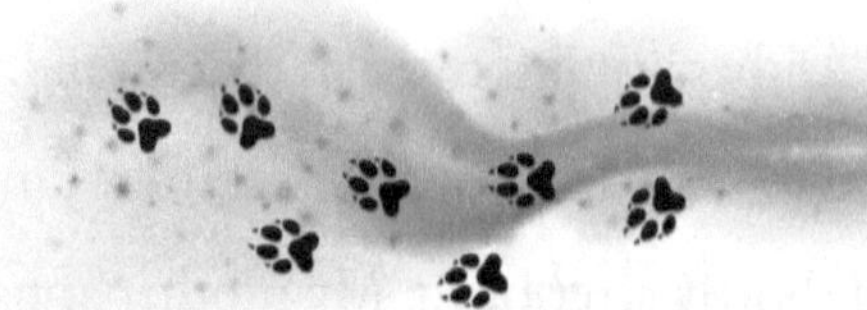

GARNET

I watch my mates as they process the bomb I just dropped on them. I wouldn't be surprised if Orym or Ry wanted to run from me. Luca and James have already told me that they're with me no matter what. And I guess this news changes everything. I had expected to fight with Father over being mated to

James. He'll still be angry, but since he's not really my father, I guess it doesn't matter much anymore.

How could Grammy lie to me for my entire life? I don't know if I can ever trust her again. Although this does explain why she made Luca hide the writing from me and why they convinced me it was all just a bad dream.

After my mates are settled, I'll have to talk to Amber again. I need to explain the dreams and show her the symbols. Maybe she'll know what they mean. For now, I have to find out what all this means to my mates. I've already started falling in love with them, and it would rip my heart out to lose any of them right now.

"Garnet, it wouldn't matter to me if you were human, a witch, a vamp, or a shifter. I care about you, and I'm not going anywhere. Bonded or not, you're mine—well, ours." Orym's sweet words bring tears to my eyes. I want to complete the bond, but I'm scared.

"Thank you. I needed to hear that. But if everyone doesn't feel the same, I promise I'll understand," I say quietly. I'm waiting for Ry to process this so he can tell me what he thinks. I can't seem to get into his head right now to hear his thoughts. From the look on his face and the way James glares at him, I'm fairly certain they're arguing.

"I can't say that I'm thrilled, but I'm not going anywhere. Orym's right; you're ours. And I won't give that up just because you're not a wolf." Ry says the words with more passion than I expect. I wonder what James said to him, but I won't ask.

"I think we should discuss something else, Red. Orym and I are at a disadvantage here. I think you should at least consider bonding with us. It would make the pack stronger. We would all be connected and able to communicate no matter what. I'm not pressuring you. I just want you to think about it," Luca insists.

"I have been thinking about it. And I know it's not fair. I'm just not ready yet. Please don't think that means you're less important to me. I just can't do it yet," I whisper. I feel like an ass because I'm denying two of my mates, but I can't make myself complete the bond yet. What if this is what pushes them away? Fuck, I need to get this figured out. "I just need a little more time. I have to adjust to everything we've learned today."

Orym takes my hand. "Garnet, it's okay. No one is going to make you do anything you're not ready for. Of course, Luca and I want to bond with you. But we will wait as long as it takes for you to be ready."

Luca starts to protest, but James stops him. "If we have to be separated at all, we'll make sure that one bonded mate is with one unbonded. That way we can all talk to Garnet. Is that a fair compromise?"

Luca nods, but I can see the disappointment in his eyes. I know that he's upset with me now, and I can't blame him. I'm upset with me too. I should just give in and complete the bond with them. But I'm terrified that I won't be able to handle all those voices in my head at once.

We talk for a bit longer before a knock sounds at the door. Orym slips off the bed and answers it, letting Amber inside. "I just wanted to see how everyone is processing your news. Vincent is settled into another guest room. I gave him a little something to help him sleep. It will also clear out the last of the mind control potion or spell that was holding him."

"I guess we're just stunned," Orym admits. "You're certain that Garnet is this missing witch? This is a lot to work through. What happens next?"

"I'm certain, though I guess we could insist on DNA tests to confirm that Gunnar isn't actually her father. Although, I don't want to be the person who asks him for that. I've seen his temper at council meetings, and would not enjoy being on the receiving end of that." The flippant way she says it pisses me off a bit.

"Where do we go from here? Provided that I've decided I believe you and once I've had time to look through my mother's journal," I ask, not giving her time to finish answering Orym's questions.

"I'd like to teach you how to use your magic. Your gifts may be completely different from any we've seen. Like I said before, I didn't know your mother personally, but I know of her powers. Without knowing who your father is, it's hard to say what powers you got. However, Ruby was a powerful witch. She was able to control the elements and would have been the territory leader if she hadn't disappeared."

"So, do you think someone took her out so she wouldn't be in charge?" Luca asks. If that's the case, I may be in more danger than we originally expected.

"It's possible. I also don't think you should tell anyone that you know about this. If someone took Ruby out, that would put a target on Garnet. And it seems as if she's already being targeted as a wolf. We don't want to make things worse."

I agree with Amber's suggestion, but I'm not sure how I feel about her teaching me magic.

Twelve

EMBRACING THE NEW ME

LUCA

WE SPEND THE NEXT few days distracting Vincent while Red trains with Amber. The four of us split our time between the two, so that Red is never alone with Amber. Whoever is keeping watch stays out of ear shot, but close enough to watch.

It's strange to see Red creating bursts of magic from thin air, but somehow it feels right. And she's really good at it, too. I think Amber has started to pressure her about our mate bond. I agree that she needs to complete it as soon as possible, but if she's not ready, there's no way to force it.

Every night, Red is exhausted and sleeps soundly. Every day, she wakes early and gets started. She trains her body as much as her magic. The five of us learn to work together as a team, our movements seamless and coordinated. After physical training, and magic training, she settles in to study Amber's books and her mother's journal. I can tell that she's upset that she'll never know her mom.

Each of us tries to help her as much as we can with studying and practicing. Amber arranges for Vincent to go home, having a couple of her trusted friends escort him. Once we're sure he's safely back home with Gunnar, we refocus on Red's training and figuring out how to save the other kidnapped people.

Amber's friends come back two days after dropping Vincent off. They bring us a package from Eli. Inside, it has new cell phones with boosted signal capabilities and a note explaining that he's already transferred everything over. All I have to do is turn each one on and it tells me who it belongs to. I love when he sends new tech. Now that we have phones that actually work this deep in the forest, we're less worried about staying as close together.

I'm still not ready to leave Red completely alone with Amber or anyone for that matter, but I'm not as worried about being ambushed. While Red trains with Amber, I call Kayden and give him an update. I'm leaving Gunnar to Orym. If I talk to him, I'll blow up and that won't help anyone. I know that James has been in touch with his brother as well.

"I don't know what we're going to do exactly. We have to find where they're holding the wolves and vamps before we can do anything. I'm sure we'll need backup, but that will have to be arranged through Amber, since this is her territory."

Kayden sighs loudly. "I figured as much. I'll have Vik talk to her. With them both being on the council, there may be some policy on this kind of thing. I'm sure if she's helping Red train, that she'll help us get our people back. Don't worry about it, Luca, we'll figure it out."

"Have you talked to Gunnar recently? Orym is calling him today."

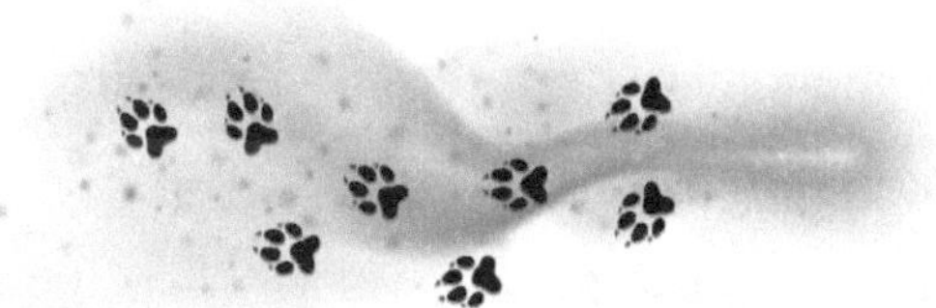

RYLAND

I know that I've been a dick to Red lately because I'm jealous of her other mates. I shouldn't be, and I'm working on it with James' help. Part of my penance is to be her practice dummy and let her shoot magic blasts at me as I run by in either my human or wolf form. Her aim is getting better, and Amber now has her attacking and splitting focus to shield me at the same time.

I get hit by a blast as Amber distracts Red. It throws me onto my side and slams me into a tree. I lay there for a minute as the pain courses through me. That one hurt. I should be happy about that because it means she's getting stronger. Instead, I'm annoyed that Amber distracted her so I'd get hit. My annoyance fades a moment later when Red races across the clearing and pulls me into her arms.

"Are you okay, Ry? I'm so sorry. I promise I'll work harder. I'll get this. I can do it." She's rambling, so I pull her down and crash my mouth to hers.

When I let her ease away from me, we're both breathless. "I'm fine. You just knocked the wind out of me, that's all. You're getting stronger."

"But I didn't mean to throw you against that tree. I was trying to shield you while I tossed stuff at you. I just can't split my focus like that. I need to work harder," she insists.

"I understand why you feel that way. I'm fine, I promise. Let's go again," I demand as I get to my feet. I still feel a little wobbly, but I won't tell her that. Instead, I force myself to shift, then nudge her with my head until she goes back to her spot.

I shake off my uneasy feeling and race by her again, not bothering to pay attention to if she's trying to split her focus. I won't make myself an easy target, but I'm not running full speed either. When she shoots a burst at me, I shift back and slide out of the way. I glance over my shoulder at her and continue to dodge.

I don't stop until I'm sure she's got her confidence back. I can't have her hesitating when she's being attacked. And Amber has decided that will be tomorrow's lesson. I stroll over and listen as she explains the strategy to Red.

"Tomorrow, I'll attack you while you attack him. You'll have to bounce between offensive and defensive pretty quickly, or risk getting hit. I won't use full power, but if I hit you, it will hurt. I need you to be mentally ready for it. After that exercise, we'll focus on learning how to control a new element. You're doing well with air and water. I'm thinking we'll add in earth tomorrow and see how it goes. Fire is the most challenging, so I'm saving it for last."

Red nods in agreement.

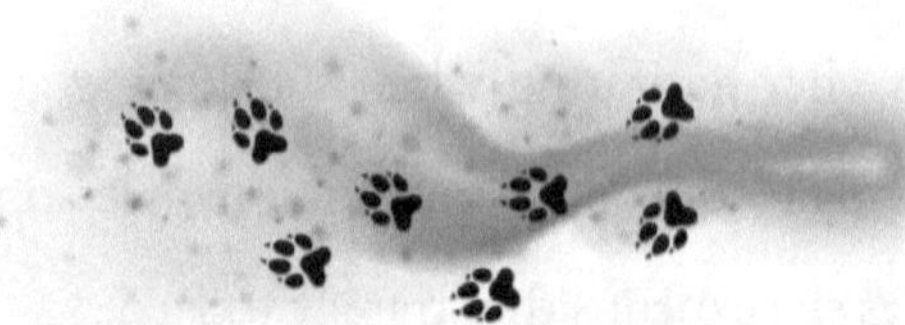

GARNET

The training schedule with Amber is intense. I've learned so much over a few short days. I feel like I'm not spending much time with any of my guys, and that makes me a little sad. They all swear that it's okay, but since I'm not even really sure what I'm training for, it doesn't make sense to me.

When Amber isn't training me, she's pressuring me about completing the bond with Orym and Luca. I've tried asking her what she knows that we don't, but she never admits anything. She's hiding something, I'm sure of it. But I have no idea what.

All I can do is absorb as much knowledge from her and the books she gives me access to while watching my back and listening to everything. I've tried to explain my fears to the guys, but James is convinced that she's helping us. I can't tell how the other three feel about her, and haven't had any real time alone with them to ask.

I spend my mornings training with Orym, Luca, or Ry—jogging, pull ups, hand-to-hand combat. Then my afternoons are with Amber, learning how to use the magic that I didn't even know I had. There's no denying that I'm a witch, not after some of the things she's taught me how to do. I can shoot lightning from my hands, push clouds across the sky, and create a vortex of water. It all scares me more than I can admit.

She claims that I'm much more powerful than she is, or than any other witch she knows. I have no idea how that's possible. No one has any idea of who my father could be, so there's no way to know if that's a factor. All I really know is that my power seems to be growing every day. I can do things that Amber claims she can't do, and that's pretty intimidating.

I struggle to master the elements, even though I can use them. Just when I think I'm learning how to split my focus to be able to attack and defend at the same time, I drop my shields or miss with my attacks. I did great for three days, then could not figure anything out. "Is burnout a thing?"

"You might be pushing too hard. Let's take the rest of the day off and relax. We can try again in the morning," Amber offers.

"We can treat you to a spa day, love," James insists. I can't help thinking that he should have asked Amber first, since we'll have to raid her supplies to do it. I've been reading about relaxation in relation to magic use.

"I have the ingredients set aside for a calming bath and a facial treatment." Amber holds up a hand. "I can see your concern on your face. I'm sure I have everything you need."

Well, I guess I don't have to worry about that now. "Thank you," I reply, letting James lead me back to the cabin.

"You relax here while I draw you a bath," he orders, nudging me toward the couch. "I'll even let you read while you wait." He motions to Luca, who brings me my mother's journal and the notebook I've been using to jot things down.

"I'll even keep you company," Luca offers, dropping to the couch next to me.

"I feel like you guys coordinated this way too easily for it to be a last-minute decision." I glare at them both.

At least James has enough sense to look embarrassed. "We were just trying to help," he defends.

"I appreciate that, but how long ago did you set this up?" I ask.

Ry walks in before they can answer me. "Two weeks. They've been planning this since we got here." He grabs an apple and joins me on the couch, giving James a chance to slip away.

"Where's Orym? I thought you two were training this morning while I worked with Amber."

He bites into the apple before answering. "He's around here somewhere." I swear that these guys are up to something, and I want to know what it is.

"What are you four up to?" I ask accusingly.

"We're just trying to take care of you, that's all," Orym says innocently as he walks into the cabin. I roll my eyes at him, but he scoops me off the couch and spins me around, then kisses me.

"Turn your brain off for a bit and let us take care of you. Then you can go back to worrying about everything." James appears in the room again and I jump, even though Orym is still holding me.

He passes me to Luca who carries me into the suite we've been living in since we got here. As soon as he sets me on my feet, Orym, Ry, and James are there. The four of them take their time stripping me down and for a minute, I think that we're going to have some fun.

Then, instead of holding me or touching me, the four of them lower me into the steaming tub. Alone. "What's going on here? I thought this was going another way."

"That might be fun, but it won't help you relax," Orym laughs.

Even with my protests, none of them will get into the tub with me. Luca starts washing my hair, while James picks up a cloth and washes my feet. Orym and Ry stand back as if they're waiting until it's their turn. The whole thing is way more erotic than it should be. My body hums at the sensations coursing through it.

When James and Luca are finished, Orym and Ry take their places and begin to wash my body. I want more than they're giving me, but no matter what I do, they refuse to let things progress the way I want. By the time the four of them are finished cleaning me, I'm relaxed but tense.

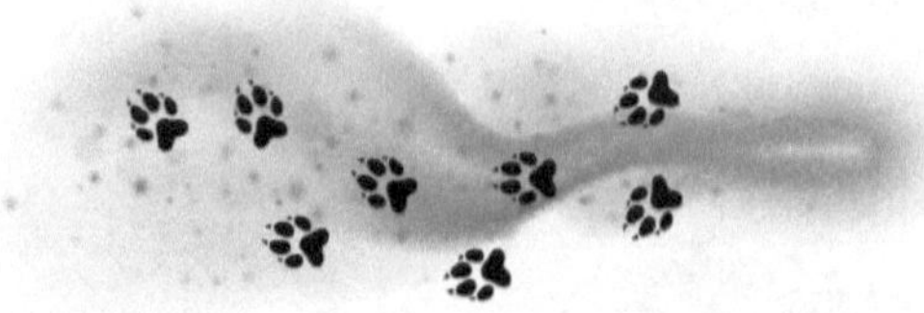

ORYM

I can tell that Garnet was not expecting to be pampered today. And I, for one, barely contained myself at the sight of her naked. It was all I could do to wash her and not try anything. As much as I want her, I will not force the mate bond on her.

She has her reasons for not wanting to complete it yet. I suspect that part of it is her distrust of Amber.

Even the raven-haired witch knows that Garnet doesn't fully trust her. And with good reason. We don't know this woman, and every effort I've made to learn about her has been met with avoidance. I have no idea how old she is or who she's related to. There is something familiar about her, though. I wouldn't be surprised to find out that she's related to Garnet somehow.

Once the pampering is done, we tuck our girl into bed with her books and notes. James offers to help her study, and Ryland actually decides to stay with them. Luca and I give her a quick kiss and leave with the intention to help Amber collect supplies and ingredients from her garden and the forest around her cabin. We don't have telepathic abilities, but I know as well as he does, that we're going to use this time to poke around and try to find out more about our witch benefactor.

"Amber?" I call out softly. She's not here. Hmm. I sniff, allowing my wolf senses to take over. "I don't think she's in the cabin."

Luca nods. "I'll keep an eye out if you want to look around." I knew he understood my plan. I'm not about to pass up time with my mate without good reason. I walk into the tiny library and start my search. I'm careful to put any books back where I found them. I'm not sure what I'm looking for, but I'll know it when I see it.

After a few minutes, I give up on the bookshelves. I turn my attention to the desk, sifting through papers that are under the open books there. Sure enough, there are notes on Garnet's progress and lists tracking what powers she's been able to use. Why would someone who's just training her need to keep this type of information?

I get Luca's attention and show him the papers. It's not exactly damning evidence of wrongdoing, but it is suspicious. I pull out my phone and scan each page. I know that Eli can figure out what this all means easier than we can, and he did offer to help. I've only talked to him on the phone, but Luca knows him and trusts him. That's good enough for me.

After the documents are sent to Eli, I flip through the birth book. There are listings for every family in the Whispering Thicket, not just witches. I find records for Luca, Ryland, and myself. Then I locate Amber's and my jaw drops. She lied.

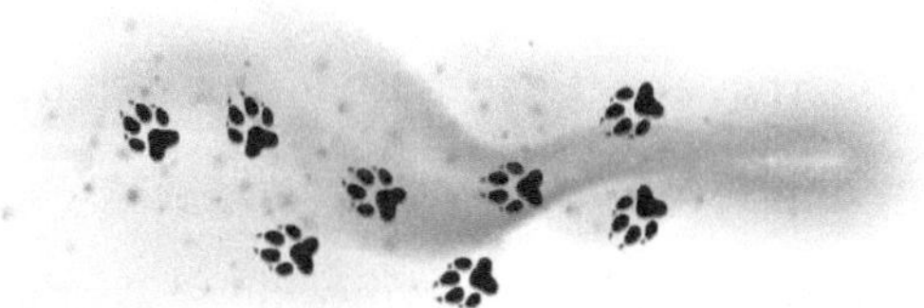

JAMES

It's hard not to give in to Garnet's advances while we're helping her bathe. But she doesn't need sex right now. She needs rest. I know that she's upset about her training going south today, and I don't want that to negatively impact her progress overall.

One bad day doesn't make you a failure, any more than one good day makes you a success. I need her to understand that.

So, I offer to help her study. We can talk about what she's reading and I can help her work out what it all means. I wish there was more I could do, but there isn't. I'm not a witch. I do think I'm the only one here who trusts Amber. She's a member of the council, and has done what she can here to help us. She even told Garnet about her mother. I don't understand why the others don't seem able to trust her.

An hour after they leave, Orym and Luca come back. "Red, you have to see this," Luca says, clearly upset.

"What?" she asks him. He hands her his phone, where he's taken photos of something. I glance over her shoulder. It's a book. Did he take pictures of one of Amber's books? That's not very polite behavior for house guests. "What is this?"

"It's proof that she lied to you. She knew your mother much more intimately than she admitted. If it's true, this means that she's your aunt," Orym explains. Wait, Amber is Garnet's aunt? Why would she lie about that?

"Why were you two snooping through our host's stuff? She hasn't done anything to make her seem untrustworthy," I insist, even though I know these four have never trusted her.

"I could tell she was hiding something. I wanted to know what it was. I can't trust someone as easily as you can, James," Orym growls. His tone is harsh, and I hate how defensive it makes me feel.

"I am on the council with her. She's an honored member. There's no reason not to trust her," I say, unsure if I'm trying to convince them or myself. Doubt creeps in, and suddenly I understand why Vik doesn't trust anyone on the council. Fuck. She lied to us. I'm not sure how to process this information.

Garnet looks at me. "James, it's okay. I understand that being on the council with her puts you in a difficult position. But I think this is enough evidence to prove that we shouldn't be here. The fact that she lied about my mother is bad. Add to that the pages of information she's keeping about each of us, and I just don't feel safe here anymore."

"We need to find the fastest route home. Wasn't she teaching you a tracking spell?" Ryland finally speaks. It's clear that he doesn't trust our host, either. I guess that makes five of us now.

"Oh, you're right. She did teach me that. I don't know if I can do it, though," Garnet says with a sigh.

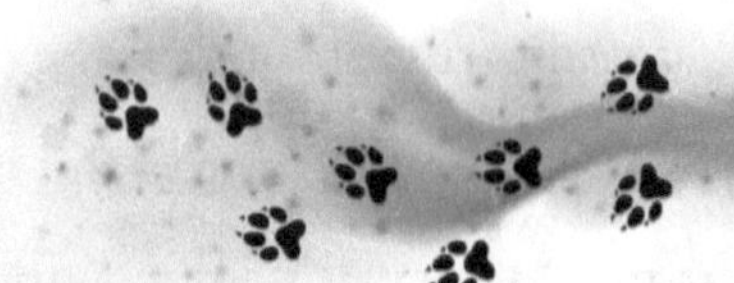

GARNET

Orym and Luca searched Amber's house to find evidence that she was lying to us. That's hard enough to process. But the fact that they actually found something to prove it, well, that's worse. She's my aunt. My mother's sister lied to me. She's still lying to me, because she's tracking my progress as if she's writing a report for someone else.

That's enough to get me moving. I pack up my clothes and the books that I've been using. I know that taking them is wrong, but I feel justified because I'm hurt. I'll make sure she gets them back when I'm finished. Perhaps Vik will return them to her at a future council meeting.

Or maybe she'll come to collect them herself, and I'll get a chance to ask her why she lied. But I already know why. She lied because she didn't think I'd trust her if she told me who she really is. And she might be right. The little bit she told me about my mother just made me want to know more. Now I can't help but wonder if she had something to do with her disappearance.

I still want to ask Grammy how I ended up being essentially adopted by Gunnar. But I'm not sure I want that answer. Because maybe Grammy knows more than she ever told me. Undoubtedly, she does, otherwise I would have known I wasn't a witch. Who can I actually trust? Is there anyone in my entire life who hasn't lied to me? I don't know. I guess that would only be my guys. As far as I know, none of them has lied to me.

I hate feeling like I can't trust anyone. As soon as we're packed, we head outside. I have no idea where Amber has gone, but I hope we don't run into her on our way out. I just want to go home. If only I knew where that really was. I shake the thought away as we walk around the back of the cabin. I have to do the tracking spell so we know which way to go.

"What am I tracking? It's usually a person, not a place. I'm not even sure I can do it at all," I admit, wringing my hands.

Each of my guys steps forward, surrounding me. "You can do this," Luca says.

"Take a deep breath and focus," Orym suggests.

"Just do your best," James offers.

Ry doesn't say anything, just takes my hand and squeezes. Somehow, knowing the four of them have so much faith in me helps. Maybe if I focus on the tree that stands in front of Ry's cabin, that will work better than focusing on the cabin itself. My studies here have shown me that plants and trees are more similar to people than I'd ever expected.

I take a deep breath and close my eyes, picturing the tree with Ry's cabin in the background. I can see every leaf, every root, every branch. And just like that, I have a path home. Or at least to Ry's place. I'm still not sure where home is, but this will work. We'll be safer there than here.

"This way," I tell them, opening my eyes and following the faint teal path that appears in front of me. "Can any of you see that?" Luca and Orym shake their heads, but Ry and James nod with wide eyes. That's an interesting benefit of the bond. "Follow that path, no matter what. It will take us back to Ry's cabin."

"They can see it because of the bond. That's amazing," Orym says. I feel a pang of guilt because I still haven't completed the bond with him or Luca. I should just give in and do it. But I don't want it to feel forced. And Amber has been pushing for me to do it, so I'm not sure I should yet. I need to do more research. Now that I know she can't be trusted, I don't want to do anything that she wants me to.

I keep my eyes open and focus on feeling for threats. I know I can throw up a shield around us as long as we stay close together. "Don't get too far away from me. I can't make a large shield, but I can protect us from magic attacks."

Ry and James respond in my head, and the other two nod. I wasn't planning to let Orym or Luca out of my sight since I can't talk to them the same way as the other two. Since they can see the path, James and Ry have taken the lead. I'm happy to let them, settling in between Luca and Orym as we walk.

I look from one to the other. "I know what you're thinking, and while I agree, I can't. Not yet. She was pushing for it too hard for that to be a coincidence. I need to know why first."

They both stare at me. "How did you know we were thinking about the bond?" Luca asks.

"Because you can't see the path, but they can," I answer.

Each of them takes one of my hands and we walk in silence for a while. Every few minutes, I close my eyes and focus on seeing the area around us. This isn't something Amber taught me, I just know that I can do it, even if I don't understand how. There are some things I just know and know how to do without any kind of training.

I guess they're natural abilities. Without knowing my mother or who my father is, I have no insight into those things. I decide just to go with my instincts and see how my magic fares. I hear something behind us and reach out again. Amber is trailing us. I can sense that she's upset, but doesn't know why we left.

THIRTEEN
AMBUSHED

JAMES

RYLAND AND I FOLLOW the path of magical energy Garnet
put out for us. This is all too much to process. How could

Amber lie to us? There has to be a reason. She can't be involved in the kidnapping of the wolves and vampires, can she? I've worked with her on the council for nearly a year now. I feel like I would have at least suspected some illegal activity. But I trusted her. With my life. And that of my mate.

I beat myself up mentally for not realizing there was something up with her. The forest is quiet here and I can't help thinking it's too quiet. But I'm not a wolf shifter, or a vamp, or a witch. I'm just a human, so I don't know if that means anything. Right now, I can't trust my instincts.

If I had, I would have seen the attack coming. Garnet is too focused on holding the spell that's showing us the path. Orym and Luca are distracted by the fact that Ryland and I can see the magic but they can't. When Ryland turns to me, I know what he's thinking. I'm sure it's because he sends the thought through the bond to Garnet and me.

We have to run. Now! I glance over my shoulder and watch as she realizes what he's said. She holds onto the other two and we all start to run. We're still following the path, but I know it's a bad idea. We're walking, or running, into a trap. Before I can express that thought, we hit an invisible barrier.

We're trapped. I stay where I am, pinned against this barrier as it closes around us. Ryland moves to the other side, where

I can see Amber strolling through the forest as if she doesn't have a care in the world. "Let us go," he growls.

"I don't understand what's happening here," she says. Even though she's trying to sound hurt, I can hear the malice in her voice. I was wrong to trust this woman, and I can clearly see that now.

"What do you want with us?" I ask.

"I want to train Garnet, of course. I've told you that. I only want to help," she insists.

"Then let us go home," Garnet says, drawing Amber's attention to herself. "If you want to help, let us go home. That's what we need right now."

"I should have known you couldn't be trusted alone in my home. What a bunch of nosey people you are." She pauses and looks at Orym. "I have my library spelled. I can see exactly what anyone touches at any time. I know exactly which books our little witchling has read, and which ones you nosed through today."

"Amber, he only did that for me. I asked him to find me a new book, but couldn't remember the title. He was looking for it when he went through things," Garnet declares.

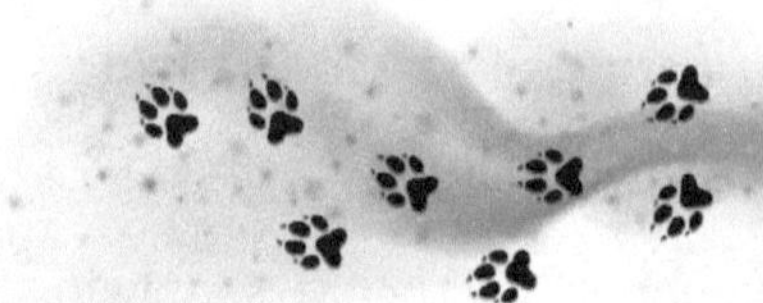

ORYM

I'm not worried about Amber being angry with me for searching her library. I suspected that she would know. That was
part of the reason I went along with Garnet's plan to leave so
suddenly. I thought we could get out of the witches' territory

before Amber caught up to us. Obviously, I was wrong. With the barrier blocking our way, we're stuck.

Garnet tries to pull Amber's attention away from me, but it only works for a moment. "Exactly what did you find, Orym?" she asks. She already knows the answer, but I won't tell her. "You can tell me now, or I can torture it out of you."

I feel her magic wrap around me and squeeze. It's hard to breathe and I can see Garnet's reaction. "I'm okay," I whisper to her.

"But you're really not," Amber smirks as her magic tightens around me. If she keeps going this way, my ribs will crack and I'll risk a punctured lung. "Now, if you were to tell me exactly what you said to your girlfriend to make her run away from me like she's scared, I'd be more likely to let you go."

"You already know what he found. *Aunt Amber.* Don't you?" Garnet snarls at her, and the admission of her title is enough to make Amber let me go. I drop to my knees, panting to catch my breath. James kneels beside me, checking for broken bones.

"Is that what upset you so much? I didn't tell you about our familial connection. You weren't ready to hear it. I took you in and protected you. I taught you how to use your magic, and this is how you repay me? By snooping through my things and running away. That's not very nice." Anger floods her tone, and I'm concerned for our safety even more than I was when she was crushing me.

"Amber, may I remind you that you are a member of the council, and you need to act accordingly. This path you're going down could be considered a declaration of war. Is that what you really want?" James stands and steps in front of all of us, facing Amber as if he isn't a human who can be easily squashed.

"James, I am aware of my position. I haven't done anything wrong here. Not yet. Now if you'll all just follow me back to my cabin, we can discuss this like civilized people." I can hear the threat in her tone. I don't see that we have a choice.

"I would prefer to speak here. I have no desire to return to your cabin or your control. I know that you've been keeping records of my power. Who are you working for?" Garnet stands tall and speaks with authority. It's pretty hot.

"I'm not working for anyone, dear niece. I simply feel the need to track your progress, that's all." Her insistence is a bit over the top, and we all know she's lying.

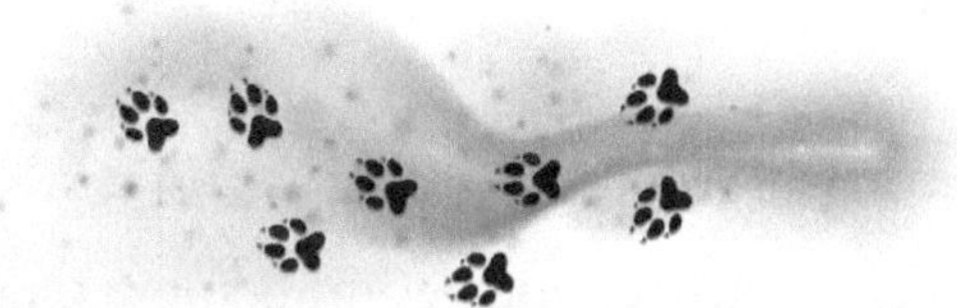

GARNET

Amber has us trapped, and there's nothing I can do to get us away from her. I wish she'd just tell us what she wants, but it seems to be a very well-guarded secret. I hope that Luca and Orym understand what I'm about to do. *James, Ry, we have to*

go with her. We'll figure out how to escape later. I have to find
out what she wants from me.

I look at Orym and Luca pleadingly. Please go along with this. I may actually have to complete our bond as soon as possible to keep us out of danger. "Fine. We'll come back to the cabin with you. But I need to know something first."

She glares at me as if I'm a pest she wants to squash. "What is it?"

"What do you get out of keeping us prisoner?" It's probably not the best approach, but I want to know. Grammy always says it never hurts to ask.

"I'm not keeping you prisoner. I'm teaching you how to be a witch. You're lucky I'm not calling the other council members about your disrespect. You entered my territory without permission, searched my house, then tried to leave without a word. It makes you look very suspicious. I am well within my rights as the territory leader to detain you and have you searched to be certain you're not stealing from me as well."

I understand the veiled threat, even if she didn't hide it very well. "So, we're not prisoners, but we can't go home?"

"I never said that, darling. Your men are welcome to leave, but you will be required to stay with me to continue your training. However, if they leave, they won't be welcomed back into the territory."

Okay, so that's how she's playing it. I could send one of them to get help, but the wards protecting the forest would keep them from returning. No matter what I do here, we're screwed. Just breathe, Garnet. We will figure out how to deal with this. At least we still have our phones from Eli.

Maybe if we keep them hidden, she won't think about taking them. "Well, that sounds a lot like we don't have a choice here. You know you can't keep us here indefinitely, right?"

"I'm not trying to, dear girl. I'm just trying to teach you and help you. I don't understand why you object so much to it. Now, let's all come back to the cabin and settle in." She turns and walks away without looking back. I know we can't continue the way we were heading, so I start to follow her.

"What are we doing?" Orym whispers as we follow Amber back to her home.

"Avoiding a fight for now. Until I'm strong enough to defeat her, or know enough to outsmart her," I explain. "We'll have to complete our bond as soon as possible." He and Luca both nod, understanding the importance. I hate that it feels like giving in to Amber, but we really don't have a choice.

As soon as we're back at the cabin, things change, though. "I can see that you can't be trusted when I'm not here. So, to ensure you cooperate and don't try to run off again, I'll be separating the five of you. And I'll be locking your rooms at night so there are no distractions to your training."

Fuck. I guess we may not get to complete the bond if she's splitting us up and locking us away. "Why would you want to separate us? That doesn't make sense. You spent a week telling me how important my mates are to my training." I know that I sound like a spoiled child, but I can't help myself.

"They still are. But now they'll be used for motivation. If you want to spend time with them, you'll have to demonstrate improvement in your magic. If you don't do well, you'll be punished." Amber's cold tone freezes me in my tracks.

"What do you mean, I'll be punished?" My heart races and sweat slicks my palms.

"I mean, I will find a suitable method to teach you that you need to listen to me. If that means torturing your mates until you comply, that's what I'll do. Do not push me again," she warns. I nod solemnly. I won't do anything that will cause my men to suffer.

"Don't you want us to complete the mate bond? You've been pushing for that as well," I mention, trying to sound casual.

"It would have been ideal, yes, but it's too late now. That will have to wait. Your training is more important." So much for manipulating her into letting me have my way. "Now, I have more errands to run, so you'll all be locked away for a while." She locks me in the room we'd been using, then I hear her tell each of my mates which room to go into. The locks click loudly, but I can't tell exactly where their rooms are.

Ry, I'm scared. I don't like this. Are you and James okay? I want to talk to Luca and Orym, but I can't.

We're fine. She didn't take our phones. I think we should use them sparingly and keep them hidden. Ry's right; I'd had the same thought myself earlier.

I send a quick group text, letting them know that I'm okay and that we need to keep the phones hidden from Amber. James offers to text his brother and see if there's anything Dec or Vik can do to help us out. My guys agree it's a good idea. I can't say one way or the other. I feel like every decision I've made recently has blown up in my face.

Even knowing that I can text them, I feel so alone. I know that's what Amber wants. She needs me to be dependent and obedient, and threatening my mates will keep me in line.

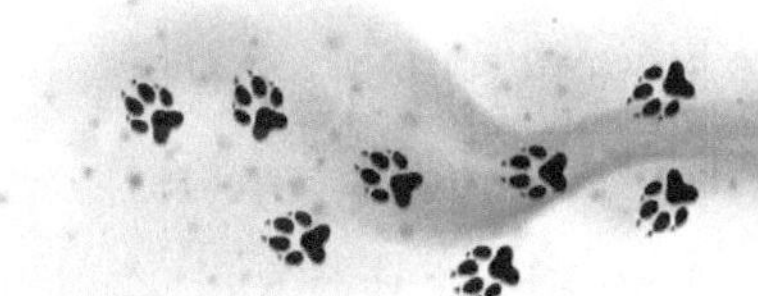

LUCA

Being able to talk to Red after we're locked up is the only good thing that's happened today. I guess I should be glad that we know the truth about Amber. Or part of it anyway. She's Red's aunt—her mother's sister. But does that mean that she had something to do with Ruby's disappearance? If so, what happened? I wish I had a way to find out.

I understand why Red didn't want to fight her way out of the forest. We probably wouldn't have won, even with three wolves and a witch. Now that we're essentially trapped here, maybe we'll find out what Amber wants with Red. Whatever it is, it can't be good.

We've agreed to hide our phones so that Amber is less likely to take them. We'll only communicate at night when we know that she's gone to bed. I hope that Red is able to focus and not worry too much about us. The not-so-veiled threat that we would be harmed if she didn't make progress fast enough did not go over my head. I'm not worried about myself, but James is human, and humans don't have advanced healing like wolves and witches, or even vamps.

He's supposed to reach out to his brother and see if we can get some help, but even that will tip Amber off that we have a form of communication. I'm not sure what the end game is here, but if Amber had something to do with Red's mom disappearing, she's dangerous.

All we can do now is wait and see what happens. I hate waiting. I want to be with my girl, comforting her. I know that she's scared. We've been best friends since we were kids. I can anticipate her emotions and actions better than anyone.

I suddenly have an idea. I wonder if Grammy can do anything to help us. She seems to just know things. Maybe a message to her would be a good idea. I send a quick text, explaining everything and letting her know that I can't respond to new messages. I ask if she can help get us out of here, but I won't hold my breath. We were the rescue team, after all. And look how that turned out.

I sigh and lean against the wall, refusing to climb into the bed. Instead, I sit where I'll be behind the door if it opens. I need to hide my phone so Amber doesn't find it. There aren't a lot of choices in this room. It has a bed, a dresser, and a half bath. I debate my options for a while before deciding.

I tear a hole in the side of the mattress, near the bottom. Then I tuck the phone into it and pull the sheet back over to hide it. That hiding place should work for now. But I'll probably need to figure out another soon.

I lean back against the wall again and close my eyes.

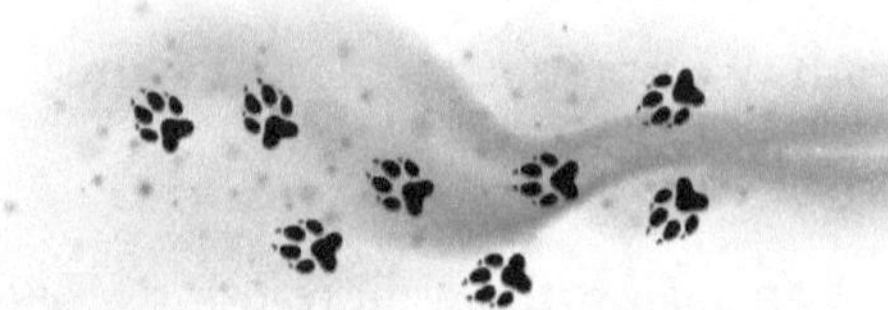

RYLAND

After we're locked away, I search the entire room for a way out. The window is sealed shut and no doubt has magic to alert our captor if we try to escape. So, I focus on the room itself. There's a door, a bed, a dresser, and a half bath. Nothing helpful at all.

When we're finished talking for the night, I have to find a place to hide my phone. I'm tempted to tuck it into my backpack and call it good, but there's always a chance Amber can come in and take it while I'm asleep. No, it needs to be somewhere she can't easily find it.

While I'm searching the room, I notice a couple of loose floorboards under the bed. I pry one up and realize that this may be the best place to store my phone. I grab an extra pair of socks from my bag and tuck the phone inside of them before placing the socks under the board. I put the wooden plank back and admire my plan. There's no way anyone would know that I'd removed it and put it back.

I stash my backpack under the sink in the bathroom, hoping that keeps Amber from noticing it. I wonder if she's planning to let us bathe while we're locked up here. It seems a little odd to me that guest bedrooms in a log cabin would have half baths, but each of the guys confirmed that theirs do as well. I wonder if Amber is more involved in the kidnapping of our people than she admitted.

It's not like making accusations at her will do any good. I stare out the window for a while, then pace back and forth around the room. I'm dying to shift and bust out the glass, but

I know it will only put Red in danger. I can't do that. I have to protect her.

How are you holding up? I know that I should let her rest, but I'm too worked up to sleep. I don't know if she'll answer. It helps to reach out.

As well as can be expected. This is all my fault. We should never have trusted her. I'm so sorry, Ry. Great, now she's blaming herself.

None of that, now, Red. This isn't anyone's fault. Except maybe Amber. That bitch knew exactly what she was doing. We'll get out of here.

I don't tell her that I have no idea how we're going to manage that. I don't tell her that I'm actually a little scared. What I do tell her is that I love her and that I'll keep her safe. And I mean it. I've fallen for her hard. I think that's what's messing with my jealousy.

I've been working on it, and I'm even feeling more comfortable with the idea that Orym is one of her mates. It's not easy, especially now that we're being kept away from each other. All I want is to hold her.

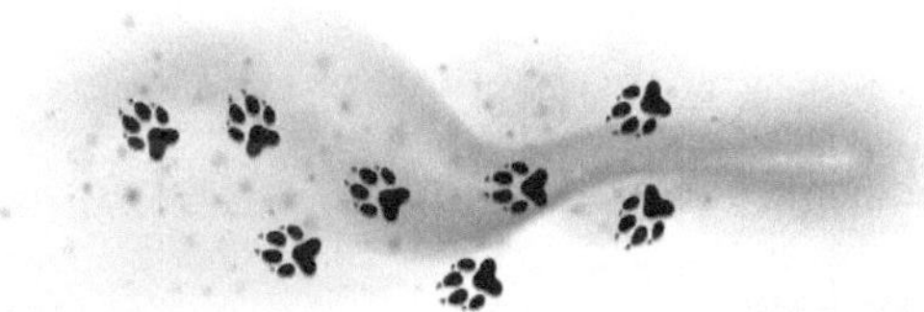

GARNET

I'm alone and terrified. I know that it's exactly what Amber wants. She said that she was going out, but since I don't trust her, I keep an eye on the door. From what my guys told me, their rooms are smaller than this one, with fewer places to hide their phones. I pull off my socks and fold them together, tucking the phone inside. Then I carefully hide them under my clothes as I put them away in the dresser.

I hope that's a good enough spot, but I don't have time to worry about it. There's too much worry in my head already. I should be doing something to find a way out of here. Instead, I'm wallowing in self-pity and wishing one of my guys could do something to save us.

That's not how this is going to go. I'm going to save us. Remembering my last training with Amber, I know what I have to work on.

She wants me to be proficient in elemental control, so I'll practice that. Then I'll practice the spells I've been copying from my mother's journal. And then I'll work on learning more symbols. The sooner I can translate my dream, the better.

I start practicing by forming a ball of water in my hand, pulling the moisture from the air around me. That part isn't hard. Then I heat the air and make it evaporate. I haven't told her I can do that yet. She hasn't given me any training in fire or any type of heat. But at least I know I won't freeze to death, as long as I can access my magic.

I drop onto the floor, sitting cross-legged. Water is by far the easiest element for me to use, so I need less practice with it.

Air is a little harder, so I need more focus. I know the window won't open, although I'm not sure how I know. With a little time and focus, I'm able to create a small vortex of air and move it around the room before letting it dissipate. Good.

Now that I'm warmed up, the next part is going to be a little harder. I concentrate on my hand, staring at it and willing my desire to spring to life. It takes longer than getting the air to cooperate, and I start to get frustrated.

Just breathe. You can do it. James' voice drifts into my head. Why the fuck didn't I bond with all four of them? Oh, yeah, because I was scared of what I'd be tying them to. There's nothing I can do about it now. I listen to James speak in my head and let his voice relax me. As he helps me focus on my breathing, I watch the tiny flower spring into being in my hand.

Its yellow petals spread and multiply, until I have a fully formed Dahlia in my hand. That wasn't so bad. I stand up and grab a vase from the dresser, filling it with water before dropping the flower's stem into it. I wonder if the flower will stick around or if it will disappear now that I've made it.

I decide to practice a little more and make three additional Dahlias, each in a different color. A teal one, a red one, and an orange one. Then I realize that I've substituted them for my mates. Well, at least I don't feel quite as lonely now.

With the flowers tucked into the vase, I sit on the floor again. Now for the hard part. Wait, before I do this, I should have a focus and a safety plan. This won't work. I head into the bathroom and sit on the edge of the tub, next to the faucet. If this gets out of hand, at least I'll have a way to get water quickly.

I place the single sheet of blank paper in the tub and stare at it. I focus my thoughts on my anger at being locked away here. I pull forth the emotions I hide from everyone. My rage fuels me, and the paper lights with flame that wasn't there a moment ago. I expected that to be more difficult than moving air or creating plants. Somehow, it was even easier than pulling water from the air.

I watch the paper burn until the only thing left is ash. Then I do it again. And again. I keep rotating through the elements until I can switch from one to the other with barely a thought. I only stop when I hear Amber return. That's when I know that she really was gone the whole time. I should have tried to escape. I should have tried to save my mates.

Instead, I did exactly what she wanted. I practiced my magic. It doesn't matter now. I know what I can do, and she doesn't have to know that I've been able to create and control fire. I quickly clean the tub, destroying any evidence of my adventure.

I'm sitting in the center of the bed when she finally comes in with a tray of food. "Here's your dinner."

"I'd like to eat with my mates," I say simply.

"You haven't earned it," she replies. I can feel the anger come off her in waves. I know that she's pissed that we tried to run.

"Would you tell me what it is that you want with me, then? And maybe explain how I can earn my mates back." I try not to sound hateful, but I can't help it. I'm as pissed as she is.

"I want you to learn. And that's exactly how you'll earn your mates back. Study. Focus. Stop trying to run away as if I'm your captor. I'm only holding you here for your own good," she insists.

I don't believe her, and I don't trust her. But I don't have a choice. "You win. I'll do it."

PRACTICE, PRACTICE, PRACTICE

RYLAND

I AM ONCE AGAIN relegated to being Red's practice dummy as Amber insists that she practice her attacks and shields. The difference this time is that Red isn't allowed to shield me, and if she misses me, Amber attacks Orym. If I don't make myself a difficult target to hit, she attacks Luca. If Red refuses to cooperate, Amber attacks James.

I'm glad that I'm the one she's attacking, because I can encourage her through the bond and let her know that I'm okay when she does hit me. *You have to focus. She's going to change things up if you don't. I know it's hard, but you have to try to hit me. You can do this.*

I want nothing more than to pull her in my arms and kiss away her fears. But I can't. None of us can touch her. Because if we do, Amber will freeze us and lock us up again.

"Do it again. Hit him this time," Amber calls out, holding an orb in her hand. I can't tell if it's a ball of electricity or something else. Either way, I don't want it to hit Orym.

I race through the clearing, dodging and weaving. *Remember, aim in front of me. Don't be afraid to hit me. I'll be fine.*

She needs the encouragement, so James joins me in telling her exactly how to hit me. In another situation, I might get upset with him for it, but this is as close to life and death as we're going to get. I hope. And Red needs to stop focusing on my health and think about her other mates.

I know you don't want to hurt him, Garnet, but Amber will let me take care of him if he does get injured. Last week, she even let me stay in his room, remember? It's okay. James' words remind me of that night I will never forget. James nursed me as my expedited healing took longer than usual. I'm not sure why Amber let us stay together, other than she was afraid she'd pushed too far and thought I was going to die.

If I did, there's no way Red would ever cooperate with her again. I think that fear is what keeps her from simply killing us to get Red alone. I get distracted by my thoughts and a bolt of magic hits me in the side, slamming me into a tree. That one hurt.

"Get up. Now or you know what will happen." Yes, I know what will happen. Luca will suffer for my insubordination. I don't want that. I struggle, but manage to get to my feet. I take three steps before I fall, face first onto the ground. I hear Luca cry out and I hate that I've failed him. I try again, but I can't do it.

I hear Amber yelling but can't make out what she's saying. I can feel Red reaching out through the bond.

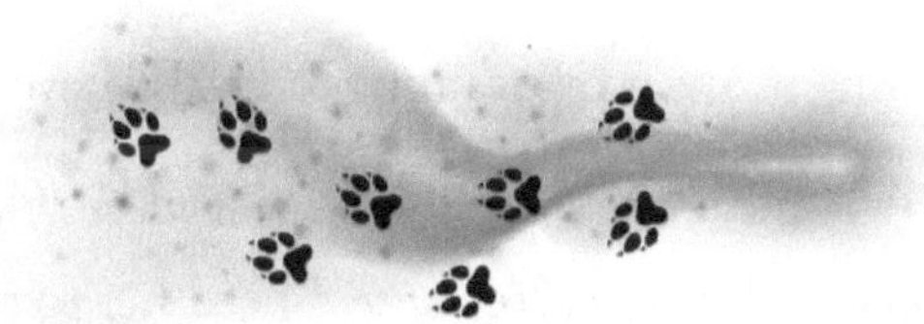

JAMES

Being an EMT has always been my calling. I hate it in this situation. Amber finally lets me go check out Ryland, after he tries to get up and come back on his own three times. When he doesn't get up, she yells at us and orders me to get him.

Luckily, I'm stronger than I look, because Ryland has a good three inches and fifty pounds on me. Before I'll even chance moving him, I have to check for injuries. Amber has been kind enough to provide me with a medical bag that I'm only allowed to touch when someone is hurt. I drop it next to Ryland and kneel to check him out.

His breathing is regular, but he's unconscious. He won't be participating in any more training today. I'll have to check him for internal injuries, too. *Garnet, he's fine. He's unconscious, but his healing is already taking over.* I need her to stay calm so I can take care of him.

"Well?" Amber calls, clearly not having any sympathy for him, even though this entire situation is her fault.

"He's knocked out. He'll recover, but he won't be able to play anymore today. Do you want me to take him inside and look after him?" For a moment, I think she's going to tell me no, but she nods.

"Take him inside and make him comfortable, then come back out here. I'll let you check on him in a while. We have more training to do," she says coldly.

I've never wanted to punch a woman in the face so badly before in my life. Instead, I grit my teeth and pick Ryland up. Once he's over my shoulder, I head into the cabin. I grab a bottle of water and head to his room. I put him in the bed and place the water beside him, where he'll find it when he wakes up. I don't want to leave, so I take my time making sure that he's settled.

When I go back out, I see that Amber has subbed Orym in for Ryland. Great, that's all I need. I'm not sure I can handle two of them injured at once. But if Garnet doesn't hit Orym, Luca will suffer. Either way, two of us will be hurt. I push my anger down, knowing that I can't attack Amber.

It doesn't matter that I'm on the council with her. She's decided exactly how this is going to play out, and so far, everything has worked in her favor. No one has come looking for us, even though my brother and his family know exactly where we are. I know that they're trying to avoid a war, but this situation is beginning to feel hopeless.

Hopefully, I'll be able to check my phone tonight and talk to Dec for a minute. Maybe if I can make him understand how serious this is, he'll step in. I'm not surprised when Orym goes down, but Amber holds up a hand to stop me from going to him.

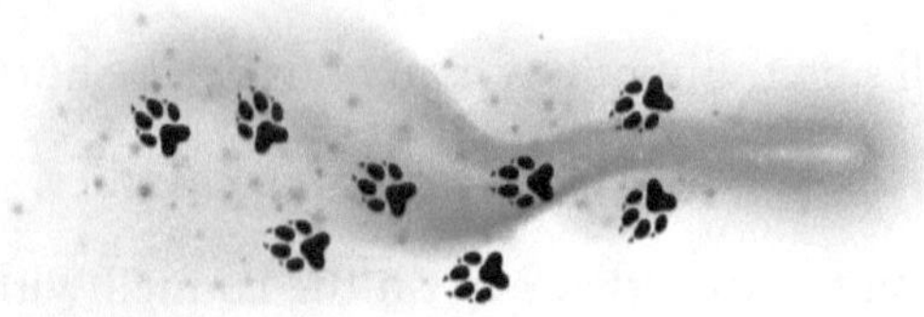

GARNET

"You have to let James check on him," I insist. Of course, Amber sees this as disrespect and slaps Luca across the face. I can't take this anymore. "If you hurt him again, I will never do what you tell me to. I'm sick of this. If you think I need to be punished, then you should hit me."

I know that I shouldn't speak out. I should do what we've been doing and wait until my magic is under control and I am certain I can beat her. But I can't stand by while she abuses my mates anymore. Electricity courses along my body, and as if by instinct, I send it shooting toward her.

Clearly Amber wasn't expecting me to fight back. The bolt wraps around her and she falls to the ground, twitching. "Please, James, make sure Orym is okay." Luca moves to stand behind me as James does what I ask. I position myself between Amber and my men. If she wants to attack them, she'll have to go through me.

"He's okay, just winded. We're not going to be able to get out of here fast enough," James admits.

"She's gonna be pissed when she comes out of this," Luca warns.

"I know. I can't handle watching her hurt you. I had to do something. I need the four of you to get out of here. You have to escape. I can keep her subdued long enough for you to get to the barrier. I'll find a way out later. Please, just go." I'm begging them to leave me. I know that they won't do it, but I wish they would.

"We can't leave you. Besides, Ryland can't travel right now," Orym says quietly.

This is the worst torture I've ever dealt with. I can't stand the thought of them getting hurt again because of me. But I'm relieved that they refuse to leave without me.

"What can we do?" I ask, hoping that they understand what I'm asking.

"Is there a way to block her magic?" James suggests. I can't remember reading anything about that, but Amber had told me that my magic had been suppressed.

"There has to be, but I don't know what it is," I admit, feeling defeated.

Luca disappears for a minute, coming back with zip ties, duct tape, and rope. "So, we tie her up and keep her subdued until she cooperates. You can research a way to stop her from using magic while she's out. We can take turns watching her."

It's a brilliant idea. If I knock her out, we can restrain her and I can go through her books. "What about the witches that are working for her?"

"Well, James, that part will get a little tricky. I think that Red can pull off telling them that Amber is busy and make them think they have to go through us." It looks like Luca has everything figured out. Except that I'm not a good liar.

He looks at me and grins. "It's not a lie. She will be busy. They don't have to know what she's busy doing." I pull him to me for a kiss. It's the first affection I've had in however many days we've been captive here since our escape attempt. I want to keep kissing him forever, but James clears his throat.

When we back away from each other, he gestures to where Amber lays on the ground. "She's coming around. You might want to zap her again," James suggests.

Orym stands up and takes my hand. "We'll figure it all out. One step at a time."

"Together," I say, stepping away from them and sending another bolt of electricity at Amber. Once I'm sure she's unconscious, I let Luca and Orym tie her up and carry her inside. With her restrained, I have free access to everything in the cabin.

"Orym, help me find books. Anything with spells or potions. Make a pile for me and I'll go through them. I'm going to check Ruby's journal again and keep an eye on her for now." I drop to the couch near the chair they've placed Amber in.

James leans down and kisses me gently. "I'm going to check on Ryland. As soon as he's awake, I'll fill him in on what's happening."

"Thank you," I whisper. I can't deal with the fact that I'm the one who hurt Ry. I know it was under duress, and I can't really blame myself, but I do. If I'd been strong enough to defeat Amber, none of this would have happened. I hate to admit that her teaching has helped me. But without it, I wouldn't have been able to knock her out.

I have to figure out exactly what she wants from me. "I'm going to look at her desk and see if there's anything that will help us there," Luca tells me. If there's a way to get out of this mess, we'll figure it out together.

I continue my search through my mother's journal. She wrote about spells and potions, but I'm not finding anything about binding powers. There has to be something. I'm getting desperate. I don't want to kill Amber, but I can't be a prisoner here anymore.

I have to find a way to be free. I wish I knew how to make that happen. A few minutes later, Luca comes back in the room holding a book and some papers. "I think I know what she was planning," he says grimly, handing me the pages and the book.

"What is all this?" I ask as I look it over.

"It looks like a spell to transfer power. I think she was testing you to see how strong you are before she found a way to make you give her your power," he explains.

I look at the book more closely. Fuck, he's right. She wants my powers.

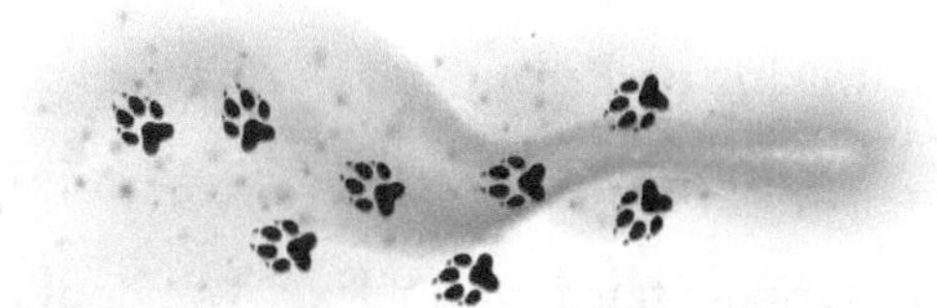

ORYM

My search of the library is a bit less fruitful than Luca's search of Amber's desk. I don't come up empty handed, though. "I found something that may be useful," I say as I walk into the living room. As I hand Garnet the book, I explain myself. "It seems like a record of magical items in the house. And it lists a pair of power blocking cuffs. In the description, it sounds like they can only be removed by the person who puts them on another person. If we can find them, we can effectively block her power."

"That's amazing. Now we just have to find them," I blurt, pulling him to me for a hard kiss. "You guys are incredible."

Now that we have some hope, things don't look as bleak. James is checking on Ryland, and we have a lead on a way to subdue Amber until we can get away. With freedom in our grasp, I'm actually starting to relax. "We should split up and search. One of us should look down here where we can keep an eye on her," I gesture to Amber tied to the chair.

I hate forcing Garnet to stay near her deranged aunt, but we need to keep Amber unconscious until we can find those cuffs.

"I've got her handled. You two start searching. Let me know if you find anything. I'll explain to James and have him help you when he's done checking on Ry." Garnet starts opening cabinets and looking through shelves in the living room.

Luca and I exchange a glance, then head off to start our search. "Where should we start?" he asks.

"Amber's bedroom?" I suggest. I think it may be the most likely place for her to hide something like what we're looking for. It would be ideal if she'd had them in a display case that was clearly marked. But that is a ridiculous thought that makes me laugh.

"What's so funny?"

"I was just wishing she had this stuff clearly labeled and on display, that's all."

Luca laughs with me for a moment. Then we enter Amber's bedroom and what we find nearly floors both of us. Amber's room actually has display cases that are clearly marked as magical items. It can't be this easy, can it? We start looking at each case, discovering that they're locked and spelled to prevent tampering. Okay, not too easy then.

We search the room and Luca finds a set of keys. Now all we need is to break the magic wards around the cases. Of course, I don't see the cuffs in any of them, but there are other items that may prove useful here. "Let's pocket the keys and keep looking. Maybe we'll find the cuffs and be able to deal with all of this later." Luca nods at my suggestion and we keep searching Amber's bedroom, hoping to find exactly what we need.

He goes into her closet and comes out with a chest.

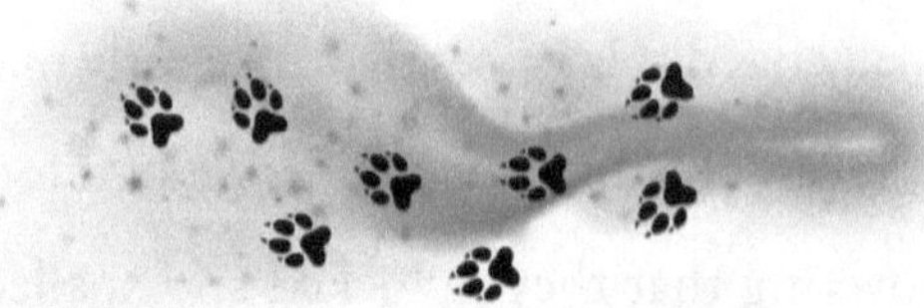

LUCA

I find a wooden chest inside Amber's closet. For a moment, I worry that it might contain sex toys or something of that nature. It's the only thing in her room that doesn't seem to be protected by magic. I carry it out of the closet and show it to

Orym. His eyes go wide when I set it on the bed and flip the latch. "Are you sure that's safe?" he asks.

I shrug. "I have no idea, but it doesn't seem to have magic around it like the cases." I open it and look through the contents. There are pictures of people I recognize and some that I don't. We find various crystals and dried flowers along with journals and spell books. And from the bottom of the chest, Orym pulls out the cuffs we've been searching for.

This is the most hope I've had in weeks. We might actually be able to get out of here. Orym and I toss everything back into the chest and take it to the living room to show Red. She's still looking through books and keeping an eye on Amber.

"I think we found them. If what the book says is correct, you'll be the only one who can put them on her," Orym explains. I set the chest on the table and open it, revealing its contents.

James walks into the room and we all freeze. Everyone is worried about Ryland. "He's resting. Most of his wounds have healed. He's sleeping the rest off now. I'm pretty sure he'll be awake for dinner."

"That's fantastic news!" Red gushes, wrapping him in a hug.

"I'm happy to hear that. Now we need to go through this chest and get those cuffs on Amber before she wakes up. There are more artifacts in her bedroom, but they're locked in display cases with magic around them. I don't know if we'll be able to get to those." I hate interrupting what little joy Red has had today, but we need to focus. I can't let our freedom be yanked away because we lost focus.

She nods. "Luca is right. We can celebrate once everything is taken care of. Let's start with the cuffs." Orym pulls them from the chest and hands them to Red. She looks them over and goes back to the book where they were listed. It explains exactly how to use them.

It only takes her a moment to figure the spell out and have them glowing with their activation. She puts them on Amber's wrists, and a faint red light surrounds Red's aunt for a moment before fading away. We won't know if they work until she wakes up and tries to use her magic. It's risky, so we keep her tied up for now.

Then the four of us go through the chest, examining the books, crystals, and flowers that have been stored in here. Red takes some notes and sets a few of the books aside.

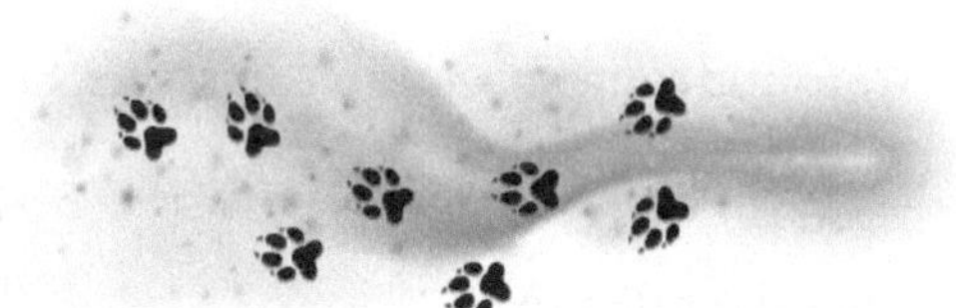

GARNET

I have a moment of panic when Ry ambles up behind me. I'm startled and jump, accidentally smacking him in the face. "Ow, fuck, that hurt," he grumbles.

"Oh, Goddess! I'm so sorry, Ry," I exclaim, pulling him into a gentle hug. I don't want to hurt him any more than I already have today.

"I'm okay now. You're not going to hurt me." He hugs me tighter and I melt against him. I realize just how affection starved I've been since Amber locked us up away from each other. "I see you've subdued her for now."

"Yeah. We found some magic blocking cuffs. Hopefully they work," Orym tells him. Ry walks over to where Amber is and kicks the chair she's tied to.

She bolts upright, wide awake and pissed. "What the fuck did you do to me?" Amber glares at me as if she can kill me with her eyes. I don't feel any magic coming from her, so the cuffs must be working.

"Nothing compared to what you had planned for me, auntie dearest," I croon, holding up the spell book that contains the power transference spell. "You were going to take my powers, weren't you?"

"Don't look at me that way. I took your mother's powers. That worked out pretty well for me, at least for a while. Then I realized that you're even more powerful than she was. You can't blame me for wanting more power. It's not like you even know what you have at your disposal, anyway." She sounds bitter and cold. I hate that I'm related to her. I'm pissed that I almost trusted her.

From the way she fights against the restraints, the cuffs are working. We'll have to keep her locked up or tied up so she can't attack us physically, but I'm okay with that. I don't mind treating her the way she's treated us.

"You can't have my powers. But if you don't stop fighting us, I'll take yours," I threaten. I'm not sure if I mean it or not, but she doesn't have to know that. Let her think I'm as cold and calculating as she is. I'll use it to my advantage.

Her eyes go wide as she considers my threat. I can see her wondering if it's worth trying to manipulate me. I could save her the trouble, but I won't. Let her try. I look forward to outsmarting her over and over. I know that she'll try to escape the first chance she gets.

I turn to Luca. "We need somewhere to lock her up so she can't escape. And we need to find her phone. I can't have her calling for help when we think we have her out of commission." He nods and heads back to her room.

"As for you, just sit there and be quiet, would ya? You're lucky Ry woke up when he did. I was planning to torture you until he did." I turn and walk back to the chest where I continue to separate the books into stacks. I'm going to have some reading to catch up on.

"You know my people will not stand for this. When they find out, they'll kill you," she cries. I turn to face her and laugh.

"Do you think we haven't considered that?" I could tell her more, but I won't. I'd rather watch her face as she thinks of every way possible that I can avoid her people attacking me. I can't kill her, or even maim her, but I can keep her out of my way for a while.

Luca comes back with her phone. "Here's this. And there are chains in her closet. If we take everything else out and search it really well, we may be able to lock her in there."

I pat his cheek before pressing a kiss to his lips. "My hero." He laughs at my joke, but I'm excited that he found a way to lock Amber up. "I think I found a soundproofing spell in one of these books. At the very least, there's an immobilize spell. We can use that along with the chains if we need to."

I glance at Amber and see fear in her eyes for the first time since we got here. Good. I want her to be scared of me. More than anything, I want to torture her and make her suffer the way she did us. But I can't. I know that my guys wouldn't be okay with that behavior. I have to do better.

"Why don't you tell me about my mother? We have some time now. It's not like you're going anywhere." I pose the question to her, but she glares at me instead of responding. "Not feeling very talkative, auntie? That's okay. I'll just read your journals and learn what I want."

"Stay out of my things. I'm warning you. You will pay for this," she threatens me again. There's no bite in her tone, though. She knows that we've beaten her. I can't help being amused by the situation. She had me under control until she started hurting my mates.

I can feel my power growing again. It's like an electric surge through me. I've felt it a few times since we got here, and each time, I've had more control and more power overall. I'd like to have someone to ask about it, but there isn't anyone around here that I would trust.

"If you don't want to tell me about Ruby, then you should probably just shut up," I say, flicking my wrist and sending sticky magic to seal her mouth. I won't keep her from breathing, but I will keep her from ruining my night.

James and Orym disappear into the kitchen, and I guess that they've decided to cook tonight. Ry doesn't leave my side, and Luca stays nearby in case he's still feeling unbalanced. The three of us settle on the couch with a few of the books I plan to read.

Fifteen
LESSONS LEARNED

LUCA

THE FIVE OF US spend the rest of the night getting everything settled. This won't be easy, but we need to know how far into everything Amber is before we make our escape. That means a few more days here. Red spends most of her time reading and practicing spells. Ryland, Orym, and I alternate keeping a watch on the perimeter of the clearing, and James makes sure our captive doesn't get away.

I know that Red is anxious about sealing our bond, but Orym and I are holding onto our hesitation. We won't let her be forced into something she's not ready for yet. Since she's the one who told us that she's not ready, neither of us is willing to let her move forward on that yet.

Amber receives a few text messages that seem to be from people who follow her. I've given Eli remote access to her phone and he's been busy figuring out her code and responding to messages. Between us, we've convinced them that she's had to go away on urgent council business. That will buy us at least a few days before anyone will come looking for her.

It gives Red more time to focus and learn what she needs to know before any possible fight can come up. Eli also manages to convince Amber's followers that we're cooperating now, and no longer need to be contained. *Once I explained what we're doing, they were all in. There is no need to prevent them from coming and going as they please. The five of them are invested in our mission.*

I shiver at the wording of that text. Somehow it worked, though. No one has bothered us. We haven't ventured out yet, other than into the clearing to practice and train, which will look normal to anyone who's still watching the cabin.

Every day, Red tries to get Amber to talk to her. I feel bad that her aunt is such a horrible person. It's worse knowing that Amber is the one who killed Ruby. Or at least, that's what she wants us to think. Who knows what actually happened? Eli is researching that too, but I don't hold out much hope for results there. The covens seem to keep all their records in a non-electronic fashion.

The five of us enjoy the peace and quiet the cabin offers, even while we understand it won't last forever. At some point, we'll have to face what Amber has been doing. There are wolves and vamps who need to be rescued and returned to their families. It's hard to stay focused on the mission when everything I ever wanted is standing in front of me. Even harder when she's feeling particularly flirty.

As badly as I want her, I don't want her to regret our bond. Orym and I have discussed it several times, and agree that we have to wait.

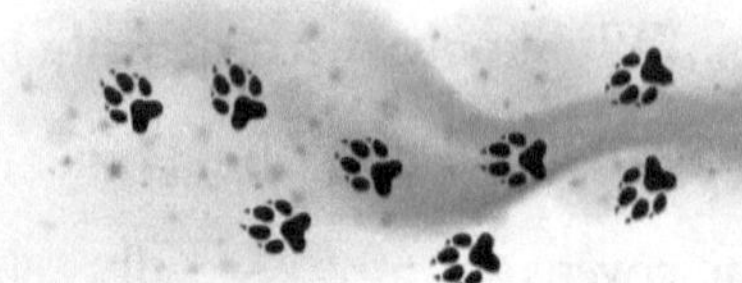

RYLAND

Watching Red argue with Amber pisses me off. The witch should be happy we haven't hurt her. She should want to talk and answer all of Red's questions. But she refuses. And Red won't let me torture her.

"Ry, we can't do that. It's not right. I know that she hurt you, but I can't let you hurt her. If she won't talk to me, then let it be. Please," Red insists. I can't refuse her, so I back down. I'm dying to shift and tear Amber's throat out, though.

James insists that we all need to keep up with physical training, so when I get frustrated, I run. Some days I end up running for hours. It takes the edge off, but doesn't make me less annoyed. I'm pleased with Red's progress with her magic. She's getting better at control and learning to split her focus when it's needed.

She's even at a point where she can knock Amber out with a wave of her hand. I don't think she understands how fucking hot she looks when she does magic without thinking about it. I'd love to say that we aren't dealing with as much sexual tension, but in reality, it's worse than it was before. Since we haven't figured out Amber's game plan, Luca and Orym don't want to complete the bond.

I think it has more to do with Red's initial hesitation, but I won't push the issue. It does mean that none of us is getting any, though, and that's another source of irritation. There are only so many times a guy can jerk off in the shower before it just doesn't do it anymore.

I agree with Luca, and I remind myself of that every time I start to get aggravated about the situation. We can't force Red into anything, and we can't let her do something that could hurt all of us in the end. Without more information, we don't know if it's safe for all of us to be bonded yet.

While I check the perimeter, Luca helps Red do more research. Orym makes lunch, and James checks on Amber again. If they would let me handle her, just once, I'd have answers. I know it. The bitch may never walk again, but I would make her talk.

That rage bubbles inside of me again, so I shift into my wolf form and race through the forest. I make sure not to get too close to the border, because if I go too far, I won't be able to get back to Red. I don't know if our bond would be enough to get me past the wards or not, but I don't want to take that chance.

She needs me, and I will not abandon her. After making sure that we're safe, and running off the majority of my rage, I return to the cabin. "Did you find anything?" I ask when I walk inside.

"Not really," Red answers quietly.

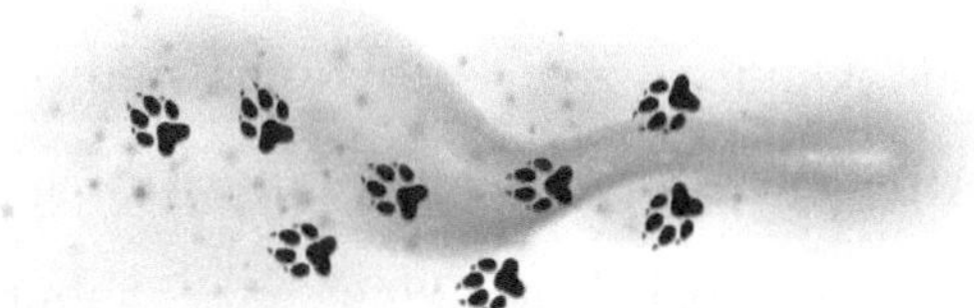

GARNET

My training seems stifled, and I'm not sure why. The only difference between when I was making progress and now is that Amber is no longer helping me. While I hate her methods, they got results. Even knowing that I have to learn this stuff to protect us isn't the same as when she was actively threatening the people I care about.

My mood sours as I go over elements again. I'm capable, and honestly, doing okay with things, but I don't feel like I'm getting better. It's a problem, and I have no idea how to fix it. I'm not about to let Amber go, so I have to deal with this myself.

I spend my mornings practicing spells and elemental conjuring. After lunch, I read and re-read everything I can, searching for answers. Then I try asking Amber about my mother and she refuses to talk. Every day is exactly the same, and I'm starting to wonder if we should just give up and go home.

Of course, now that I know I'm not actually a cursed wolf shifter, I don't exactly know where home is. I miss Grammy, but I don't know that I can trust her anymore. Everyone I know has lied to me my entire life. Or they were lied to as well.

I've always felt like I didn't fit in, and I guess this is why. I really don't fit in anywhere. I'm a witch who was literally raised by wolves. I laugh at that for a moment before the weight of it all hits me. I'm alone. Except for my guys. They are the only family I have left. And I can't seem to convince two of them to claim me.

I know this is just an off day, and I'm feeling sorry for myself. I know that I'm better than this, but I can't help how I'm feeling right now. I need to gather my thoughts and refocus my efforts. Training will do no good today if I'm not focused. And right now, I can't.

I walk into the cabin in search of someone to make me feel better. James is dealing with Amber; Ry is patrolling the grounds. That leaves Luca or Orym. Well, I guess that takes sex as a relaxation method off the table. They've both made it clear that we're not bonding right now. Not until we know why Amber was pushing so hard for it.

I sigh when I walk through the cabin and don't find any of them. Where are they? I thought Luca was going to handle lunch. Orym should be around here somewhere. I've looked everywhere but the attic, and I'm not going up there right now. It's dark and creepy.

Maybe I'll just take a shower and see how I'm feeling after. I peek my head in on James and see that he's trying to get Amber to talk to him. It's sweet how he's trying to help. Hopefully he'll get her to talk. *I'm going to shower. Just wanted to check on things here first.* I talk to him telepathically so that I don't have to let Amber know I'm here.

No progress, but I'm still trying. His response is depressing too, but fits the mood of the day. Feeling defeated, I retreat to the bedroom we've claimed and head into the bathroom. The hot water feels nice against my skin and I start to relax a little. Before I realize what I'm doing, I've started playing with the water, creating things from it and moving them around. For some reason, it makes me feel better.

When the water starts to cool, I use magic to heat it with very little effort. It seems as if I can do things with my magic today, just not the things I thought I should be doing. But using magic to keep myself warm and entertained is working, so I don't stop.

The bathroom door opens and I jump a little in surprise. A peek around the curtain tells me that it's just Orym checking on me. "You startled me."

"Sorry. Luca finished making lunch, and you've been in here for a while. I wanted to make sure you're okay. Ryland and James thought you were upset about something. Can I help?" His offer makes my heart skip a beat. I can think of several things I'd like his help with.

"I don't know. I'm having a bad day. Magic isn't cooperating, and that made me think about missing home. Then I realized that I don't really have a home anymore. I don't fit in anywhere." I don't mean to unload it all on him, but it feels better now that I have.

He grabs a towel and turns the shower off. Once he has me wrapped up in the towel, he carries me over to stand on the rug in front of the sink. Orym grabs another towel and starts to dry me off. His gentle touch isn't sexual at all, but still sets me on fire. But I know nothing is going to happen. I even understand why. After all, it was my idea to wait. And bonding now feels rushed and pressured, so I won't push. I want these things to happen naturally.

After he dries me off, Orym starts to brush my hair. With my tangles taken care of, he carries me to the bedroom and finds my softest pajamas. It's barely lunch time, and he seems to be getting me ready for bed. "What are you doing?"

"No one can have a bad day when they're wearing comfy pjs. It's a fact," he insists. I dress in the shirt and pants he hands me, then I let him carry me to the kitchen for lunch.

These guys are a little over the top sometimes, but I like it. I don't mind being carried around or having someone cook for me. Everyone sits around the table and we eat in comfortable silence.

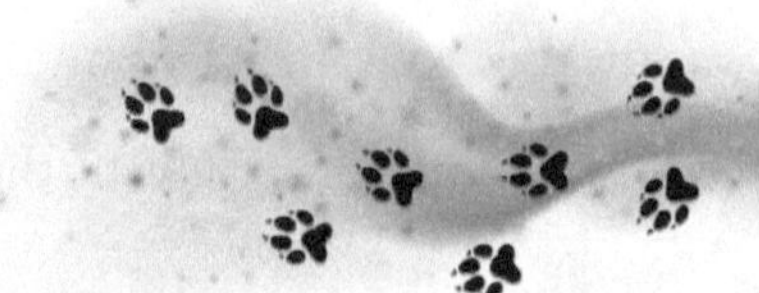

JAMES

Garnet seems more relaxed after her shower, but I'm still worried about her. I think it would be beneficial for her to complete the bonds with Luca and Orym. It's not my place to push for that, so I keep my mouth shut. She has to make that decision herself. Or rather, with them. Since Amber pushed so hard for it, I know there are risks. I've been trying to get her to talk to me, and may have actually gotten some useful information out of her today.

I'm not sure she realizes that she told me anything, but I'd prefer to research it before I tell Garnet. After lunch, Ryland insists that she train with him outside for a while. It'll be a good distraction for her, and allow me time to do my research. I wait until they go outside, then turn to Luca and Orym. "Would one of you keep an eye on Amber for me for a while? I have some research I need to do."

"Sure, but what are you researching? Did she tell you something?" Luca asks.

"I want to verify it first. I can't give Garnet false hope. Either way, I'll explain at dinner," I offer. He nods and goes to check on our prisoner.

"If you need help, let me know," Orym offers.

"I will. If you could just make sure she stays outside for a while, that would be great. I don't know how much training she's up for. If she gets upset or frustrated, maybe a walk would help." With his agreement to help, I head for the attic. I know from our earlier exploration that there are more books and notes up there.

Earlier, Amber mentioned something about a family tome that contained certain spells. It was in passing, and she didn't seem to realize that she'd given me any useful information. There is a chance that she's lying, and knows what she said, but I don't think so. It doesn't matter, because I want to find the book and check it for myself.

If there really is a spell that will give Garnet full access to her powers, she deserves to know about it. It's up to me to verify that such a spell actually exists. The door creaks as it swings open. I open the curtains to let light in, and start sifting through books. At first, I find a few that appear to be about elemental control. I set those aside to take downstairs for Garnet.

None of these are what I'm looking for, though. I can't give up. She needs this book, and I want to be the one who finds it for her. I'm the only human here, and sometimes I feel like I'm not enough for her. I want to prove that I can be useful.

It's obvious that the bookshelves don't have anything helpful on them. So, I start searching other things in the room. I find it in a chest in the corner.

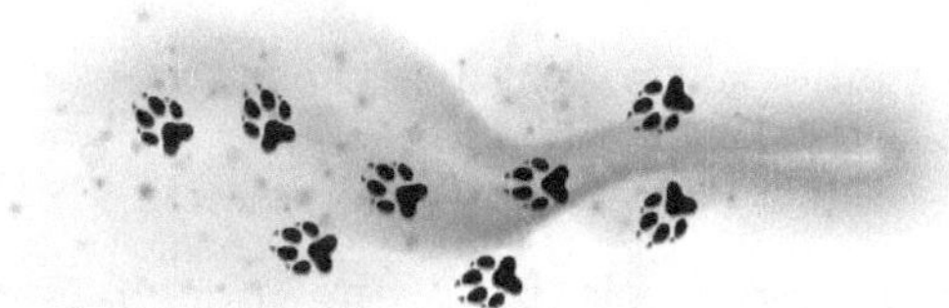

ORYM

Keeping Garnet busy isn't nearly as hard as I had expected it to be. I can think of better ways to distract her, but since we're not bonding yet, those are off the table. I watch her spar with Ryland for a while, then join them. She has to be able to handle multiple attackers at once, and we practice those scenarios for a while.

I can see that she's getting tired, and don't want to push her too hard. We don't need her to get injured or blocked. "Why don't we take a walk and relax for a little while before we train some more?" I can tell that Ryland has me figured out and expect him to tell her.

"That sounds like a great idea. The three of us could use a break. We can walk down and take a dip in the lake. I found it on one of my patrols. It's secure enough, especially since Amber's thugs think we're on their side now." Swimming is a great way to relax. I wonder for a moment if Garnet will agree, or if she'll want to go back into the house and see what Luca and James are up to.

"That sounds really nice, actually. Should we get Luca and James?" she asks.

Ryland answers before I can. "James is seeing to our guest, and Luca was cleaning up the kitchen. If we wait for them, it'll take too long. Come on, it won't hurt to spend a little time with us, will it?"

She laughs. "No, it won't. I just don't want anyone to be left out." I can see the guilt pass over her features at the thought that Luca and I are already being left out.

"We'll figure all of that out soon enough, love. Let's just go relax for a bit." I sling an arm over her shoulder and steer her in the direction Ryland gestures. I'll have to remember to thank him for helping me. He gives me a knowing look over her head and I nod my thanks.

At least I know that he's actively helping me. That should give James the time he needs. I hope he's onto something helpful. But I guess we'll find out at dinner.

Ryland shows us where the lake is, and it's gorgeous. Garnet's face lights up and I can see the tension in her melt away. This is exactly what she needed. It doesn't matter that she's in flannel pajamas, she seems more free than she has in weeks. She even races away from us toward the water, giving us a moment to speak quietly.

"Thank you," I say.

"Happy to help. You'll fill me in later?" he asks, keeping his voice low.

"James needed a bit. He'll explain at dinner," I offer. Ryland nods.

"Then let's distract our girl, shall we?" I'm surprised at how well we've been getting along. I can't even remember why I hated him so much before.

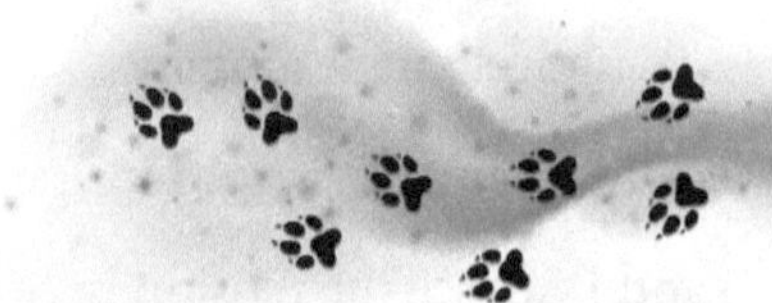

GARNET

I know that Orym and Ryland are trying to distract me, but I don't know why. Taking a break from training sounds good, so I don't argue. I decide that they don't even need to know that I'm onto them. I let my genuine pleasure take over at the sight of the lake. I'm not in the mood for a swim, but I love being this close to a natural source of water.

The flowers around the lake are beautiful, too. I string a few together to make a crown and drop it on my head. I let myself really relax for a little while. It's not easy to forget what we're doing, but I allow it, just for a bit.

I see Ry and Orym talking. I could try to read lips or use magic to see what they're talking about, but I'll let them have their secret. At least they're getting along. I never thought I'd see the day when the two of them would conspire together. They've hated each other for years, though no one really knows why. I'm not even sure that they do.

I take in the solace of the lake and lay in the grass. It's so peaceful here, and I wish I could bottle this feeling up to have with me later when I need it. When Orym and Ry join me, I play with my elemental magic a bit. I pull a trail of water from the lake and make it dance above us. Then I mix a gust of air with it, creating a small hurricane. It's easy to combine air and water. Adding the other two elements is what usually stumps me.

This time is different. I manage to drop the vortex into the sand beside the lake and pick up a little bit of the light brown earth. I debate for a moment before hitting the whole thing with a bolt of lightning, setting it on fire. When the flames disappear, a small circle of glass remains. I know that's a chemical reaction of the lightning and sand, but it's perfectly circular and polished. That has to be an effect of the magic.

"That's strange, isn't it?" Ry asks, picking it up and handing it to me. The glass should be hot, but it's cold to the touch. Hmm. Very curious.

"It is. I've never done anything like that before. I wonder if that means this piece of glass is significant somehow," I ponder.

"We should keep it, just in case," Orym offers, slipping the palm sized circle in his pocket. "But you're supposed to be relaxing here, not creating things with magic." He sounds as if he's chastising a child who's misbehaved.

I laugh at him for a moment. "I was relaxing. That was me playing around with the magic instead of training. Maybe that's the problem."

Both men look at me, confused. "What do you mean?" Ry asks.

"I've been trying too hard. I need to relax and play with it to get better results. I can't take everything so seriously all the time. We've been pushing so hard to find answers and figure out how to control my magic. Maybe the answer is to not try so hard," I offer.

I can see that they're considering my thought. Without thinking, I start the process again. I want to see if I can replicate those results. Within just a few minutes, there's another identical circle of polished glass. There seems to be some sort of significance to it, though I'm not sure why.

I just feel like this glass is meant to help us somehow. I have no idea what it can be used for, but it's pretty. And sometimes that has to be enough. I feel compelled to make one for each of us. Maybe my subconscious knows something I don't. Perhaps it's something I've read and forgotten. Or I just like the way the little circles of glass look and want each of us to have one. I don't know. I don't question it, instead, let myself work on instinct. That isn't something I've done until now, either.

I'd begun to think I didn't have any instincts. Growing up away from my family made me feel different from everyone. But maybe I'm not that different after all. Maybe I just have to give myself the freedom to try things and see what happens.

"Thanks for getting me to take a break. I don't know if these will help us, but something tells me they're important. It could just be the mixing of different elements. I'm not sure, but I have a good feeling about things now."

Both men smile at me, and I marvel at how lucky I am to have both of them. It's especially impressive that until a few weeks ago, they would have been punching each other if anyone had made them sit this close together. Now we're starting to operate like a real family. I hope we can finish all of this soon. I want to see what the Goddess has in store for us. But first, we have to figure out Amber's plan and find out what she wants with my powers. I don't know how we'll do that since she won't talk to me.

I have to trust that the Goddess will help us in her own way. She's set us on this path for a reason, and we have to trust that she knows what she's doing. Each of us has a part to play, and the sooner we accept that, the better everything will work. It's almost like she speaks the words into my soul. I have a newfound hope and positive feeling that everything is going to work out the way it's supposed to. We will find the missing wolves and vamps, and we will save them.

I can't explain how I know it, but I do. We will not fail this mission.

SMALL SUCCESSES

JAMES

As promised, I explain my search of the attic at dinner. I expect someone to be upset that I didn't discuss it with everyone first, but it doesn't happen.

"Did you find what you were looking for?" Ryland asks.

"I think I did. Plus, I found several more spell books that I think will come in handy too. I brought all the books down, along with the chest where I found the spell I was looking for." I gesture to the counter where I put everything.

Garnet picks up one of the books and flips through it. "I can see how this one will be beneficial. If they're all like this, then you've found a goldmine."

"If you think that one is good, check this out." I pull the ancient tome from the chest and place it into her hands. "It has an unbinding spell in it. And several others that might give us some insight into Amber's motives."

I'm relieved that Garnet decided to knock her out so that we could all have some time together. After I hand her the spell book, I show her the journals I found as well. "I don't know that any of this is relevant, but it looks like these are Amber's personal journals. I haven't read much of it because I'm not sure if we're violating her privacy or not. I figured I would leave that up to you, since you are her niece."

"I'll check them out. Maybe she wrote about why she's so anxious for me to complete the mate bond," Garnet says. As soon as the words leave her mouth, her eyes go wide and her hands cover her face. She's been very careful not to talk about that, and I'm sure she's embarrassed that she brought it up.

"Hey," Luca gently pulls her hands from her face. "It's okay. You don't have to worry about us. We know you care. We're yours, bonded or not. Right, Orym?"

"Without a doubt," Orym agrees. I know that none of them like to talk about it though. It reminds them that Ryland and I are already bonded with Garnet. I don't regret it, but it was also completely accidental.

"Let's get back to the matter at hand. We need to review these spells and make sure they're what we need," Ryland pulls our focus back to the spell books. There will be time to figure the rest out later, and he knows it.

"I'll start reviewing her journals tomorrow. We have to learn more about why the witches are taking wolves and vampires too. That's the only way we'll be able to save them." Garnet sounds more steady as her attention returns to the spell book in her hand. I hope that the unbinding spell is something that she can do herself. If we need another witch for it, we'll be screwed. It's not like Amber's followers will help us out.

Unless...no, that would never work.

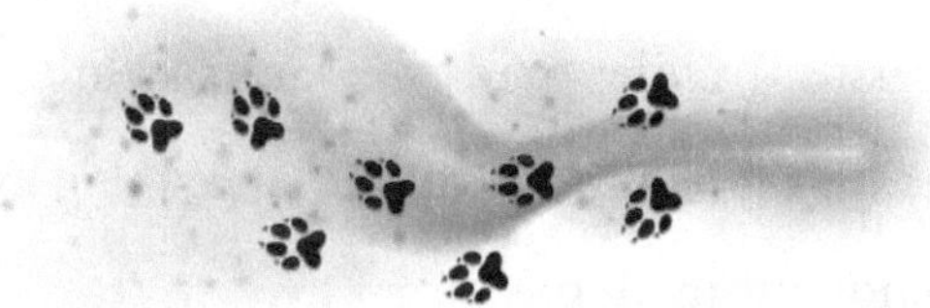

LUCA

The pain on Red's face when she mentions the mate bond is enough to make me cringe. I want to erase all of her pain and replace it with nothing but happiness. Unfortunately, we have a little while to wait for that. I don't have a magic wand to wave and make it all go away. It's not what she needs right now anyway.

Everyone settles into their regular nightly routine, and I take the opportunity to sit with Red as she studies the spell that could help us the most. "Do you need me to do anything?" I offer, rubbing a hand down her arm.

"If you really want to help, you could start on one of Amber's journals. I understand why James didn't want to read it, but I won't have time to go over everything myself. If you don't mind, just mark the parts I need to read." I nod at her suggestion and grab a couple of the journals and a notepad.

Settling on the couch next to her feels like the most natural thing in the world. We work in silence for a while. Amber's private thoughts are even worse than her public ones. I can tell from her writing that she hates most other supernatural beings. It seems as if that may be the whole reason for the kidnappings. But I still suspect there's more to it than that.

I continue reading, marking spots that I think Red and the others need to see. Most of it is nonsense, though. This journal paints a picture of a jealous little sister, who desperately wants to be special. Her powers are mediocre, but her aspirations are phenomenal. As a child, Amber wanted to be exactly what she is, or was before Red showed up. She wanted to control the territory as the most powerful witch in it.

When we showed up, Red ruined that for her. The second journal describes in detail the torture and interrogation of Red's mother, Ruby. Amber wanted her sister to tell her where the baby was. Ruby refused, and she paid for that refusal with her life. She didn't die until her little sister had stripped her powers and transferred them to herself, though. And from her words on these pages, Amber relished the pain she inflicted on Ruby. She enjoyed torturing her, and was sad when her sister died, only because she couldn't continue to hurt her.

I make a note to not tell Red about that part and keep reading. Amber wrote the spells she used and their effects in detail, so the journal was also another spell book. She detailed ingredients for potions and how those potions worked. Some of this is pretty useful stuff. I wonder if I can remove the pages about Ruby and just let Red read the rest.

"I think I can do this unbinding spell tomorrow," she announces after studying it and reading through a few other pages in that book for a while.

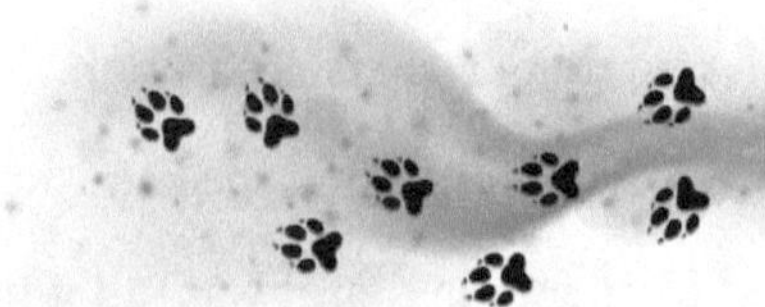

GARNET

I read through the spell book that contains the unbinding spell several times before I finally understand it. The book itself isn't that confusing, it's the way Amber wrote the spells in it. The pages aren't in order, and I have to decipher the correct order before I can understand how to do the spell I need. I'll have to find the candles, incense, and crystals required for it. But once I have the pages marked in order, I make a list of what I need.

I think we can gather all the supplies from inside the cabin. Then I can do the spell in the clearing. As soon as the spell is complete, I'll have to have my guys take care of me. The book details the effects of a power surge like the one I expect. It's going to be rough and probably pretty painful.

"I think I can do this unbinding spell tomorrow," I say to Luca, drawing his attention away from Amber's journals that he's been reading. I can tell that he's reading something he doesn't want to share with me from his face. He's never been able to lie to me, and this won't be any different.

"What is it?" I ask, putting my hand on his arm and pulling the book toward me.

He shakes his head. "Don't. Seriously, some of this shit is pretty bad. Amber is more than a little crazy. Did you find a binding spell in there? I think we're gonna need one to keep her from coming after you again."

I can tell that he's upset by what he's reading, and that makes me angry. "I haven't, but I think I can rework the unbinding spell. Or I could just use the power stripping spell that she was going to use on me." I don't really want to take her powers for myself, but if that's the only choice I have, I will. I'm done playing nice with her. After all of her bullshit while she claimed to be training me, I've decided that I'm going to treat her the way she's treated me.

"You'd really strip her powers permanently?" Luca looks shocked to hear me say that.

I nod. "If that's the only way to be sure she'll leave us alone, then yes, I will," I respond without hesitation. Our freedom is too important for me to pause. I have to be willing to fight for our future, and be as ruthless as those we're going to have to fight against. I'm not even sure I'll be able to do it, but I have to try.

"I guess I never expected that from you," he says quietly.

"Does that disappoint you?" I ask, suddenly scared that he'll decide that he doesn't want to be with me. The idea that I could lose Luca tears me apart in a way I never thought was possible.

"Not even a little. It just surprised me, that's all," he assures me.

"I don't want to hurt her. I'd rather not have to. But she may not give us a choice. And she never once hesitated to hurt one of you to get me to cooperate. Why should I treat her differently?" I ask him. I don't want to fight with him.

I'm scared that we're on uneven ground right now anyway. I should drop it and avoid this topic, but I can't.

"You shouldn't. I just didn't expect you to be the one who decided to hurt her. I figured it would have to be Ryland, Orym, or myself. You know that we would do that for you." It wasn't a question. And he's right, I do know that. It's just hard to wrap my head around everything.

"Did you find anything to explain why she was so adamant about us bonding as soon as possible?" I'm not sure I want the answer, but I can't stop myself from asking this question either.

"Not yet. Everything she has in her journals about fated mates indicates that the bond makes you stronger and gives you more power. If we had already bonded, she wouldn't have been able to control you as easily." He closes the books and turns toward me. "Do you think she was pushing so hard so that you *wouldn't* do it?"

"I don't know. I've thought about that possibility. I don't want to put you at risk if I don't have to. If there's something we don't know about why she pushed so hard. It's bad enough I'm worried about James and Ry. I can't handle being terrified that something will happen to all of you." I know how that sounds, and I don't like it. But it's true. If I could take back bonding with any of them, I would, at least until I knew what Amber's game plan was.

"I hate that she's poisoned you against us. I know it's not exactly that, but that's how it feels sometimes. No matter how you phrase it, Ryland and James share something with you that Orym and I don't. I'm not angry. And I'm not trying to manipulate you. I'm just telling you how it feels." I can hear the sadness in his voice. He doubts my feelings for him.

"Luca," I begin, but he holds up a hand.

"Red, it's okay. Really. We understand your reasons for waiting. I just hope you're right about them." He stands up and walks out of the room, leaving the journals on the counter next to the rest of the books. How did I manage to fuck this up so badly?

After Luca leaves me alone, I take a deep breath and go back to my notes. I know him well enough to know that going after him won't help. Nothing I can say will fix this. I have to figure Amber's motives out so that it's safe to bond with my mates. That is the only way to make this right.

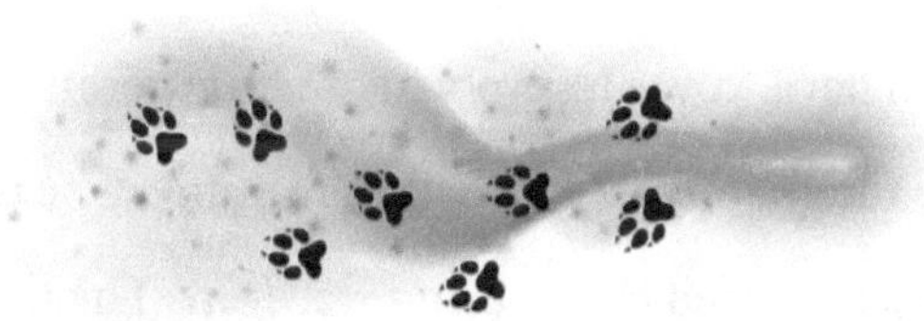

ORYM

After cleaning the kitchen, I head outside with Ryland for a run around the property. I have to run this sexual frustration off, because jerking off isn't doing it for me. As soon as I step outside, I shift into my wolf form. Settling into my pale gray fur is my comfort zone. I feel completely at home in my animal form, just like I'm sure Ryland and Luca do.

I stroll up to Ryland, taking in his jet-black fur and larger stature. I'm proof that you don't have to be the biggest guy around to be tough. Maybe that's been our problem all along. I've always been a little intimidated by Ryland's size. I'll never admit that to anyone, though.

We run hard, covering every inch of the perimeter. We call it a patrol, and that's part of what we're doing. The rest is getting some much-needed exercise and freedom. The fact that we're still at this cabin is nearly the same as being locked up. We can't leave yet because Garnet doesn't have everything she needs.

And I feel like we're no closer to being able to rescue the abducted wolves and vamps than we were before we knew that Amber is involved. We still haven't figured out exactly who she's working with. There has to be a wolf or two working with her, otherwise there's no way she'd be able to effectively take them from their homes.

I let my mind wander, puzzling over everything as we run. Before I realize, we've stopped at the small lake that's near the cabin. There's no one around, so I'm not sure why Ryland is stopping. When he shifts, I do the same. He must need to talk to me about something.

"What's up?" I ask, looking around. This place looks a lot different when the sun is setting than it does at noon. It's kind of creepy.

"Do you think we'll ever get to go home? I didn't want to talk about it where the others could hear. I know Red has a lot on her mind, and I don't want to guilt her." Wow, is Ryland actually thinking about someone else for a change? I'm impressed.

"I think she'll find what she needs in those books James found. Then we'll be one step closer to going home. But you know that she has mixed feelings about that now, right? She doesn't know where she belongs, since she discovered that she's a witch, not a wolf."

Ryland starts to pace in front of the lake. "I get that. I'm just feeling antsy here. Even if we don't go back to the pack lands, we can't stay here indefinitely. The forest doesn't want us here. Can't you feel it?"

I shake my head. "I'm not sure what you're talking about. I don't feel anything." I wonder if he's somehow more sensitive to the magic than I am.

"It feels like there's something pushing me to leave."

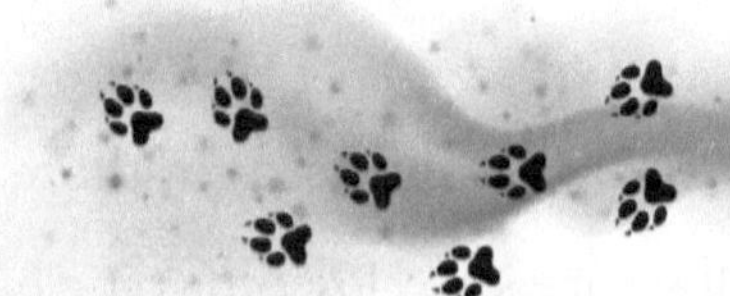

RYLAND

I take a chance, telling Orym how I'm feeling. There is something in this forest that wants me gone. It wants all of us to leave and never come back. I just don't know what it is. I'm starting to wonder if I'm being paranoid. "It feels like there's something pushing me to leave."

"But what could do that? The trees are alive, yeah, but not like that. It's not like the forest itself can do that," he says. Logically, I know that. But I can't brush off this feeling. Something is in this forest and it wants us gone.

"I don't know. It's just a feeling I can't shake. I think we should get out of here as soon as possible." It won't help telling him that. We both know that Red needs to be here to learn how to use her magic, and we need to figure out where the witches are holding the wolves and vamps.

"We will. She needs more time to figure her powers out. Plus, we have to find the missing wolves. Once everyone is safe, we'll be able to go home."

I can't argue with that. "We need to start searching for the victims. There's no way to save them if we don't know where they are."

"Do you want to patrol farther out, then?" I can't believe that Orym is just going along with my plan like we're friends. That feels strange too.

"I think that's the best option. If anyone stops us, we tell them that Amber asked us to keep an eye on things out here while she's away," I offer. That excuse makes the most sense, and Orym seems to agree.

After deciding it was better to stick together, we shift and start our search. At first, we take a jog around the perimeter, then expand a few yards at a time. We have to keep an eye out for the territory boundary, even though I'm sure we're not close to it. If we accidentally get stuck on the other side of it, that would be bad.

We make several circles, expanding our radius out as far as we're comfortable. I stop running when we get close to the first cabin we came across when we entered the forest. There are people here now. Orym halts behind me and we both shift. "Why'd you stop?" he asks.

I point at the cabin through the trees. "People."

"Not just people," he says when he takes a closer look. "Some of those are wolves and maybe some vamps too."

We duck down and watch for as long as we're comfortable. I note how many people are coming and going freely while Orym keeps track of how many have weapons. Why do witches need guns? This is an added layer to the already complicated web we've been trying to tear down.

By the time we head back to the cabin, it's dark. The only way to find the path is to shift.

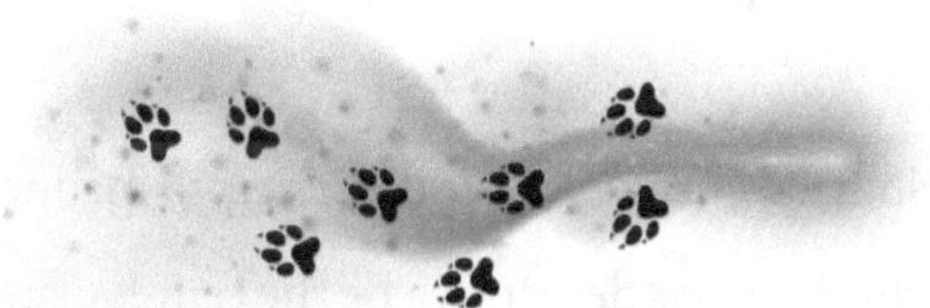

GARNET

With my notes complete and Luca upset with me, I decide to start reading Amber's journals. I purposefully avoid the two that Luca started with, since there was something in one of them that he didn't want me to see. I might as well not make him more upset.

As I read, I feel like I'm actually learning something about my now estranged aunt. She had claimed to be a lot younger than my mother, but that isn't true. I have no idea how she's maintained her looks, because she appears to be about my age. In reality, she's old enough to be my mother herself. Which makes her somewhere in her fifties, while looking thirty. That fact alone is impressive, or it would be if she wasn't so terrifying.

Each journal chronicles her descent into madness. She was a jealous child, always desiring to be the center of attention. She grew into a bitter teenager who resented her sister's powers. From there, things got worse when Ruby got pregnant with me. Amber did everything she could to find out who my father was, but my mother refused to tell her.

I can't help thinking that my mother knew how dangerous her little sister was, even then. That's the only explanation for her keeping that secret. She was trying to protect me. Just like her giving me to Grammy was for my protection. I can't find anything in my mother's journal about giving me up, but that has to be what happened. Unless it was my father who did it after Ruby was killed. I hadn't thought of that before. Grammy could know my real father.

That's a matter for later. I can't dwell on that right now. I have to focus on figuring out Amber's end game. Her journals get progressively worse, and she details everything.

Each dark deed that corrupted her soul is written in gory detail in her journals. Some of it makes me feel sick. Other parts terrify me even more than I thought possible. I'm glad I got to read them, though, because it helps me understand her better. It doesn't matter, really, but it will serve to remind me that she used to be a normal person with a pure soul.

She had a chance for redemption, but chose to follow a dark path. And using that dark magic changed her. The woman I met, the one I know, is not Amber. Not the one my mother grew up with at least. So much has happened to her. There are so many things she's done. I can't even think about it because a lot of it turns my stomach.

I force myself to keep reading, stopping when I get to the journals that Luca started with. I know that I should just let it go and stop reading, but I have to know. I pick one up and read it quickly. It's worse than any of the others. She details plans of murder and stealing people's powers, then goes into further detail after the fact.

How can I be related to this monster? What if I'm no better than she is? I told Luca while he was reading this that I would take her powers if I had to. Fuck. He must think I'm horrible like her. Pain washes over me and I drop to the floor. I can't stop the tears that start to fall. I don't want to be like her. I can't be, can I?

Even if I did bind or remove her powers, it would be to protect people, not to use them for myself. I'm still sitting in the floor with her journal in my lap, crying, when Orym and Ry get back from their patrol.

"Red, what happened?" Ry drops to the floor next to me.

Orym kneels on my other side. "Are you okay?"

I can feel the panic rolling off of both men. "I'm fine. I was reading Amber's journals. She's a monster."

"It can't be that bad, can it?" Orym wants to give everyone the benefit of the doubt. But it won't work this time.

"She wrote about her plans to kill people, then wrote about how she felt as they died by her hand. She liked it. A lot." I can't tell them more than that, because I know it will make me sick.

"So, we can't just leave her here when we go, can we?" Ry asks.

I shake my head. "I don't think so. But I'm not sure what we can do with her." I don't want to think about it either because I worry anything I do will make me as much of a monster as she is. But I don't tell him that.

"There's a spell to strip her powers. We can do that and tie her up. We'll take her to the council and see what they say about it. Then there's no chance of her escaping," Ry offers. I should be shocked that he's on my side, but honestly, I expect him to suggest worse.

"Is that all you found?" Orym asks, and I know what he really wants to know.

"I haven't found her most recent journals yet. I don't know why she pushed us so hard to complete the bond. And I really do want to."

He cuts me off, not letting me finish. "It's okay. Luca and I can handle waiting. Even if that means you need to have some alone time with James and Ryland. We'll be fine. We're not going anywhere."

No matter how many times they say it, I still feel bad about it. There is nothing I can do about it, though. Well, there is one thing, but what if completing the bond ruins everything? No, I can't do that yet. I have to make sure that it won't somehow give Amber the upper hand here.

"We found the kidnapped wolves and vamps," Ry says, effectively changing the subject.

BREAKTHROUGH

RYLAND

I EXPLAIN TO RED exactly where we found them, and she laughs. "I know it's not funny, but the fact that they're keeping them exactly where we first discovered them, kinda is."

"I know that you're trying to get everything ready for the rescue and be as prepared as possible. How close are you?" Orym asks. I still think we should just go free the wolves and involve the council if we have to, but he disagrees. He insists that Red has to be ready to use her magic before we act.

"I don't know. I found the unbinding spell, and I'm going to do it tomorrow. But I don't know how hard it's gonna hit me. I may be okay and have complete control. I may not. The entries about it are confusing." Her lack of confidence shakes me to my core. I want to protect her and keep her safe, but I can't.

"We need to get those prisoners out of there now. We can't afford to wait," I say, helping Red to her feet.

"Of course, we do. But Garnet has to be ready. We'll never make it out of the forest without her," Orym argues. I don't want to fight with him, but I need both of them to see my point.

"I agree with Ry. If we wait until I'm ready, it'll never happen. But I would feel better about it if I did the unbinding spell first. Can we agree to wait until tomorrow at least?" she asks, threading her fingers through mine.

I nod, knowing I can't argue with her request. "What can I do to help with the unbinding?" She hands me a list of ingredients and supplies.

"I just have to get all this together. Most of it is in the kitchen. It's one of a hand full of spells that aren't dependent on the phase of the moon or time of day. I can do it whenever and wherever. I'll use the clearing, since we don't know exactly what will happen." She's so calm about the whole thing. We have no idea how this spell will affect her, but she's willing to do it and take that risk. For us.

"Are we all going to be able to be there with you at least?" My heart races at the thought that I can't be there when I know that she'll need me.

She smiles sweetly. "I hope that you'll all be out in the clearing with me when I do the spell. I'll feel safer that way."

I pull her into my arms and kiss her forehead. I can't wait until all of this is over and we can move on with our lives. The five of us have so much we need to discuss and deal with, but we can't do any of that until the prisoners are safe and we're back home.

She hugs me back, then I let Orym take her from my arms.

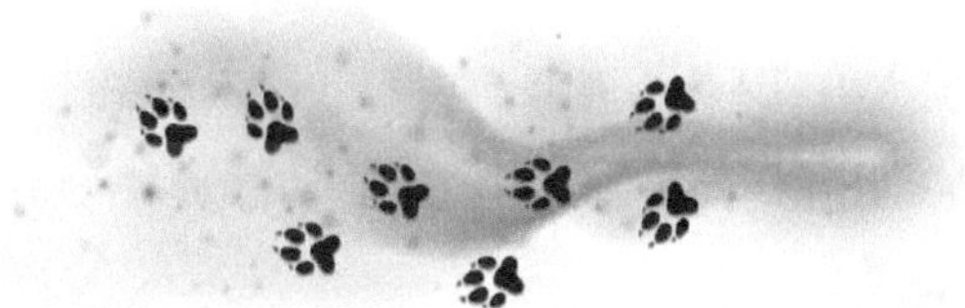

JAMES

I have no idea what Amber is up to, but I can tell she's trying to get information from me. With the cuffs on, she can't use her magic. She has to rely on other methods of manipulation. "Are you sure there's nothing going on? It seems like you're all getting ready for something," she says.

"Just eat your dinner. Don't worry about what we may or may not be planning," I reply, holding the fork up for her to take a bite. I can't let her feed herself without untying her, and I'm not about to do that. We've taken great pains to secure her and remove anything she can use as a weapon or to escape.

I want nothing more than to walk away and let her rot, but I know that Garnet doesn't want that. At least not right now.

"If you want to talk, why don't you tell me why your people kidnapped those wolves and vamps," I offer after a few minutes of silence.

Amber smiles at me. To anyone who doesn't know her, it would seem to be a sweet smile, but I can see the darkness in her. "I have no idea what you're talking about, darling."

Of course, she doesn't. But I didn't tell her that I'd figured out what she tried to hide yesterday. She doesn't know that I've found her journals and spell books that were hidden in the attic. I figure she doesn't need to know yet. At some point, Garnet will tell her.

Garnet tells me that she found the spell she needs and that she's going to perform it tomorrow. That's a relief. The sooner we can be done with this, the better. I won't be able to fully relax until Amber is locked away and awaiting trial by the council. Since part of her crimes were against me, another council member, I should be able to enact justice myself. It's my right. But I won't. I'll wait and let the council decide what to do with her.

I have to refocus on feeding Amber, as I catch myself getting distracted. "Just eat, then. It'll be time to sleep soon."

"Are you ever going to let me sleep in my own bed again?" she asks, batting her eyelashes at me. I know that this particular manipulation attempt is designed to make me think she's innocent. It won't work.

"Maybe. That just depends on you." My response is curt and unemotional. I won't let her bait me, and I'm not about to let her sleep in her bed. She'll stay locked in this closet just like every night since we tied her up.

"Oh, come on. What do I have to do to show you that I'm no longer a threat? With these lovely bracelets my niece gave me, I can't even do the most basic magic. What could I possibly do to you if you let me sleep in my bed?"

"That's enough food. Good night."

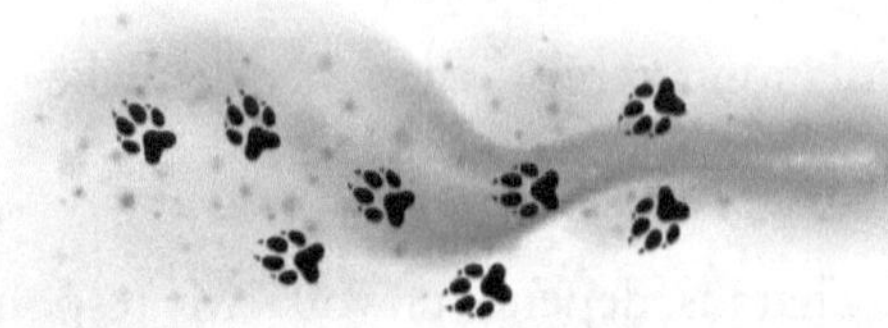

GARNET

After talking to Orym and Ry, I feel better about things. We know where the missing wolves and vampires are being held. We have a plan in place to rescue them. Everything is going the way we need it to. Things are almost too perfect. Almost.

Luca still isn't talking to me, and I don't know how to fix things with him. I don't really want to talk to the other guys about it. I want to keep some privacy between them. It's hard, though. Because I want to share and get their advice. But I can't do that to Luca. If they took my side, then he'd be alienated. And if they didn't, then I'd be hurt.

So, I hold my tongue and don't mention the quarrel. "Okay, we know how we're gonna hit them. Where's Luca? He needs to know this too." Ry starts looking around for him.

"I'm not sure where he went," I admit.

"I'll catch him up later, then," he says. I'm certain he can tell what's happened, but he doesn't ask about it or push for more information.

With the plan laid out, everyone decides that we should turn in early. I know I won't be able to sleep until I've at least tried to fix things with Luca. I look for him in the house, but can't find him. I sigh, walking outside to hunt him down.

I can't believe how badly I'm screwing everything up. Luca has been my best friend my entire life, and I manage to alienate him in one afternoon, just by saying something completely stupid. I all but told him that he wasn't as important to me as James and Ry are. And that's not true. Each of my mates is important. I need them all.

I walk carefully down the path that leads to the lake. Hopefully he's there. I've looked everywhere else that I can think of. But I guess if he doesn't want to be found, I won't find him. I get to the lake, and there's no one around.

Luca, where did you go? I know that he can't hear my thoughts, but I can't stop myself from thinking it at him.

Do you need some help finding him, Red? Ry offers. I can tell that the only reason he responds is that I was projecting the thought.

Yes, please. I won't be able to sleep until I talk to him.

Before I can tell him where I am, I hear two sets of wolf paws racing toward me. I forgot that mates can track each other easier. Plus, Ry and Orym are the best trackers I know. For a minute, I think it's Luca with Ry. Then I realize how much Orym and Luca look alike in their wolf forms. I know it's not Luca when the gray wolf stops short of tackling me.

My disappointment must be obvious, because they instantly shift back. "Did we scare you?" Orym asks, pulling me into a hug.

"I thought you were him for a minute," I admit, holding back a sob.

"Oh, honey," he says as he rubs his hand up and down my back. "You don't have to tell us what happened between the two of you. But if you want to talk, we'll listen. James is making sure Amber is locked up, then he's coming to help."

"Thank you," I reply, letting myself melt into his embrace. I allow myself a moment of comfort, then pull away so we can start looking for Luca.

"Where could he have gone?" Ry asks. He pulls out his phone and tries to call. After a minute or two, he frowns and lowers the phone. "It goes straight to voicemail. Something is wrong here, and I don't know exactly what it is."

We split up to search the area, making sure to stay within sight of each other. When James meets up with us, Ry and Orym decide to go a little further out. They promise to stay together and insist that James and I do too. I don't object. It's not safe here, even if Amber's people think we're working with them.

It's dark when we finally give up on finding him tonight. He must be off somewhere hiding. There's no other explanation for him vanishing. I upset him, and now I have to suffer by worrying because he's gone. When he comes back in the morning, I'm going to punch him, then kiss him, then punch him again.

I don't sleep well, even though I'm sandwiched between Orym and Ry, with James on Ry's other side. I toss and turn, only getting a few minutes of rest at a time. I have no idea how the three of them sleep through it, but somehow, they do.

I carefully climb out of the bed at first light. Laying here won't help me any, but maybe doing that unbinding spell will. I get dressed quickly and gather my supplies. Then I head outside to the clearing. With any luck, Luca will come back while I'm working.

I draw my circle on the ground with salt. Then I place the spell ingredients around the cauldron that stands in the center of the circle. I consult the spell book as I work, making sure that I'm following the instructions exactly. I can't afford to screw this up. If I do, I might lose what little control I have over my magic.

After everything is laid out, I carefully double and triple check the placement of each item. I go over the words in my head again and again. I can't make any mistakes here. This has to be exactly right.

I take a moment to center myself, wishing Luca was here. He's always been the best at calming me down when I'm nervous about anything. I take a few deep breaths, willing my heart to slow down and forcing my breathing to regulate.

I have one shot here.

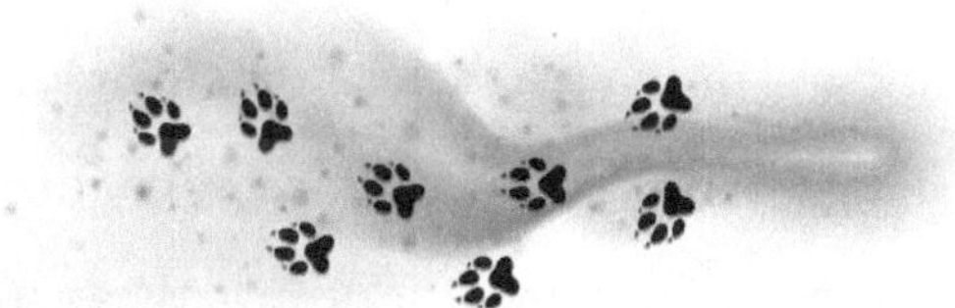

LUCA

Red's words sting me. She's never been so cold and unfeeling toward me before. I know that if I don't walk away, I'm going to cry. Or worse, I'll scream at her and make her feel guilty about not bonding with me. I don't want it to happen that way.

I want her to want to bond with me. I don't know why she doesn't want to. I thought we were close. She's been my best friend for as long as I can remember. I can't stay in this cabin right now. She's too close.

I shift as soon as I'm out the door. I run, not paying attention to where I'm heading. I just need to get away. I get further away from the cabin than I mean to before I stop running. I'm panting and my muscles ache. I should head back so I can shower and go to bed. I should probably confront her about this and get everything out in the open between us. But I can't do that yet. It's still too raw.

I know that I shouldn't feel that way. Red is my fated mate. We're destined to be together. So, what if she has other mates too? Why should that matter? It shouldn't matter if I'm the last one she bonds with or the first. I know that we will bond at some point. I'm being immature and childish about this.

I talk myself into heading back toward the cabin. I sniff the air, looking for the right direction to head in. I know I'm not close to the border, so I don't have to worry about accidentally going across the boundary.

Well, all I can do is track my way back now. I sniff the ground, searching for the path I took to get here. When I find it, I start racing back toward my family. I run until I'm sure

I should be close, then I stop to sniff around again. That's strange. It's like my scent is just gone. Did I make a wrong turn somewhere? I shake that thought away and look for the trail again. I think I've found it, so I take off running again. It's getting dark, which would make it harder to see if I shifted back.

I run a while longer, trying to follow the path back to the cabin. When I stop again, I realize that something is really wrong. I don't recognize this part of the forest. Somehow, I've gone deeper into the woods instead of heading back toward the cabin. How did I manage that?

I've gotten turned around and now I'm lost. How? I'm so busy trying to figure out where I am that I'm not paying enough attention. I step onto the net that scoops me off the ground, and I'm trapped. Fuck. I manage to shift back in the tight space, but I can't figure out how to get free.

"You might as well stop struggling, wolf."

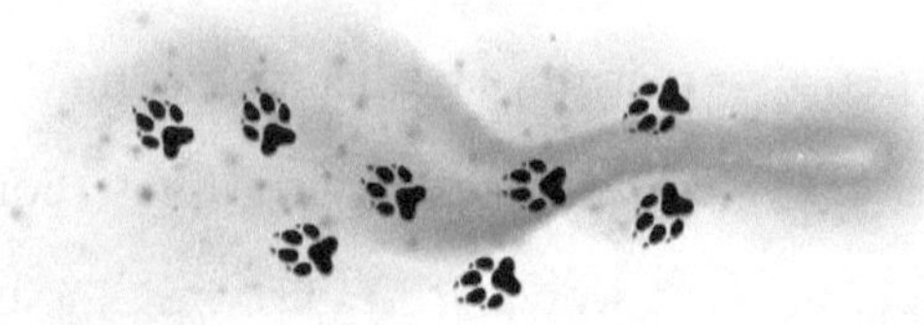

ORYM

I wake early, noticing that Garnet is no longer laying in the center of the bed. I jump from the bed and dress quickly. I hope she hasn't gone looking for Luca again. We agreed that none of us would go out alone. I run out the front door and see her in the clearing. She's doing the spell without us.

Part of me is hurt, but I understand that she feels like every-thing is spiraling and she needs to do something to get herself under control. This may be the exact thing she needs. I can't stand in the way of that. But I can get just close enough to make sure she's safe without interfering.

I drop onto the bottom step of the porch, my eyes glued to what she's doing. I can hear her chanting something but can't make out what she's saying. It doesn't matter, I know what the pages said. She has to call her powers back to her, breaking the binding that was placed on her.

I'm amazed at how strong she is. This woman that the God-dess has chosen for me—she's been through so much, but she refuses to give up. She keeps pushing forward. And I know that Garnet wants to save everyone. She feels like it's her purpose. Maybe it is. I don't know how she does it. I wouldn't be nearly as resilient without her.

Even without our bond completed, I'm falling for her. I knew that I would from the moment her lips first touched mine. It also explains why I was always so drawn to her, even before we knew that we were fated. I can't imagine feeling that way about multiple people. She must be so overwhelmed all the time.

I want to take her away from here and protect her from all the dangers that life has. I know that I can't, but that doesn't make the desire any less. Even if I suggested it, she'd say no. Garnet will face whatever is thrown at her, and she'll overcome it all. I know she will.

I watch as she completes the spell. For a moment, nothing happens. Then a column of bright light surrounds her. She stands there with her arms outstretched, absorbing it all. The light seems to be pouring into her, filling her up.

Is this her power returning? Did the spell go wrong? Fuck, if this kills her, I will never forgive myself. I race to her, stopping when I see that she's still standing and she's in the center of the circle. I know from her explanation that I can't cross that circle until she finishes the spell. If something goes wrong, I'll have to wait until I'm sure she's finished or until I'm sure something is wrong.

I stand there, tortured, watching this light fill her up. She's glowing, and her face is contorted in pain. I want to reach out, but I promised her that I would wait.

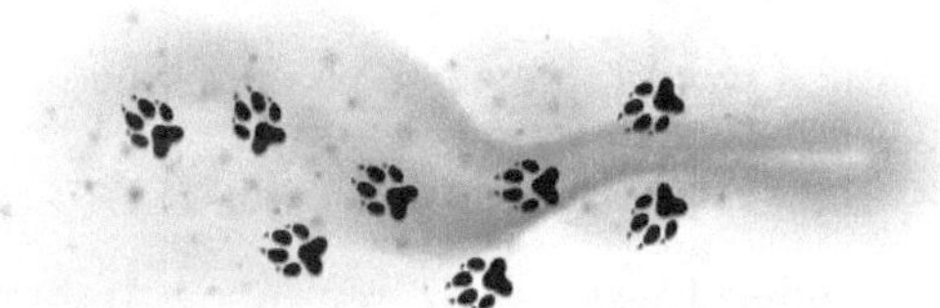

GARNET

I start the chant after adding the ingredients in order into the cauldron at my feet. I feel the exact moment when my power is unlocked. It's like it wasn't bound inside of me, but locked away somewhere else. It all rushes back to me at once.

I'm frozen in place, my arms outstretched, absorbing the magic into my skin. I have to close my eyes because the light is so bright. I sense someone approaching, but can't see who it is. It can't be Ry or James, because I would know from our bond. That means it has to be Luca or Orym. Since we didn't find Luca last night, I'm guessing it's Orym.

It doesn't matter who it is, because I can't stop what's happening to me. I wouldn't even if I could. The pain is extreme, but somehow it feels right. This magic is part of me. It was taken away when I was a baby, removing the very thing that made me who I am.

I know without a doubt that I am a witch. Not just any witch, though. There's something different about this magic. I can't explain it, but it doesn't feel the same as the magic I've been working with. I would love to talk to Luca about this, but I don't know where he is.

Something inside of me knows that he's in danger, though. I can feel my senses opening to a point of misery. The light is too bright, the sun is too hot, I can smell everything, and there's so much noise. It's overloading my senses. I feel like I'm being ripped in half.

If this is how I die, my one regret will be not bonding with all of my mates. I should have listened to Amber when I had the chance. At this moment, I'm certain that her insistence that I complete the bonds was designed to make sure I didn't. She was playing me, and I let her do it.

I know things that I couldn't possibly know. I can see Orym watching as this happens. He's dying to reach for me, but he won't, because he promised to let me do this spell no matter what. I can feel his anguish at watching me suffer.

I feel the moment when James wakes up and rushes out the door. Ry is two steps behind him. I see what they see, and it's terrifying. I'm frozen in place, surrounded by blinding light. It looks like I'm being consumed and could explode at any moment.

Focus, Garnet. I can't get distracted. I have to gather my magic and get it under control. I can't. The pain is too much. If I stand here any longer, I'm going to combust. *Move; get out of this circle.* But I can't move. All I can do is surrender to these sensations and let the magic do whatever it's going to do.

I draw in a ragged breath and feel the flames burn into my lungs. I didn't even realize that I was on fire. Icy water follows the burning. A cool breeze whips around me and the earth quakes beneath my feet. I feel my soul rip open and absorb it all. But something is missing. Something is wrong here.

The pain that tears through me is too much. I can't stand it. It's as if my body is rejecting the magic, but the magic won't let me go. This is how I'm going to die. In just a moment, I won't be here at all. I'll be reduced to ash. What can I do to fight it? I have no idea.

I look through James' eyes again for a moment. They're seeing what I'm feeling. It looks as if I'm building up to an explosion. I did something wrong and I don't know how to fix it. It's too late for me. This is the end. I can feel the darkness creeping in.

I break the connection for a moment, giving myself a moment to breathe. I don't need to watch what happens next. It's bad enough I have to feel it. Ry and James rush forward, determined to pull me from the circle and stop what's happening to me.

Orym stops them, convincing them to join hands and surround the circle. They have to stretch, and end up too close to the flames that dance on my skin. But his plan works. The moment they close their circle around mine, the pain eases. The light is still bright, impossible to see through. I can tell that I'm not on fire anymore, though.

My body finally cooperates and begins to absorb the magic. I can feel my soul knitting back together. By the time the light fades, I'm nearly whole again. I know that the parts that still feel broken are because of the uncompleted bonds.

Right now, I know that I will live long enough to take care of that. Then I'll be even more powerful. Then I'll be whole. I can't explain the sensation that washes over me as the light finally fades away. I blink, struggling to see once the brightness is gone.

"Garnet? Are you okay?" Orym asks quietly. I know he doesn't want to interrupt the spell, and that he's concerned.

"I think so. I have to close the circle," I mutter. I hope that they understand. If I don't close the circle, the magic could leave me again. I don't know how much more painful that would be, and don't want to find out.

I work quickly but move slowly. I feel invigorated but sluggish. It's like my energy was filled to capacity, but then I was dropped into a vat of honey and told to run out of it. My arms and legs feel heavy and my mind is racing.

I understand the runes I've been seeing in my dreams, and I know what we need to do.

REGROUP AND RESCUE

LUCA

I HANG THERE, IN the net, for a while after the witches find me. "You might as well stop struggling, wolf." That voice echoes in my head. I know now how the witches have been able to kidnap so many wolves so easily. They have an inside man. Red was right the other day when she said she saw Levi. But it's not just him.

Lobo is the one who told me to stop struggling. He grew up with us. He trained with us. But I guess as Levi's grandson, there's no reason for him to be loyal to us. I wonder how many more wolves Amber has on her side by using Levi as a lieutenant in her little army.

It doesn't matter. The only thing that will do is make it harder to determine who needs rescued and who needs arrested. I fumble in my pocket for my phone, but I can't find it. Did I lose it somewhere?

Fuck. I bet Red is freaking out right now. I've been gone for hours. And even if I was upset with her, she'd never just accept that I took off. I fight against the ropes again. I have to get out of here and back to her. She needs me. Red is going to do that unbinding spell in the morning and I need to be there to make sure nothing goes wrong.

The moment I start tugging and shifting to break free of this net, something hits me. I'm not sure if it was a large stick or a bolt of magic. "I said, 'stop struggling.' Surely you understand what that means."

"Come on, Lobo, let me out of here. We come from the same region."

He hits the net again, and I realize it's a large stick. Well, that answers that. And apparently Lobo doesn't care that we're technically all part of the larger pack. Great. I guess I'll just add my name to the list of wolves who need rescued.

Okay, Luca, just breathe. This situation is bad, but you know there are four people who will be looking for you. They won't give up until they find you. Just breathe and stay alert. I have to give myself a pep talk to stay focused.

There's no point in trying to escape right now. Lobo is my guard, and he's clearly working for whoever is in charge. Maybe I can find out if that's Amber or not.

"Lobo, can I ask you something?"

He growls, but nods. "If it makes you stop trying to escape, sure. You won't be any good to us if I have to hurt you anyway."

Well, that's something. "Who are you working for here? And why are you doing all of this?"

"Don't worry about who's in charge. I have enough authority to take you out if needed. As for the why? Well, that's another story altogether. If you live long enough, you'll get the answers you want."

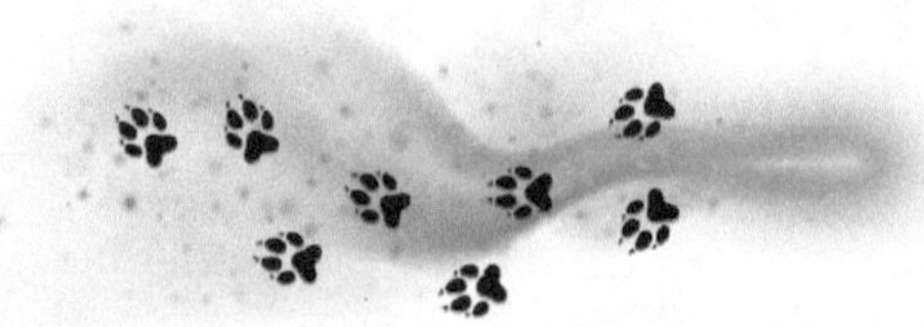

RYLAND

Once Red has unlocked her powers and recovered from the aftermath, we sit down and talk about our next step. We're going home today, by way of the cabin where the wolves are being held. James goes to check on Amber while the rest of us take care of breakfast. No one was thinking of food when we were startled awake by Red's pain.

James calls me along the bond. *Ryland, I need you to come here. Don't tell the others yet.* That's kind of cryptic. I shrug and stroll out of the kitchen. I'd already started coffee, and that was the extent of my breakfast responsibility this morning.

I walk into Amber's room and instantly know why he called to me. "Where the fuck is she?" I growl.

He shakes his head. "I don't know. But she got away with some of the relics from the displays, so I'm guessing she had help. And it looks like she's still wearing the cuffs. That means the magic used wasn't hers. I don't know how they knew she was locked up here."

"They must have had some sort of code that we didn't know about," I say, checking the room to see how they got her out. It looks like the window was pried open. That must have happened while Red was doing her spell this morning. Or while we were looking for Luca last night.

"I didn't check on her last night. This is my fault. Now what are we going to do?" James is beating himself up about this. I can feel his guilt through the bond. Which means that Red will feel it too.

As if he summoned her, Red rushes into the room and wraps her arms around James. "What's wrong? What happened?"

"Amber escaped. We're gonna have to move quicker than we expected. We need to go now if we hope to rescue everyone." I don't mind taking charge, but I have to admit, I don't want to leave without finding Luca.

"Do you think they took Luca? How else would they know that Amber was being held prisoner?" Red's thought makes sense, but Luca would never give us up like that.

"I don't know, but we'll find him. And the others. We'll bring them home and take care of Amber. She won't win this," I assure them both. "We might as well have a quick breakfast and fill Orym in."

Back in the kitchen, we catch Orym up on what's happened and the updated plan. "If she found a way to escape and take artifacts with her, does that mean she has her magic back too?"

"We don't know, but the cuffs aren't supposed to work that way. Right now, we'll operate on the idea that she found a way and will be using her magic against us," Red says, her voice trembling. I know that she's worried about Luca, and the situation in general. "Let's go."

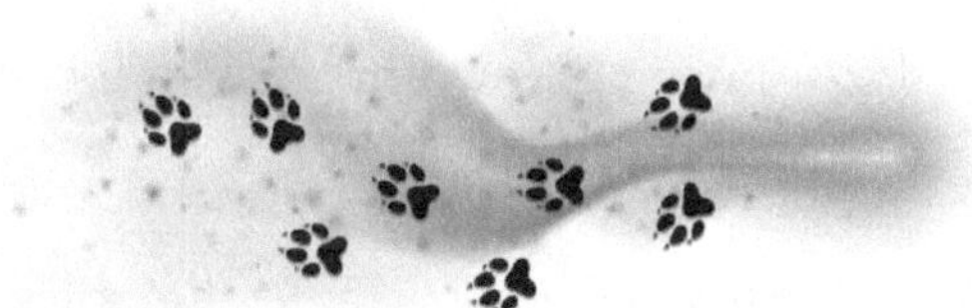

GARNET

Wolfing down breakfast and packing quickly give me some-thing to focus on besides Amber escaping and Luca going missing. With any luck, he'll be at the cabin with the rest of the kidnapped people. Just when I think things are finally going our way, this happens. Goddess help me, I don't know how much more I can take.

I need this done and over with. I want nothing more than to go home and claim my mates. Then we can figure out exactly how this will work. Gunnar may force us to leave the forest. I don't know where we'd go, but that's within his rights as territory leader. And to think, I was terrified I'd get exiled for being fated to a human. Now I'm scared it'll be because I'm not even a wolf.

Even knowing that he's not my father, I'm still scared of him too. But more than that, I'm angry. All these years, he treated me like I was less. He made me think I was broken, when really, I was just different. Part of me can't wait to face my bully. The rest is concerned that he'll shift and rip me apart.

I can't focus on that right now. I have to keep my head in the game. I was supposed to have more time to get used to my full powers, but that's not happening now. All I can do is try my best and hope it's enough. I take a deep breath and walk out the door, meeting three of my mates outside.

"Let's move," Ry says, taking charge again. Honestly, I'm relieved. I half expected them all to look to me for guidance, and I'm not ready for that yet. I'm struggling to keep it to-gether. All I want is to break down because Luca is missing and

Amber's escaped. I want to curl up in a ball and cry because we haven't saved the vampires and wolves yet.

But I can't do that. My men won't let me. I'm so glad I have them to lean on. Without their strength, I wouldn't be able to do this. I would have caved at the first moment something went wrong.

We start our trek, heading toward home, while still moving in the direction of the cabin where Ry and Orym saw the wolves yesterday. My nerves are going crazy and I start to feel sick. When we get to the edge of the clearing where that cabin stands, it's eerily quiet. "No. No, no, no, no. They were here yesterday. They can't be gone." I hear someone screaming, then a hand clamps over my mouth. Oh, I was screaming.

"Garnet, love, you have to pull it together. We can't draw attention to ourselves right now," James whispers against my ear.

"Stay together, take a look around. Then we're heading home. We'll regroup and get backup to come back," Orym insists. Ry nods at him. James is behind me, so I can't see his reaction.

I'm okay now, I promise. I tell James and Ry through the bond. Ry motions for James to let me go. "I'm sorry," I breathe when he does.

"It's okay, Red. We just need to stay focused. It's gonna be okay," Ry assures me. How can he possibly know that? For all we know, Amber had all the wolves and vamps killed the minute she escaped and that's why we can't find them now. I don't speak my fears, refusing to give them a chance to come true.

We search the area, inside and outside the cabin, and find nothing. There is no trace of the people who were held here. We have no idea where they were taken or even who held them here. As we finish up, there's a rustling in the trees nearby.

The four of us stop and stare as Levi and a few of his pack-mates stroll out of the trees as if they belong here. I instantly put up a protective shield. "So, it's true then," Levi utters half to himself.

"What are you doing here, Levi?" Orym asks. I realize that this was his mission all along, and he's taken turns letting everyone else run it. That trust he has in us warms my heart.

"I'm doing what I have to in order to protect my family, Orym. I would expect you to understand that," he responds.

I don't trust him. Something is off here. I can tell that my mates agree with that thought by the way they tense when Levi takes a step closer. "We don't want any trouble. Just let the prisoners go and we'll leave you alone."

"What prisoners? Do you kids see any prisoners here?" he asks his crew. Of course, they laugh and shake their heads.

"Where's Luca?" I ask, barely holding back the rage that's begging me to attack him.

"Well, little girl, I have no idea where your boy toy ran off to. Maybe he wasn't too keen on sharing and decided to find someone else to follow around," Levi snarls. He's cruel and harsh. Even though my heart knows better, his words sting.

Luca would never voluntarily leave me, would he? Was he that upset about me not bonding with him that he ran away from me? I can't afford to dwell on that idea right now. I have to find him. If he doesn't want me, he can tell me himself.

"Levi, we're not here to fight. We just want to go home. We'd like to take our kin with us. Do you know where he is?" Ry steps forward, blocking me from Levi. I can't tell if he's protecting me or the old man. I'm not really sure which of us needs it more.

James takes my hand and pulls me close to him. They can feel my anger through the bond. I'm itching to attack.

"We don't have him. He may be with the leaders, but I don't know where they are right now."

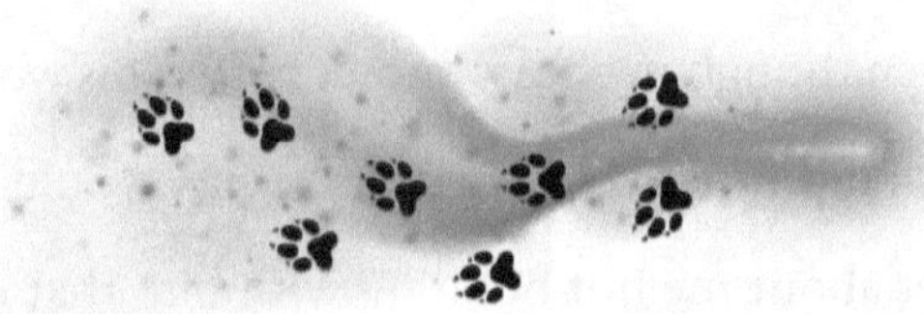

JAMES

I hold onto Garnet as if my life depends on it. Perhaps it does. She's practically foaming at the mouth to attack these guys. I think they're wolves, from the way Ryland and Orym talk to them. I know that I won't be any help negotiating with or questioning these guys. Instead, I focus on keeping Garnet calm and preventing her from starting a war.

Are you sure these guys have Luca? I ask her, making sure to block Ryland so he can focus on what he's doing.

I am. I can't explain how I know; I just do. We had a disagreement yesterday and they must have grabbed him when he went to get air.

I hate that we all seem to run off when we get upset. We definitely need to work on that. *Okay, I can accept that. We'll find him. You have to stay calm, though. We can't attack them if they have Luca. That won't end well for him, right?*

She nods, and I know that she'll hold back. With the change in posture, I know I've missed something in the conversation. Levi looks tense, as if he's deciding whether they should attack or not. Garnet holds onto the shield she put around us. The blue glow of her magic is mesmerizing.

I have to pay attention. Now that I've got her settled, I have to figure out what's going on here. "I already told you; we don't have your boy. Now, if you're set on leaving the territory, let us escort you. These woods aren't safe, you know."

Are they really going to let us go? I find that hard to believe. Amber was so set on Garnet staying, even before she revealed that she was the one behind the kidnappings. There has to be something more that they want from her. Maybe he's trying to lull us into a false sense of trust here. Ryland and I exchange a glance, and I know that he's thinking the same thing.

"We'll go, but we don't need an escort. I have to tell you, Levi, if I find out that you did take Luca, you'll pay. As a matter of fact, if he's not home by sundown, I'm going to assume that you lied and you do have him. Then I'll gather a small army and be back to get him." Ryland's threat sends a shiver of cold down my spine.

I know he means every word. I hope for their sakes that they send Luca home. Even as I have the thought, I know that they won't. This will end up being a war. I'm not sure any of us is ready for that.

"You'd better get moving then, hadn't you?" Levi snarls, and I'm sure he's barely holding back his shift. It reminds me of a feral wolf about to attack.

I'm not usually one to run from a fight, but I can recognize when I can't win.

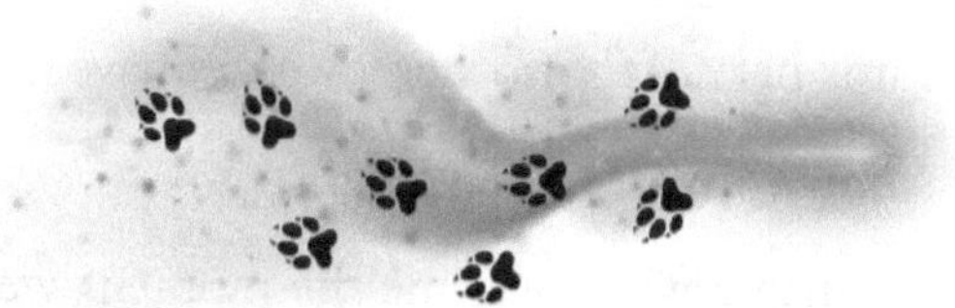

ORYM

Levi insists that they don't have Luca, but I can tell he's lying. I wonder if they're trying to brainwash him to their side. That would hurt Garnet the most. I'm glad that James has stayed by her side. If she drops this shield, we'll be way too exposed.

Levi and his group watch as we turn to leave. I keep an eye behind us while Ryland leads us out of the clearing. This place isn't safe. We need to leave now. Maybe this feeling is what Ryland was telling me about before. I feel it now, the forest's desire for us to be gone.

We race toward the barrier that will take us to safety. Safety is a relative term at this point, but it will be safer on the other side than it is here. At least there, we can have Gunnar show up with some wolves if there's a fight.

I feel the magic wash over me the moment we step across that boundary. It feels like coming home. I wonder if it's the opposite for Garnet, since she knows now that she's not one of us. My heart aches for her, because of what she's learned and what she's lost.

I know that having her magic is better for her than it being suppressed. I'm worried though, that she'll give up. Luca has been her best friend our entire lives. They've never been apart, except for during Gunnar's 'punishments' when he split them up in an attempt to break one or the other of them. I have to chuckle at that, because nothing he did could keep them apart.

They would always sneak away and hang out, no matter how bad the consequences after. And none of us would tell on them either. Somehow, we knew they were meant to be together.

A pang of guilt hits me. I'm her mate too, so I shouldn't feel guilty. I feel like it's partially my fault that he ran off. I know it's ridiculous, but if I'd insisted that he go with Ryland and myself, he wouldn't have been there to argue with Garnet.

She hasn't told us that's what happened, but it's the only thing that makes sense. Once we find him, I'll figure out how to fix this for them. I won't give up until he's back with us. Garnet deserves that. I'll do my best to take his place while he's gone. I know it won't be enough, but she needs all of us to lean on.

We don't stop running until we make it back to Ryland's cabin. We only stop there long enough to drop off our packs and clean up a little. Garnet wants to talk to Gunnar, and I think that's the best idea. Besides, we need to check on Vincent too. If he even made it back like Amber said.

"It won't hurt to shower and put on clean clothes. We have at least that much time," Ryland assures her.

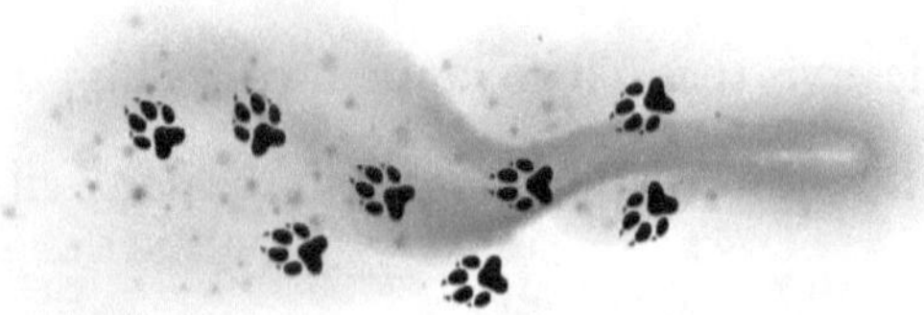

GARNET

I don't want to take time to clean up, but I know how dirty we are from running through the woods all day. So, I let Ry push me into it. Each of us showers and finds clean clothes, then we go off to find Gunnar. It's so strange to not think of him as my father, even though Luca figured it out a long time ago.

Luca. My heart hurts just thinking of him. I have to push it away. The only way to get him back is to keep moving forward. Talking to Gunnar and Vincent is the first step. James insists on helping me shower and get dressed. I can't argue with him. These three have been so amazing to me, taking care of me and keeping me focused.

I still miss Luca, but it's like they're trying to make up for that loss. I can't think of it like that. We will get him back. We have to. I can't live without him. Just like I couldn't live without these three.

Orym brushes my hair, then we're ready to go. I can't help noticing how no one is out in the camp as we walk through. It seems odd, since normally this would be the most active area for free time. Training should have ended a couple of hours ago, and people would be gathered for a bonfire and social time.

We get to the cabin I grew up in, and I hesitate. Do I knock? Or just walk in? It feels strange to be back here after being away for a few weeks and learning about my past. I knock on the door and jump when Grammy opens it quickly. "Come in, we have much to discuss," she says, stepping out of the way for us to enter.

"Is Gunnar here? We need to talk to him," I ask.

"So, you've learned the truth. He'll be along in a bit. He's got a group out searching for Vincent. They've done that every day since you left. We weren't sure if you were coming back or not."

"Wait, Vincent isn't here, either? That bitch," I growl. I never should have trusted her. I feel completely stupid.

"Don't blame yourself, child. This situation is not your fault, no matter what she told you," Grammy says.

"I don't know how I'm supposed to feel about everything. Why did you lie to me all these years?" I know this isn't the time, but I can't stop the question.

She shakes her head. "I never meant to lie. I was protecting you. Your mother was a beautiful soul, and she trusted me with her most precious gift. Gunnar was pissed that I agreed to hide you, but he went along with it because he had no choice. It was easy enough to convince everyone that you were his, since his wife had just died. She'd been sick for a while, and we were able to make them all think it had been because of pregnancy. It wasn't, but that isn't important."

Grammy wipes tears from her eyes and continues. "I wanted to tell you as you got older. I could see how much not being able to shift hurt you. I should have let you know that it wasn't you. But I couldn't tell you. It wasn't safe. I see now that was a mistake."

"Grammy, they took Luca. She said that they brought Vincent back here. But it was all a lie. I don't know what she wanted with me, but she's escaped and everything is falling apart." I sob and the old woman pulls me into her arms.

At this moment, it doesn't matter that she lied. This is my grandmother, the woman who raised me, the woman who loves me more than anyone else ever has. I let myself relax into her embrace and cry it out.

"It's okay child. We'll fix it all. Just breathe." She strokes my back as I cry. "Now, would you boys fill in some of what she just blurted out. I'm a little lost here."

Ry explains everything, with a little help from Orym and James. "And that brings us here. We need Gunnar to gather some wolves so we can go back and rescue the ones who've been taken. Including Luca. Because after talking to Levi, I'm sure they have him. I'm also sure they aren't going to care about my threat. If we want him back, we'll have to go get him."

"I see. That is a lot to go through in such a short time. But you have your powers now, and that will help. You'll need to learn how to use them. I'm guessing you brought some of Amber's books with you?" Grammy eases me away from where I've been clinging to her.

"Yes. I have several books at Ry's place. I've been studying them, and I'm making progress. But I just unlocked my full magic. I haven't even had a chance to use it yet." There wasn't time to test anything, and I think Grammy understands that.

"I want you boys to take Red home and take care of her tonight. If she's up to it, you should complete your bond, Orym. It'll make her stronger, and make finding Luca easier. I'm sorry I wasn't the one to explain things, dear. But I'm here to help now." She hugs me tightly again and I can feel her love engulf me.

"Thank you, Grammy. I couldn't do this without you," I insist.

"You could, but you don't have to. I'll talk to Gunnar when he gets back. He won't be happy about this, but we'll gather some wolves to help with the rescue. It'll take some time to plan this out, though. Don't be disappointed when we don't leave tomorrow."

"But Luca," I start. Grammy holds up a hand to stop me.

"They won't hurt him. At least not without you being in a position to watch."

NINETEEN
PREPARATIONS

ORYM

GRAMMY'S WORDS HURT GARNET. It doesn't matter that she tells the truth. It's still painful to hear that Luca will be used against us. We take her back to Ryland's place and settle her in to rest. She's not happy about it, and I don't blame her. There are far better things we can be doing right now to prepare instead of napping. But she's upset and none of us know how to deal with that.

Once she's settled in, we meet in the living room to discuss the situation. "I think we should call my brother and see what kind of help they can provide. We shouldn't be completely dependent on Gunnar and his whims," James insists.

"I think you're right. We shouldn't depend entirely on either faction. Maybe Vik can enlist the council's help too," Ryland suggests.

James walks off to make the call, and Ryland turns to me. "Do you think they'd really hurt Luca just to punish Red?"

"I do. But we're not gonna let it get to that point. We're gonna find him and get him back before they have a chance to hurt him." I don't know how, but I'll do everything I can to fix this for Garnet. She deserves to rest easy knowing that her mates will take care of her.

"I like that plan. But we're gonna need lots of backup for this. We don't even know how many witches there are total. That gives them an advantage."

"It does," I admit, "But they don't know that we can easily team up with vamps, either." At least I hope they don't, but I don't say that out loud.

"All we can do now is wait for Gunnar to get back with us. I hope that Grammy pleads our case as well as possible. He's not an understanding man, and he'll be pissed that we had Vincent and lost him." Ryland seems more upset about that than he should be. I'm sure he blames himself for Vincent being taken again. We trusted Amber because she seemed to be on our side. We should have known better. That's in the past, and can't be changed.

"You know that wasn't your fault, right?" I ask, forcing him to look at me. I can see the pain in his eyes. "You didn't lose Vincent. We all thought Amber was helping us. Well, everyone but Garnet. She didn't really trust her at all."

I understand his guilt because I harbor my own. "I know, but I still feel responsible. I'm trying to prove I'd make a good alpha, and I'm screwing it up left and right."

"You'd make a great alpha. And we'll decide that together, once everyone is bonded. For now, don't take the weight of the world on your shoulders, okay? We'll handle everything together," I suggest. I'd love to be the pack alpha, but I'm not willing to fight over it. Just being with Garnet is enough.

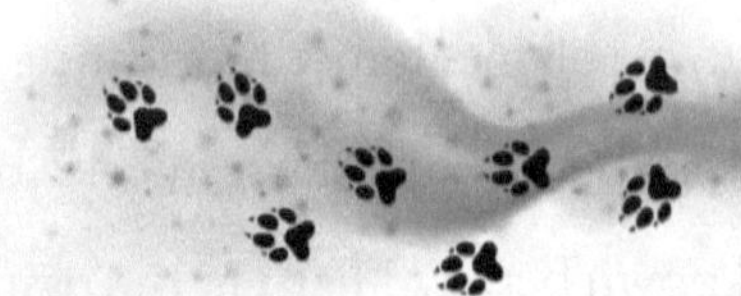

RYLAND

Before we can finish our conversation, there's a knock on the door. James wouldn't knock, would he? I go to the door and find Gunnar glaring at me. "What did you fuck up this time?" he growls as he barges into my home.

"Alpha, it's nice of you to come see us," I say, taking a breath to get my anger in check. Gunnar is always disrespectful and this is nothing for me to get upset about. As soon as the door closes, Red comes out of the bedroom.

"Gunnar," she says in acknowledgement. I watch his face and notice that he almost corrects her, then stops himself. That's a new development.

"Witch," he snarls.

I step forward and put my hand on his chest, then notice that Orym is standing right behind me. "You will speak to our mate with respect. She is not one of your wolves. If you want to disrespect us, that's your right as alpha. But you will not disrespect her, ever again."

To my surprise, he looks at me, then Orym, and hangs his head. "My apologies."

"Thank you. I assume Grammy told you what happened?" I gesture to the living room, offering him a seat. Gunnar sits, but I can tell that he's uncomfortable.

"She did. She claims that you found Vincent and sent him home with an escort. But he never arrived. And she says that Luca was taken too." There is animosity in his voice, but I let it go. One apology is all I'll ever get from him, and I know it.

"We trusted Amber, but she lied to us," Red says. Gunnar makes a face at her, but doesn't interrupt. "She said that she would have her people bring Vincent back home. It's obvious that she didn't do that."

Orym pulls Red into his arms. She's getting upset at Gunnar, and we need her to stay in control of her magic. Since James and Luca are usually the ones who comfort her, I'm glad Orym steps in.

"Did you know that Amber is Red's aunt?" I ask. It's not my story to tell, and I hope she doesn't get upset with me, but I have to know.

He shakes his head, and surprise crosses his face. "What?" he asks, then mutters to himself, "I guess that explains a lot."

"What do you mean?" Orym looks at him intently.

"I mean, she was always asking about Red. She wanted to know what she was interested in and that kind of thing. It was odd, but I just figured she was looking for a way to get on my good side."

As if Gunnar had one. "And you didn't think that was a red flag that needed to be shared?"

"It's my pack, and I decide what needs to be shared. You're lucky I let her hide here. I could have turned her away and my mother for accepting her. Instead, I gave her a place to live."

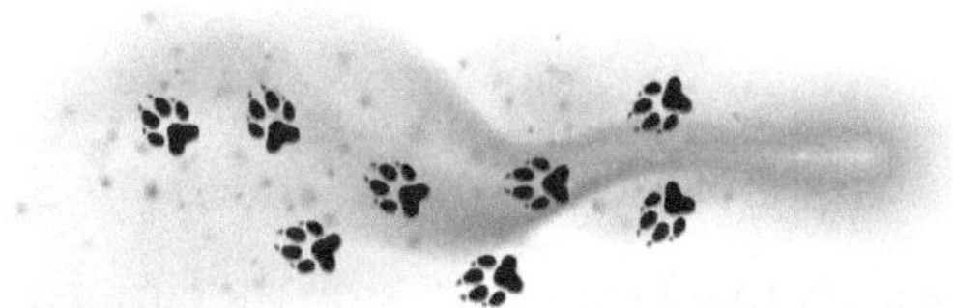

GARNET

"Yes, you gave me a place to live. And you treated me like a defective wolf my entire life. So, thank you for that." I know I'm letting my anger take over. Orym takes a step back as electricity darts across my skin.

With the full force of my magic inside of me, and no idea how to completely control it, I know that I should take a breath and calm myself down. I also know that with Gunnar sitting in front of me, I can't. He's done way too much to cause me pain.

"I did the best I could with you, and you know it," he claims.

"Then your best wasn't good enough," I toss back. Electricity crackles around me, moving faster. I hear the door open, and arms wrap around me from behind. James. He sucks in a sharp breath before I manage to stop the current.

I turn to face him, and he smiles at me. "You okay, love?"

I take a deep breath. "I am now. Thanks. Did I hurt you?"

"Nah, I'm good." I know that he's lying, but I don't push the issue. He hugs me close, not letting me take a good look at his arms. I'm sure that I burnt him, but he doesn't let me go.

Why would you do that? I hurt you. I insist in his head.

Yeah, but you didn't hurt him. That's the important part. I'm fine. Take a breath and focus. We need his help. James grins at me, then says out loud, "Dec is gonna talk to the others and see what they can do to help us. He can't guarantee anything, but he thinks that Vik and Eli have enough vamps in their employ to send us a small army. But Eli and Kayden will want to plan the whole thing out, so it may be a few days before they're ready to go."

That puts a damper on our plans. And since it's almost nightfall, it doesn't look like Levi took our threat about sending Luca home seriously. I tune out part of the conversation as Gunnar glares at me in James' arms. Surely Grammy told him that I have four mates and that these three are most of them. I don't care what he thinks. I know how he feels about humans, and I know that if I really was his daughter, he would be pissed that I'm mated to a human.

But, since I'm not actually his daughter, his opinion no longer matters. Okay, it shouldn't matter. Part of me is still that little girl who really wants her daddy's approval. I need that part to catch up to the rest of me that knows he's not my dad.

I wrap my arms possessively around James, letting him hold me while my men discuss the plan of attack with Gunnar. I'm relieved that Dec thinks they can help us, but annoyed that it's gonna take a few days to get everything organized. Luca has been gone for too long already.

What if he thinks we're not coming for him? I can't handle him being away from me and alone. My heart is breaking. I have to go after him, but I know that I can't do that without help. It won't do any good to get caught too.

"I'll gather the wolves and let them know that the vamps are taking point on this. Yes, it pisses me off. But I understand why it needs to be that way. Viktor has more pull with the council than I do. Probably because I'm an asshole. Yes, I know that too. It doesn't change anything," Gunnar says as he gets up to leave. He pauses at the door, and for a moment, I think I see regret cross his features. I wonder what he's thinking, but before I can ask, he slips out the door.

He'll send a text letting Ry and Orym know when to show up for the meeting. I won't be invited, or even allowed to attend. That'll be strange. Maybe I'll convince James to go to the city with me while they have their meeting. I'd like to see Delilah and talk to her about everything.

She's the only girlfriend I've ever really had, and she treats me more like a little sister. It's funny, in a village full of wolves, being raised with them, you'd think some of them would have been nice to me. Sadly, you'd be wrong. They tolerated me because of who they thought my father was. I wonder how they'll react to the news that I'm not one of them.

That would be something to see, but I won't be there. Wolves only, and all that. It doesn't matter. I have other things to focus on. After Gunnar leaves, everyone turns to me. "What the fuck was that?" Ry asks.

"What?" I counter. I know what he's talking about, but I really don't want to discuss it.

"You know what he's talking about. Don't avoid the question. What happened there?" Orym takes Ry's side, and I find that I'm not a fan of that.

"You two let her get angry. One of you should have stepped in and done exactly what I did. I knew that she would drop the magic the second it started to burn me," James chastises them. I laugh because he's getting after them as if they've done something wrong. None of us knows how to deal with my powers.

"How can you get upset with them over this?" I'm still laughing, and they're looking at me as if I've lost my mind. Perhaps I have. It doesn't matter, though, because James is right. Someone had to step in, or I would have attacked Gunnar. It would have been foolish and two of my mates would have paid the price. I can't let that happen again. "I'll work on it. I can't go around attacking people who piss me off."

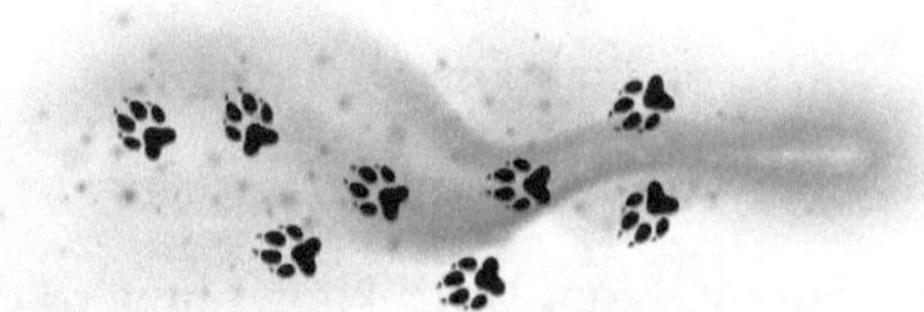

JAMES

I can't help being annoyed that neither Ryland nor Orym thought to place themselves in a position for Garnet to hurt them so she would realize how close she was to losing control. It doesn't matter now, but I know letting her attack Gunnar would have been a bad idea.

Knowing that we'll be waiting at least a few days for everything to be organized makes everyone antsy. I don't like it, but there's nothing I can do to get the vamps or wolves to move faster. I'm sure that Eli needs time to gather tech that will help us be successful in our mission.

I hate how Gunnar talked to everyone, especially Garnet. I wanted to rip his throat out, and I'm the least violent person here. I don't know how Orym and Ryland managed to hold themselves back. It was all I could do to focus on calming her down instead of attacking him myself. Hell, if Luca was here, he probably would have attacked the old man. Luca. That's why she's so emotional and struggling to control herself.

I already miss Luca, so I know that feeling is amplified in Garnet. With how close they are, she's got to be miserable. We should do something to take her mind off him. I have ideas, but I'm not sure if any of them are viable.

Personally, I'd like to fuck her until she can't walk. That would definitely take her mind off Luca for a little while anyway. I don't know that sex is what she needs, though. I'll have to test the waters and see if I can figure out what she does need.

"We should take the night off." I make the announcement, stepping away from Garnet and dropping onto the couch. "Dinner, a movie, and relaxing. That's what we should do tonight. It'll help everyone refocus on the goal and come at it fresh."

I can see them considering my statement. Something flashes in Orym's eyes, and I suspect I know what he'd like to do to relax. I'm all for it, but I don't know that Garnet will be. His gaze meets mine, and I nod.

"Let us take care of you tonight, Garnet," he offers. I glance at Ryland and see that he understands what Orym is thinking. We'll do what we can to help him out, and if she's not ready, I know that he'll back off.

Garnet smiles at us. It's sad and doesn't reach her eyes, but she's trying. "That sounds good." I'm relieved that she doesn't want to try and plan out the attack tonight. Hopefully she'll go along with Eli and Vik's plans and we'll get the wolves on board too. We have to work as a team to save the kidnapping victims.

Ryland disappears into the kitchen to make something for dinner, I assume. Orym walks over to the book case and starts looking at movies. Garnet looks over his shoulder, determined to help.

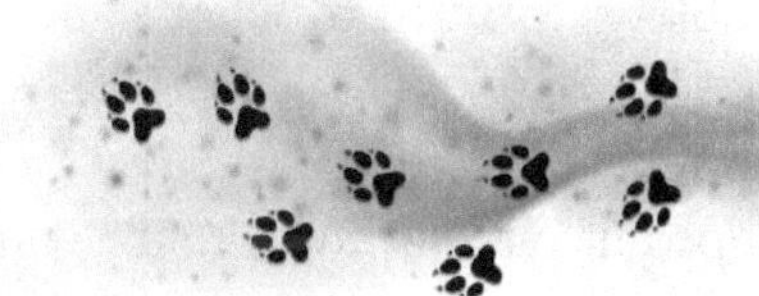

LUCA

I don't get any answers out of Lobo, but he finally lowers the net to the ground when someone brings him a collar. Fuck. That looks a lot like the cuffs we put on Amber, but in collar form. I'm not looking forward to what's about to happen. Sure enough, as soon as he lowers me enough to reach my neck, the collar is snapped in place. I know that I couldn't run if I wanted to.

This isn't exactly like the cuffs though. Those had to be put on by a witch, and can only be removed by the same witch. Lobo is a wolf like me, so this uses different magic. "What's this for?" I ask, not expecting him to answer.

"It's so you do what I tell you," he says simply.

That's what I was afraid of. "What is it you want me to do?" I know that I should shut my mouth and be happy that I'm not tangled in that net anymore, but I'm terrified about what this could possibly mean.

"I want you to obey. You can't run away. You can't leave the witches' territory with that on, either. It has a failsafe that will electrocute you if you try." He smirks at that statement, as if he expected me to try to run away anyway.

"I see. So, I'm just gonna follow you around now?"

"Pretty much. You can carry stuff for me." Great. I get to be his grunt. Just what I was hoping for. I hope that Red and the guys managed to get back home. I would ask, but what if they hadn't tried yet because they were looking for me? I can't risk messing that up for them.

Lobo leads me back to a camp where other wolves and vamps are wearing similar collars. Wait, is that Vincent? Yeah, that tracks. Why would Amber have sent him home like she told us when she's the one kidnapping everyone? I wish we'd been more cautious about this whole thing from the start, but it's too late now. Lobo sends me to help Vincent gather firewood.

"I thought you got sent home," I tell him.

"Nope. Since whatever spell they had controlling me was broken, they gave me a fancy collar like yours," he responds. I wonder what he's been through, since he's not being a colossal dick anymore.

"They're gonna come for us," I say.

"I hope they don't," he replies.

"Why not?"

"Because that's what she wants. She wants Red to come back, so she can lock her up like us. There's something going on here that's really bad. Like dozens of dead vamps and wolves, bad. I've been trying to find out what she's planning, but they're really secretive about it all. When Amber came back, she couldn't use her magic, and she's pissed about it." With Vincent's explanation, I understand more of what's going on here, but there are still mysteries. Lobo walks over and we stop talking.

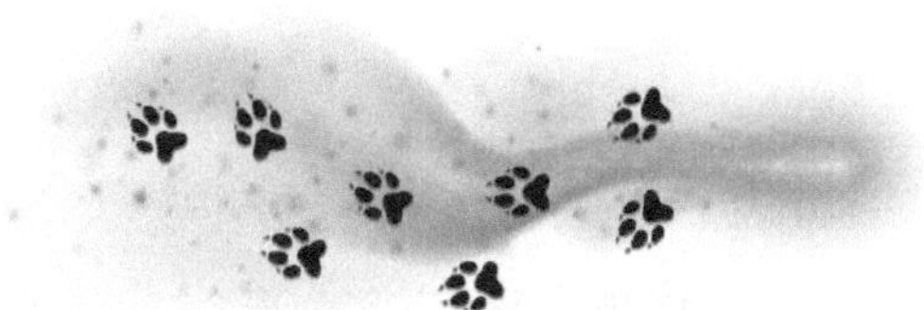

GARNET

Dinner and a movie seem to be just what I need to take my mind off things for a while. I'm surprised that Ry remembers how much I love tacos. Then Orym picks out my favorite cheesy sci-fi movie for us to watch. It's almost like having Luca here with me. But the biggest surprise is how both Ry and James give me space to snuggle up with Orym on the couch.

I can't deny the desire that builds in me at his closeness. This is the first opportunity we've had to be alone without Amber nearby. I find myself fantasizing about the things I want to do to Orym instead of paying attention to the movie. When he puts his arm around my shoulders, I shift a little, resting my back on his naked chest.

I can feel his breath on my neck, and it sends a shiver down my spine. The lights are low, and no one is paying attention to us. It would be so easy to tease him. But with our bond, James and Ry would absolutely know what was happening. As if he's reading my mind, Orym slides his hand down my side and rests it on my hip.

His breath is ragged against my skin, matching my own. We stay like that for a few minutes, watching the movie, pretending that we're not on the verge of falling off a cliff of passion.

Out of nowhere, James stands up. "I'm wiped. You guys finish the movie. I'm gonna go to bed." He kisses me gently and heads to the bedroom. I look at Orym and Ry, but neither of them looks suspicious of what just happened.

My heart is racing at Orym's closeness. His fingers start to trace my hip and I struggle to draw in a breath. I don't want him to stop.

A moment later, Ry stretches and yawns loudly. "I think James has the right idea. I'm going to sleep. Enjoy the end of the movie." He kisses me hard, then walks away, turning off the light on his way out of the room. Did they plan this? Do I care?

"I guess it's just you and me," Orym whispers against my ear. "Unless you're tired too."

"I'm not," I breathe. His fingers start to trace my hip again, stroking the waistband of my pajama shorts. I shiver, leaning more into him. He pulls me onto his lap and presses his lips to mine. I moan at the contact and he slips his tongue in to stroke mine. Now that I'm on top of him, I can feel how hard he is. I hum as he kisses me.

Orym eases me back on the couch, so I'm beside him. He scoots up so he can continue to kiss me. His lips move from mine to my neck and back. He's barely touching me, and I want more. I need him. I need to complete our bond. My body is practically begging for it.

"Orym, please," I pant. He tightens his grip on me and kisses me again. When he stops, we're both breathless.

"Garnet, you have to tell me what you want. I won't push, but if we start, I won't be able to stop. I want you too much. But I don't want to claim you if you're not ready." I can hear his control straining against his desire.

"I want you, Orym. I want to claim you and be claimed by you. Please." As soon as the words are out of my mouth, he claims it again.

His hands finally start to move again, stroking my cheek, then moving down my chest. He barely grazes my breasts before trailing down my stomach. He stops short, just before he gets where I want him. I whimper and he chuckles. Orym traces a figure eight pattern next to my waistband, then moves his hand to the leg opening of my shorts.

I suck in a sharp breath at the barely there touch. He strokes his finger along the material, sliding it just under the edge. He's almost touching me exactly where I need him. I shift my hips, but he doesn't move his hand.

It looks like I'm going to have to move things along myself. I slip my hand between us and grab the waistband of his pants. He growls playfully in my ear, then nips at my neck. I reach into his pants and grip his cock. I stroke it slowly from root to tip, rubbing my thumb over the pre-cum that lingers there.

His groan makes me smile. I like knowing I have that kind of power over him. He kisses me as I stroke him. Then he slides a finger under my shorts, teasing my pussy. I stroke him faster, and that does the trick. He dips a finger inside of me, and I nearly come undone.

I keep up my pace stroking him, pushing him closer to his release. He distracts me by pulling his finger out of me and rubbing it up my opening to my clit. He circles my sensitive nub a few times, then slips two fingers inside of me again. I know that I'm drenched and so close to coming. He keeps alternating between sliding his fingers into me and rubbing my clit until I fall of that edge. He kisses me, swallowing my moans of pleasure.

Satisfied that I'm ready, he pulls my shorts off, then my top, before shedding his pants. Before I can prepare myself, he thrusts into me, fully seating himself in one go. My breath catches in my chest as another orgasm hits me full force.

That doesn't stop Orym from fucking me hard. He thrusts into me and pulls almost all the way out before thrusting in again. The pace he sets is fast, but I like it. Within only a few more minutes, I come again. This time, I bite his shoulder, marking him as mine. That triggers his orgasm, and he bites down on my neck. I feel our bond snap into place.

TWENTY
EPILOGUE

GARNET

A FEW DAYS TURNS into a week. That turns into two weeks. I'm not sure at this point that we'll ever be ready to launch our rescue mission. I don't regret bonding with Orym, but I do regret not bonding with Luca.

We've been practicing my magic, and apparently, I can find my mates when they're not near me. But it only works through the bond.

I'm going into the city today to meet with Delilah. She's been helping me figure out my powers. It's easier to practice with her, since Eli has sparring rooms, and tech that can keep me from hurting anyone too badly. Besides, Delilah is a hybrid, so she has super-fast healing.

Are you sure you don't want us to stick around? Orym asks before pressing a kiss to my forehead.

I'm good. Nothing can happen to me here. Besides, the guys need to talk to you three about the mission. I'm just gonna play with Delilah a bit. You won't be gone long. This is the one place where I don't worry about my guys or me. Eli has Midnight locked down. It's like a fortress.

Just call for us if you need us. James' voice in my head makes me smile.

I will. Now go. I kiss each of them before shoving them out the door.

"I don't want to know what you four were talking about, do I?" Delilah laughs.

I shake my head. "They're paranoid about something happening. I had to make them leave." She laughs, clearly understanding the issue.

"Mine are the same way. Men." She rolls her eyes. "I guess we should get started. Where we left off last time?"

I nod, shaking my body to loosen up. It should be terrifying to know that a vampire-wolf hybrid is about to attack me, but I'm not worried. Delilah won't hold back, but I know that I can defend myself. We've practiced this several times. Even if she bites me, it won't turn me, because she's not a full wolf or vamp. Grammy assured us that hybrids don't have the ability to change others.

I close my eyes and center myself, keeping them closed to test my other senses. I should be able to hear her before she attacks. Hopefully, early enough that I can dodge. I count my breaths and wait with my eyes closed. It's hard not to peek, but I know that she's not going to attack while I'm looking.

I decide to cheat a little, pushing into her head so I can see through her eyes. I haven't told her yet that I can do this. The fewer people who know, the better. We've been documenting my powers and abilities since we started working together. I have a journal that I write in daily, but Eli insisted that it be electronic and use his privacy software. I agreed, because that keeps anyone else but me out of it. I can write whatever I want and no one will ever know unless I decide to let them read it.

Of course, I have Eli back it up to his secure server, and he has the encryption codes. I trust him not to read it. I've come to consider Delilah and her men my family. I trust them with my life, and the lives of my men. They're going to help me get Luca back.

If I wasn't looking at myself through Delilah's eyes, she would have hit me that time. "Good dodge. You waited longer that time, too." Her praise makes me smile. Yeah, it pays to keep some secrets.

"I'm going to try something different this time. Let me know if it works," I say.

"What do you mean?" she asks. I shake my head and watch as she jumps at me to attack. I throw a blast at her and push her back ten feet. She flops onto the floor and laughs. "I'd say that worked."

"That actually wasn't what I was trying to do. Let's go again," I order. She lunges toward me and I move her body from the inside, turning her around so that she vaults herself away from me. Her surprised squeal has me opening my eyes and watching her fall.

"How did you do that? It felt like you were inside my body controlling it," she gasps.

"I kind of was," I admit. "It's a new thing I'm working on. I've been practicing with the guys. Of course, it's easy to get in their heads because of our bond. It takes a little more concentration with other people."

"You can't tell anyone else about this," she admonishes me.

"You and my guys are the only ones who know. I wasn't even going to tell you, but your face was priceless and I couldn't resist." I laugh as I admit what I've been doing.

"Okay, that is way cool. Just promise me that you won't tell anyone else. I'm serious. I know that you're the bad ass witch who's gonna save us all, but I need to protect you."

"You're not my mom, D," I tell her.

"No, I'm more like your super cool older sister," she insists. Then she pulls me in for a hug. I am so thankful for these people.

"Thank you," I say in her ear.

"For what? You're doing most of the work here."

"You guys didn't have to help us. I just want you to know how much we appreciate it."

She smiles at me. "You're family. I mean, you are mated to my brother-in-law, after all." I laugh at her joke. Fated mates doesn't exactly work like being married, but it's close enough.

"Good point. I am rather fond of James."

Since we're finished with training for the day, we head upstairs to see if the guys are done with their meeting.

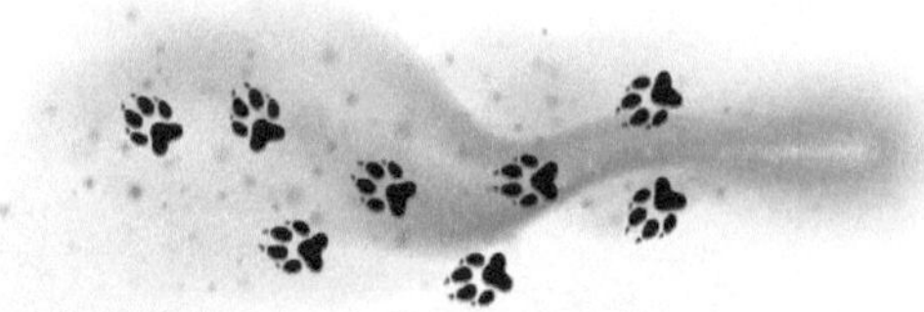

RYLAND

Our meeting takes five minutes. Vik wanted to go over the plan again, but we all know what we have to do. Eli is sending micro drones in to survey the area and find where the prisoners are being held before we go across the border.

Red has to be the one to bring the border down. I'm not sure that she can do it, but Dec insists that she can. How does he know? I have no idea. But I like the confidence he has in my mate. Maybe he and James have discussed it. It doesn't matter either way. We will do what we have to in order to rescue Luca.

Vik and I have been butting heads over who's going to lead the charge. I want to show my mate that I can be the alpha she needs. Yes, he has more experience and is more prepared. But I'm not ready to concede yet.

"Do I need to kick your ass, little wolf?" he asks with a smirk. I know he won't hurt me, but I'm tempted to fight him for the lead position.

"That sounds like a good way to decide this," I shoot back. He peels his suit jacket off just as the doors open.

Red and Delilah stroll in. Fuck. There goes that plan. No way will they go along with this. "What are you two doing?" Delilah asks.

"The little wolf wants to challenge me to see who leads the troops into the forest when it's time," Vik says, still smirking.

Both girls look at each other and shrug. "Sounds like a plan. Get to it," Red says. Delilah nods her agreement. What the fuck just happened here? They're okay with us fighting. This seems too good to be true.

Everyone stands back, giving us the center of the room. Vik and I circle each other a few times before he lunges at me. I shift into my wolf form and dodge him easily. I don't realize that he's backing me into a corner and I'll be stuck there. My wolf form is too big to maneuver in this room quickly.

Within minutes, he has me pinned to the ground and I have no choice but to give in. Begrudgingly, I shift back and tap out. I hate that he won so easily, but at least I can say I tried.

"Good effort, little wolf. I think we should lead the charge together," Vik announces. For me, that's almost as good as a victory.

"Thanks, that would be great," I agree. I'm still amazed at how quickly these vampires welcomed us into their family. I guess that's probably because James and Dec are actually brothers, but it doesn't feel forced or fake.

I'm glad that Red has them, since she lost the man she thought was her father. Grammy still tries to be part of her life, but Red is hesitant. She's still hurt about being lied to, and I don't blame her.

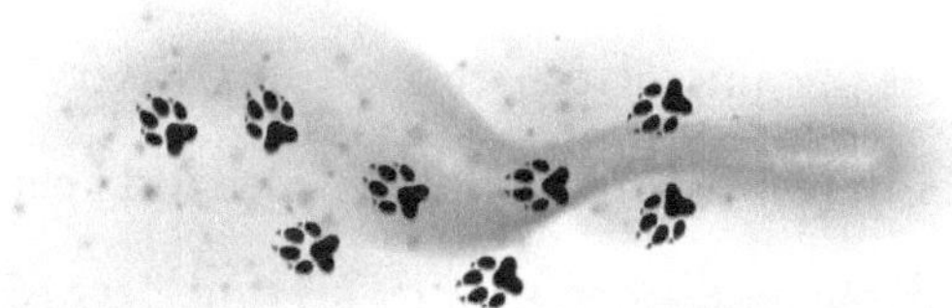

JAMES

Ryland's challenge of Vik lasts for five minutes. Apparently, it's enough to impress the vampire, and he offers to share command. It's a sweet gesture, no doubt maneuvered by Delilah. But I'm not telling anyone that. My brother's mate is very diplomatic, and can be good at forcing compromise.

I grin at her knowingly, but she shrugs. I'm happy for the change I see in Garnet. She's more relaxed and gaining confidence every day. Her control is better as well. Delilah works with her on her magic during the day, and I work on meditation with her in the evenings.

Everyone here is working together smoothly. Well, as smoothly as possible. Vik and Ryland still butt heads a lot. But you can see the mutual respect there. Orym is trying to learn as much about tech from Eli as he can. Dec and I get to hang out while we're here. Kayden spreads his time between all of us. I think if Luca was here, they'd be together talking about cars or something.

We all feel Luca's absence in our own way. And we're helping Garnet deal with it the best we can. Eli's surveillance tech is helping with that too. He's able to spy on the witches without them noticing. The drones he's using are insect sized. They blend with the forest, and are nearly invisible. Because of him, we know where the camp is right now. We're anticipating them moving again. It seems random, but I'm sure there's a pattern to when and where they move the camp. We just haven't figured it out yet.

I'm confident that we will. I don't know how long it will take, but at least we have eyes on them now. The tiny drones see everything. Eli won't let Garnet see the recordings, and after our meeting today, I'm glad.

They've been torturing the captives at random. We can't tell exactly why or how they choose, but a lot of times, Luca steps between the captors and whoever they're beating on. That gets him abused the worst of all. I'm sure that he understands what he's doing, but that doesn't make it any less painful to watch.

He hasn't told her yet that he has the drones in place. All she knows is that they exist and will be used to get us to the right place. We can't afford her losing control because she finds out that he's being tortured. I hate keeping things from her, but this one can't be helped.

I walk over to Garnet and kiss her, pulling her against me. I do it as a distraction, so that Eli can get the monitors turned off before she sees the surveillance footage on the left screen. I pour myself into the kiss until she's putty in my arms. "What was that for?" she asks when I finally let her go.

"I missed you," I respond, even though we were only apart for maybe half an hour.

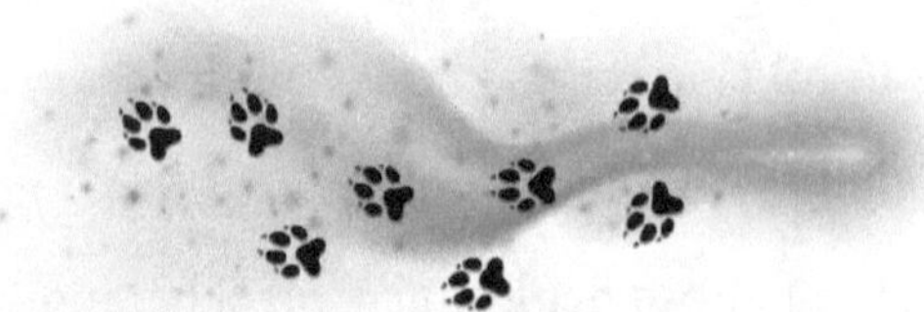

ORYM

I realize that James is distracting Garnet so we can turn off the monitors on the wall. When he turns her away from them, I motion to Eli and he shuts them off. He understands why she can't know about them yet. She'll go nuclear and we'll have to clean up the mess.

Once the monitors are off, he lets her go. She's suspicious, but doesn't know exactly what we're hiding. I don't want to tip her off, so I stay where I am, talking to Eli about how the drones will work on the day of our attack.

"With these drones, we'll be able to pinpoint exactly where they're keeping the prisoners and how many guards we'll be dealing with." He directs my attention to the schematics for the drones, showing me again how they work. We both know it's overkill, but neither of us want to be on the receiving end of Garnet's wrath.

She walks over and wraps her arms around my waist, tucking her head into the crook of my neck. "What are you two nerds talking about over here?"

"Eli was just showing me the schematics for the drones and explaining how they work," I say.

"Why do that when we could just watch the footage on these monitors?" Fuck. She knows. How does she know?

"Come on, Orym. You guys can't hide anything from me. I've known for days that you have eyes on the camp. And that they move it every few days." She pauses, then continues, "And that they've been beating Luca."

"I'm sorry, love. We just wanted to give you time to train. We weren't intending to hide it," I defend.

She shakes her head. "I know. I'm okay. It hurts, but getting upset about it won't help. I have to channel that rage into my training and take them all down when we get there. If I'm not mistaken, they'll move the camp again tomorrow."

"Wait, how do you know that? It's been so irregular. We haven't been able to figure out the pattern," Eli interjects.

"They move with every phase of the moon. How did you guys not see that?" Delilah adds. She's been paying attention too. Damn, I thought we'd kept this from both of them. But I guess if one knew, they'd tell the other. It really wasn't the best plan we'd ever had.

"Wow, I guess we should discuss these things with the ladies next time," Dec says, walking over to Delilah and hugging her. "We'd still be lost if it wasn't for you two."

"Well, we did figure it out together. The trick was waiting for you guys to admit you didn't know what they were doing. And figuring out how to tell you that we knew about the footage," Garnet admits.

I can't believe we had so little faith in her. She knew long enough to figure out the pattern, and didn't lose her shit over it. I won't underestimate her again.

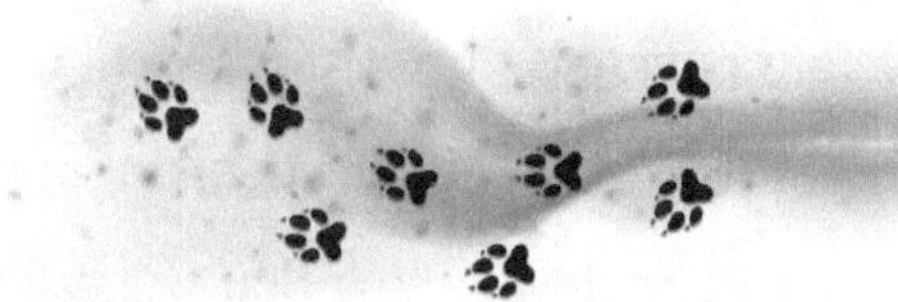

LUCA

The whip cracks as it slams into my back again. I bite back my scream. I don't know if I'm going to survive this. I can't think like that right now, though. Red. I have to focus on Red. She needs me. I have to stay strong for her. I must do what she would, and protect these people.

I take every opportunity I'm given to do chores assigned to someone else. Then I do what I can to make sure I'm the one who gets beaten instead of anyone who's weaker than me. I have no idea what they're planning, or what they do with the people who disappear and don't come back.

I'm trying to find out. I need to be in a position to pass along information to whoever comes after us. I still don't know if Red and the guys made it out of the forest. They could be prisoners at the cabin again. No one is talking about them, so I don't ask. I refuse to do anything that will call attention to them.

The flesh on my back splits as the whip tears through it again. I've lost count of how many lashes this is, or how many are to come. It doesn't matter. If I can't remain conscious for all of them, my captors will stop when I pass out from the pain. For whatever reason, they want me alive. I've heard Lobo say that when I started a fight with one of the guards.

"You can beat him, but we're not allowed to kill him. She wants this one alive," he'd said.

I consider that as the whip comes down on me again. I feel the warm, sticky blood drip from my wounds. After this, they'll let one of the vampires tend to me. The cost for their help will be my blood. I'll happily pay, because when they're finished feeding, they'll bring me food and clean my lash marks.

Sometimes it feels like playing Russian roulette, though. How much blood does it take to entice a vampire to kill a wolf? I have no idea. I guess I'll find out if they go too far with my beatings. At this point, I might welcome death as a friend.

I can't let myself think that way. What I'm doing here is too important. I'm gathering intel and protecting people who need it. I should be surprised when Vincent starts doing the same; standing up for those who aren't equipped to fight back.

I try to stop him, because I know that these monsters who are holding us captive won't kill me. They've never offered the same protection to him. But he won't listen. "If you can stand up for people, so can I. Luca, I've never done anything to help anyone. Let me do this." His words echo in my head as the whip comes down on me again.

I feel the darkness close in on me, and I welcome it.

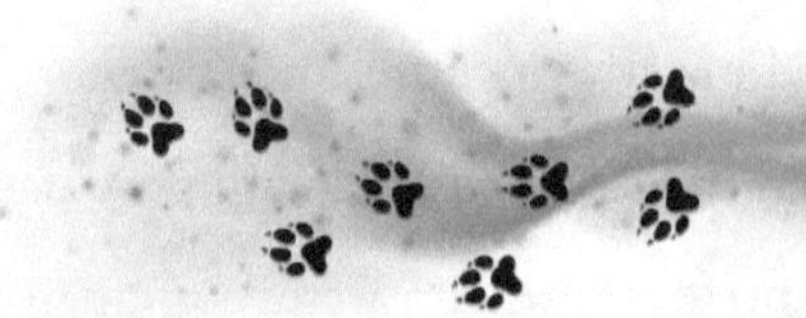

GARNET

It's a relief to admit that I know what's happening to Luca. I hate hiding things from any of my mates. But Delilah and I needed time to figure out the pattern. When she pulled up the video a few days ago, I'd steeled myself against what she showed me. I refused to feel anything. I watched it as if that wasn't my best friend being beaten within an inch of his life in every single frame.

After watching the videos, I think Grammy is right, though. Amber will keep him alive until I'm there. Then she'll use him to hurt me. I hold onto that thought as we train today. I let the rage I feel fill me up. If I detonate like a nuclear bomb, I know that Eli's sparring room can handle it.

I've insisted that we use dummies today. I won't chance hurting someone that I care about. But I do want to see what happens when I lose control. My guys agreed to stay out, and Delilah's guys agreed to make them comply.

"Are you sure about this?" Delilah's voice comes through the earpiece I wear. I know they can see what happens in here and they can hear through the mic in my earpiece.

"I'm sure, D. It's fine. We have to know. This isn't something we can wait and see when we're trying to rescue these captives. I won't risk people's lives if I'm not stable enough to do this." I'm tired of this argument already, because I've had it with each of my guys, each of D's guys, and now D herself.

"Okay. We're just worried about you, that's all," she replies. I nod, then shake myself. I need to be as relaxed as possible before we start.

I close my eyes and take a deep breath. "I'm ready." When I open my eyes, the screens on the walls light up, showing the surveillance videos of Luca and other captives being beaten for whatever reason. Tears stream down my face.

"I can turn it off at any time, Red," Kayden's voice sounds in my ear. I shake my head.

"Don't." I need to watch this. I need to feel it all. I have to let myself feel it all. "Turn the sound up." As soon as I make the request, I'm bombarded with the screams of those who are being whipped and beaten. Except Luca. He never makes a sound, until just before he collapses from the pain.

Then I hear a single word, and I'm destroyed. "Red." My nickname, the one I hate, the one he says the way a lover says their beloved's name, falls from his lips as he hits the ground. I know he's not dead, because this is the first video of what they've done to him.

But the tears increase anyway. I couldn't stop them if I tried. It doesn't matter. I don't need to see any more. I let my tears fall as the rage builds. I know from before that electricity dances across my skin. This time I don't even try to hold back. The power builds, moving faster.

I sense the glow before I see it. Power builds at my feet and moves up my body. My hair flows behind me as if I'm standing in a storm with the wind blowing at my face. It feels like I'm being burnt up from the inside out. Between the electricity and the flames, I think I might die. I don't stop.

I can't stop. I have to know. And if this does kill me, then maybe that will be the thing that stops Amber. I know that if something happens to me, they'll get Luca back. Ry, Orym, and James have promised to save him no matter what.

They won't let these people suffer any longer than they have to. This will all be over soon. I scream as the power builds inside of me, before blasting out and destroying everything in the room. I'm on fire, burning from the inside out. Pain engulfs me and I drop to my knees.

"Red? Red, please. Are you okay?" I don't know how many times they've called my name, both in my head and over the earpiece. I brace my hands on the floor and push myself up. I nod and force myself to my feet.

The tears still fall. The fire still burns through me. But when I look at my hands, they're fine. I've not been touched by the flames. The room I'm in has been decimated, as if a bomb went off. Parts of the ceiling and walls are falling down. Flames kiss the walls.

Debris floats in the air. I close my eyes and force myself to control my power. I douse the flames with my own tears.

"Garnet, we don't have visual. Are you okay?" Orym's voice this time.

"I'm here," I manage. I can't say more. Not right now. The pain is still tearing through me. But if Luca can take all those beatings to protect people, I can handle this. I will save him. No one will stop me.

I stand there for another moment, assessing the damage I've done to Eli's indestructible room. I guess he won't be calling it that anymore. Perhaps, nearly indestructible would be a better moniker. Maybe I'll suggest that.

I look around the room, focusing on the areas closest to me and comparing them to the furthest away. I know what test we need to do next. "Eli, can you reset this room by tomorrow?" My voice sounds cold and dark.

"Of course," he responds.

"Good. We need to do this again, but with some minor alterations." I don't explain my thoughts. Eli already knows what I want to do. He and Vik have been planning this long enough to know what will happen when we go after the captives. I'll have to face off with my aunt. And I'm nearly ready. It won't be long now. I will have my mate back and save her victims.

I'm coming for you, Amber.

THE STORY CONTINUES...

In **Wolf Caged! Pre-Order** your copy here: https://books2read.com/HoF2-WC

After accidentally bonding with two of my mates, I discovered secrets that were kept from me. These things have changed my life—I can't go back to what I was now that I know what I am.

I'm committed to stopping Amber and her followers. They're still kidnapping wolves and vampires, and now they've started taking humans, too. We're stuck trying to figure out what they hope to accomplish.

Amber crosses a line when she takes one of my mates. I will find her, and I will save him, no matter the cost.

I've lost my family, but found myself. I have to figure out exactly what that means. I know there are more answers waiting for me, and I must find them. My obsession may chase everyone away.

When we start finding bodies, things get urgent. Since they've taken one of my mates, it's personal. I have to save Luca before it's too late.

ACKNOWLEDGMENTS

I would like to thank:

My Alpha and Beta Teams who try hard to keep me on track;

My Editing Team who does their best to make sure my books make sense and have as few typos as possible;

My Cover Artist, Lara at Wynter Designs, who's responsible for the gorgeous images on the front of this book

and My ARC Team, who catch some of the things the rest of us miss.

ABOUT THE AUTHOR

M.P. Starkweather is a wife, mother, author, poet, casual online gamer, self-proclaimed fan-girl, and full-time nerd. She writes free-form poetry, paranormal romance, sci-fi romance, reverse harem romance, and is branching out into contemporary romance. In her free time, she enjoys writing, reading, Dungeons & Dragons, table top games with her husband and friends, and playing with her son. M.P. also enjoys tv, movies, and music across various genres.

To get the most up-to-date information about her latest releases and book signings, check out www.mpstarkweather .com and join her newsletter, or follow her on your favorite social media site.

ALSO BY M.P. STARKWEATHER

Standalones - Contemporary RH OV

Cold Princes

Knot My Valentine

The Pack Next Door – Contemporary RH OV series

Princess or Knot

Fiancée or Knot

Queen or Knot

Vampires at Midnight - Paranormal RH series

Blood Moon

Blood Lost

Blood War

A Vampires at Midnight and Hunters of the Forest Crossover Novella - Paranormal RH, free with newsletter sign up

Blood Wolf

Hunters of the Forest - Paranormal RH series

Wolf Bane

Wolf Caged

Wolf Moon

The Legend of Khaine Academy – Paranormal RH Academy series
The Awakening (pre-order coming soon!)
Forged by Magic - Sci-fi/Fantasy M/F series

Hidden

Betrayed

Saved

Daydreams and Sunsets - a collection of poetry

Daydreams and Sunsets

www.ingramcontent.com/pod-product-compliance
Lightning Source LLC
Chambersburg PA
CBHW021327310726
48971CB00001B/18